Archie®

Love Showdown

30th Anniversary
SPECIAL EDITION

Publisher / Co-CEO: Jon Goldwater
President / Editor-In-Chief: Mike Pellerito
Chief Creative Officer: Roberto Aguirre-Sacasa
Chief Operating Officer: William Mooar
Chief Financial Officer: Robert Wintle
Senior Vice President: Jonathan Betancourt
Senior Director of Editorial: Jamie Lee Rotante
Production Manager: Stephen Oswald
Art Director: Vincent Lovallo
Lead Designer: Kari McLachlan
Associate Editor: Carlos Antunes
Co-CEO: Nancy Silberkleit

♥ Written by

DAN PARENT, BILL GOLLIHER,
GEORGE GLADIR, & FRANK DOYLE

Art by ♥

DAN DECARLO, STAN GOLDBERG, DOUG CRANE,
DAN PARENT, BILL GOLLIHER, PAT KENNEDY,
VINCENT DECARLO, RUDY LAPICK, JACK MORELLI,
JIM AMASH, HENRY SCARPELLI, KEN SELIG, ALISON FLOOD,
MIKE ESPOSITO, JON D'AGOSTINO, VICKIE WILLIAMS,
BILL YOSHIDA, & BARRY GROSSMAN

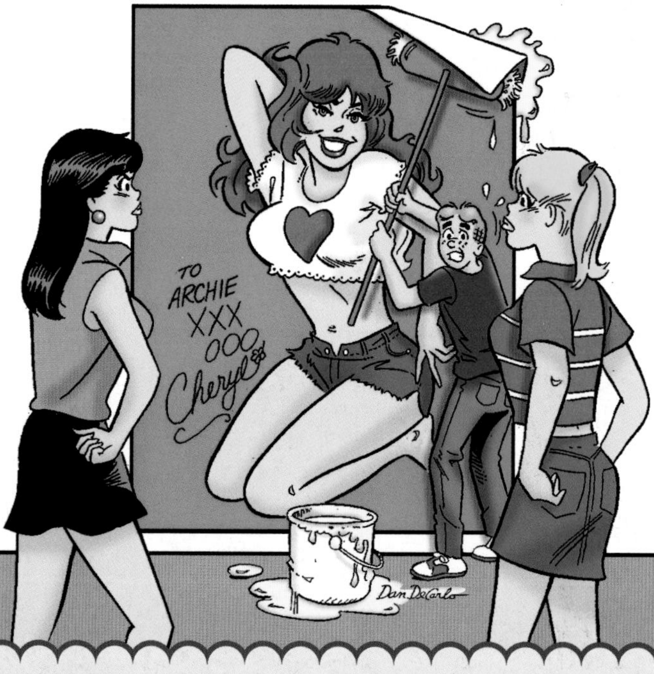
TO ARCHIE XXX OOO Cheryl
Dan DeCarlo

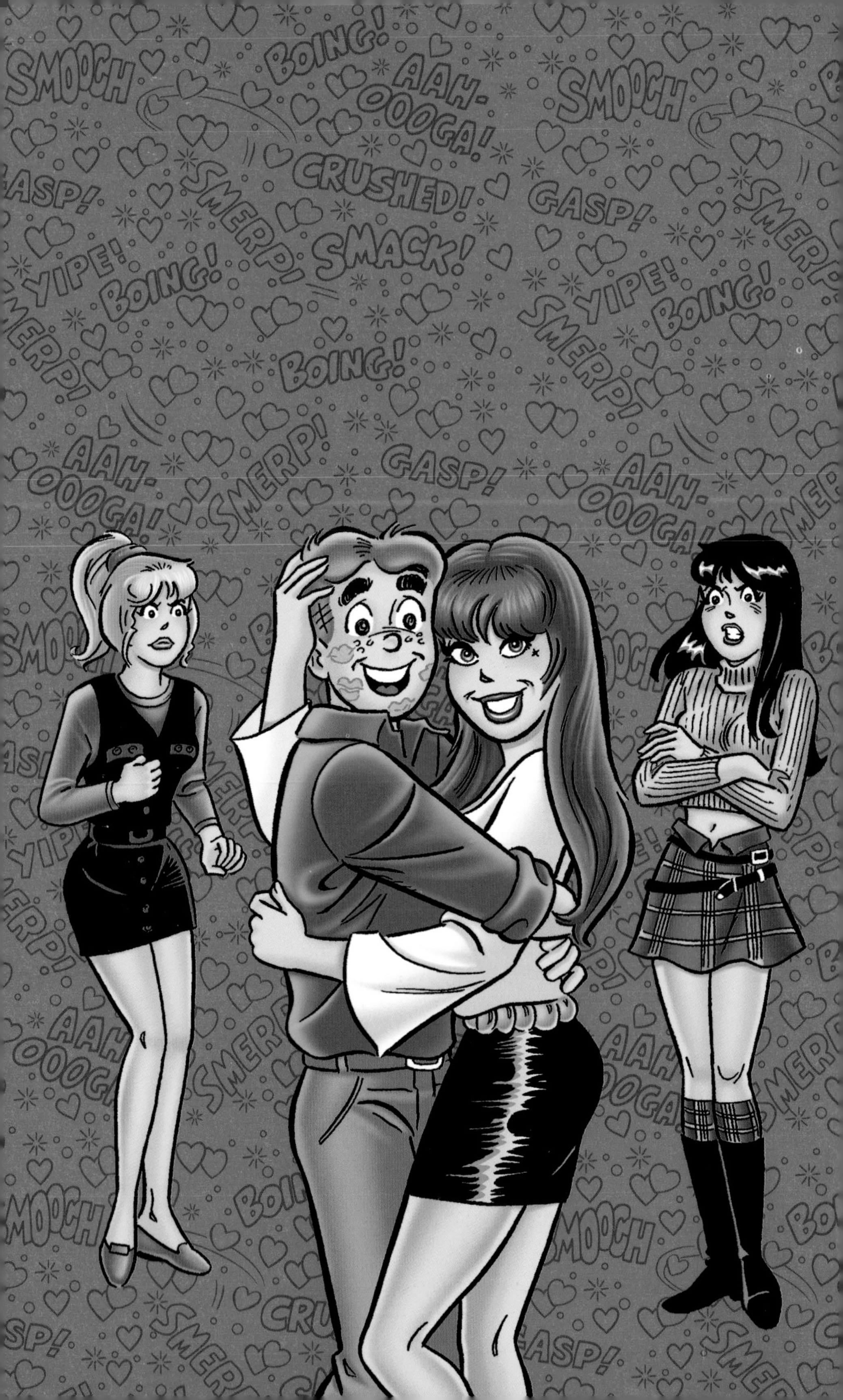

SMOOCH
BOING!
AAH-OOOGA!
SMOOCH
CRUSHED!
SMERP!
GASP!
SMACK!
YIPE!
BOING!
YIPE!
BOING!
SMERP!
BOING!
AAH-OOOGA!
SMERP!
GASP!
AAH-OOOGA!
SMOOCH

Table of Contents

♥ ARCHIE LOVE SHOWDOWN ♥

Chapter One

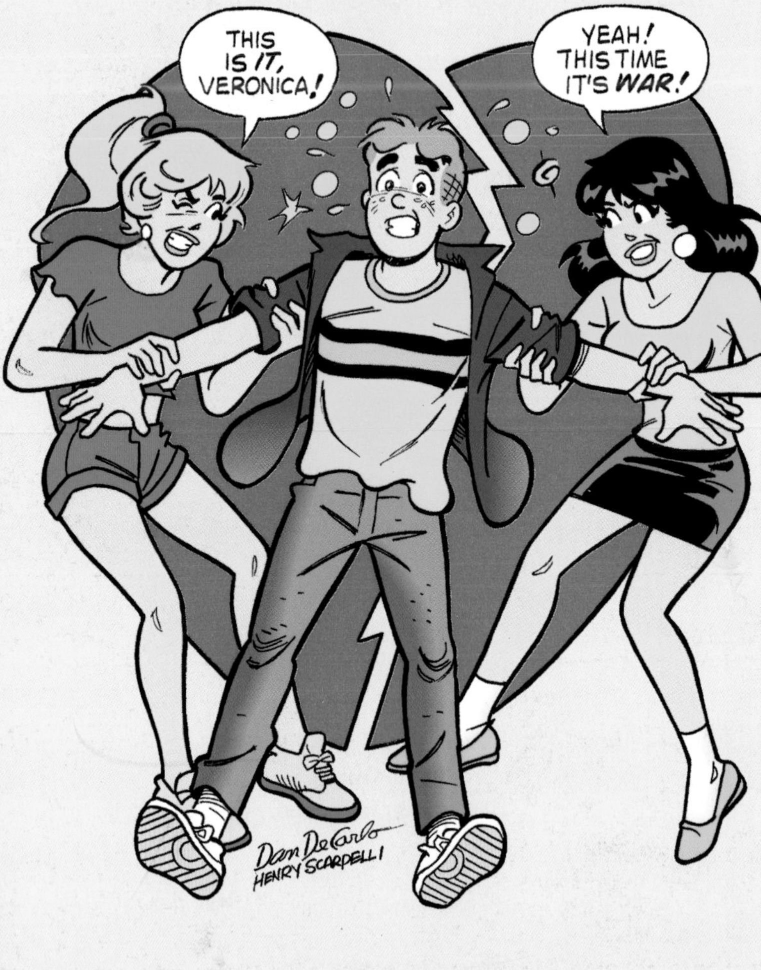
THIS IS *IT*, VERONICA!
YEAH! THIS TIME IT'S *WAR*!
Dan DeCarlo
HENRY SCARPELLI

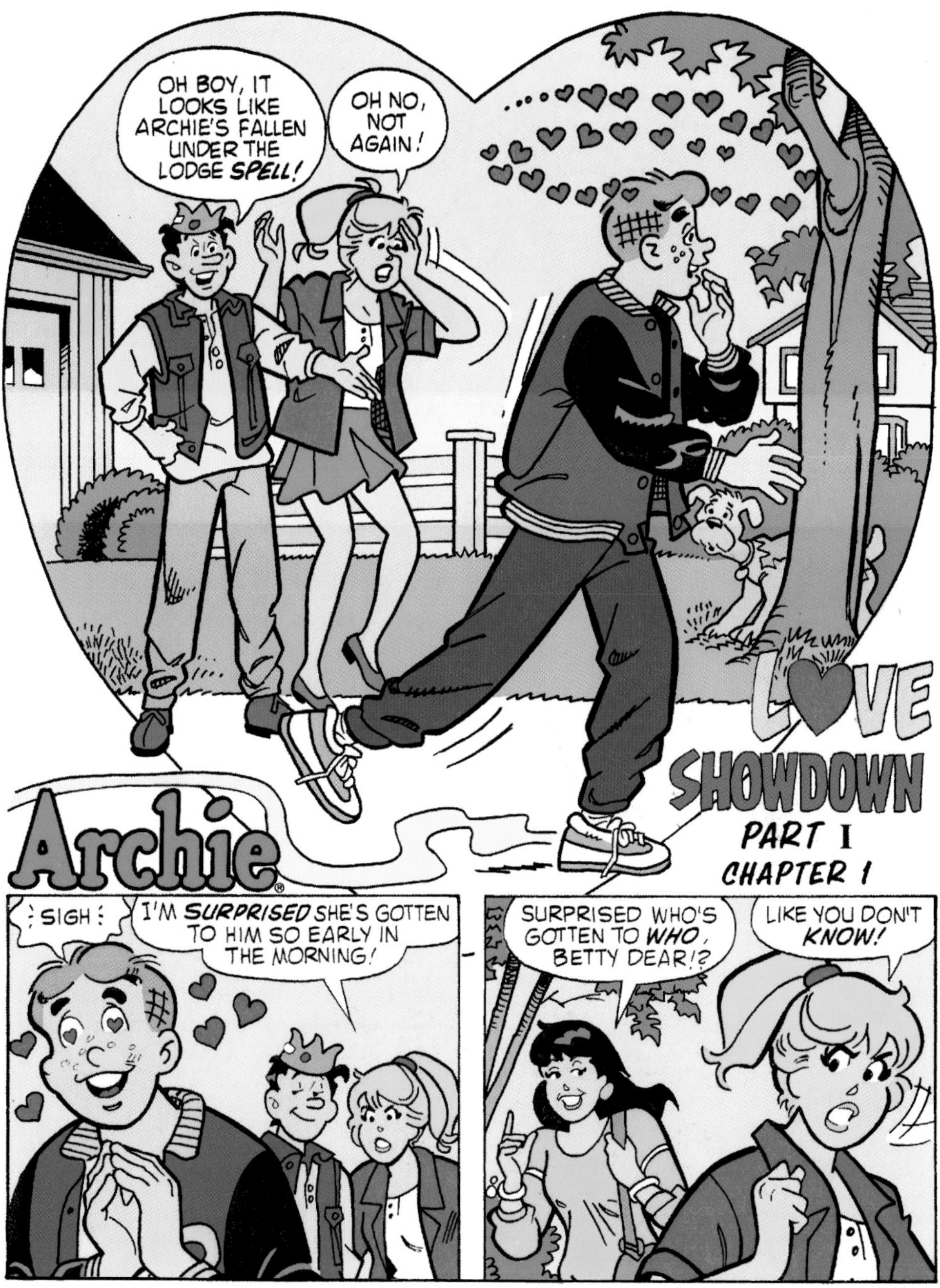
OH BOY, IT LOOKS LIKE ARCHIE'S FALLEN UNDER THE LODGE SPELL!
OH NO, NOT AGAIN!
Archie
LOVE SHOWDOWN
PART I
CHAPTER 1
SIGH
I'M SURPRISED SHE'S GOTTEN TO HIM SO EARLY IN THE MORNING!
SURPRISED WHO'S GOTTEN TO WHO, BETTY DEAR!?
LIKE YOU DON'T KNOW!

ORIGINALLY PRINTED IN ARCHIE #429, NOVEMBER 1994

DAN PARENT • STAN GOLDBERG • HENRY SCARPELLI • BILL YOSHIDA • BARRY GROSSMAN

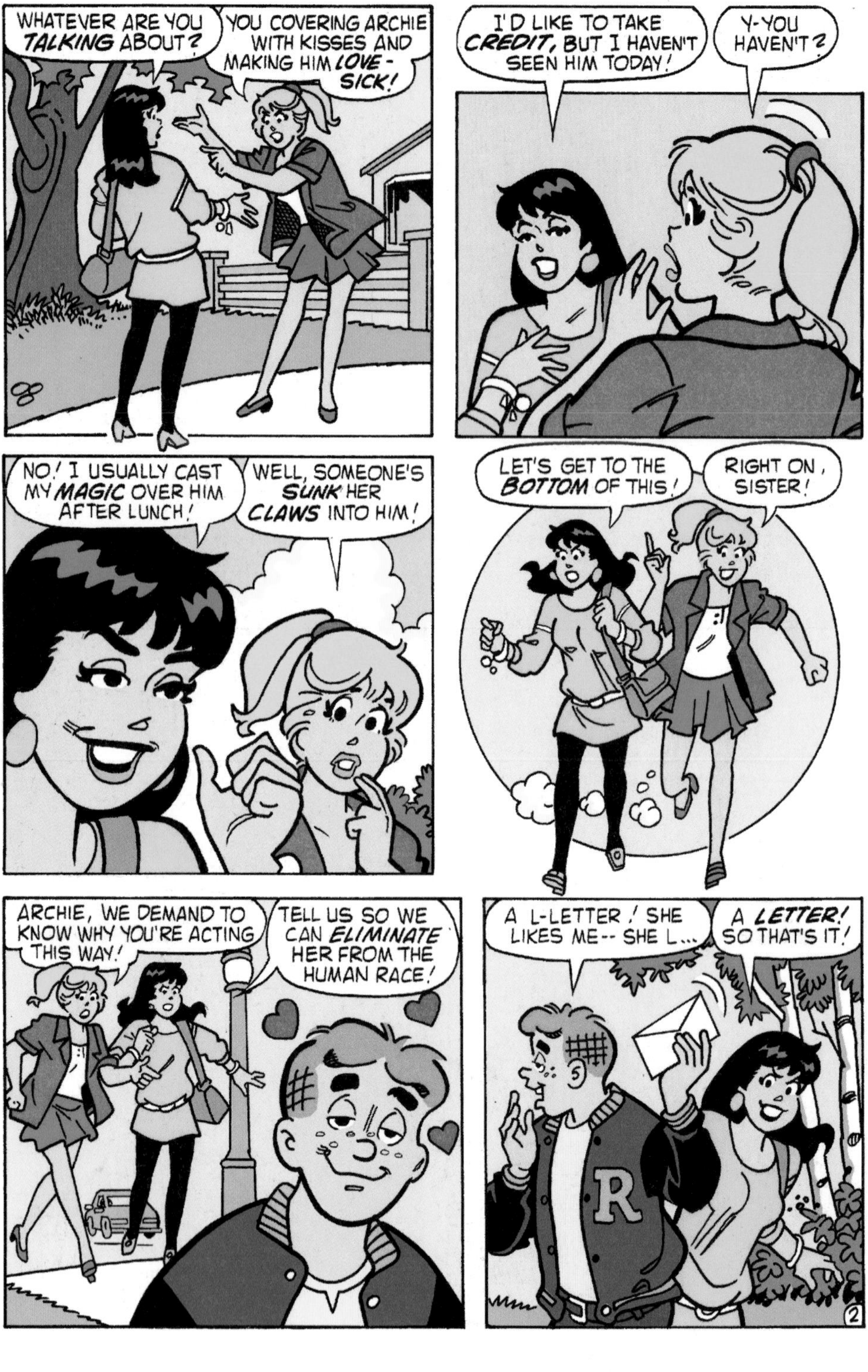
WHATEVER ARE YOU TALKING ABOUT?
YOU COVERING ARCHIE WITH KISSES AND MAKING HIM LOVE-SICK!
I'D LIKE TO TAKE CREDIT, BUT I HAVEN'T SEEN HIM TODAY!
Y-YOU HAVEN'T?
NO! I USUALLY CAST MY MAGIC OVER HIM AFTER LUNCH!
WELL, SOMEONE'S SUNK HER CLAWS INTO HIM!
LET'S GET TO THE BOTTOM OF THIS!
RIGHT ON, SISTER!
ARCHIE, WE DEMAND TO KNOW WHY YOU'RE ACTING THIS WAY!
TELL US SO WE CAN ELIMINATE HER FROM THE HUMAN RACE!
A L-LETTER! SHE LIKES ME-- SHE L...
A LETTER! SO THAT'S IT!
R
2

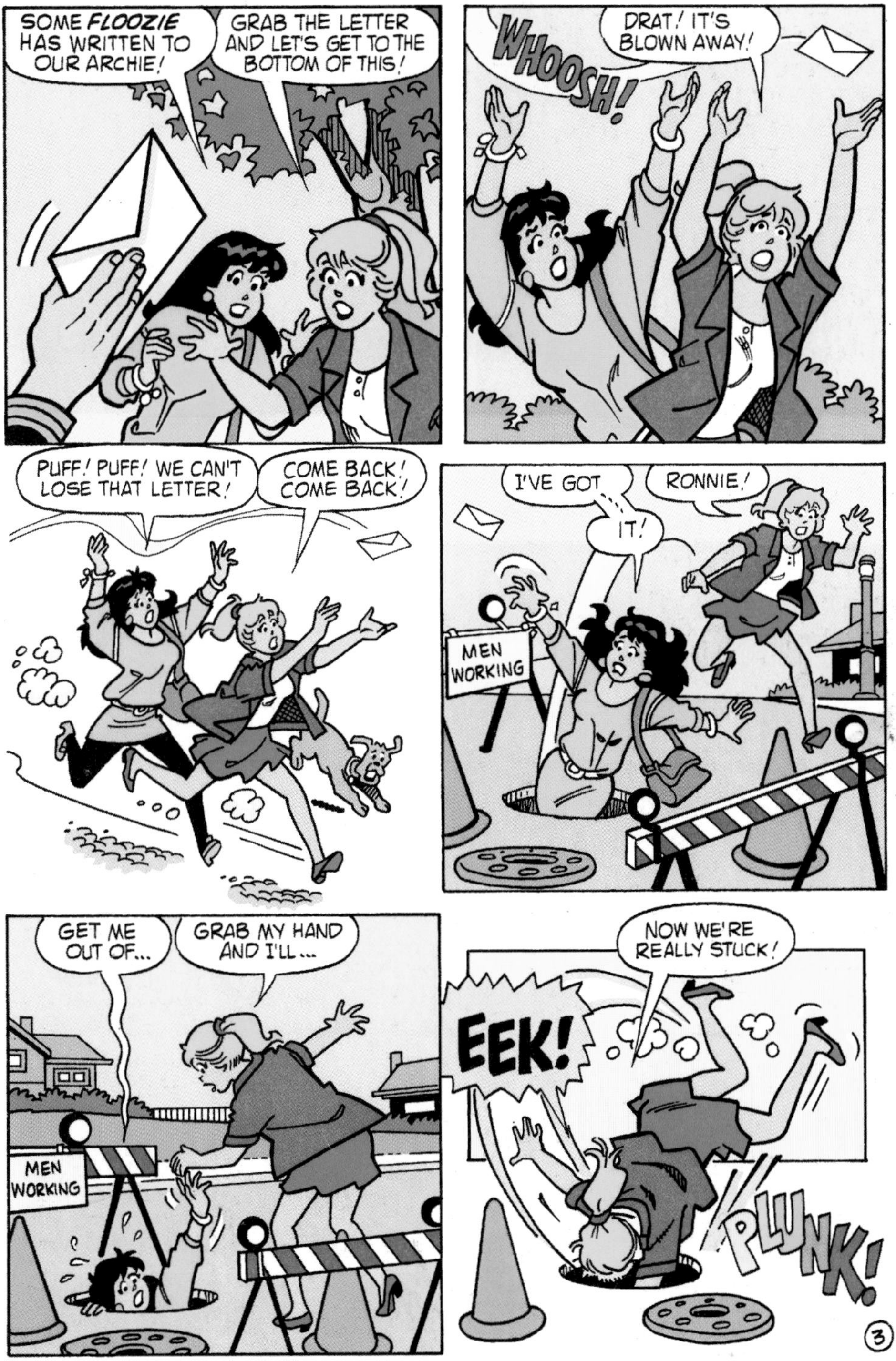
SOME FLOOZIE HAS WRITTEN TO OUR ARCHIE!
GRAB THE LETTER AND LET'S GET TO THE BOTTOM OF THIS!
WHOOSH!
DRAT! IT'S BLOWN AWAY!
PUFF! PUFF! WE CAN'T LOSE THAT LETTER!
COME BACK! COME BACK!
I'VE GOT
IT!
RONNIE!
MEN WORKING
GET ME OUT OF...
GRAB MY HAND AND I'LL...
MEN WORKING
NOW WE'RE REALLY STUCK!
EEK!
PLUNK!
3

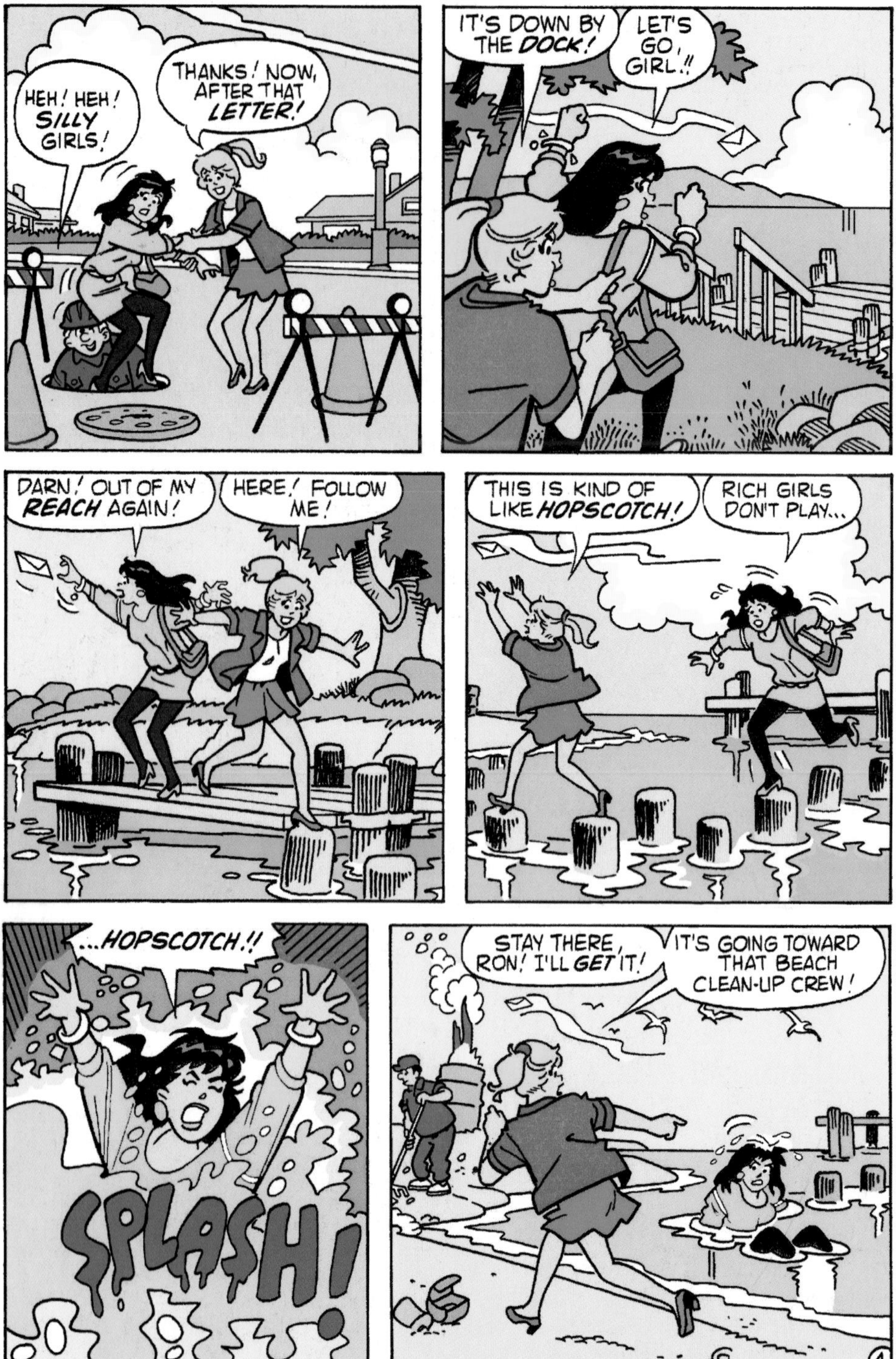
HEH! HEH! SILLY GIRLS!
THANKS! NOW, AFTER THAT LETTER!
IT'S DOWN BY THE DOCK!
LET'S GO, GIRL!!
DARN! OUT OF MY REACH AGAIN!
HERE! FOLLOW ME!
THIS IS KIND OF LIKE HOPSCOTCH!
RICH GIRLS DON'T PLAY...
...HOPSCOTCH!!
SPLASH!
STAY THERE, RON! I'LL GET IT!
IT'S GOING TOWARD THAT BEACH CLEAN-UP CREW!
4

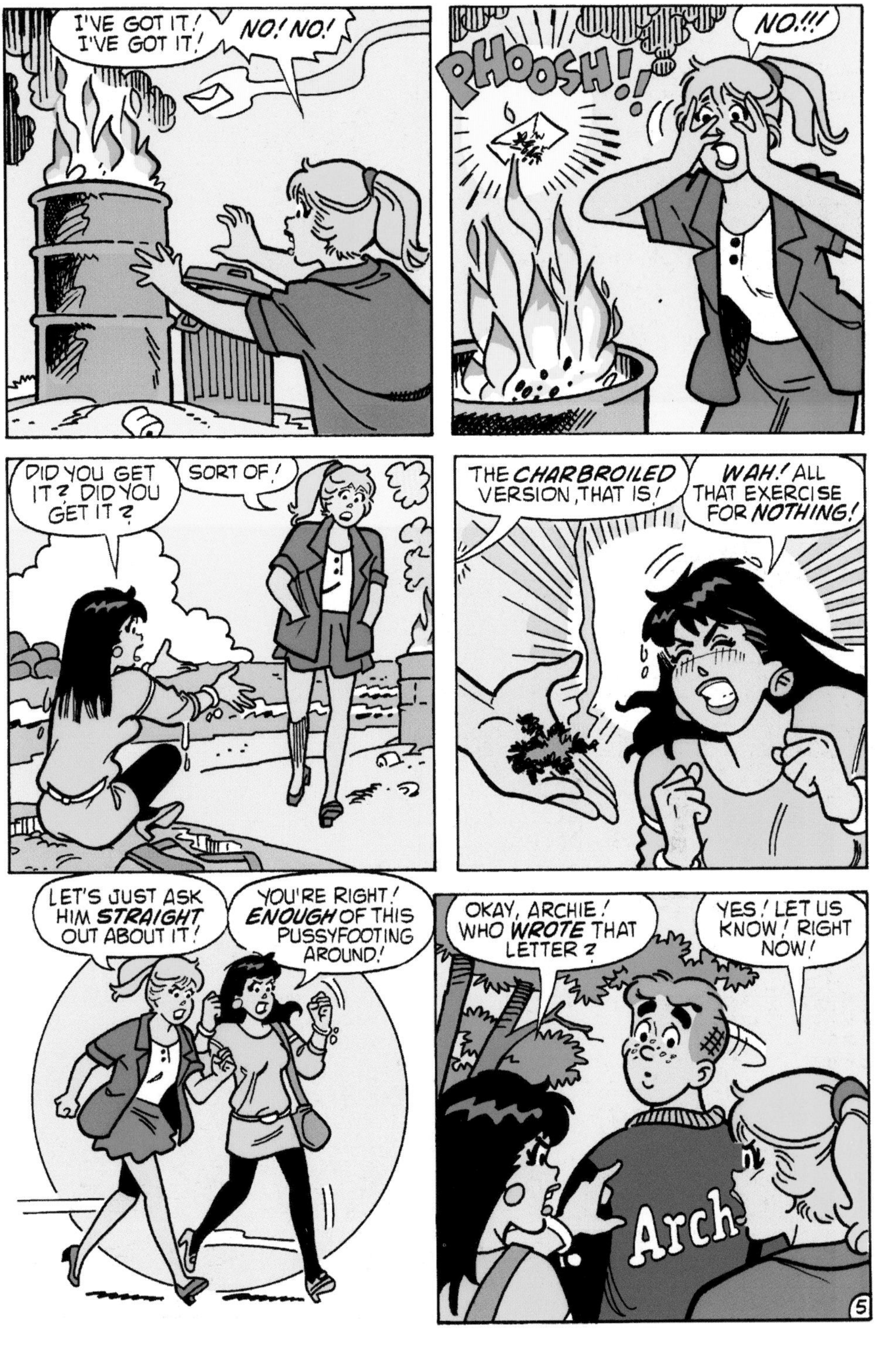

I'VE GOT IT! I'VE GOT IT!
NO! NO!
PHOOSH!
NO!!!
DID YOU GET IT? DID YOU GET IT?
SORT OF!
THE CHARBROILED VERSION, THAT IS!
WAH! ALL THAT EXERCISE FOR NOTHING!
LET'S JUST ASK HIM STRAIGHT OUT ABOUT IT!
YOU'RE RIGHT! ENOUGH OF THIS PUSSYFOOTING AROUND!
OKAY, ARCHIE! WHO WROTE THAT LETTER?
YES! LET US KNOW! RIGHT NOW!
Arch
5

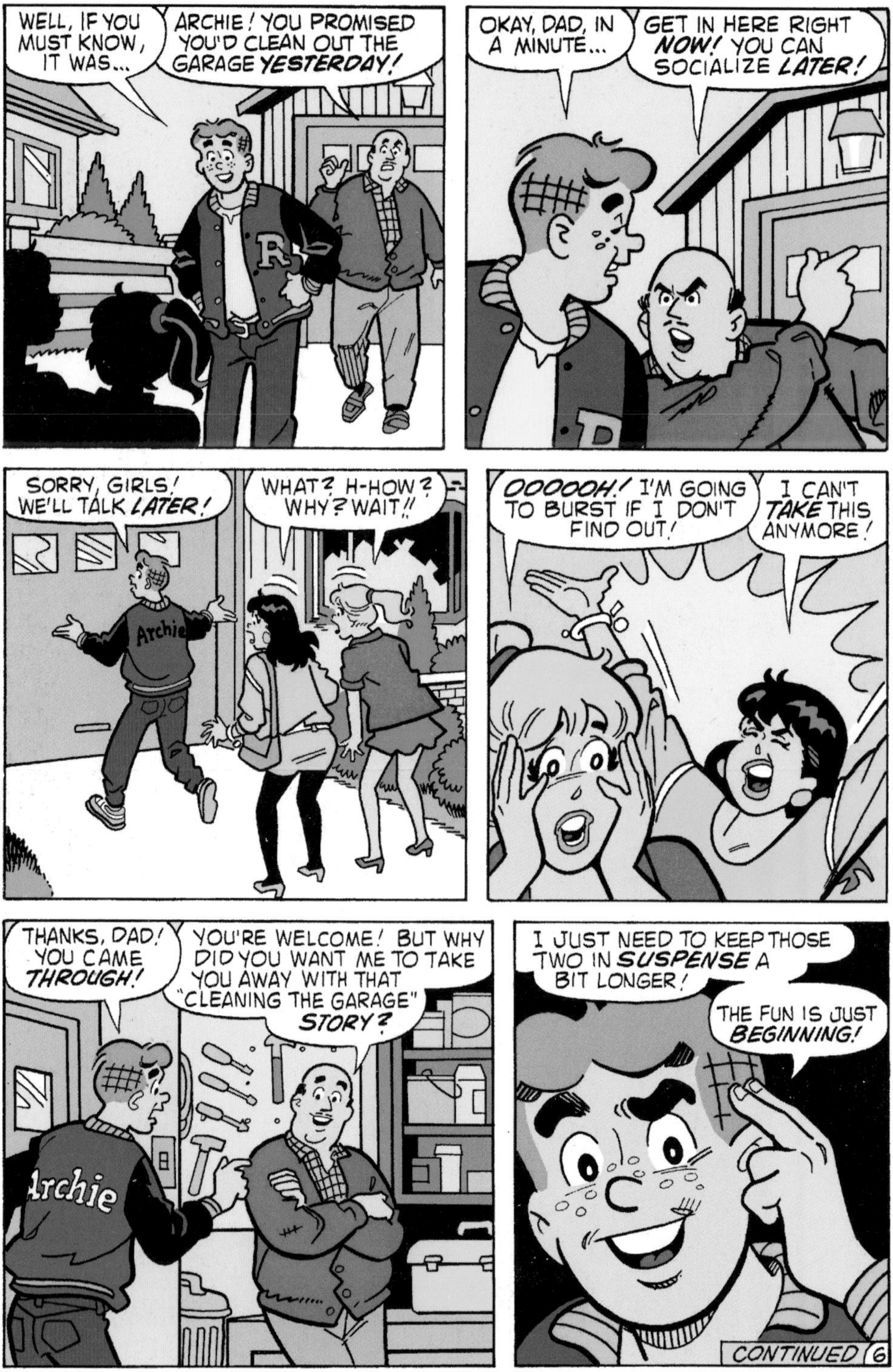

WELL, IF YOU MUST KNOW, IT WAS...
ARCHIE! YOU PROMISED YOU'D CLEAN OUT THE GARAGE YESTERDAY!
OKAY, DAD, IN A MINUTE...
GET IN HERE RIGHT NOW! YOU CAN SOCIALIZE LATER!
SORRY, GIRLS! WE'LL TALK LATER!
WHAT? H-HOW? WHY? WAIT!!
Archie
OOOOOOH! I'M GOING TO BURST IF I DON'T FIND OUT!
I CAN'T TAKE THIS ANYMORE!
THANKS, DAD! YOU CAME THROUGH!
YOU'RE WELCOME! BUT WHY DID YOU WANT ME TO TAKE YOU AWAY WITH THAT "CLEANING THE GARAGE" STORY?
Archie
I JUST NEED TO KEEP THOSE TWO IN SUSPENSE A BIT LONGER!
THE FUN IS JUST BEGINNING!
CONTINUED 6

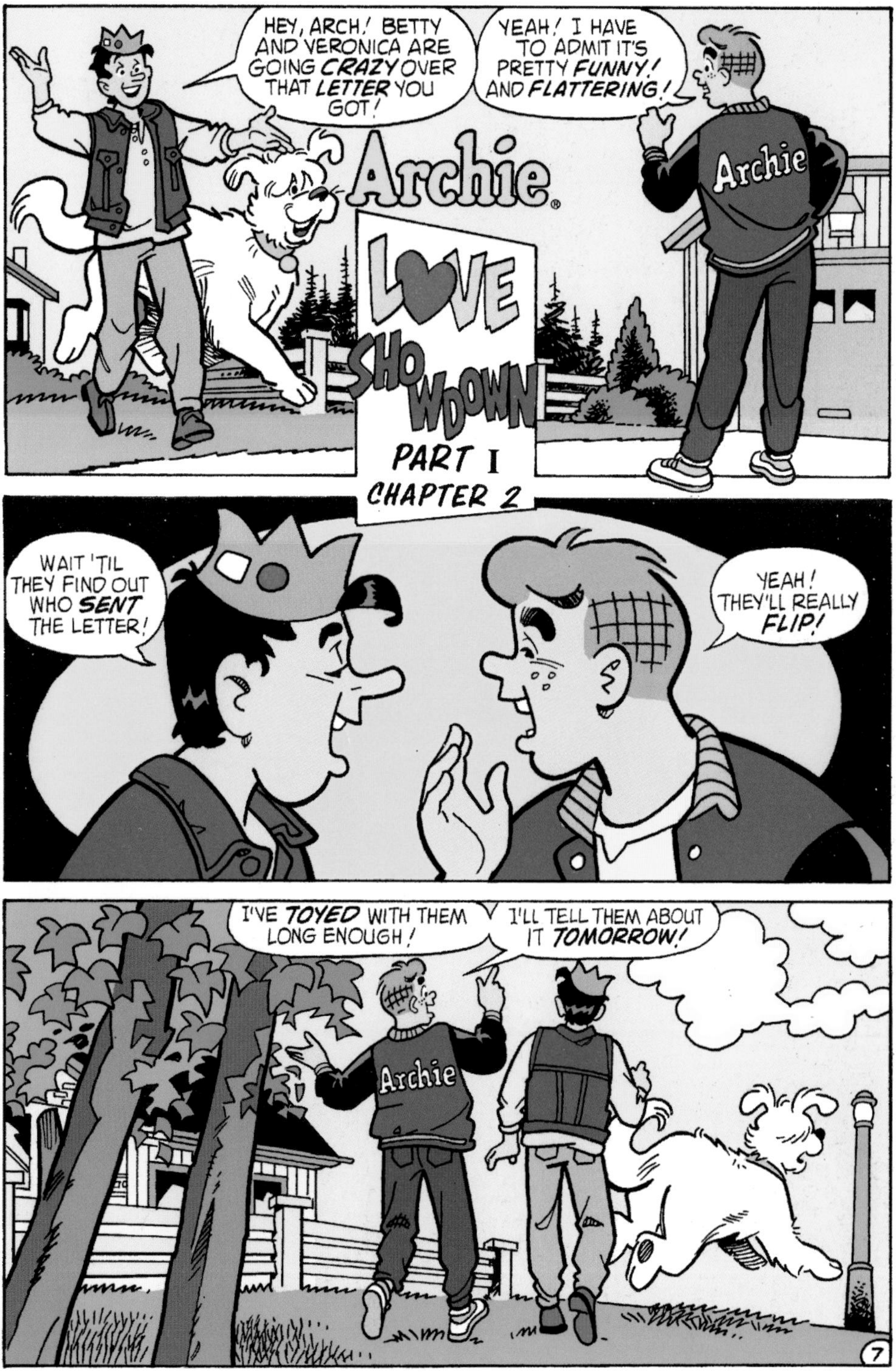
HEY, ARCH! BETTY AND VERONICA ARE GOING CRAZY OVER THAT LETTER YOU GOT!
YEAH! I HAVE TO ADMIT IT'S PRETTY FUNNY! AND FLATTERING!
Archie
Archie
LOVE SHOWDOWN
PART I
CHAPTER 2
WAIT 'TIL THEY FIND OUT WHO SENT THE LETTER!
YEAH! THEY'LL REALLY FLIP!
I'VE TOYED WITH THEM LONG ENOUGH!
I'LL TELL THEM ABOUT IT TOMORROW!
Archie
7

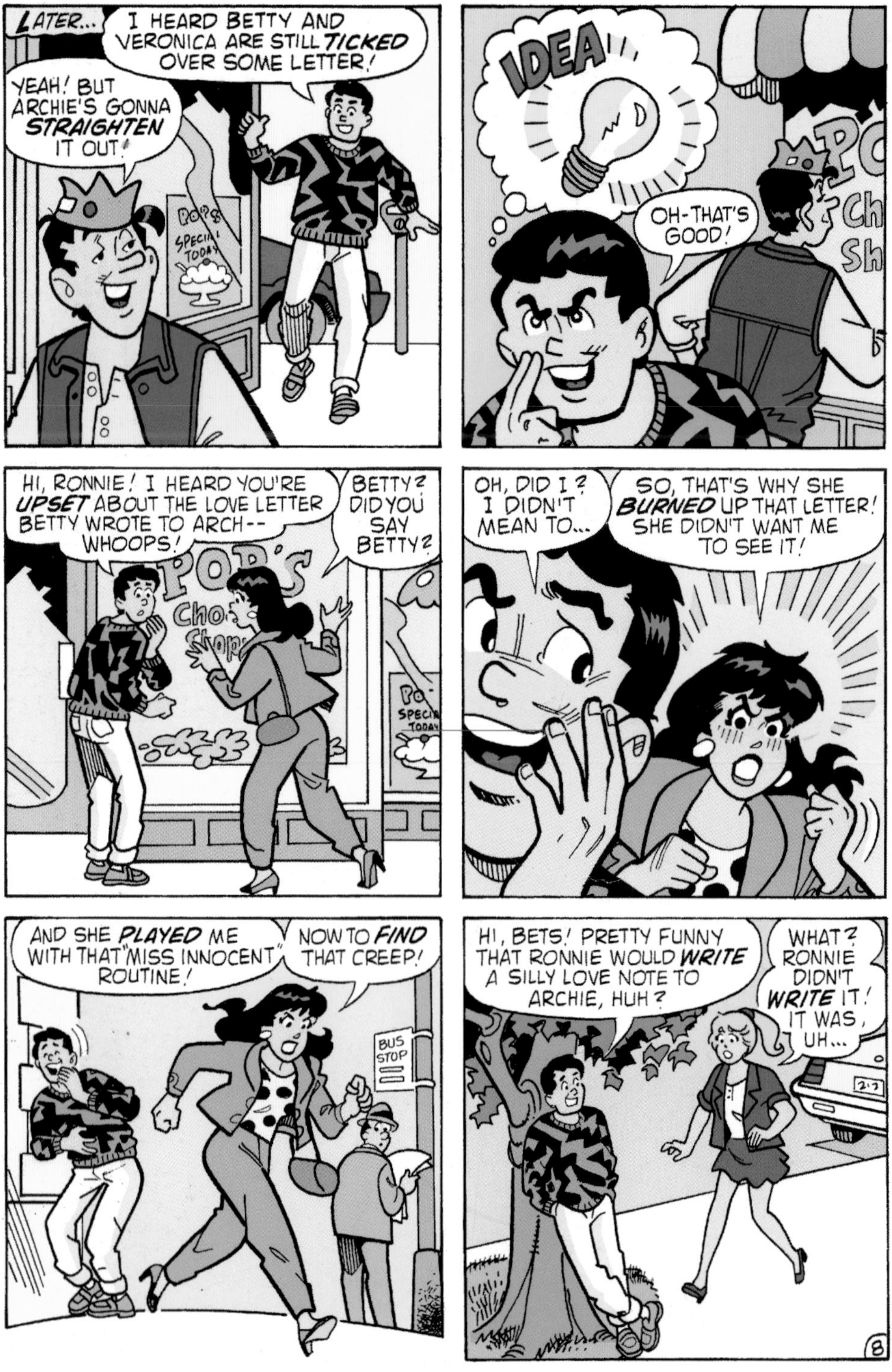
LATER...
I HEARD BETTY AND VERONICA ARE STILL TICKED OVER SOME LETTER!
YEAH! BUT ARCHIE'S GONNA STRAIGHTEN IT OUT!
POP'S SPECIAL TODAY
IDEA
OH-THAT'S GOOD!
HI, RONNIE! I HEARD YOU'RE UPSET ABOUT THE LOVE LETTER BETTY WROTE TO ARCH-- WHOOPS!
BETTY? DID YOU SAY BETTY?
OH, DID I? I DIDN'T MEAN TO...
SO, THAT'S WHY SHE BURNED UP THAT LETTER! SHE DIDN'T WANT ME TO SEE IT!
AND SHE PLAYED ME WITH THAT "MISS INNOCENT" ROUTINE!
NOW TO FIND THAT CREEP!
BUS STOP
HI, BETS! PRETTY FUNNY THAT RONNIE WOULD WRITE A SILLY LOVE NOTE TO ARCHIE, HUH?
WHAT? RONNIE DIDN'T WRITE IT! IT WAS, UH...
8

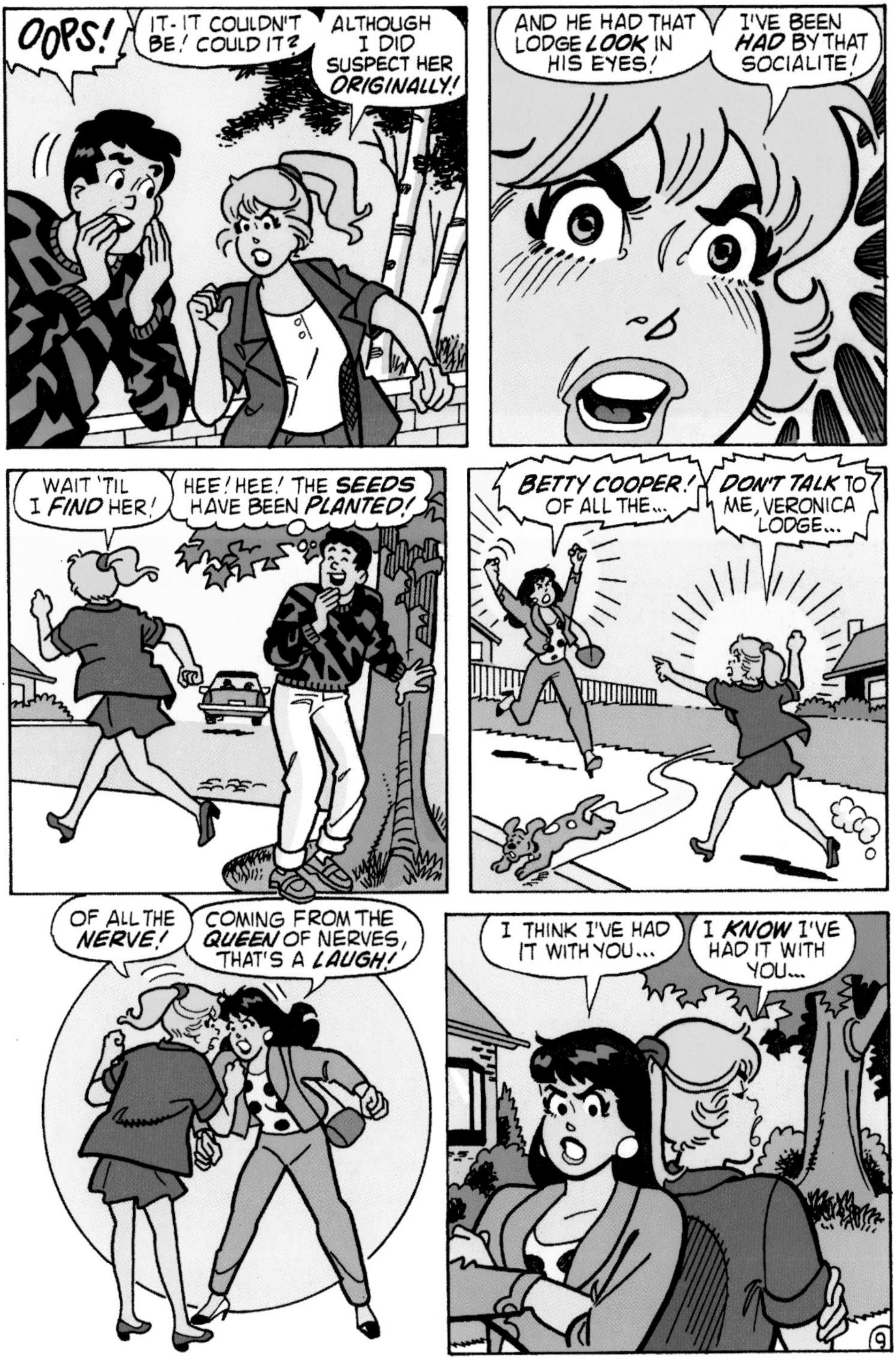
OOPS!
IT- IT COULDN'T BE! COULD IT?
ALTHOUGH I DID SUSPECT HER ORIGINALLY!
AND HE HAD THAT LODGE LOOK IN HIS EYES!
I'VE BEEN HAD BY THAT SOCIALITE!
WAIT 'TIL I FIND HER!
HEE! HEE! THE SEEDS HAVE BEEN PLANTED!
BETTY COOPER! OF ALL THE...
DON'T TALK TO ME, VERONICA LODGE...
OF ALL THE NERVE!
COMING FROM THE QUEEN OF NERVES, THAT'S A LAUGH!
I THINK I'VE HAD IT WITH YOU...
I KNOW I'VE HAD IT WITH YOU...
9

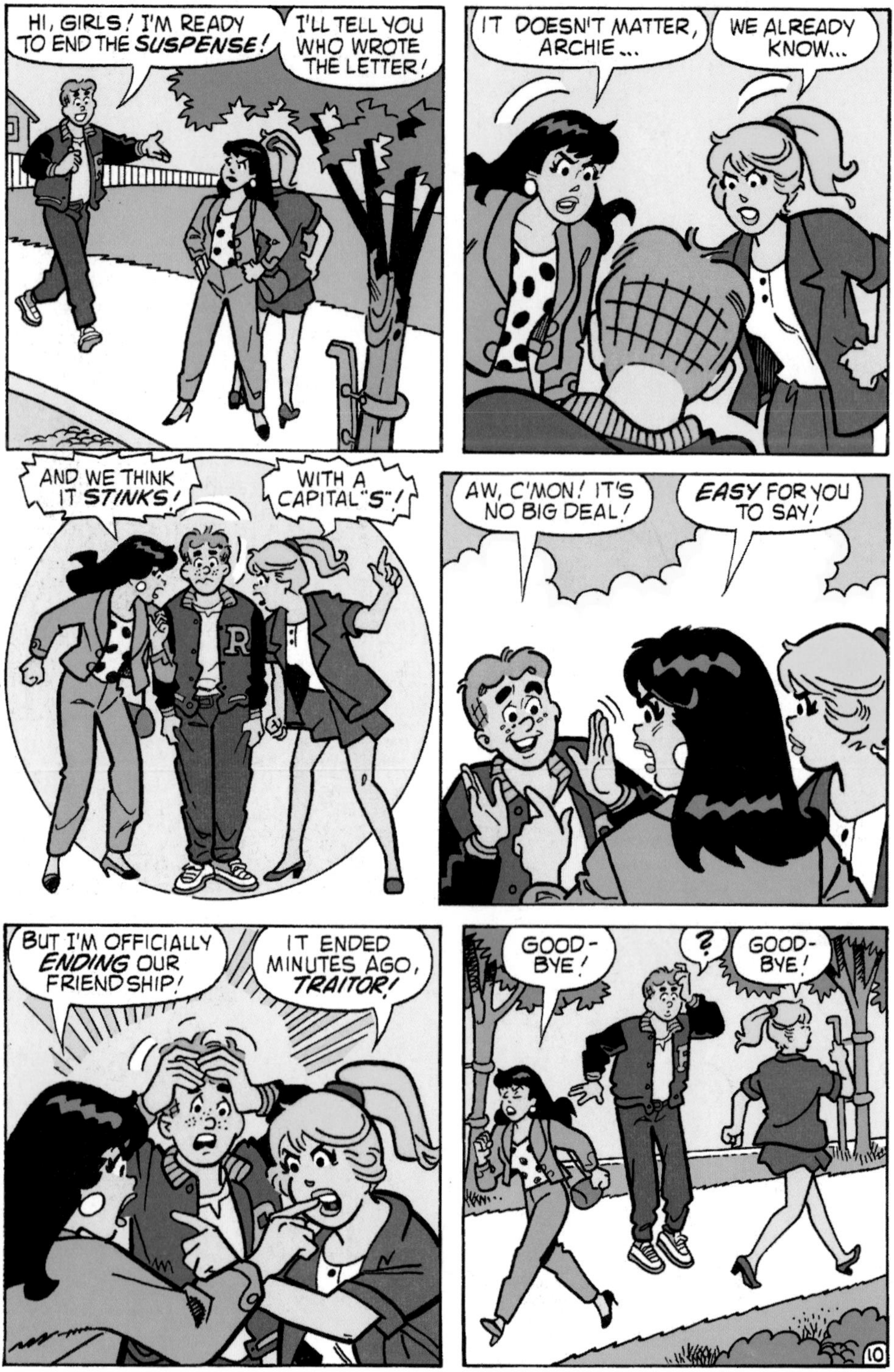
HI, GIRLS! I'M READY TO END THE SUSPENSE!
I'LL TELL YOU WHO WROTE THE LETTER!
IT DOESN'T MATTER, ARCHIE...
WE ALREADY KNOW...
AND WE THINK IT STINKS!
WITH A CAPITAL "S"!
AW, C'MON! IT'S NO BIG DEAL!
EASY FOR YOU TO SAY!
BUT I'M OFFICIALLY ENDING OUR FRIENDSHIP!
IT ENDED MINUTES AGO, TRAITOR!
GOOD-BYE!
?
GOOD-BYE!
10

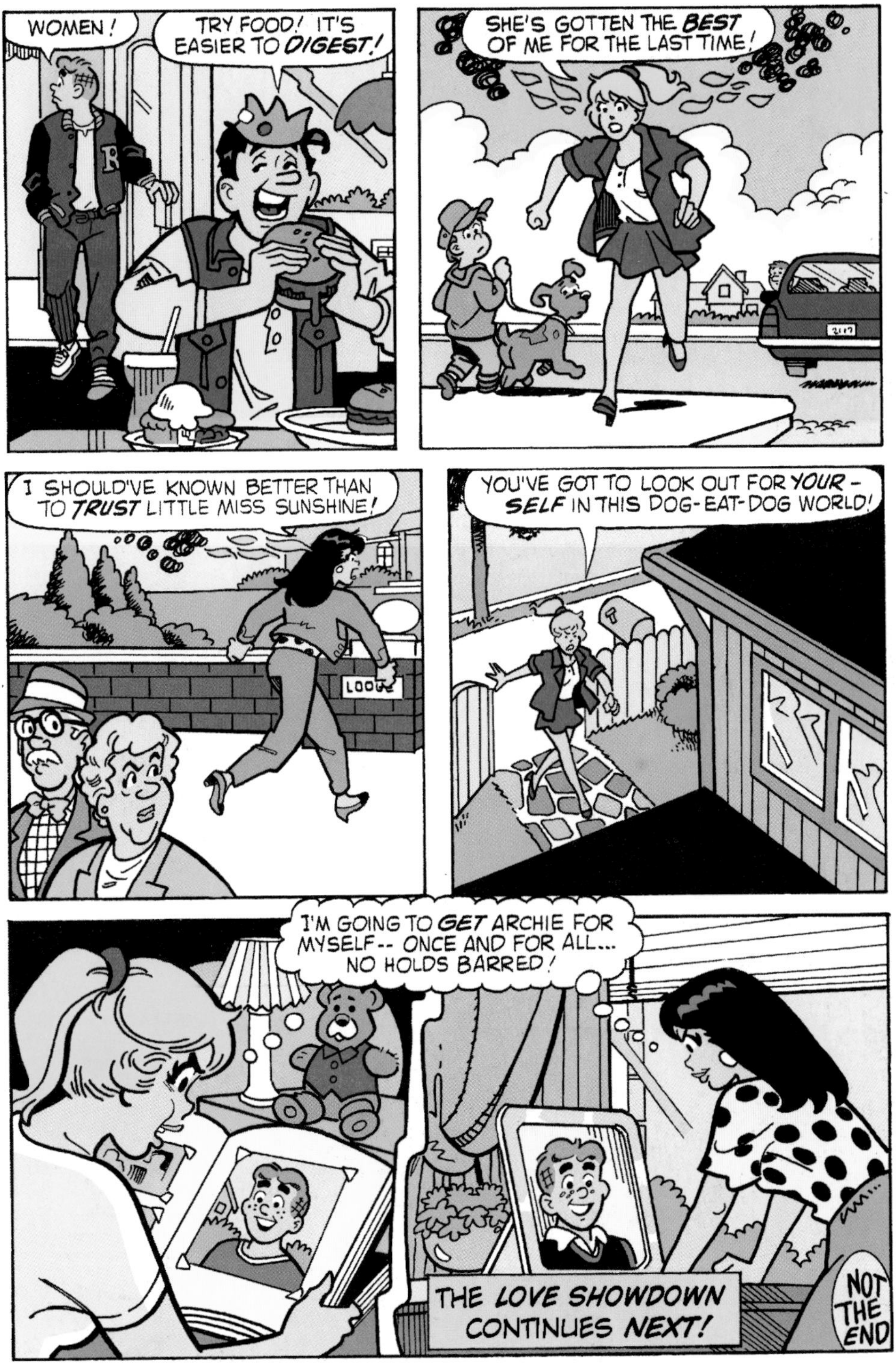
WOMEN!
TRY FOOD! IT'S EASIER TO DIGEST!
SHE'S GOTTEN THE BEST OF ME FOR THE LAST TIME!
I SHOULD'VE KNOWN BETTER THAN TO TRUST LITTLE MISS SUNSHINE!
LODGE
YOU'VE GOT TO LOOK OUT FOR YOURSELF IN THIS DOG-EAT-DOG WORLD!
I'M GOING TO GET ARCHIE FOR MYSELF-- ONCE AND FOR ALL... NO HOLDS BARRED!
THE LOVE SHOWDOWN CONTINUES NEXT!
NOT THE END

♥ ARCHIE LOVE SHOWDOWN ♥

Chapter Two

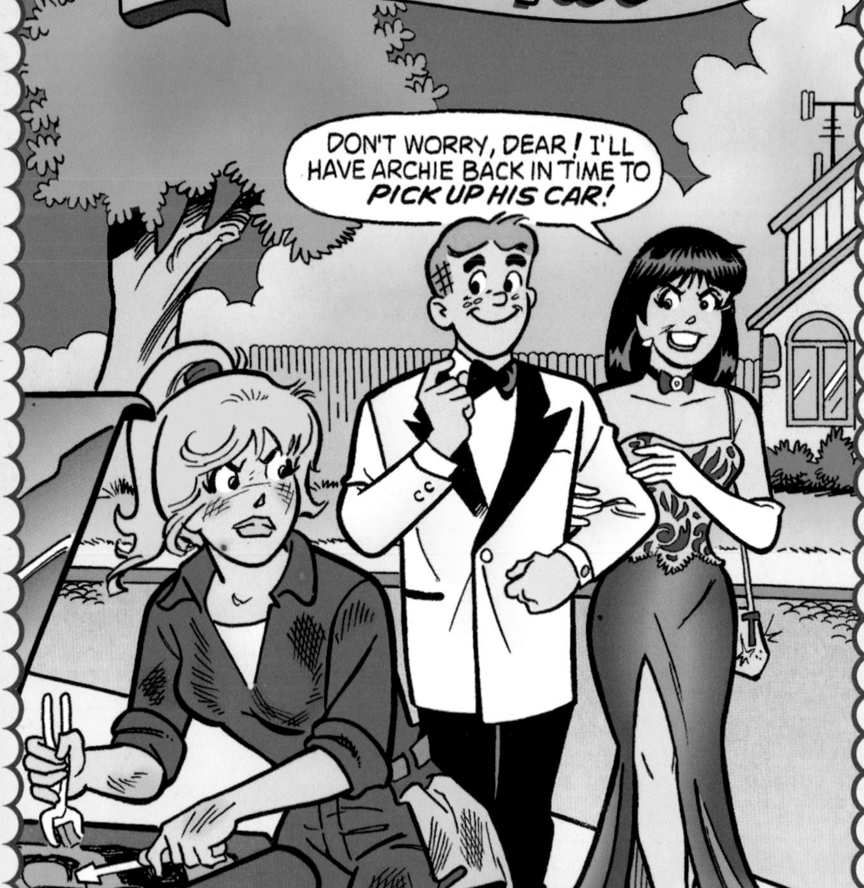

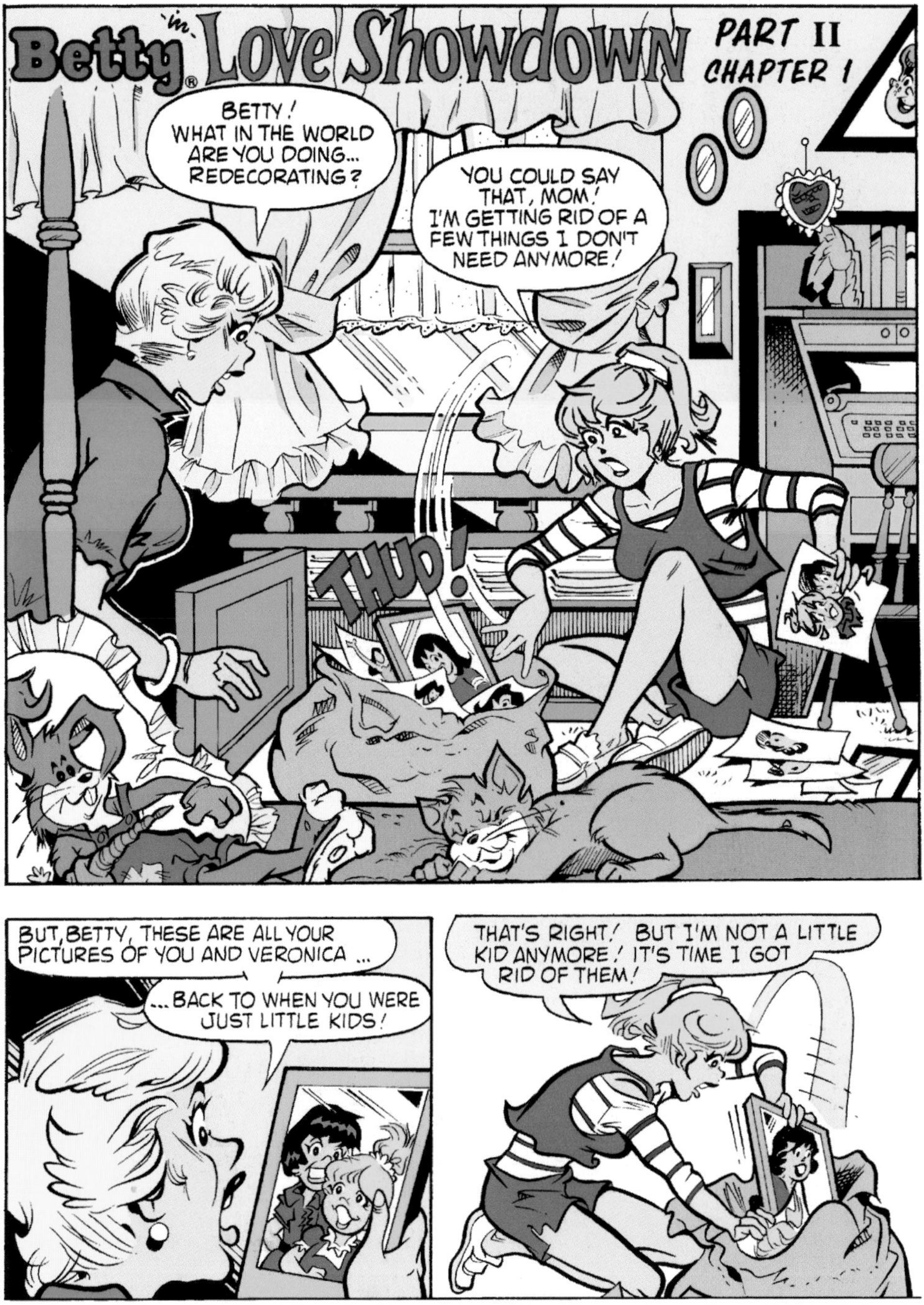
Betty in Love Showdown
PART II
CHAPTER 1
BETTY! WHAT IN THE WORLD ARE YOU DOING... REDECORATING?
YOU COULD SAY THAT, MOM! I'M GETTING RID OF A FEW THINGS I DON'T NEED ANYMORE!
THUD!
BUT, BETTY, THESE ARE ALL YOUR PICTURES OF YOU AND VERONICA ...
... BACK TO WHEN YOU WERE JUST LITTLE KIDS!
THAT'S RIGHT! BUT I'M NOT A LITTLE KID ANYMORE! IT'S TIME I GOT RID OF THEM!

ORIGINALLY PRINTED IN BETTY #19, NOVEMBER 1994

BILL GOLLIHER • DOUG CRANE • KEN SELIG • BILL YOSHIDA • BARRY GROSSMAN

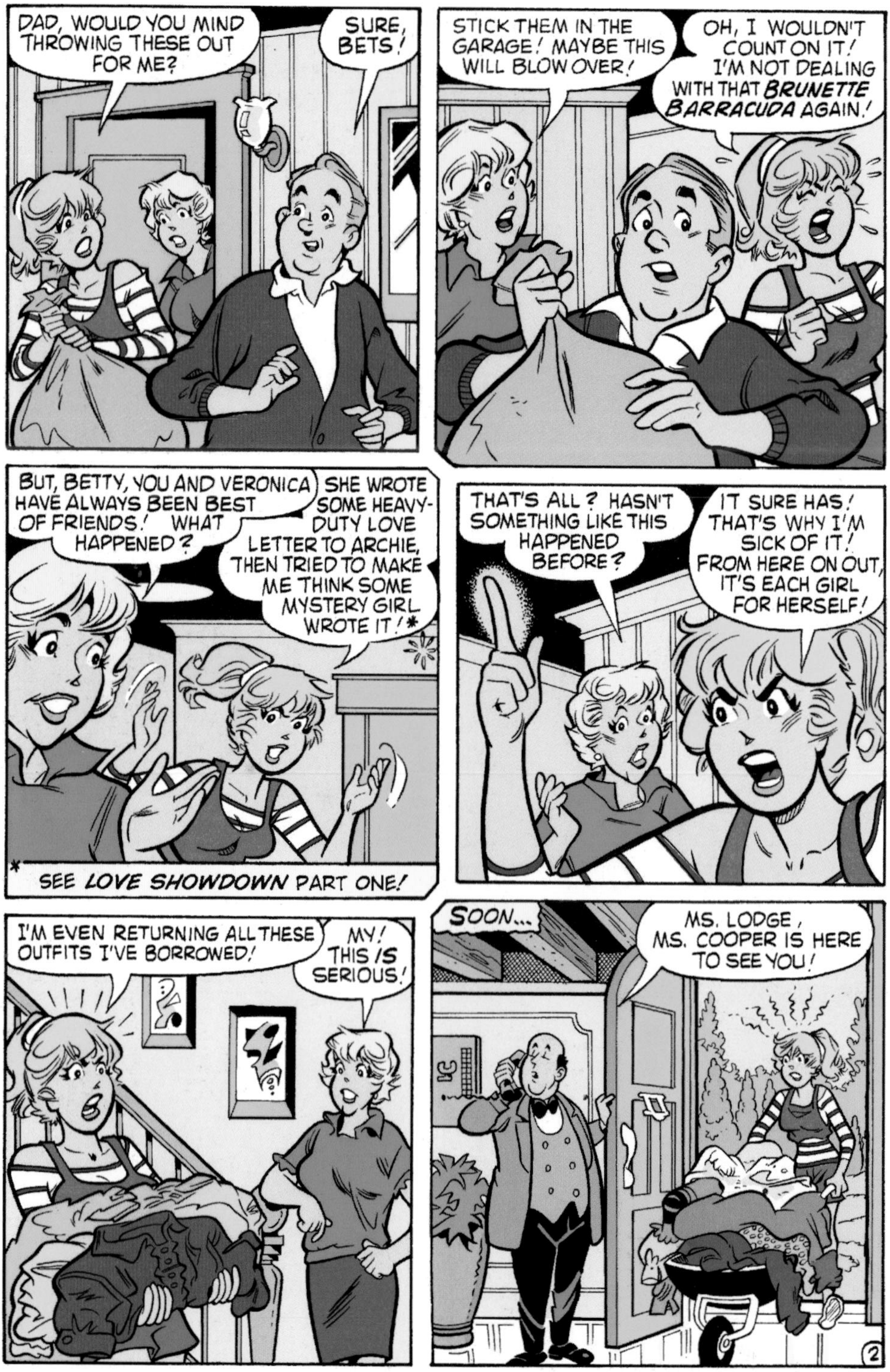
DAD, WOULD YOU MIND THROWING THESE OUT FOR ME?
SURE, BETS!
STICK THEM IN THE GARAGE! MAYBE THIS WILL BLOW OVER!
OH, I WOULDN'T COUNT ON IT! I'M NOT DEALING WITH THAT BRUNETTE BARRACUDA AGAIN!
BUT, BETTY, YOU AND VERONICA HAVE ALWAYS BEEN BEST OF FRIENDS! WHAT HAPPENED?
SHE WROTE SOME HEAVY-DUTY LOVE LETTER TO ARCHIE, THEN TRIED TO MAKE ME THINK SOME MYSTERY GIRL WROTE IT!*
* SEE LOVE SHOWDOWN PART ONE!
THAT'S ALL? HASN'T SOMETHING LIKE THIS HAPPENED BEFORE?
IT SURE HAS! THAT'S WHY I'M SICK OF IT! FROM HERE ON OUT, IT'S EACH GIRL FOR HERSELF!
I'M EVEN RETURNING ALL THESE OUTFITS I'VE BORROWED!
MY! THIS IS SERIOUS!
SOON...
MS. LODGE, MS. COOPER IS HERE TO SEE YOU!
2

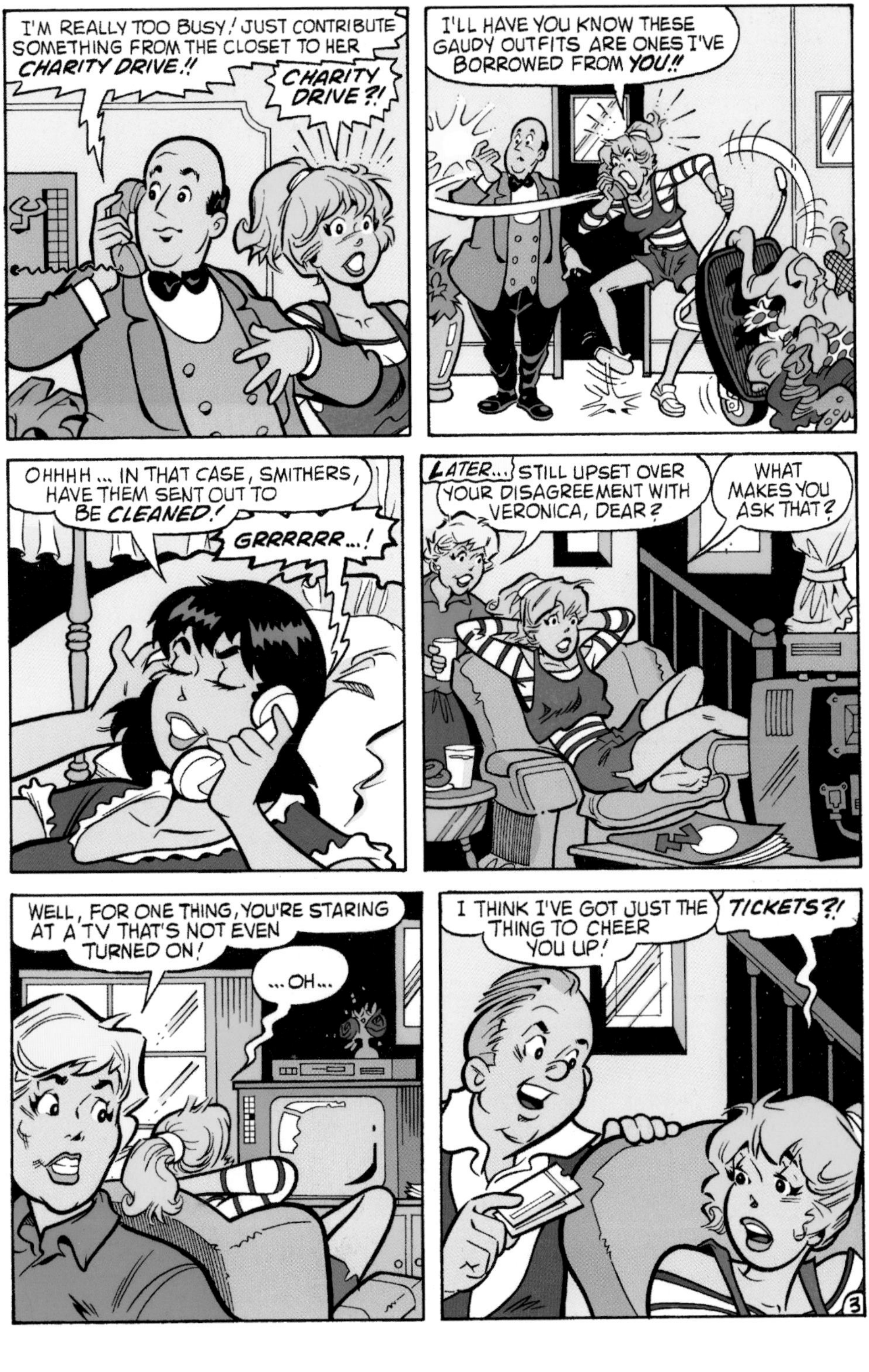

I'M REALLY TOO BUSY! JUST CONTRIBUTE SOMETHING FROM THE CLOSET TO HER CHARITY DRIVE!!
CHARITY DRIVE?!
I'LL HAVE YOU KNOW THESE GAUDY OUTFITS ARE ONES I'VE BORROWED FROM YOU!!
OHHHH ... IN THAT CASE, SMITHERS, HAVE THEM SENT OUT TO BE CLEANED!
GRRRRRR...!
LATER...
STILL UPSET OVER YOUR DISAGREEMENT WITH VERONICA, DEAR?
WHAT MAKES YOU ASK THAT?
WELL, FOR ONE THING, YOU'RE STARING AT A TV THAT'S NOT EVEN TURNED ON!
...OH...
I THINK I'VE GOT JUST THE THING TO CHEER YOU UP!
TICKETS?!
3

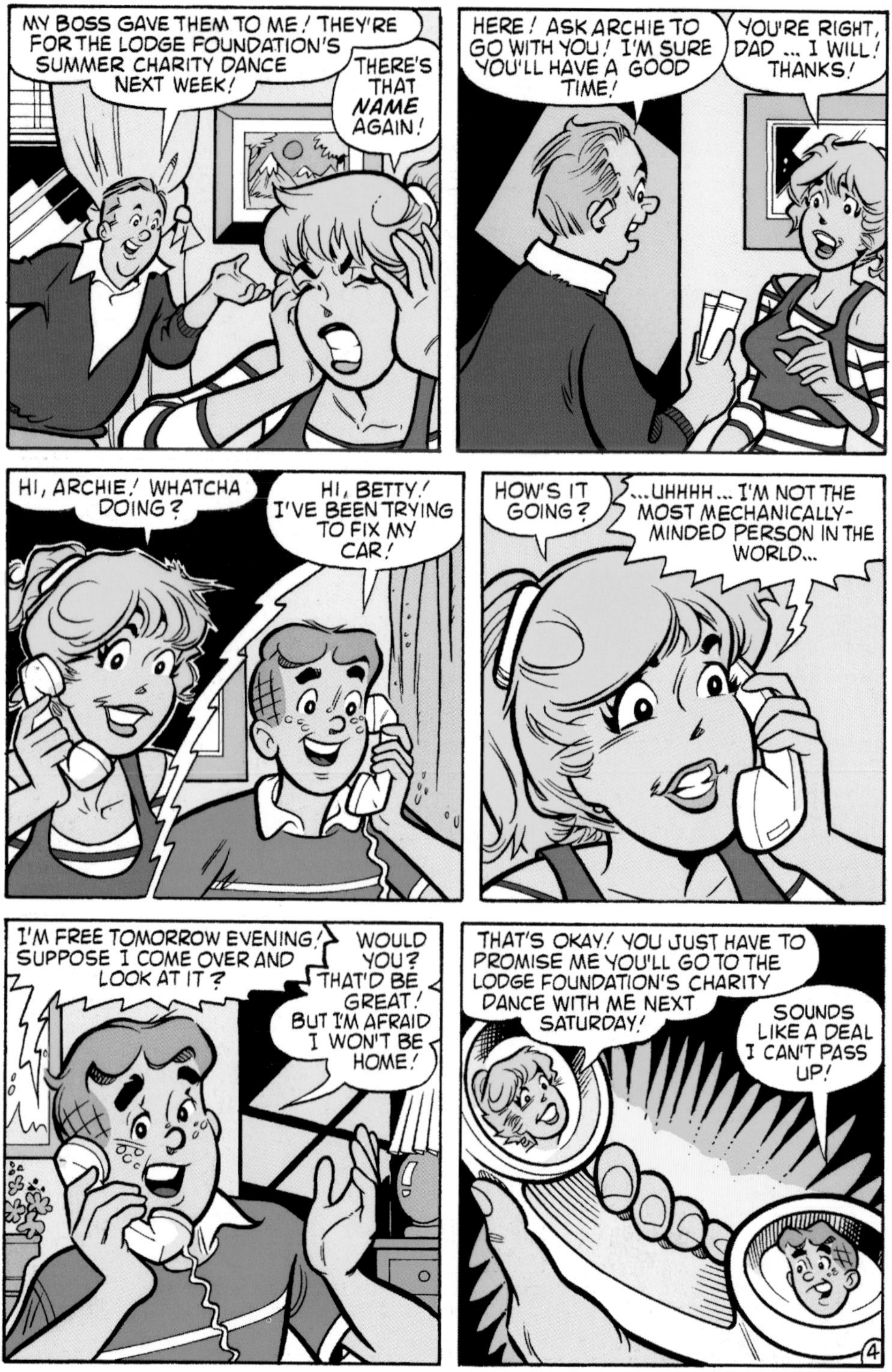
MY BOSS GAVE THEM TO ME! THEY'RE FOR THE LODGE FOUNDATION'S SUMMER CHARITY DANCE NEXT WEEK!
THERE'S THAT NAME AGAIN!
HERE! ASK ARCHIE TO GO WITH YOU! I'M SURE YOU'LL HAVE A GOOD TIME!
YOU'RE RIGHT, DAD ... I WILL! THANKS!
HI, ARCHIE! WHATCHA DOING?
HI, BETTY! I'VE BEEN TRYING TO FIX MY CAR!
HOW'S IT GOING?
...UHHHH ... I'M NOT THE MOST MECHANICALLY-MINDED PERSON IN THE WORLD...
I'M FREE TOMORROW EVENING! SUPPOSE I COME OVER AND LOOK AT IT?
WOULD YOU? THAT'D BE GREAT! BUT I'M AFRAID I WON'T BE HOME!
THAT'S OKAY! YOU JUST HAVE TO PROMISE ME YOU'LL GO TO THE LODGE FOUNDATION'S CHARITY DANCE WITH ME NEXT SATURDAY!
SOUNDS LIKE A DEAL I CAN'T PASS UP!
4

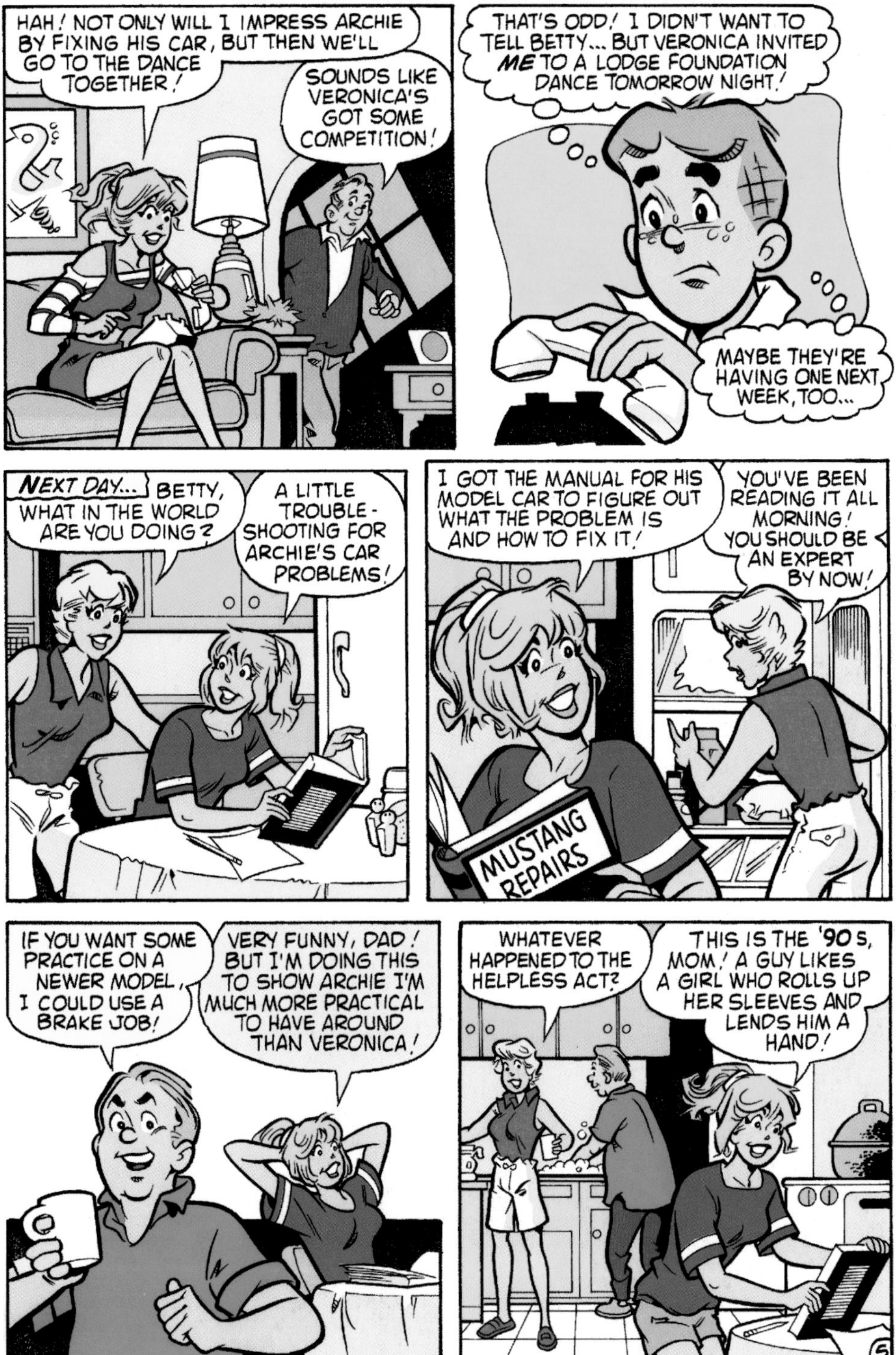
HAH! NOT ONLY WILL I IMPRESS ARCHIE BY FIXING HIS CAR, BUT THEN WE'LL GO TO THE DANCE TOGETHER!
SOUNDS LIKE VERONICA'S GOT SOME COMPETITION!
THAT'S ODD! I DIDN'T WANT TO TELL BETTY... BUT VERONICA INVITED ME TO A LODGE FOUNDATION DANCE TOMORROW NIGHT!
MAYBE THEY'RE HAVING ONE NEXT WEEK, TOO...
NEXT DAY...
BETTY, WHAT IN THE WORLD ARE YOU DOING?
A LITTLE TROUBLE-SHOOTING FOR ARCHIE'S CAR PROBLEMS!
I GOT THE MANUAL FOR HIS MODEL CAR TO FIGURE OUT WHAT THE PROBLEM IS AND HOW TO FIX IT!
YOU'VE BEEN READING IT ALL MORNING! YOU SHOULD BE AN EXPERT BY NOW!
MUSTANG REPAIRS
IF YOU WANT SOME PRACTICE ON A NEWER MODEL, I COULD USE A BRAKE JOB!
VERY FUNNY, DAD! BUT I'M DOING THIS TO SHOW ARCHIE I'M MUCH MORE PRACTICAL TO HAVE AROUND THAN VERONICA!
WHATEVER HAPPENED TO THE HELPLESS ACT?
THIS IS THE '90S, MOM! A GUY LIKES A GIRL WHO ROLLS UP HER SLEEVES AND LENDS HIM A HAND!
5

SEE YOU TWO LATER! I'VE GOT A JOB TO DO!

DO YOU THINK THE HOSPITAL GAVE US MR. GOODWRENCH'S BABY BY MISTAKE?

HI, ARCH! HOW'RE YOU DOING?

NOT TOO GOOD! THIS THING STILL HAS ME STUMPED...

WELL, I'VE BEEN DOING A LITTLE STUDYING AND I THINK I KNOW WHERE YOUR PROBLEM IS!

YOU'VE GOT TO BE KIDDING!

SOON... AH-HAH! JUST AS I THOUGHT!

WHAT IS IT?

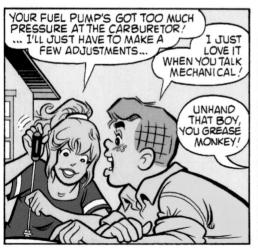

YOUR FUEL PUMP'S GOT TOO MUCH PRESSURE AT THE CARBURETOR! ...I'LL JUST HAVE TO MAKE A FEW ADJUSTMENTS...

I JUST LOVE IT WHEN YOU TALK MECHANICAL!

UNHAND THAT BOY, YOU GREASE MONKEY!

I'VE GOT DIBS ON HIM TONIGHT!

VERONICA!?!

CONTINUED ...

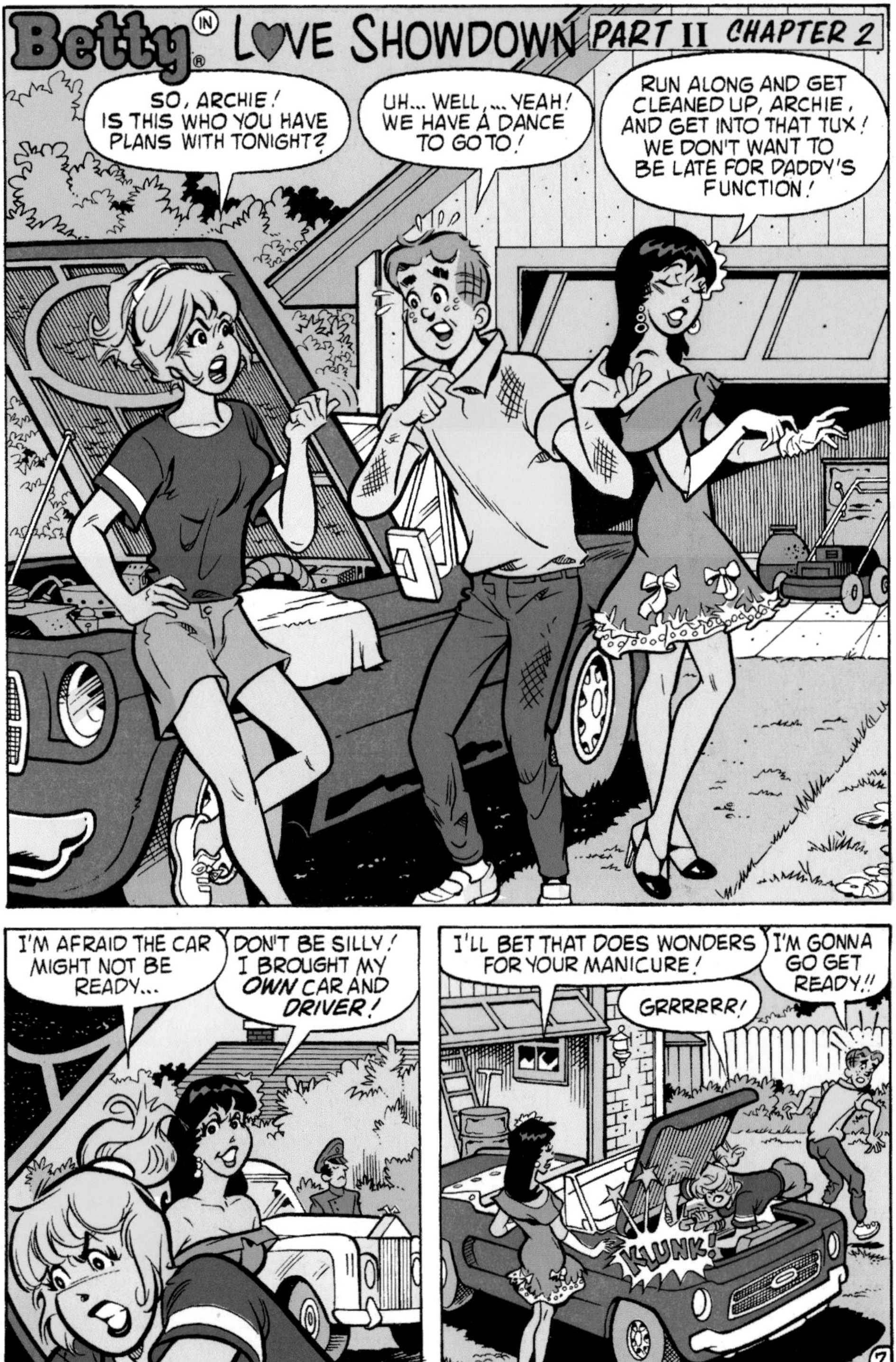
Betty IN LOVE SHOWDOWN PART II CHAPTER 2
SO, ARCHIE! IS THIS WHO YOU HAVE PLANS WITH TONIGHT?
UH... WELL,... YEAH! WE HAVE A DANCE TO GO TO!
RUN ALONG AND GET CLEANED UP, ARCHIE, AND GET INTO THAT TUX! WE DON'T WANT TO BE LATE FOR DADDY'S FUNCTION!
I'M AFRAID THE CAR MIGHT NOT BE READY...
DON'T BE SILLY! I BROUGHT MY OWN CAR AND DRIVER!
I'LL BET THAT DOES WONDERS FOR YOUR MANICURE!
GRRRRRR!
I'M GONNA GO GET READY!!
KLUNK!
7

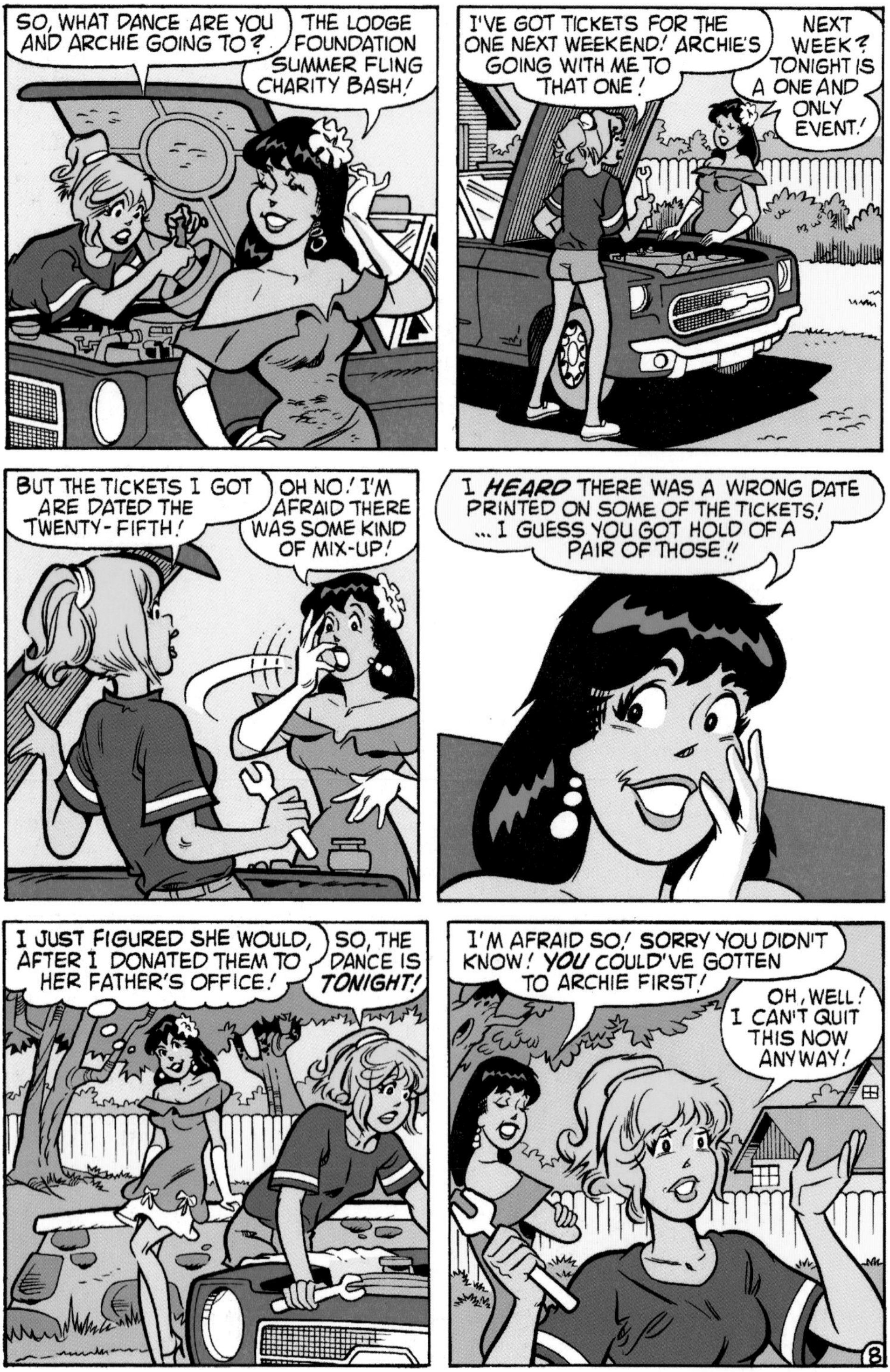
SO, WHAT DANCE ARE YOU AND ARCHIE GOING TO?
THE LODGE FOUNDATION SUMMER FLING CHARITY BASH!
I'VE GOT TICKETS FOR THE ONE NEXT WEEKEND! ARCHIE'S GOING WITH ME TO THAT ONE!
NEXT WEEK? TONIGHT IS A ONE AND ONLY EVENT!
BUT THE TICKETS I GOT ARE DATED THE TWENTY-FIFTH!
OH NO! I'M AFRAID THERE WAS SOME KIND OF MIX-UP!
I HEARD THERE WAS A WRONG DATE PRINTED ON SOME OF THE TICKETS! ... I GUESS YOU GOT HOLD OF A PAIR OF THOSE!!
I JUST FIGURED SHE WOULD, AFTER I DONATED THEM TO HER FATHER'S OFFICE!
SO, THE DANCE IS TONIGHT!
I'M AFRAID SO! SORRY YOU DIDN'T KNOW! YOU COULD'VE GOTTEN TO ARCHIE FIRST!
OH, WELL! I CAN'T QUIT THIS NOW ANYWAY!
8

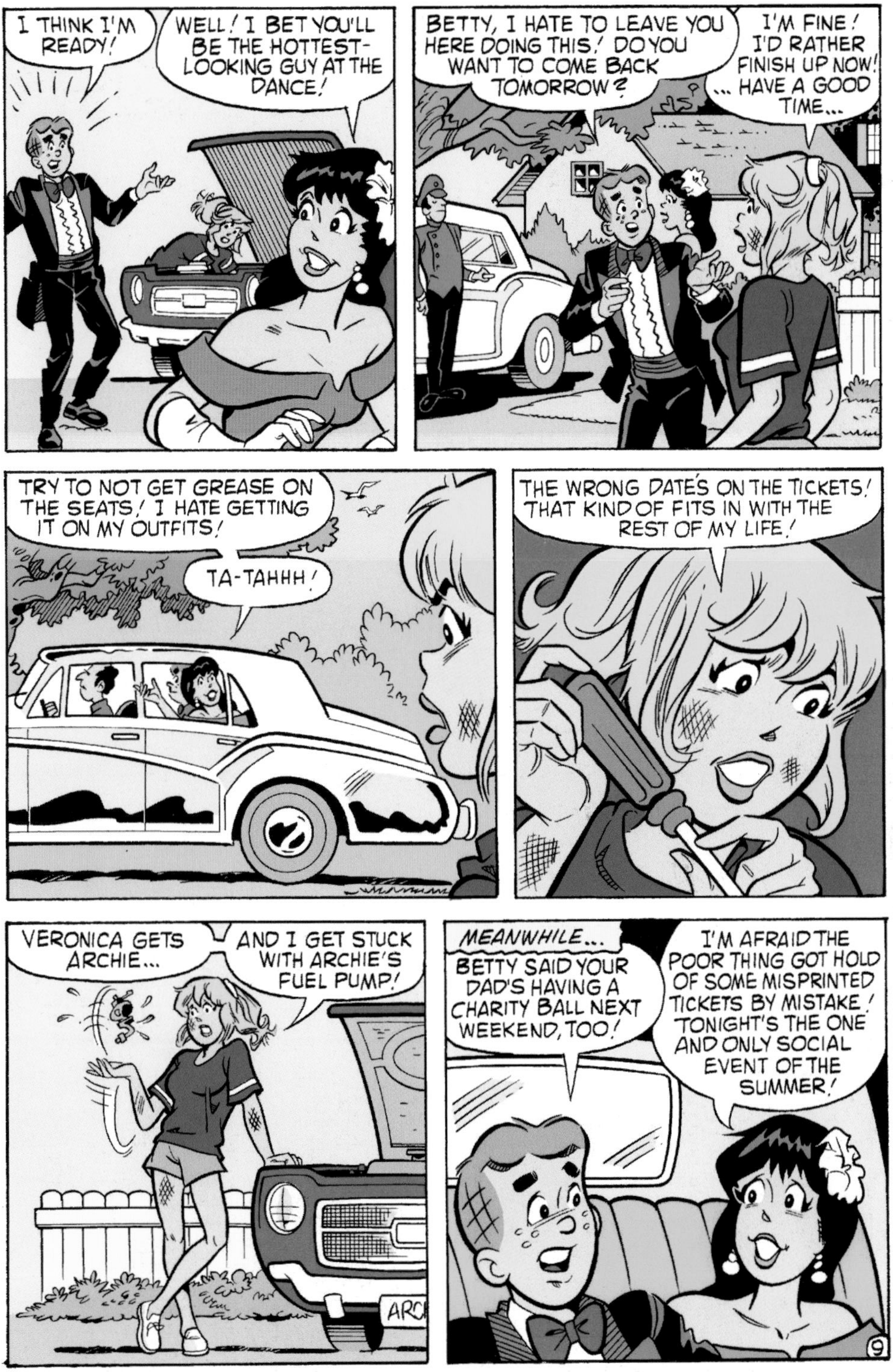

I THINK I'M READY!
WELL! I BET YOU'LL BE THE HOTTEST-LOOKING GUY AT THE DANCE!
BETTY, I HATE TO LEAVE YOU HERE DOING THIS! DO YOU WANT TO COME BACK TOMORROW?
I'M FINE! I'D RATHER FINISH UP NOW! ... HAVE A GOOD TIME...
TRY TO NOT GET GREASE ON THE SEATS! I HATE GETTING IT ON MY OUTFITS!
TA-TAHHH!
THE WRONG DATE'S ON THE TICKETS! THAT KIND OF FITS IN WITH THE REST OF MY LIFE!
VERONICA GETS ARCHIE...
AND I GET STUCK WITH ARCHIE'S FUEL PUMP!
ARC
MEANWHILE...
BETTY SAID YOUR DAD'S HAVING A CHARITY BALL NEXT WEEKEND, TOO!
I'M AFRAID THE POOR THING GOT HOLD OF SOME MISPRINTED TICKETS BY MISTAKE! TONIGHT'S THE ONE AND ONLY SOCIAL EVENT OF THE SUMMER!
9

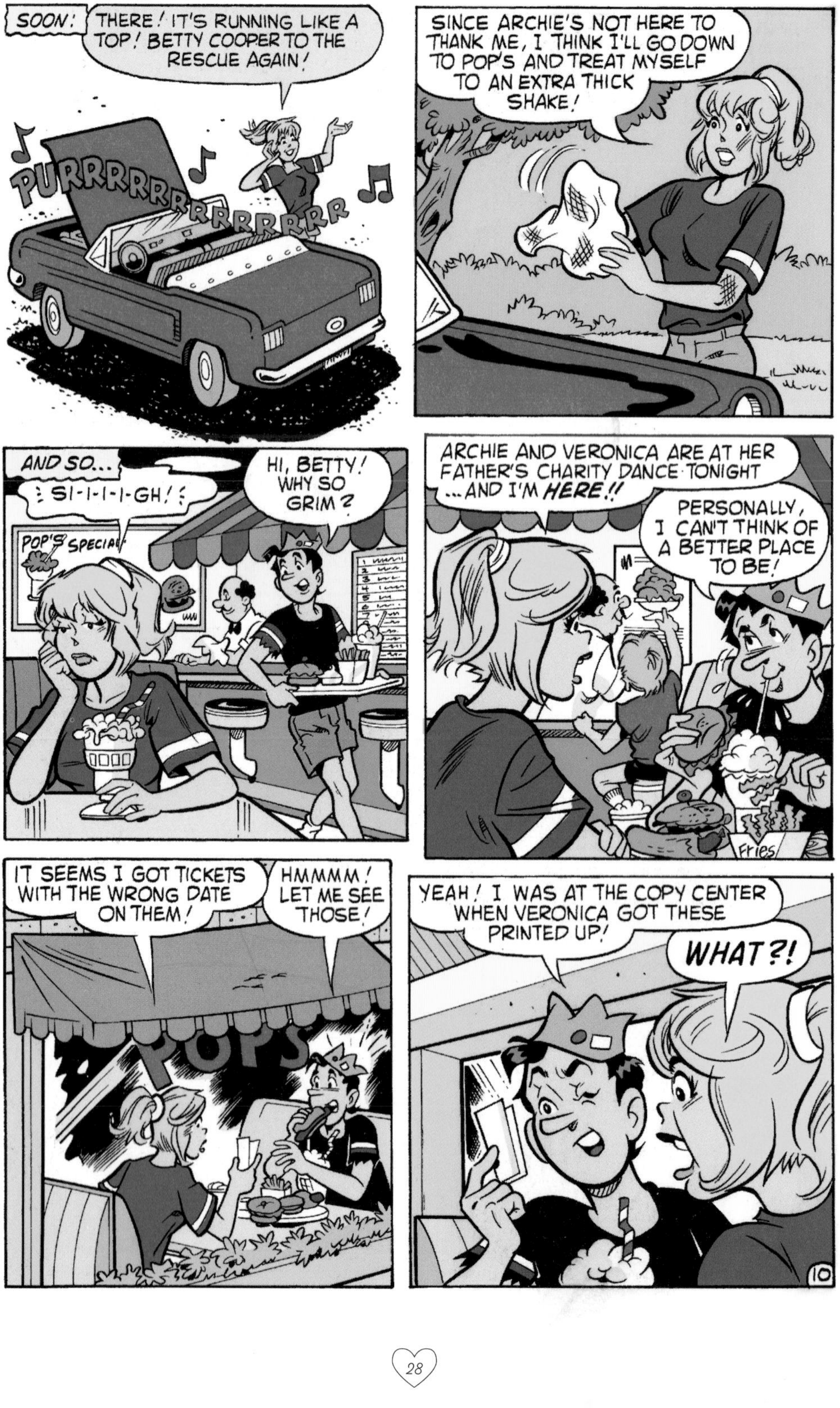
SOON:
THERE! IT'S RUNNING LIKE A TOP! BETTY COOPER TO THE RESCUE AGAIN!
PURRRRRRRRRRRRRRRR
SINCE ARCHIE'S NOT HERE TO THANK ME, I THINK I'LL GO DOWN TO POP'S AND TREAT MYSELF TO AN EXTRA THICK SHAKE!
AND SO...
SI-I-I-I-GH!
POP'S SPECIAL
HI, BETTY! WHY SO GRIM?
ARCHIE AND VERONICA ARE AT HER FATHER'S CHARITY DANCE TONIGHT ...AND I'M HERE!!
PERSONALLY, I CAN'T THINK OF A BETTER PLACE TO BE!
Fries
IT SEEMS I GOT TICKETS WITH THE WRONG DATE ON THEM!
HMMMM! LET ME SEE THOSE!
POP'S
YEAH! I WAS AT THE COPY CENTER WHEN VERONICA GOT THESE PRINTED UP!
WHAT?!
10

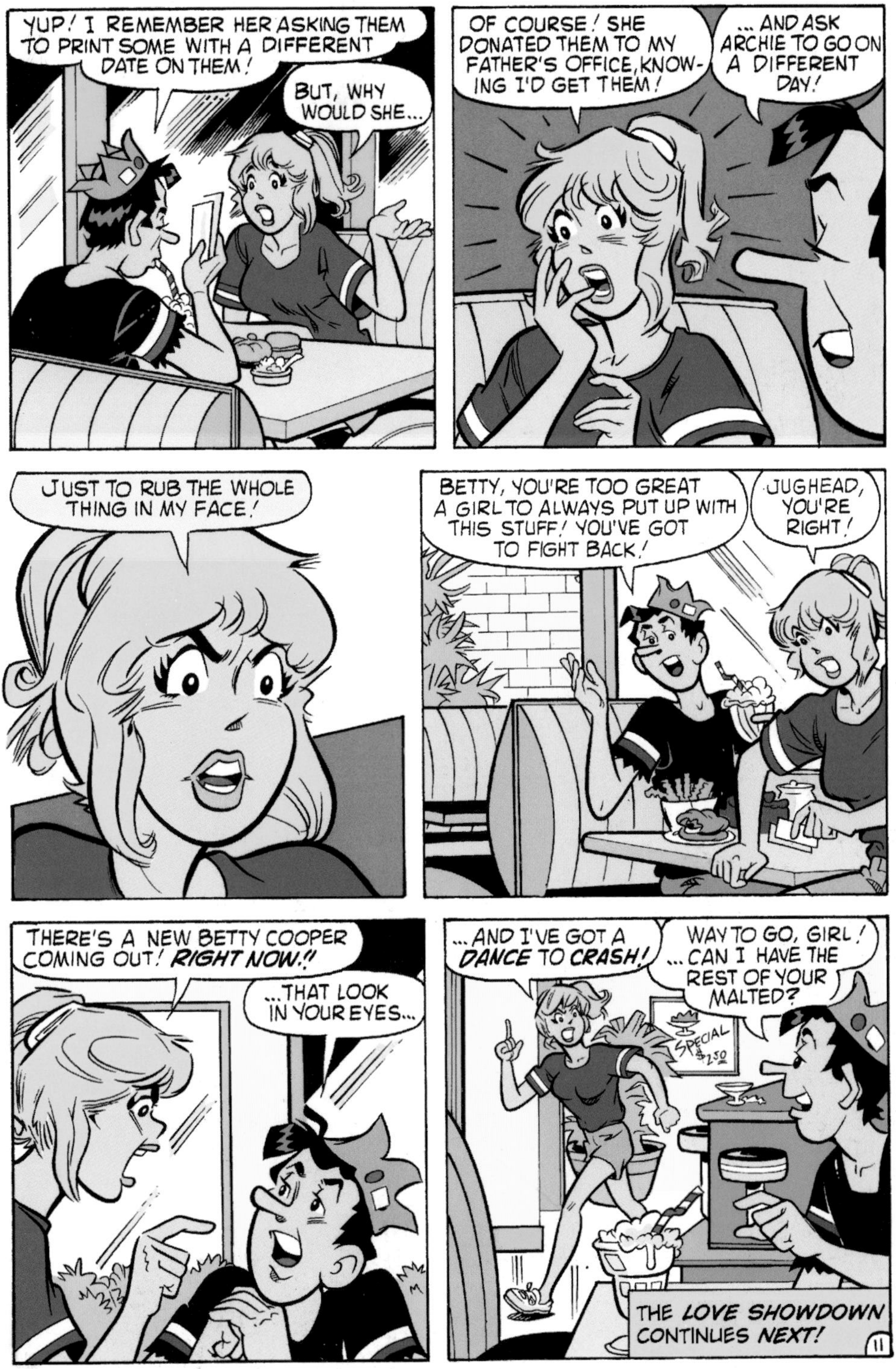
YUP! I REMEMBER HER ASKING THEM TO PRINT SOME WITH A DIFFERENT DATE ON THEM!
BUT, WHY WOULD SHE...
OF COURSE! SHE DONATED THEM TO MY FATHER'S OFFICE, KNOWING I'D GET THEM!
... AND ASK ARCHIE TO GO ON A DIFFERENT DAY!
JUST TO RUB THE WHOLE THING IN MY FACE!
BETTY, YOU'RE TOO GREAT A GIRL TO ALWAYS PUT UP WITH THIS STUFF! YOU'VE GOT TO FIGHT BACK!
JUGHEAD, YOU'RE RIGHT!
THERE'S A NEW BETTY COOPER COMING OUT! RIGHT NOW!!
...THAT LOOK IN YOUR EYES...
...AND I'VE GOT A DANCE TO CRASH!
WAY TO GO, GIRL! ...CAN I HAVE THE REST OF YOUR MALTED?
SPECIAL $2.50
THE LOVE SHOWDOWN CONTINUES NEXT!
11

♥ ARCHIE LOVE SHOWDOWN ♥

Chapter Three

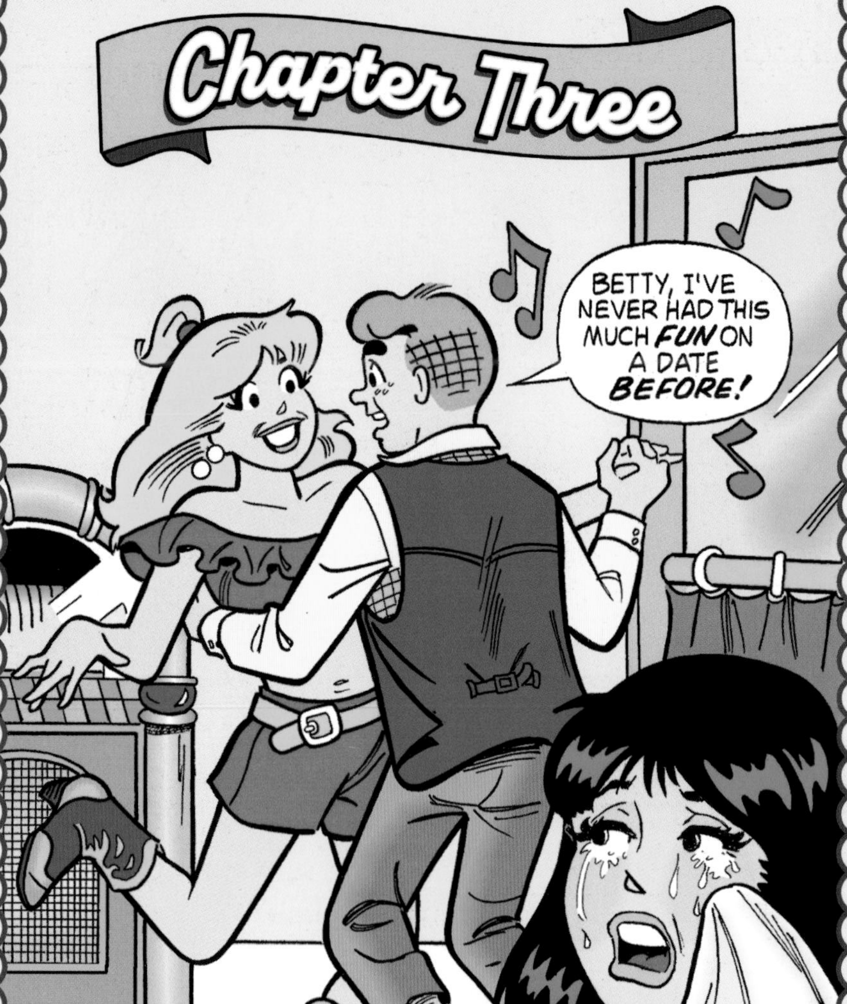

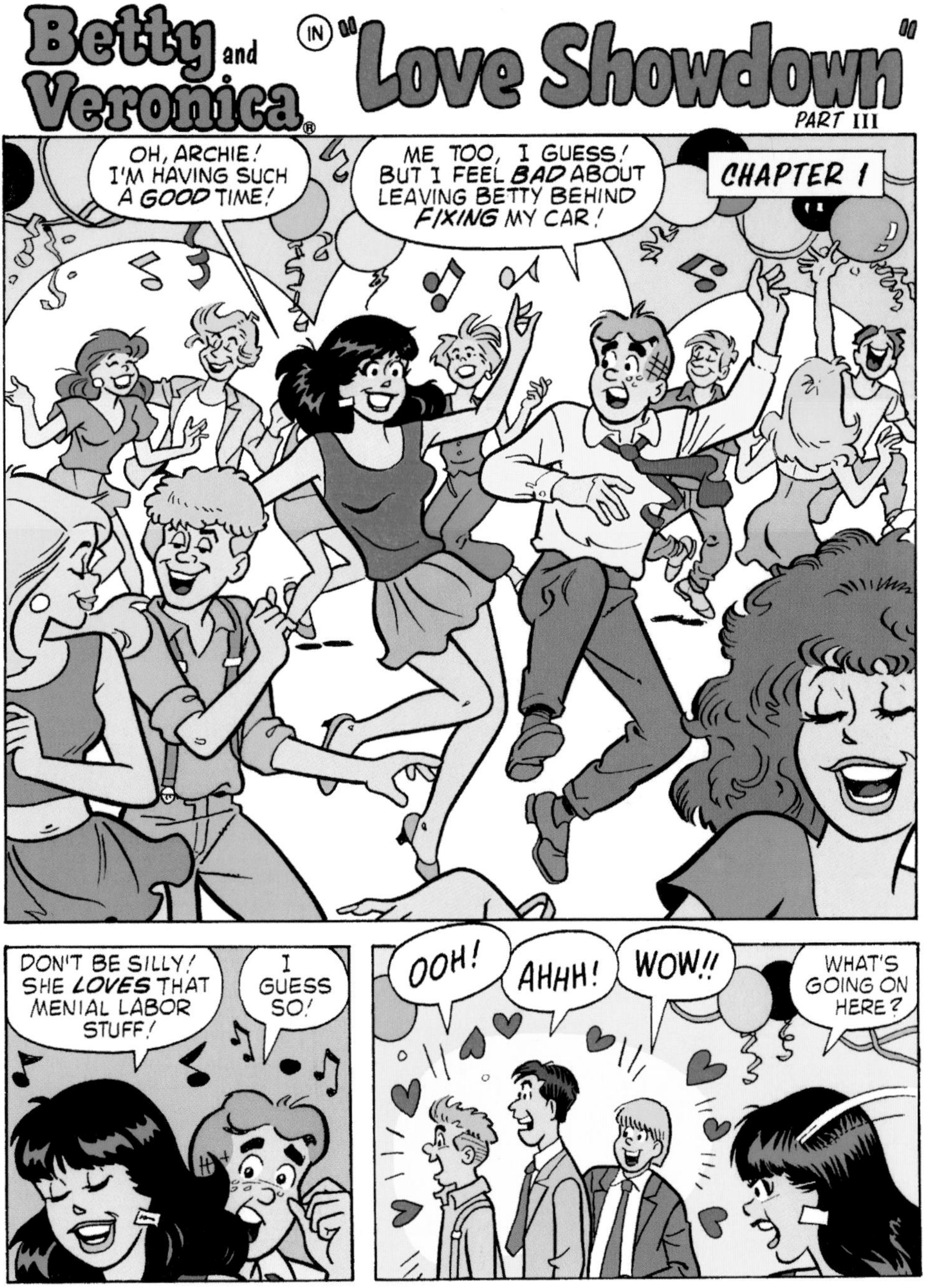
Betty and Veronica
IN "Love Showdown"
PART III
CHAPTER 1
OH, ARCHIE! I'M HAVING SUCH A GOOD TIME!
ME TOO, I GUESS! BUT I FEEL BAD ABOUT LEAVING BETTY BEHIND FIXING MY CAR!
DON'T BE SILLY! SHE LOVES THAT MENIAL LABOR STUFF!
I GUESS SO!
OOH!
AHHH!
WOW!!
WHAT'S GOING ON HERE?

ORIGINALLY PRINTED IN BETTY AND VERONICA #82, DECEMBER 1994

DAN PARENT • DAN DECARLO • ALISON FLOOD • BILL YOSHIDA • BARRY GROSSMAN

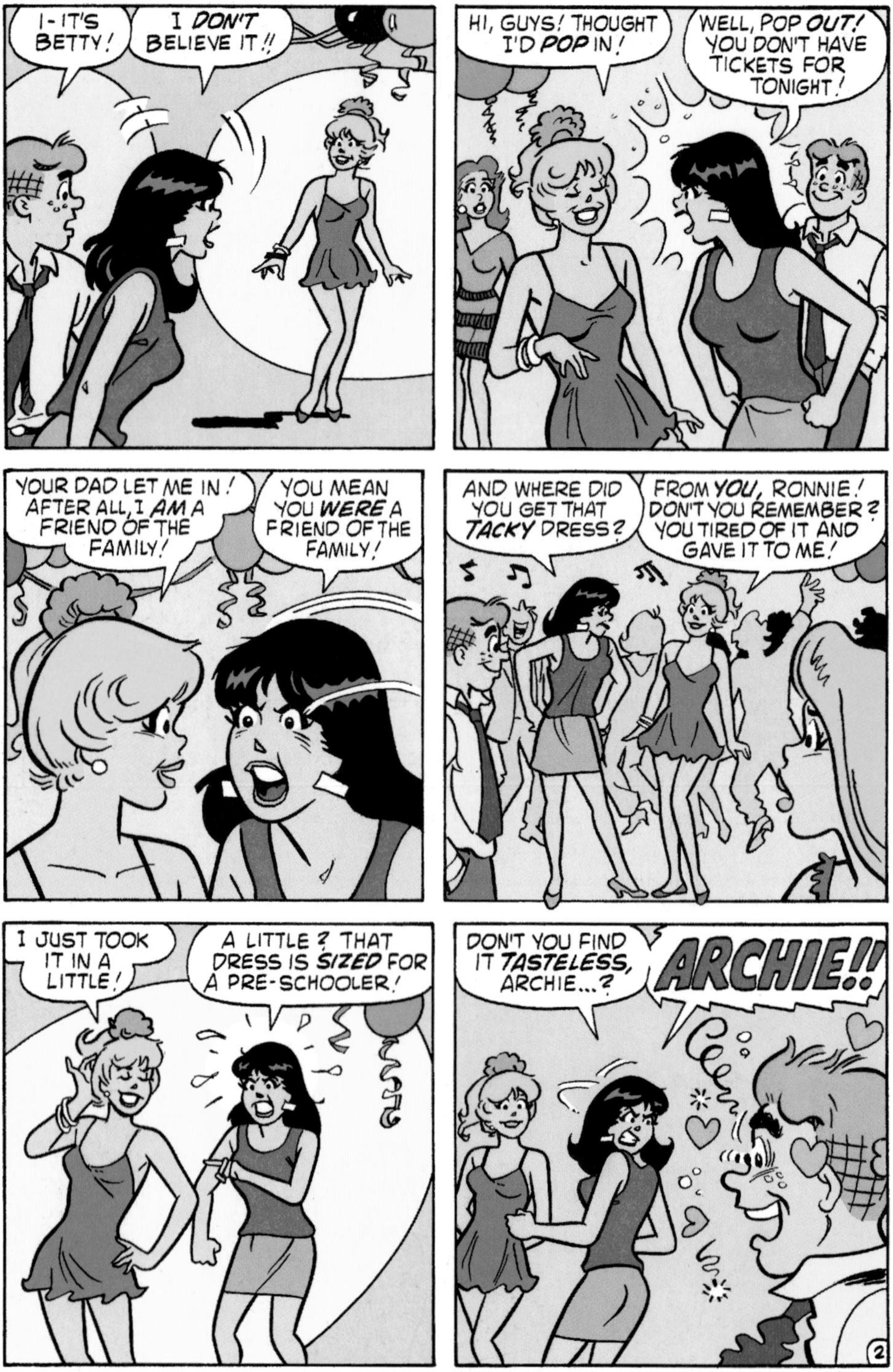
I-IT'S BETTY!
I DON'T BELIEVE IT!!
HI, GUYS! THOUGHT I'D POP IN!
WELL, POP OUT! YOU DON'T HAVE TICKETS FOR TONIGHT!
YOUR DAD LET ME IN! AFTER ALL, I AM A FRIEND OF THE FAMILY!
YOU MEAN YOU WERE A FRIEND OF THE FAMILY!
AND WHERE DID YOU GET THAT TACKY DRESS?
FROM YOU, RONNIE! DON'T YOU REMEMBER? YOU TIRED OF IT AND GAVE IT TO ME!
I JUST TOOK IT IN A LITTLE!
A LITTLE? THAT DRESS IS SIZED FOR A PRE-SCHOOLER!
DON'T YOU FIND IT TASTELESS, ARCHIE...?
ARCHIE!!
2

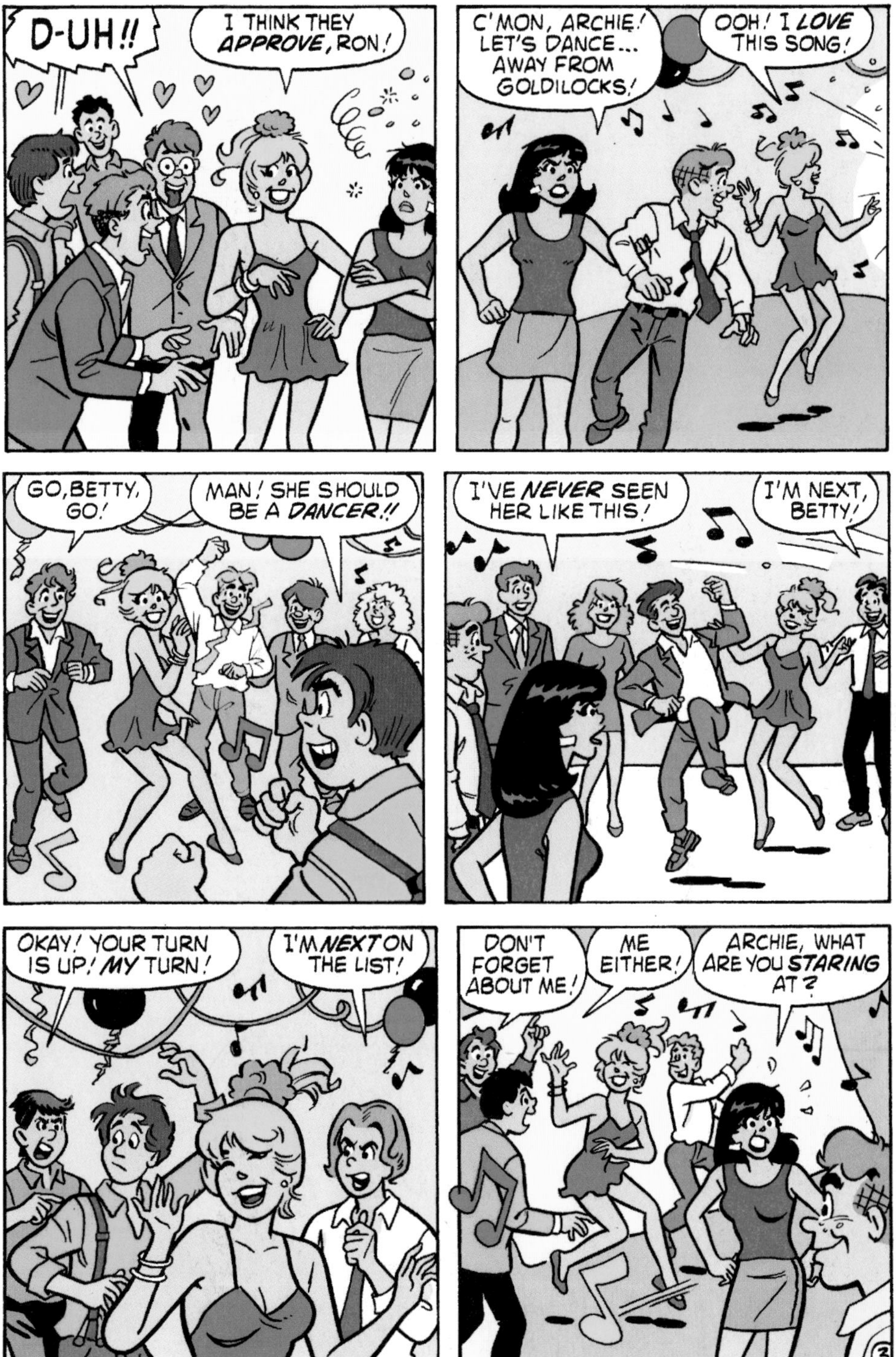
D-UH!!
I THINK THEY *APPROVE*, RON!
C'MON, ARCHIE! LET'S DANCE... AWAY FROM GOLDILOCKS!
OOH! I *LOVE* THIS SONG!
GO, BETTY, GO!
MAN! SHE SHOULD BE A *DANCER*!!
I'VE *NEVER* SEEN HER LIKE THIS!
I'M NEXT, BETTY!
OKAY! YOUR TURN IS UP! *MY* TURN!
I'M *NEXT* ON THE LIST!
DON'T FORGET ABOUT ME!
ME EITHER!
ARCHIE, WHAT ARE YOU *STARING* AT?
3

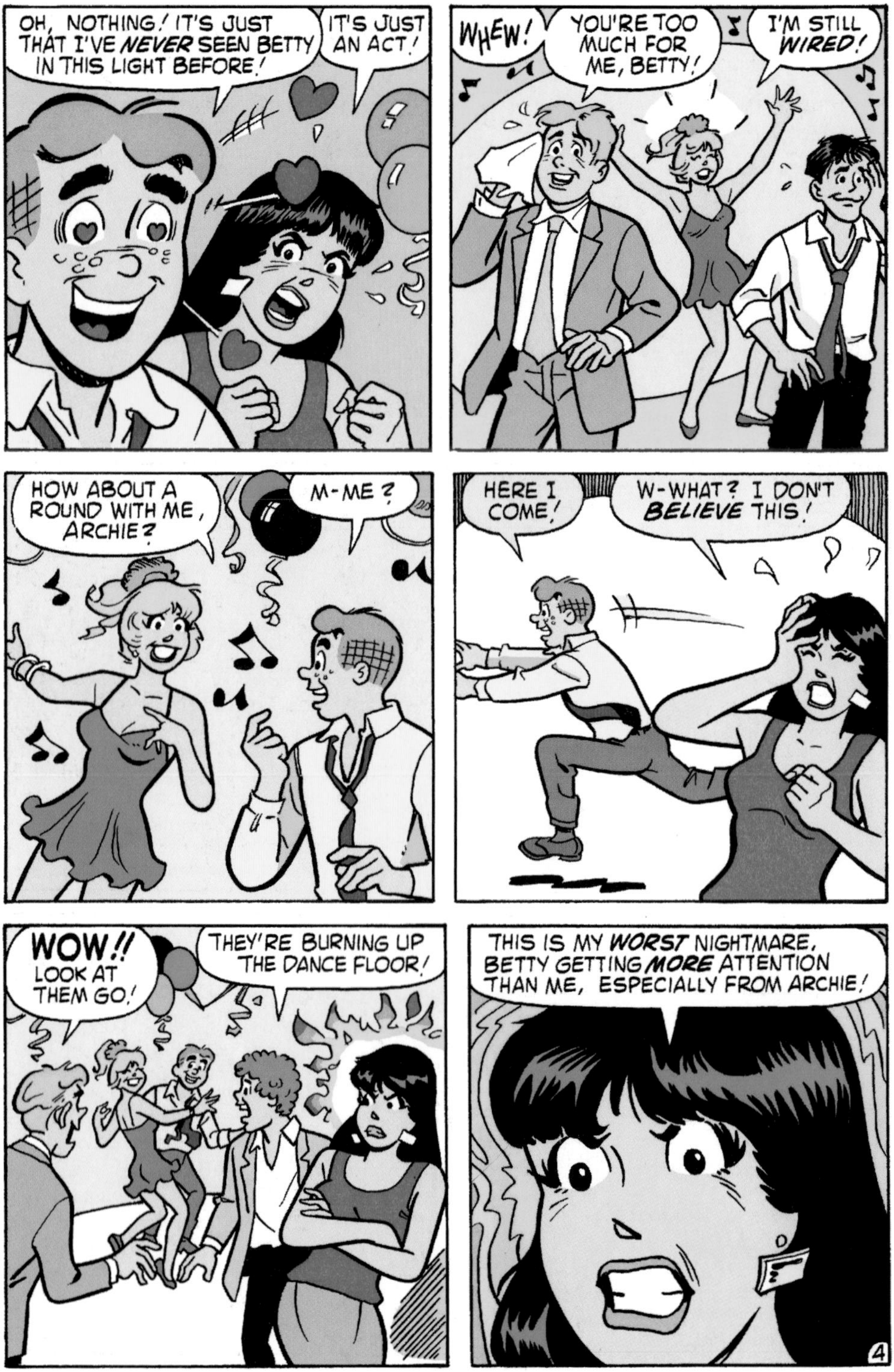
OH, NOTHING! IT'S JUST THAT I'VE NEVER SEEN BETTY IN THIS LIGHT BEFORE!
IT'S JUST AN ACT!
WHEW!
YOU'RE TOO MUCH FOR ME, BETTY!
I'M STILL WIRED!
HOW ABOUT A ROUND WITH ME, ARCHIE?
M-ME?
HERE I COME!
W-WHAT? I DON'T BELIEVE THIS!
WOW!! LOOK AT THEM GO!
THEY'RE BURNING UP THE DANCE FLOOR!
THIS IS MY WORST NIGHTMARE, BETTY GETTING MORE ATTENTION THAN ME, ESPECIALLY FROM ARCHIE!
4

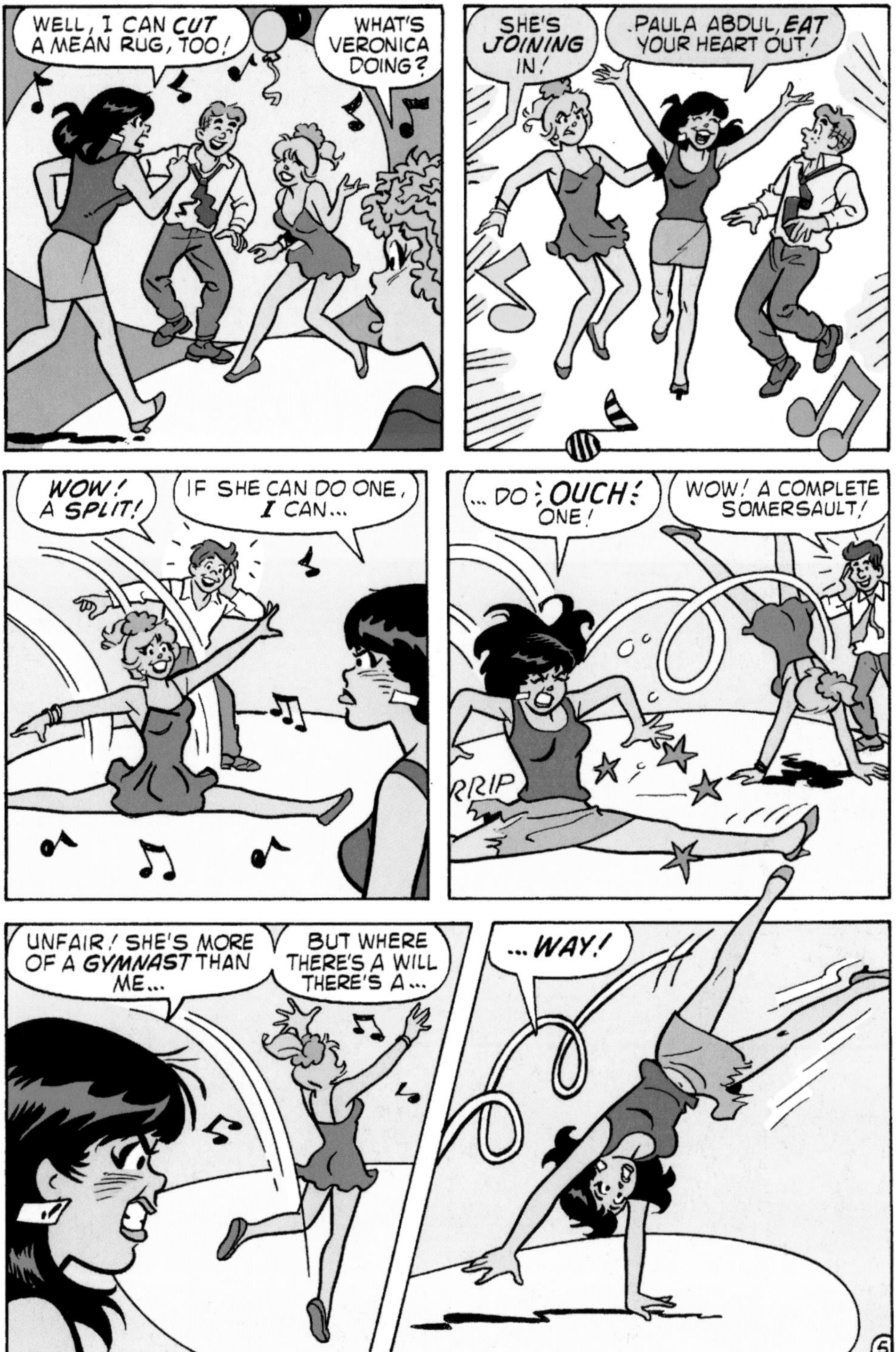
WELL, I CAN CUT A MEAN RUG, TOO!
WHAT'S VERONICA DOING?
SHE'S JOINING IN!
PAULA ABDUL, EAT YOUR HEART OUT!
WOW! A SPLIT!
IF SHE CAN DO ONE, I CAN...
... DO OUCH! ONE!
RRIP
WOW! A COMPLETE SOMERSAULT!
UNFAIR! SHE'S MORE OF A GYMNAST THAN ME...
BUT WHERE THERE'S A WILL THERE'S A...
...WAY!
5

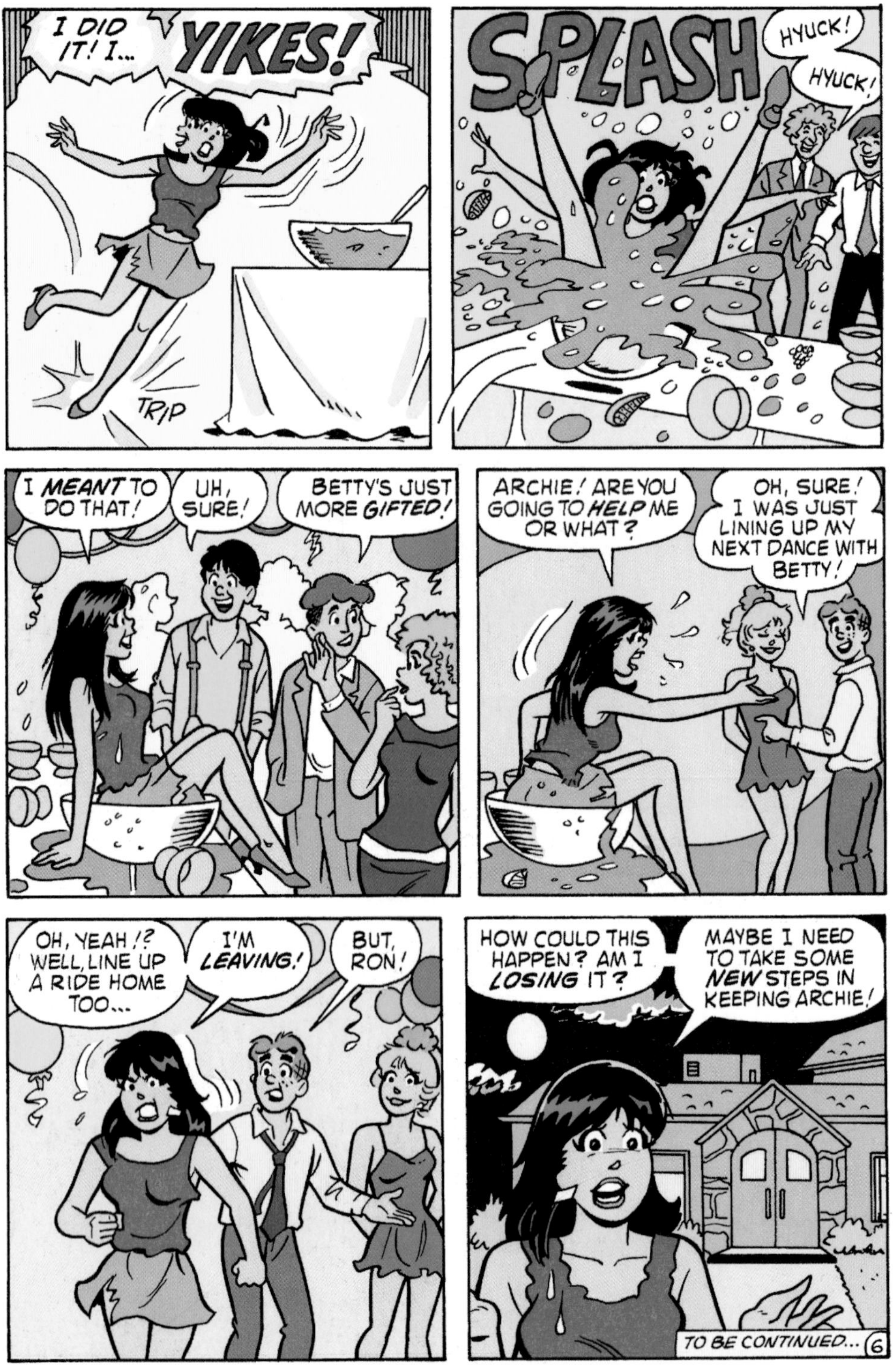
I DID IT! I...
YIKES!
TRIP
SPLASH
HYUCK!
HYUCK!
I MEANT TO DO THAT!
UH, SURE!
BETTY'S JUST MORE GIFTED!
ARCHIE! ARE YOU GOING TO HELP ME OR WHAT?
OH, SURE! I WAS JUST LINING UP MY NEXT DANCE WITH BETTY!
OH, YEAH!? WELL, LINE UP A RIDE HOME TOO...
I'M LEAVING!
BUT, RON!
HOW COULD THIS HAPPEN? AM I LOSING IT?
MAYBE I NEED TO TAKE SOME NEW STEPS IN KEEPING ARCHIE!
TO BE CONTINUED...
6

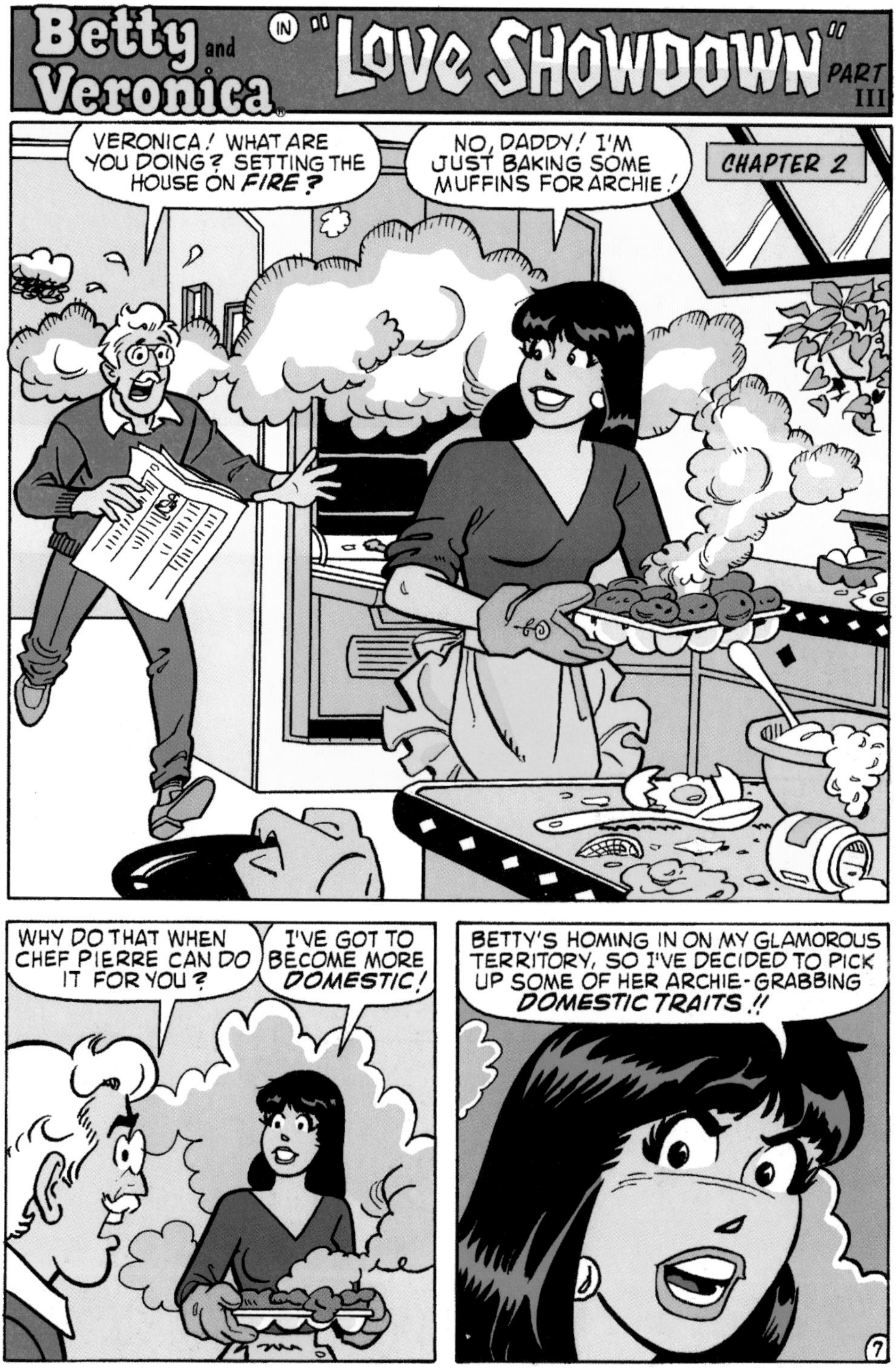

Betty and Veronica
IN "LOVE SHOWDOWN" PART III
CHAPTER 2
VERONICA! WHAT ARE YOU DOING? SETTING THE HOUSE ON FIRE?
NO, DADDY! I'M JUST BAKING SOME MUFFINS FOR ARCHIE!
WHY DO THAT WHEN CHEF PIERRE CAN DO IT FOR YOU?
I'VE GOT TO BECOME MORE DOMESTIC!
BETTY'S HOMING IN ON MY GLAMOROUS TERRITORY, SO I'VE DECIDED TO PICK UP SOME OF HER ARCHIE-GRABBING DOMESTIC TRAITS!!
7

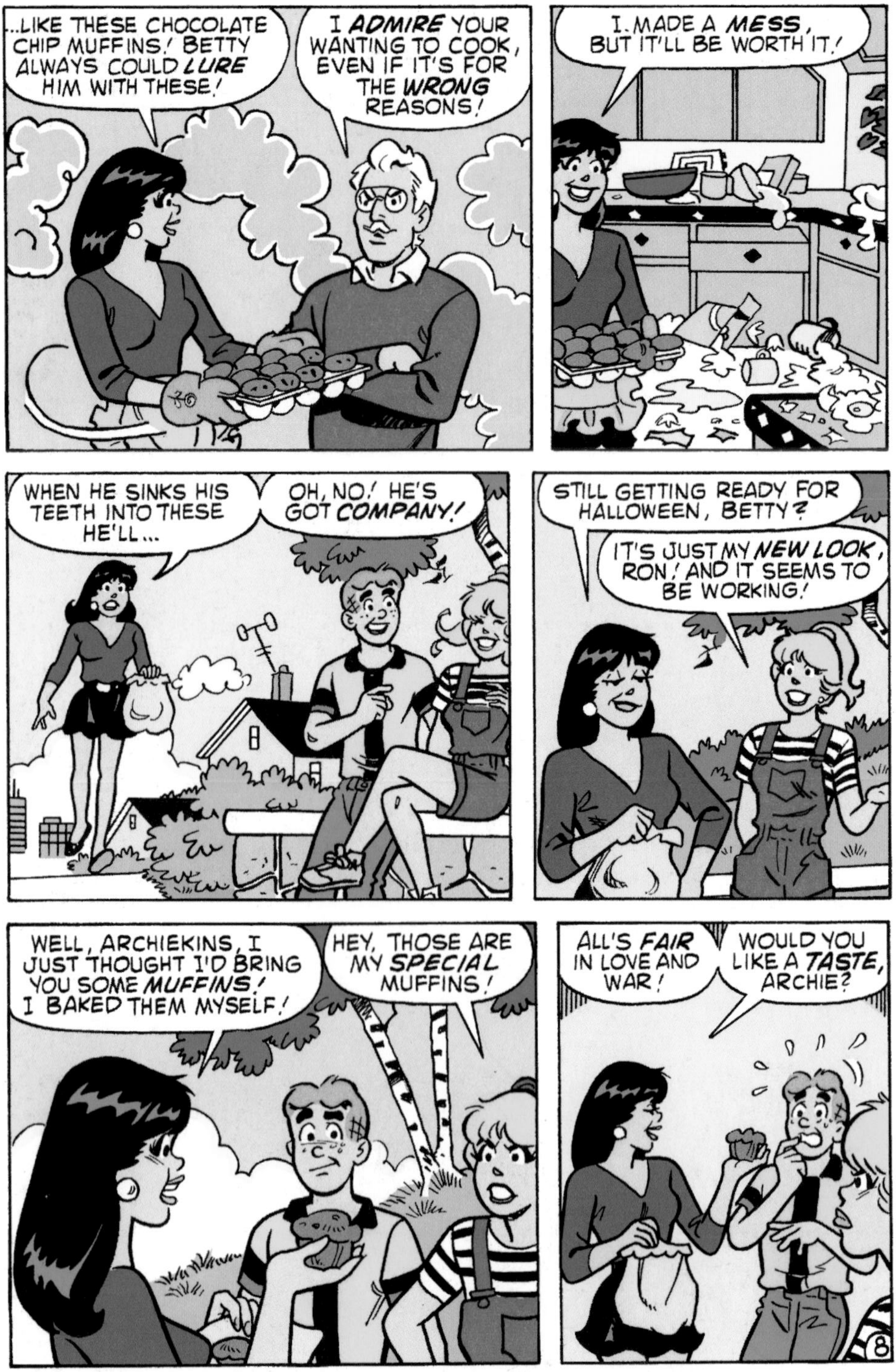
...LIKE THESE CHOCOLATE CHIP MUFFINS! BETTY ALWAYS COULD LURE HIM WITH THESE!
I ADMIRE YOUR WANTING TO COOK, EVEN IF IT'S FOR THE WRONG REASONS!
I MADE A MESS, BUT IT'LL BE WORTH IT!
WHEN HE SINKS HIS TEETH INTO THESE HE'LL...
OH, NO! HE'S GOT COMPANY!
STILL GETTING READY FOR HALLOWEEN, BETTY?
IT'S JUST MY NEW LOOK, RON! AND IT SEEMS TO BE WORKING!
WELL, ARCHIEKINS, I JUST THOUGHT I'D BRING YOU SOME MUFFINS! I BAKED THEM MYSELF!
HEY, THOSE ARE MY SPECIAL MUFFINS!
ALL'S FAIR IN LOVE AND WAR!
WOULD YOU LIKE A TASTE, ARCHIE?
8

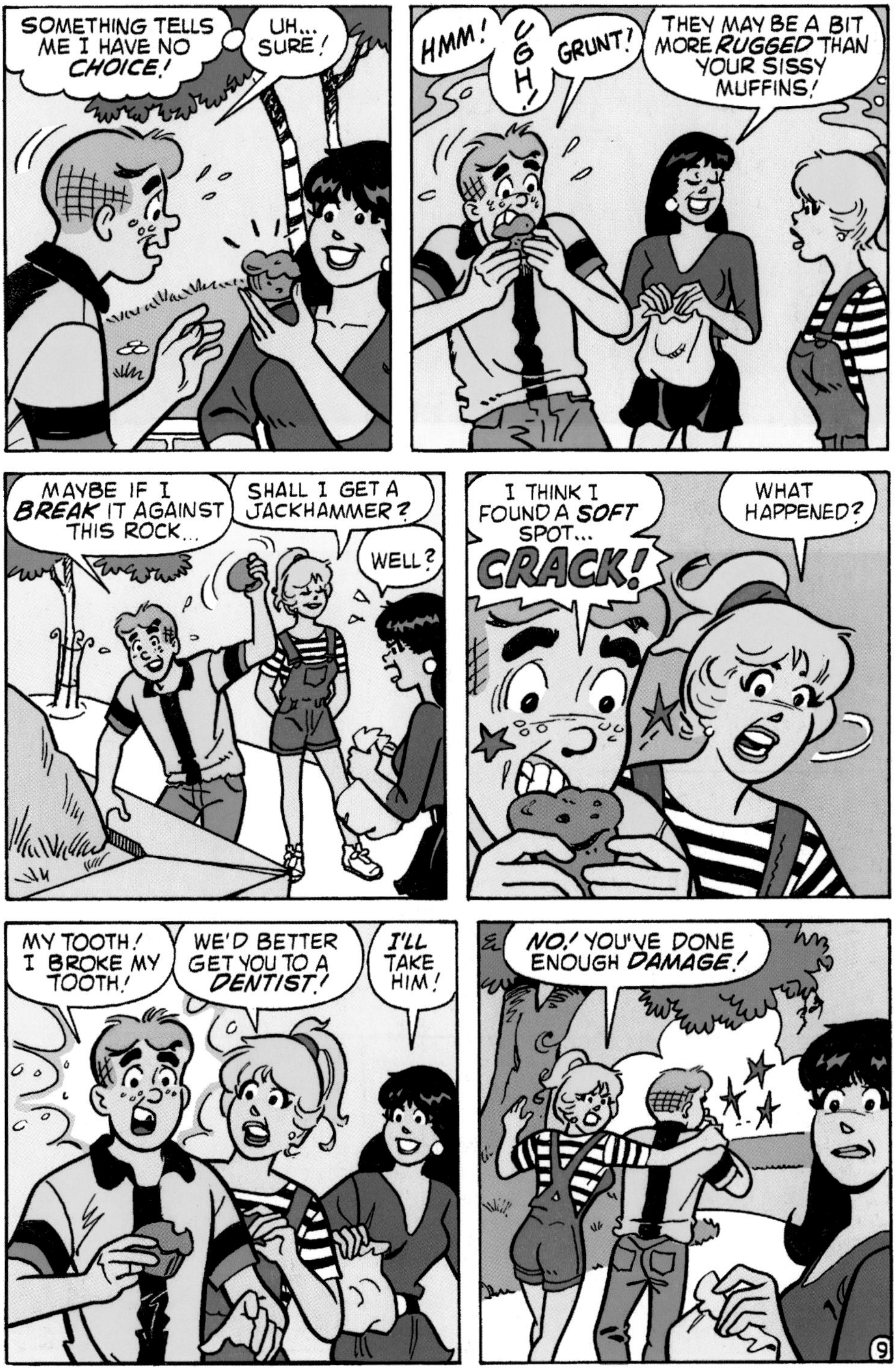
SOMETHING TELLS ME I HAVE NO CHOICE!
UH... SURE!
HMM!
UGH!
GRUNT!
THEY MAY BE A BIT MORE RUGGED THAN YOUR SISSY MUFFINS!
MAYBE IF I BREAK IT AGAINST THIS ROCK...
SHALL I GET A JACKHAMMER?
WELL?
I THINK I FOUND A SOFT SPOT...
CRACK!
WHAT HAPPENED?
MY TOOTH! I BROKE MY TOOTH!
WE'D BETTER GET YOU TO A DENTIST!
I'LL TAKE HIM!
NO! YOU'VE DONE ENOUGH DAMAGE!
9

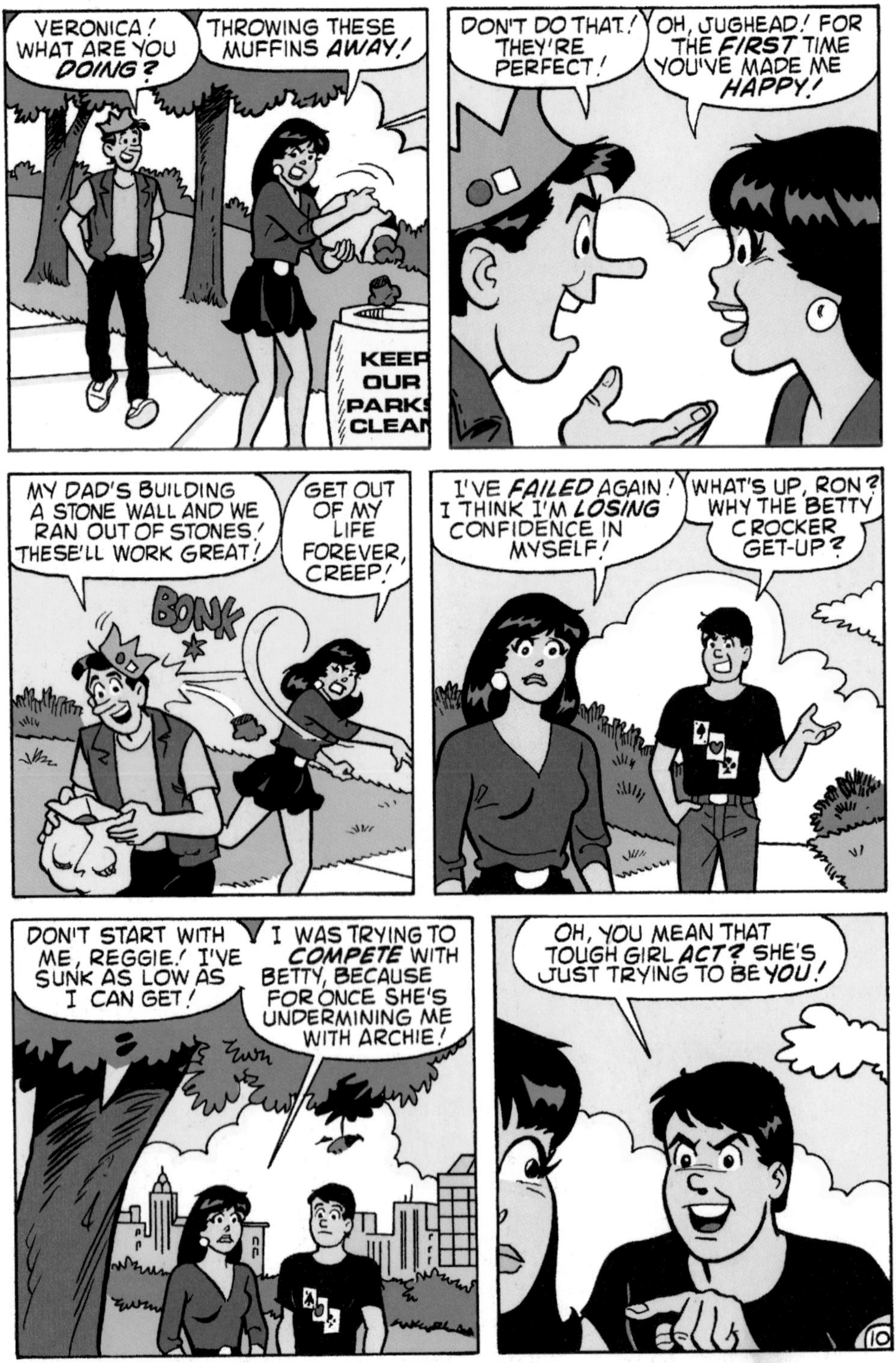
VERONICA! WHAT ARE YOU DOING?
THROWING THESE MUFFINS AWAY!
KEEP OUR PARKS CLEAN
DON'T DO THAT! THEY'RE PERFECT!
OH, JUGHEAD! FOR THE FIRST TIME YOU'VE MADE ME HAPPY!
MY DAD'S BUILDING A STONE WALL AND WE RAN OUT OF STONES! THESE'LL WORK GREAT!
GET OUT OF MY LIFE FOREVER, CREEP!
BONK
I'VE FAILED AGAIN! I THINK I'M LOSING CONFIDENCE IN MYSELF!
WHAT'S UP, RON? WHY THE BETTY CROCKER GET-UP?
DON'T START WITH ME, REGGIE! I'VE SUNK AS LOW AS I CAN GET!
I WAS TRYING TO COMPETE WITH BETTY, BECAUSE FOR ONCE SHE'S UNDERMINING ME WITH ARCHIE!
OH, YOU MEAN THAT TOUGH GIRL ACT? SHE'S JUST TRYING TO BE YOU!
10

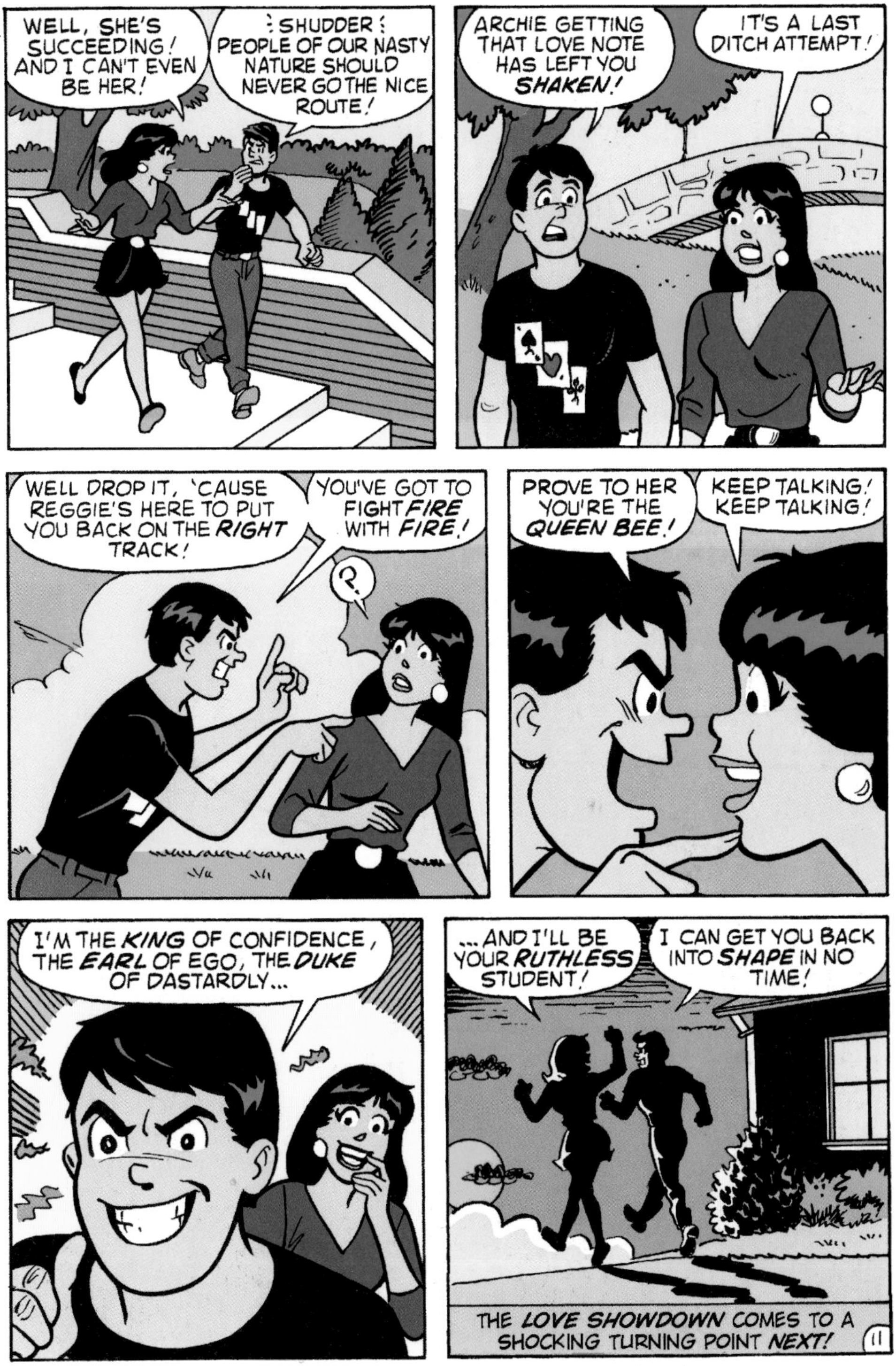
WELL, SHE'S SUCCEEDING! AND I CAN'T EVEN BE HER!
SHUDDER PEOPLE OF OUR NASTY NATURE SHOULD NEVER GO THE NICE ROUTE!
ARCHIE GETTING THAT LOVE NOTE HAS LEFT YOU SHAKEN!
IT'S A LAST DITCH ATTEMPT!
WELL DROP IT, 'CAUSE REGGIE'S HERE TO PUT YOU BACK ON THE RIGHT TRACK!
YOU'VE GOT TO FIGHT FIRE WITH FIRE!
?
PROVE TO HER YOU'RE THE QUEEN BEE!
KEEP TALKING! KEEP TALKING!
I'M THE KING OF CONFIDENCE, THE EARL OF EGO, THE DUKE OF DASTARDLY...
...AND I'LL BE YOUR RUTHLESS STUDENT!
I CAN GET YOU BACK INTO SHAPE IN NO TIME!
THE LOVE SHOWDOWN COMES TO A SHOCKING TURNING POINT NEXT!
11

ARCHIE LOVE SHOWDOWN
Chapter Four
UNHAND THAT REDHEAD, BLONDIE! THE OLD VERONICA IS BACK!
SUNDAE $1.25
BANANA SPLITS $1.75
Dan DeCarlo
HENRY SCARDELLI

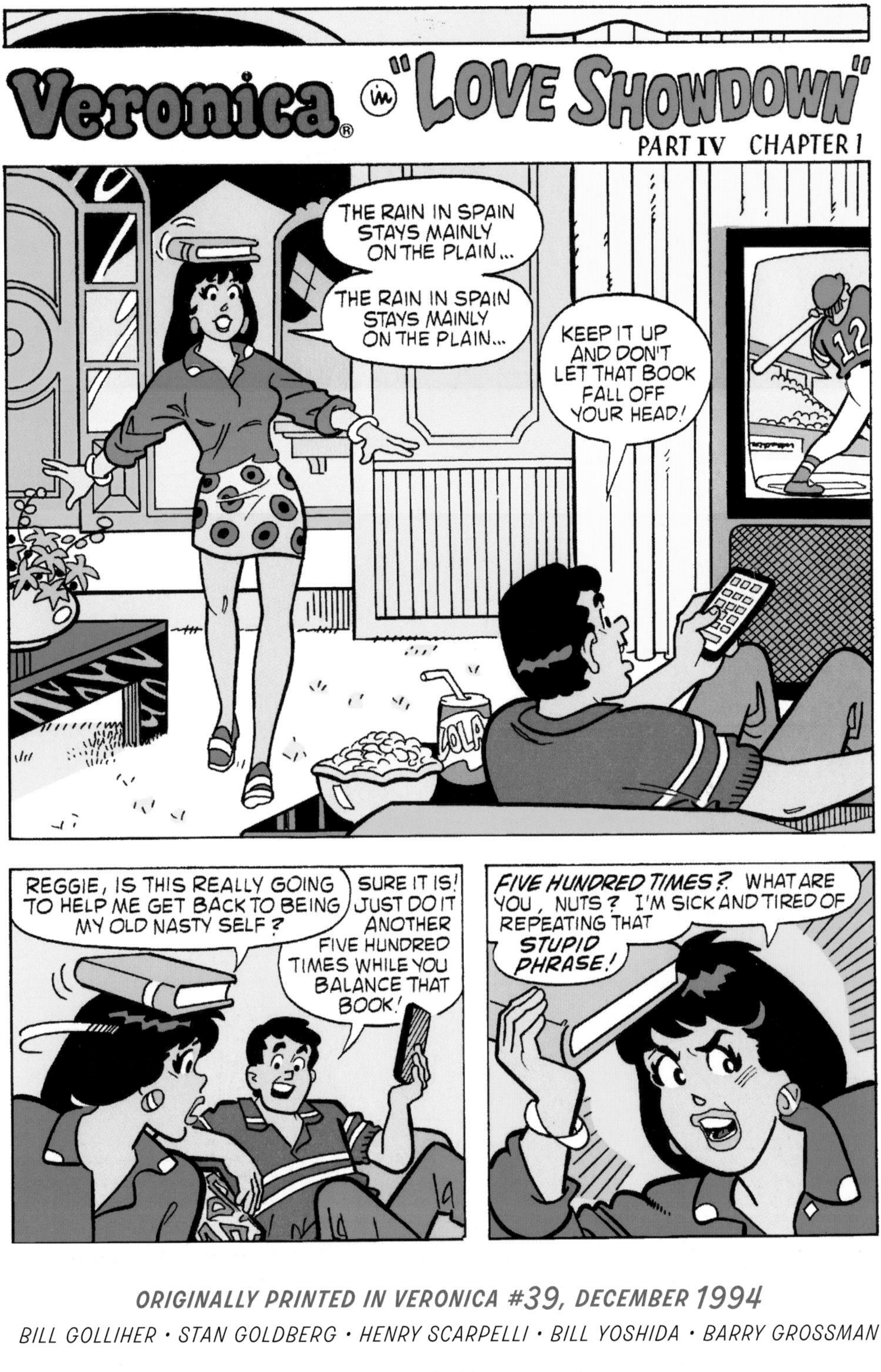
Veronica in "LOVE SHOWDOWN"
PART IV CHAPTER 1
THE RAIN IN SPAIN STAYS MAINLY ON THE PLAIN...
THE RAIN IN SPAIN STAYS MAINLY ON THE PLAIN...
KEEP IT UP AND DON'T LET THAT BOOK FALL OFF YOUR HEAD!
REGGIE, IS THIS REALLY GOING TO HELP ME GET BACK TO BEING MY OLD NASTY SELF?
SURE IT IS! JUST DO IT ANOTHER FIVE HUNDRED TIMES WHILE YOU BALANCE THAT BOOK!
FIVE HUNDRED TIMES? WHAT ARE YOU, NUTS? I'M SICK AND TIRED OF REPEATING THAT STUPID PHRASE!

ORIGINALLY PRINTED IN VERONICA #39, DECEMBER 1994

BILL GOLLIHER • STAN GOLDBERG • HENRY SCARPELLI • BILL YOSHIDA • BARRY GROSSMAN

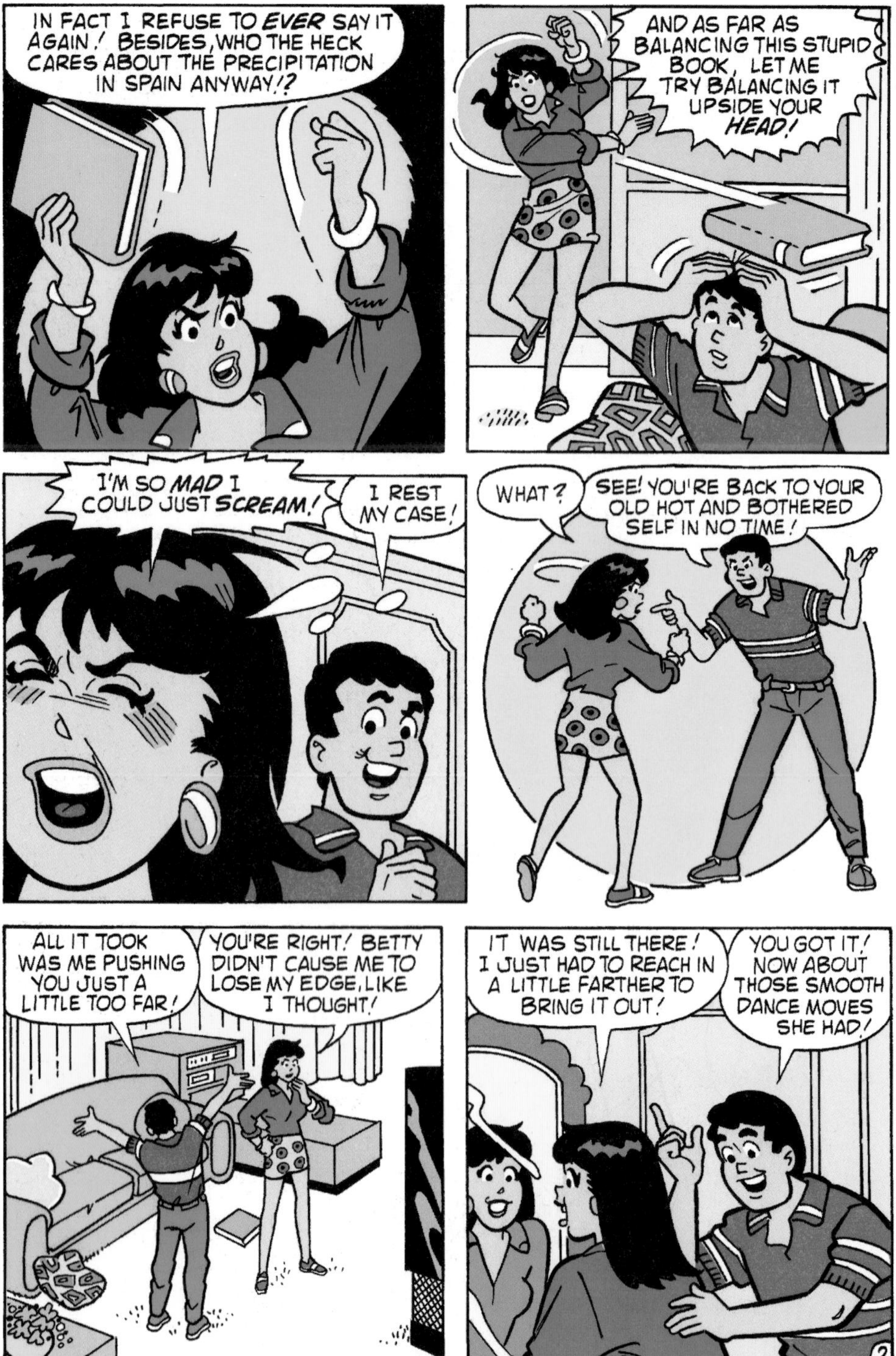
IN FACT I REFUSE TO EVER SAY IT AGAIN! BESIDES, WHO THE HECK CARES ABOUT THE PRECIPITATION IN SPAIN ANYWAY!?
AND AS FAR AS BALANCING THIS STUPID BOOK, LET ME TRY BALANCING IT UPSIDE YOUR HEAD!
I'M SO MAD I COULD JUST SCREAM!
I REST MY CASE!
WHAT?
SEE! YOU'RE BACK TO YOUR OLD HOT AND BOTHERED SELF IN NO TIME!
ALL IT TOOK WAS ME PUSHING YOU JUST A LITTLE TOO FAR!
YOU'RE RIGHT! BETTY DIDN'T CAUSE ME TO LOSE MY EDGE, LIKE I THOUGHT!
IT WAS STILL THERE! I JUST HAD TO REACH IN A LITTLE FARTHER TO BRING IT OUT!
YOU GOT IT! NOW ABOUT THOSE SMOOTH DANCE MOVES SHE HAD!
2

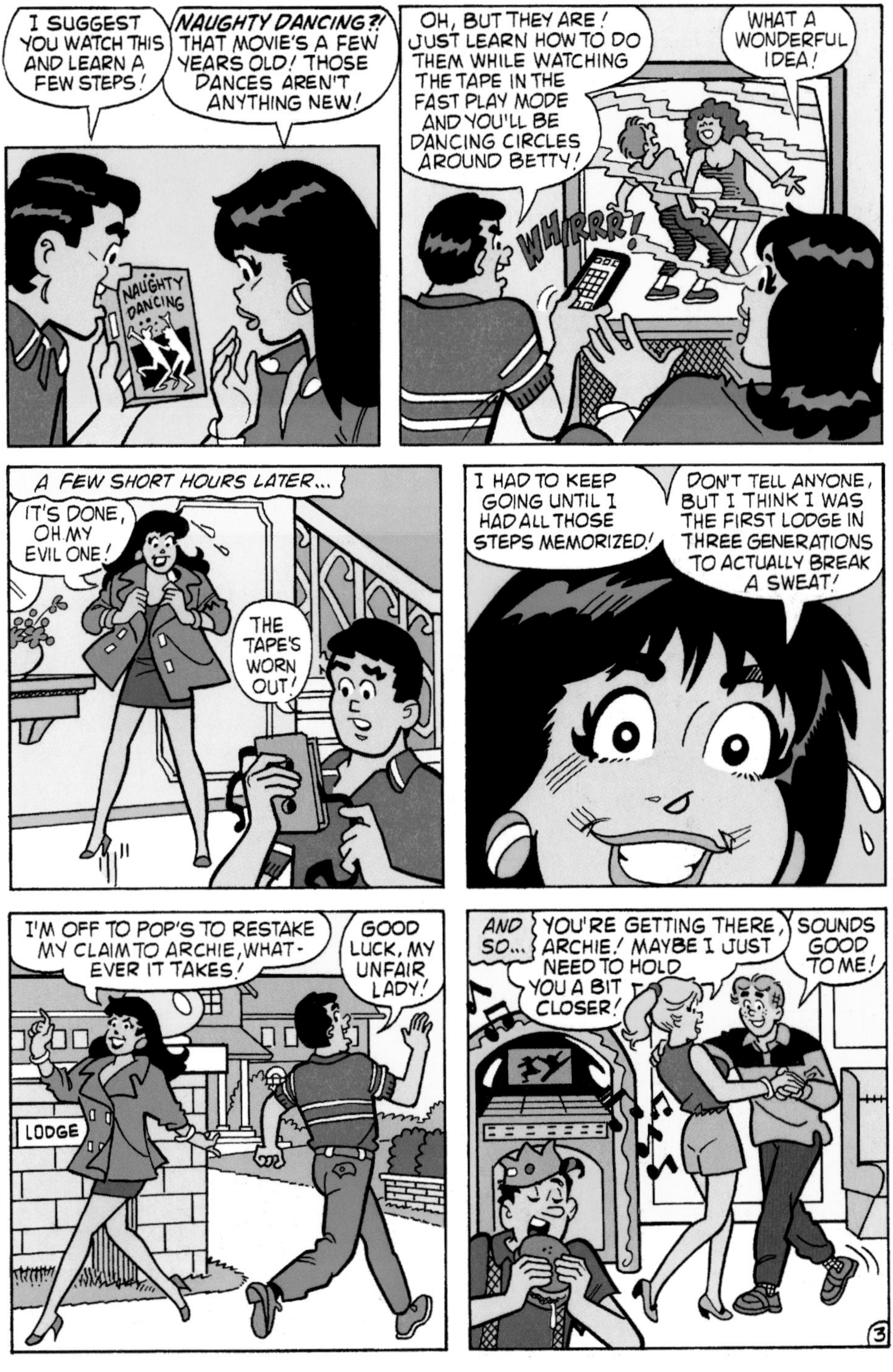
I SUGGEST YOU WATCH THIS AND LEARN A FEW STEPS!
NAUGHTY DANCING?! THAT MOVIE'S A FEW YEARS OLD! THOSE DANCES AREN'T ANYTHING NEW!
NAUGHTY DANCING
OH, BUT THEY ARE! JUST LEARN HOW TO DO THEM WHILE WATCHING THE TAPE IN THE FAST PLAY MODE AND YOU'LL BE DANCING CIRCLES AROUND BETTY!
WHAT A WONDERFUL IDEA!
WHIRRR!
A FEW SHORT HOURS LATER...
IT'S DONE, OH MY EVIL ONE!
THE TAPE'S WORN OUT!
I HAD TO KEEP GOING UNTIL I HAD ALL THOSE STEPS MEMORIZED!
DON'T TELL ANYONE, BUT I THINK I WAS THE FIRST LODGE IN THREE GENERATIONS TO ACTUALLY BREAK A SWEAT!
I'M OFF TO POP'S TO RESTAKE MY CLAIM TO ARCHIE, WHAT-EVER IT TAKES!
GOOD LUCK, MY UNFAIR LADY!
LODGE
AND SO...
YOU'RE GETTING THERE, ARCHIE! MAYBE I JUST NEED TO HOLD YOU A BIT CLOSER!
SOUNDS GOOD TO ME!
3

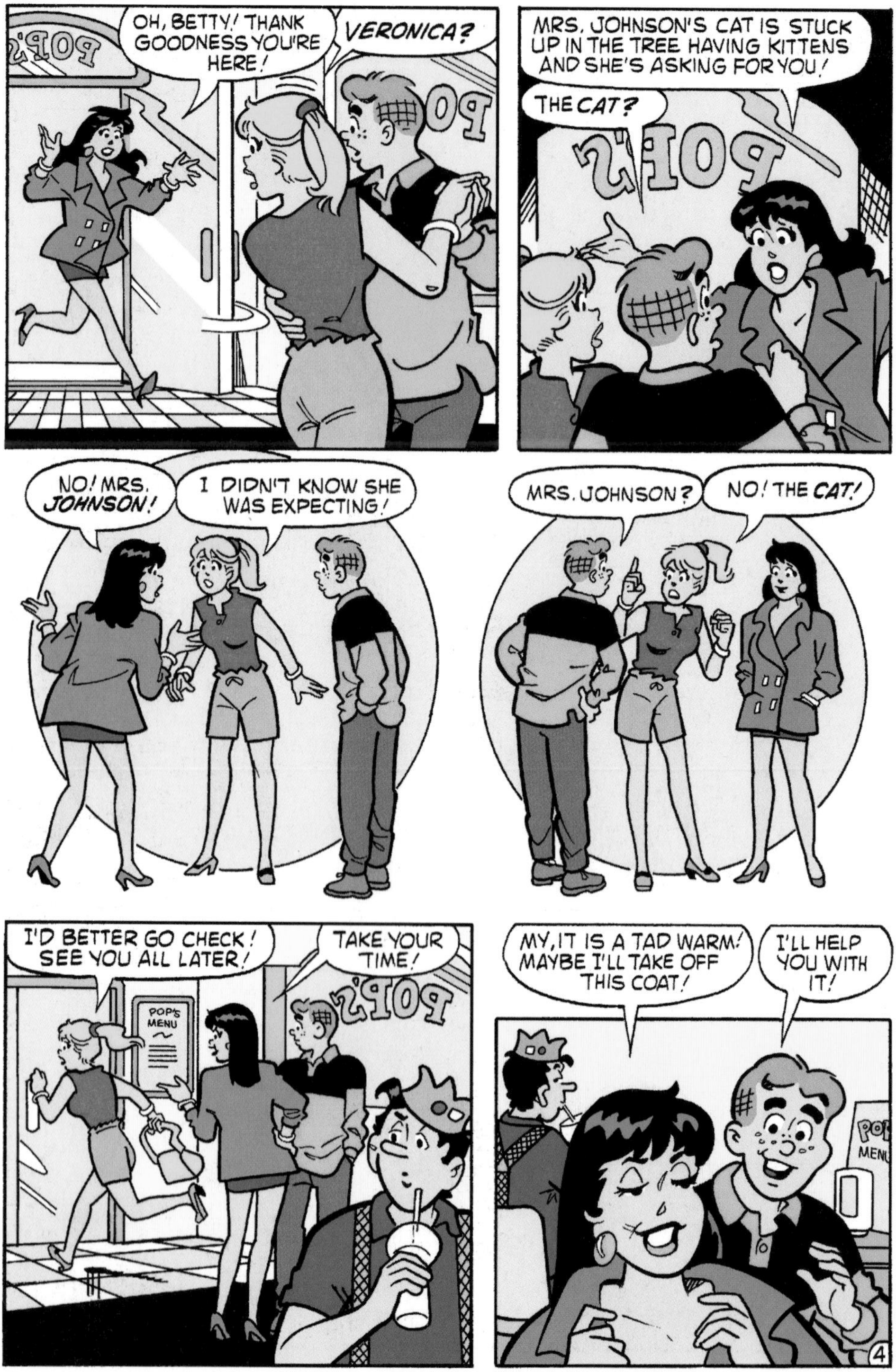
OH, BETTY! THANK GOODNESS YOU'RE HERE!
VERONICA?
POP'S
MRS. JOHNSON'S CAT IS STUCK UP IN THE TREE HAVING KITTENS AND SHE'S ASKING FOR YOU!
THE CAT?
POP'S
NO! MRS. JOHNSON!
I DIDN'T KNOW SHE WAS EXPECTING!
MRS. JOHNSON?
NO! THE CAT!
I'D BETTER GO CHECK! SEE YOU ALL LATER!
TAKE YOUR TIME!
POP'S MENU
POP'S
MY, IT IS A TAD WARM! MAYBE I'LL TAKE OFF THIS COAT!
I'LL HELP YOU WITH IT!
4

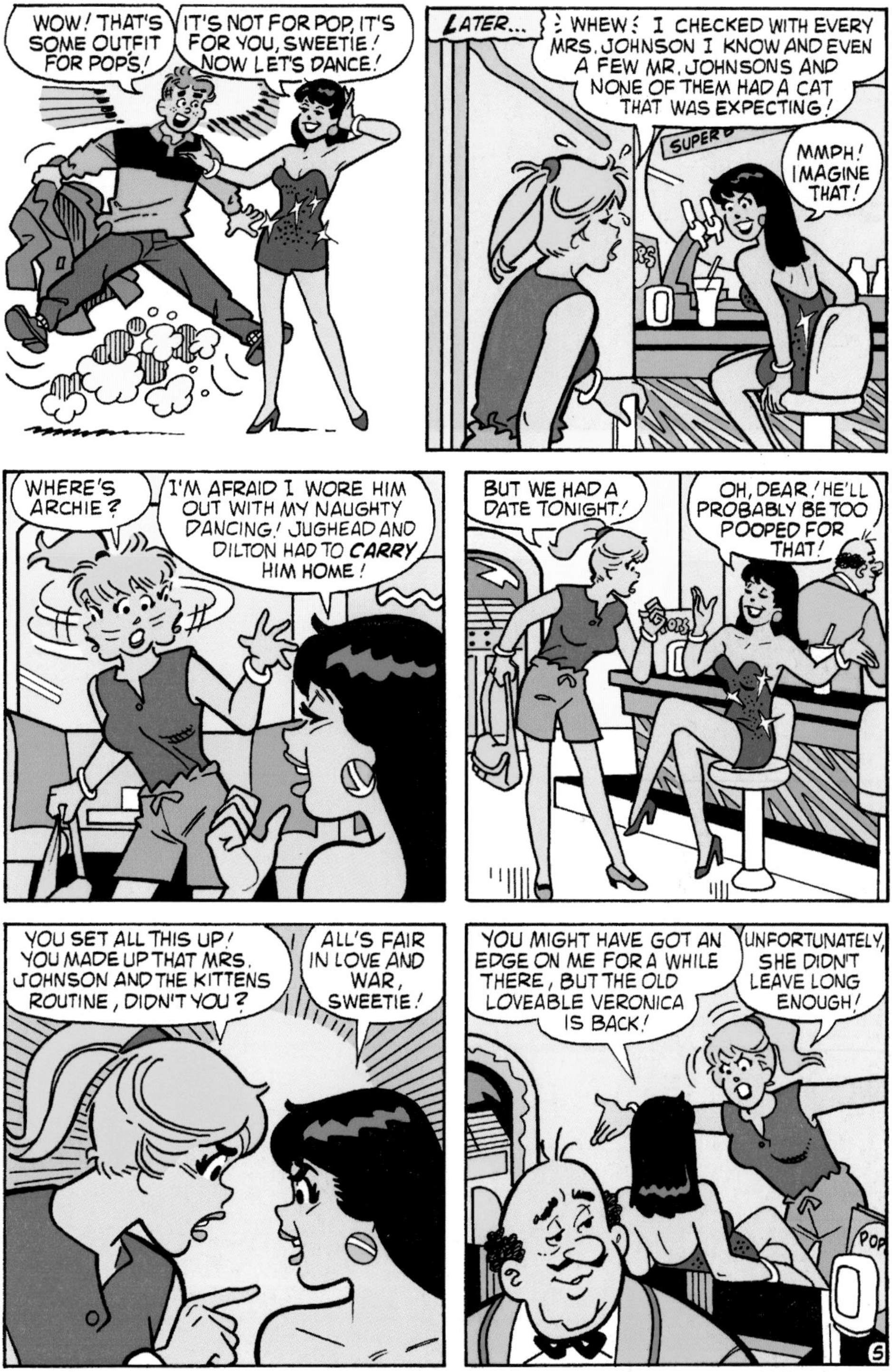

WOW! THAT'S SOME OUTFIT FOR POP'S!
IT'S NOT FOR POP, IT'S FOR YOU, SWEETIE! NOW LET'S DANCE!
LATER...
WHEW! I CHECKED WITH EVERY MRS. JOHNSON I KNOW AND EVEN A FEW MR. JOHNSONS AND NONE OF THEM HAD A CAT THAT WAS EXPECTING!
MMPH! IMAGINE THAT!
WHERE'S ARCHIE?
I'M AFRAID I WORE HIM OUT WITH MY NAUGHTY DANCING! JUGHEAD AND DILTON HAD TO CARRY HIM HOME!
BUT WE HAD A DATE TONIGHT!
OH, DEAR! HE'LL PROBABLY BE TOO POOPED FOR THAT!
YOU SET ALL THIS UP! YOU MADE UP THAT MRS. JOHNSON AND THE KITTENS ROUTINE, DIDN'T YOU?
ALL'S FAIR IN LOVE AND WAR, SWEETIE!
YOU MIGHT HAVE GOT AN EDGE ON ME FOR A WHILE THERE, BUT THE OLD LOVEABLE VERONICA IS BACK!
UNFORTUNATELY, SHE DIDN'T LEAVE LONG ENOUGH!
5

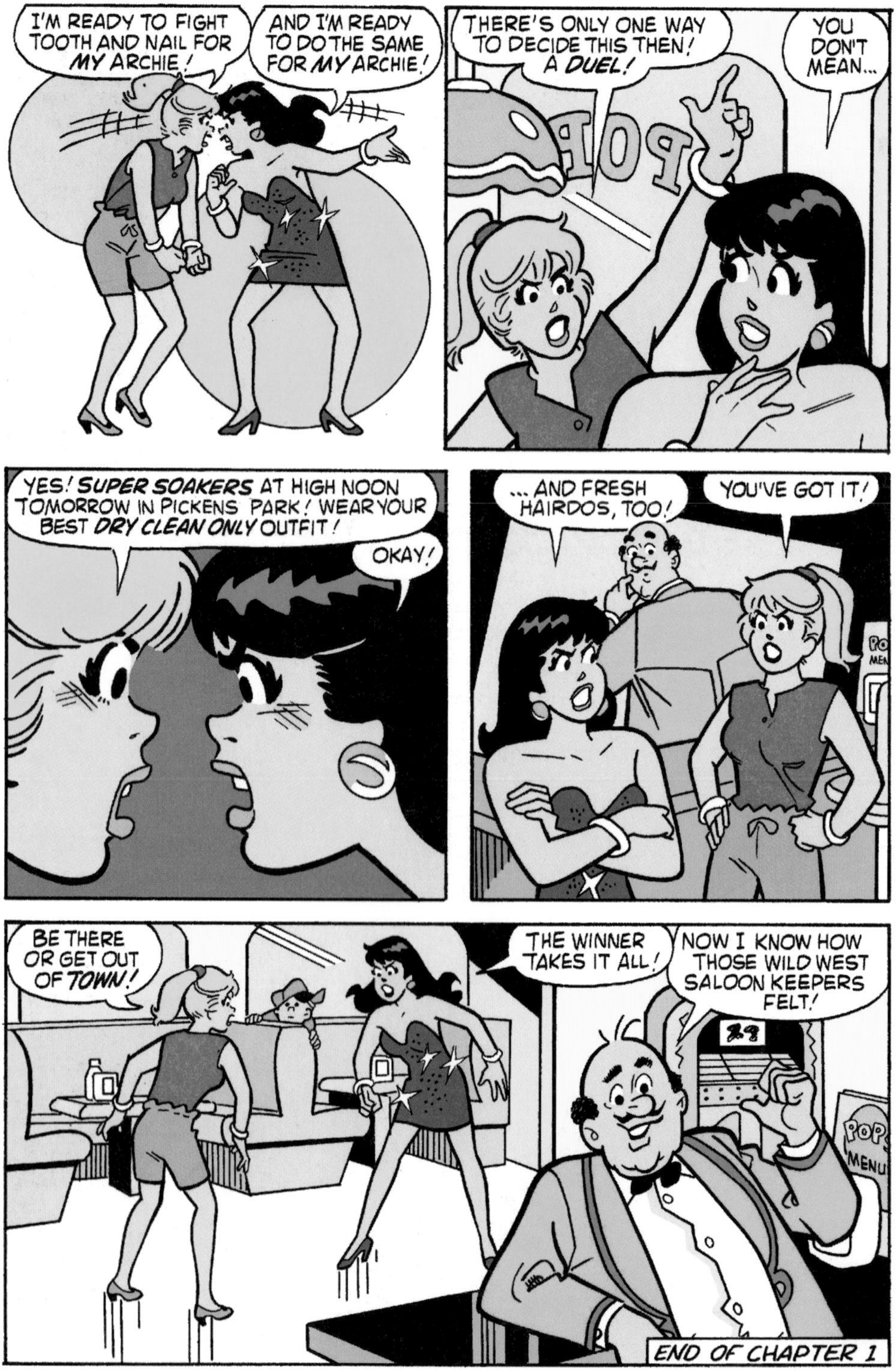
I'M READY TO FIGHT TOOTH AND NAIL FOR MY ARCHIE!
AND I'M READY TO DO THE SAME FOR MY ARCHIE!
THERE'S ONLY ONE WAY TO DECIDE THIS THEN! A DUEL!
YOU DON'T MEAN...
POP
YES! SUPER SOAKERS AT HIGH NOON TOMORROW IN PICKENS PARK! WEAR YOUR BEST DRY CLEAN ONLY OUTFIT!
OKAY!
... AND FRESH HAIRDOS, TOO!
YOU'VE GOT IT!
BE THERE OR GET OUT OF TOWN!
THE WINNER TAKES IT ALL!
NOW I KNOW HOW THOSE WILD WEST SALOON KEEPERS FELT!
POP'S MENU
END OF CHAPTER 1

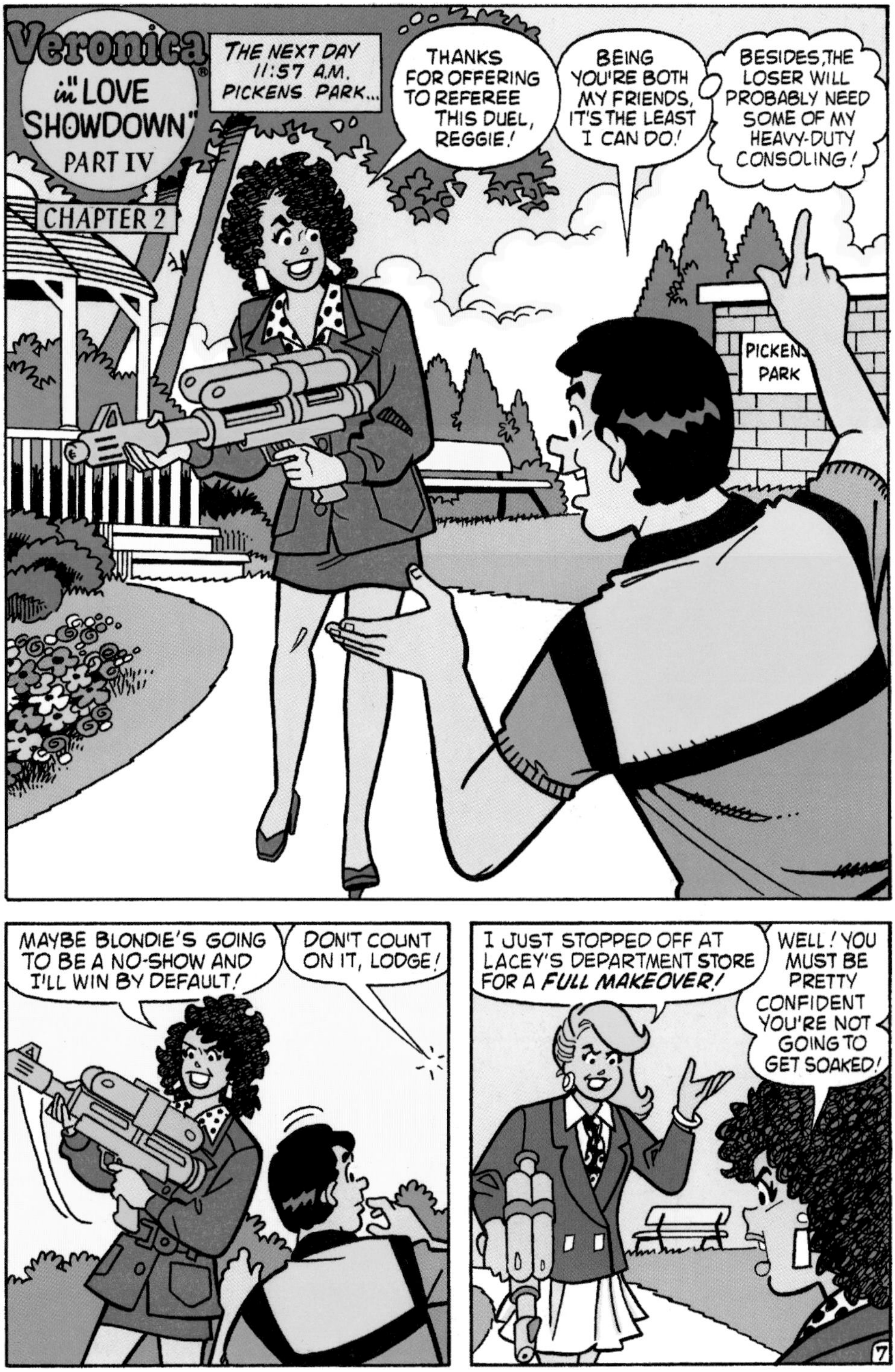
Veronica in "LOVE SHOWDOWN" PART IV
CHAPTER 2
THE NEXT DAY 11:57 A.M. PICKENS PARK...
THANKS FOR OFFERING TO REFEREE THIS DUEL, REGGIE!
BEING YOU'RE BOTH MY FRIENDS, IT'S THE LEAST I CAN DO!
BESIDES, THE LOSER WILL PROBABLY NEED SOME OF MY HEAVY-DUTY CONSOLING!
PICKENS PARK
MAYBE BLONDIE'S GOING TO BE A NO-SHOW AND I'LL WIN BY DEFAULT!
DON'T COUNT ON IT, LODGE!
I JUST STOPPED OFF AT LACEY'S DEPARTMENT STORE FOR A *FULL MAKEOVER!*
WELL! YOU MUST BE PRETTY CONFIDENT YOU'RE NOT GOING TO GET SOAKED!
7

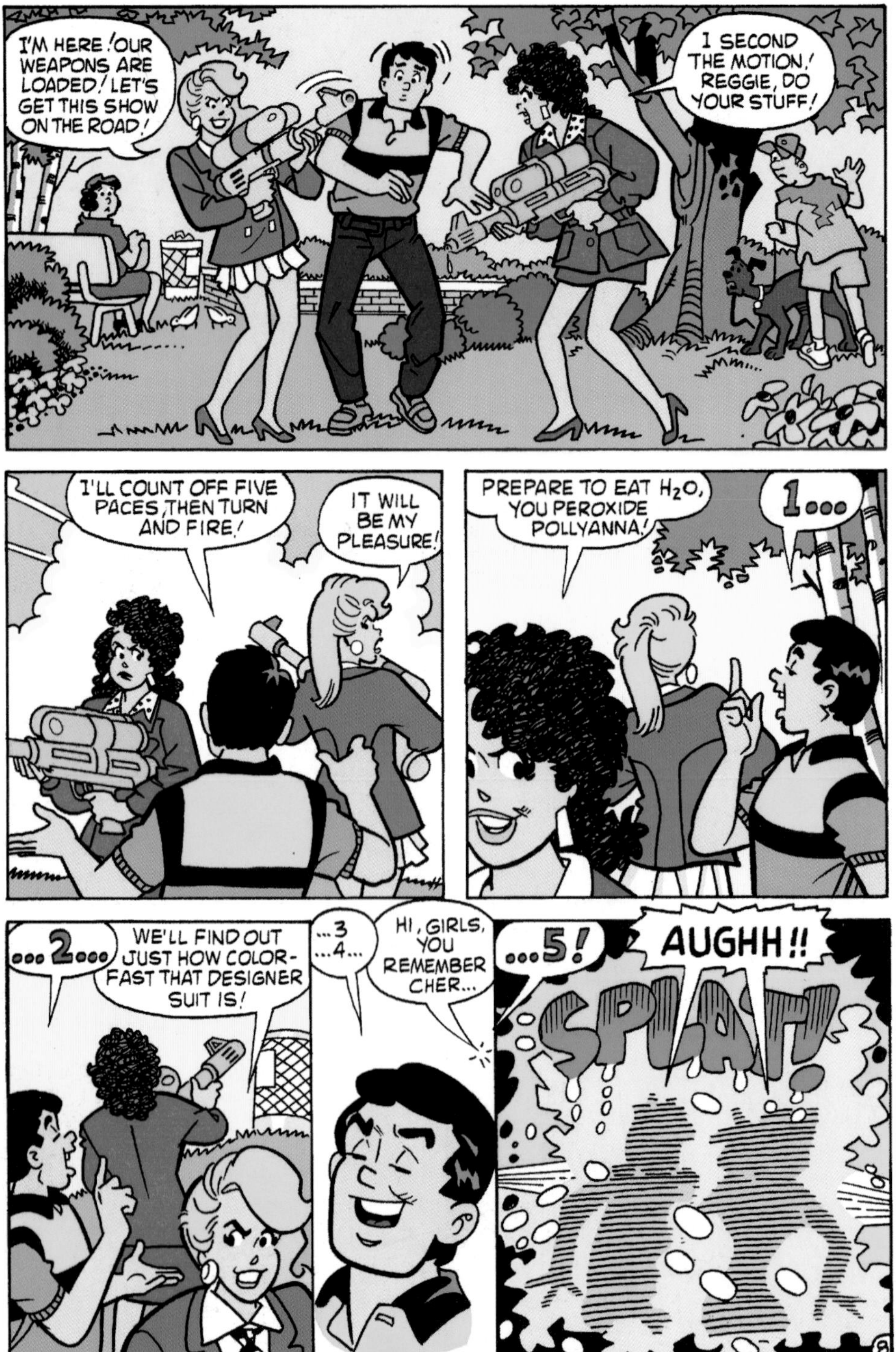
I'M HERE! OUR WEAPONS ARE LOADED! LET'S GET THIS SHOW ON THE ROAD!
I SECOND THE MOTION! REGGIE, DO YOUR STUFF!
I'LL COUNT OFF FIVE PACES, THEN TURN AND FIRE!
IT WILL BE MY PLEASURE!
PREPARE TO EAT H_2O, YOU PEROXIDE POLLYANNA!
1...
...2...
WE'LL FIND OUT JUST HOW COLOR-FAST THAT DESIGNER SUIT IS!
...3
...4...
HI, GIRLS, YOU REMEMBER CHER...
...5!
AUGHH!!
SPLAT!
8

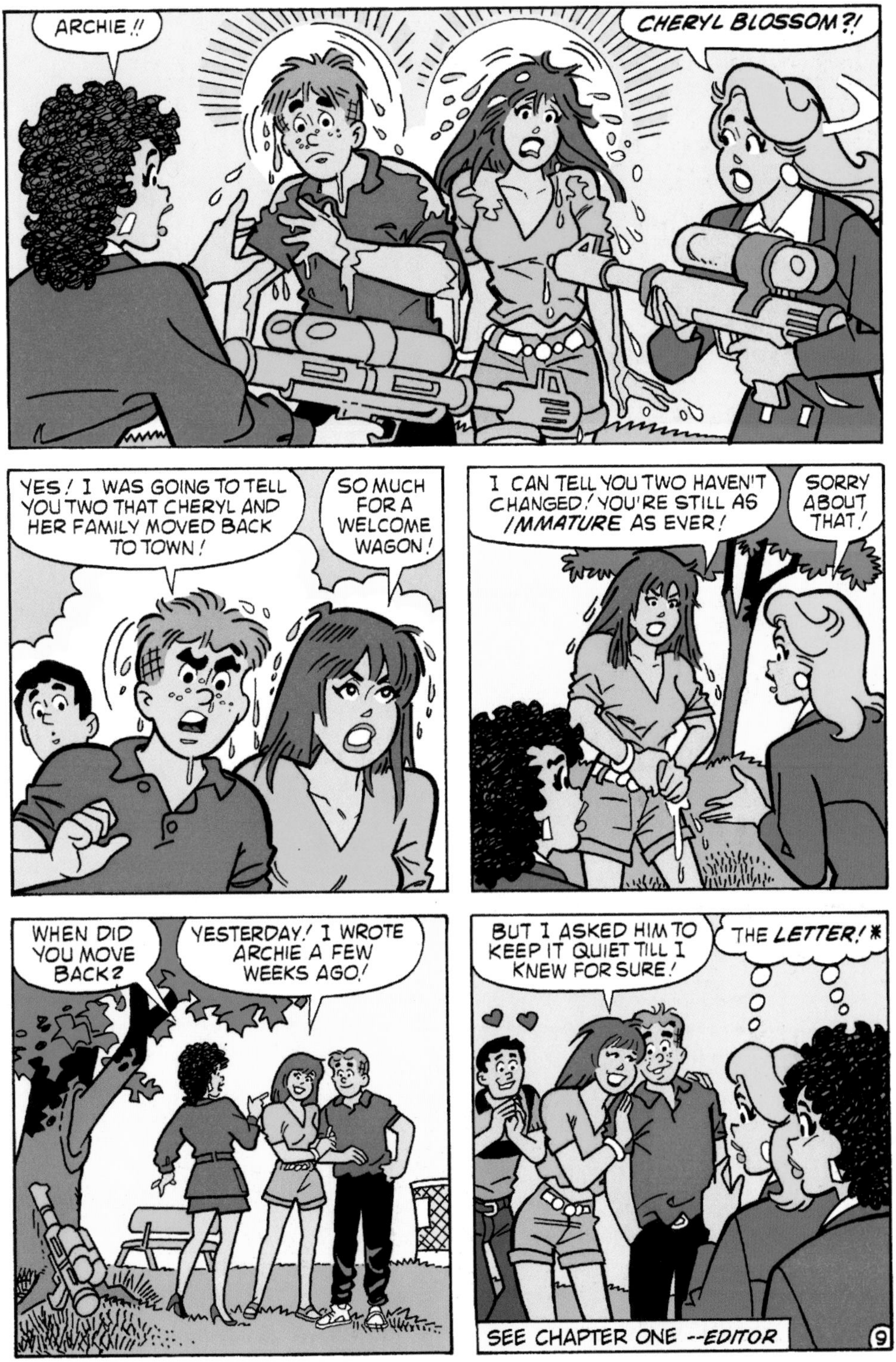
ARCHIE!!
CHERYL BLOSSOM?!
YES! I WAS GOING TO TELL YOU TWO THAT CHERYL AND HER FAMILY MOVED BACK TO TOWN!
SO MUCH FOR A WELCOME WAGON!
I CAN TELL YOU TWO HAVEN'T CHANGED! YOU'RE STILL AS *IMMATURE* AS EVER!
SORRY ABOUT THAT!
WHEN DID YOU MOVE BACK?
YESTERDAY! I WROTE ARCHIE A FEW WEEKS AGO!
BUT I ASKED HIM TO KEEP IT QUIET TILL I KNEW FOR SURE!
THE *LETTER*! *
SEE CHAPTER ONE --*EDITOR*
9

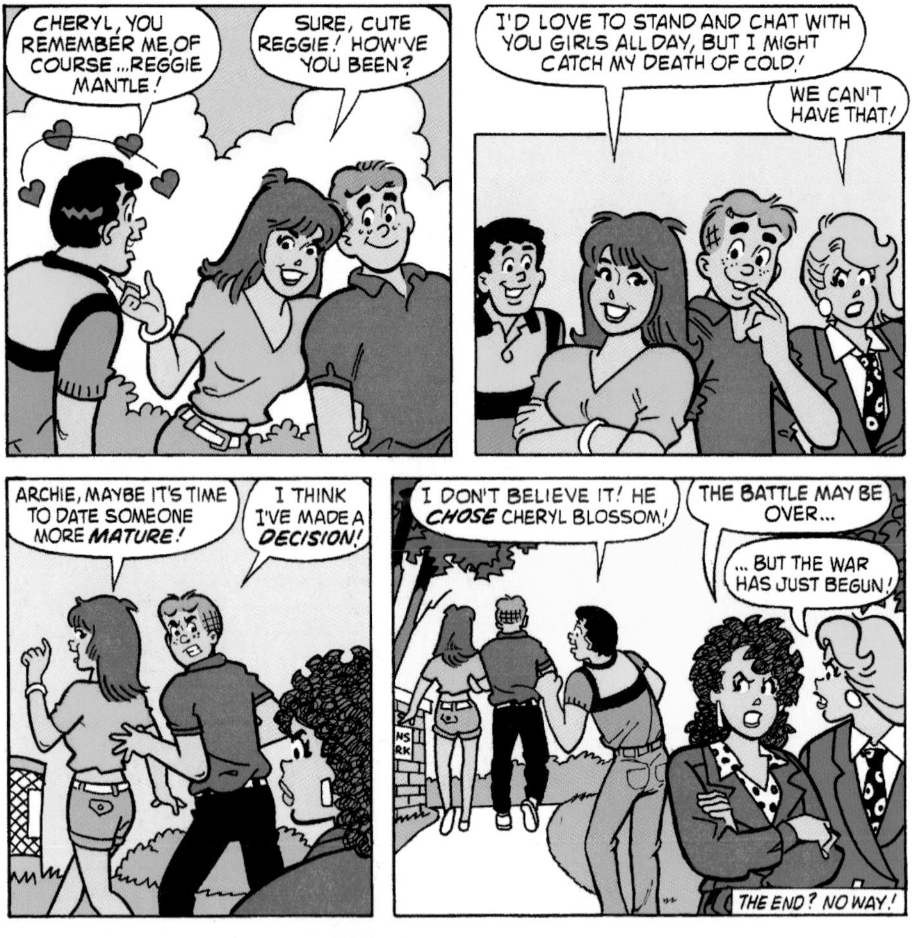
CHERYL, YOU REMEMBER ME, OF COURSE ...REGGIE MANTLE!
SURE, CUTE REGGIE! HOW'VE YOU BEEN?
I'D LOVE TO STAND AND CHAT WITH YOU GIRLS ALL DAY, BUT I MIGHT CATCH MY DEATH OF COLD!
WE CAN'T HAVE THAT!
ARCHIE, MAYBE IT'S TIME TO DATE SOMEONE MORE MATURE!
I THINK I'VE MADE A DECISION!
I DON'T BELIEVE IT! HE CHOSE CHERYL BLOSSOM!
THE BATTLE MAY BE OVER...
... BUT THE WAR HAS JUST BEGUN!
THE END? NO WAY!

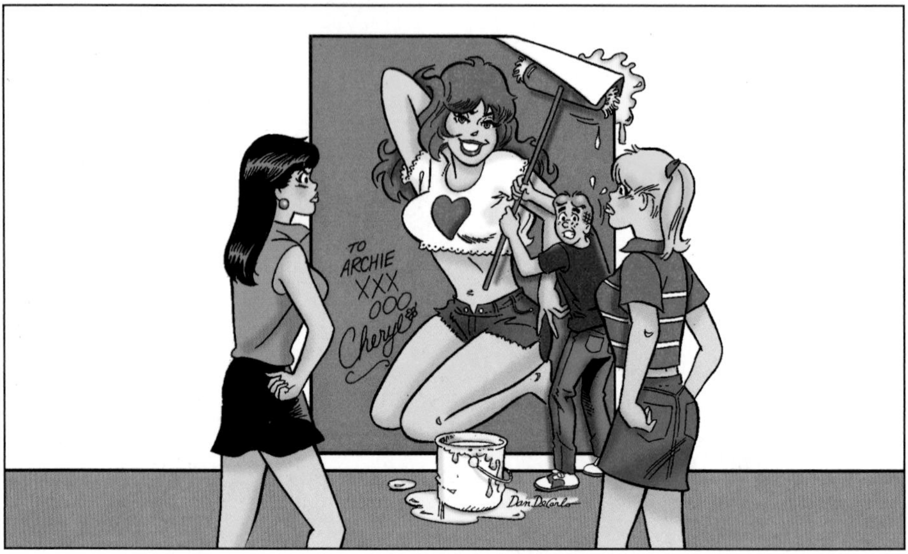
TO ARCHIE XXX OOO Cheryl
Dan DeCarlo

♥ ARCHIE LOVE SHOWDOWN ♥

Chapter Five

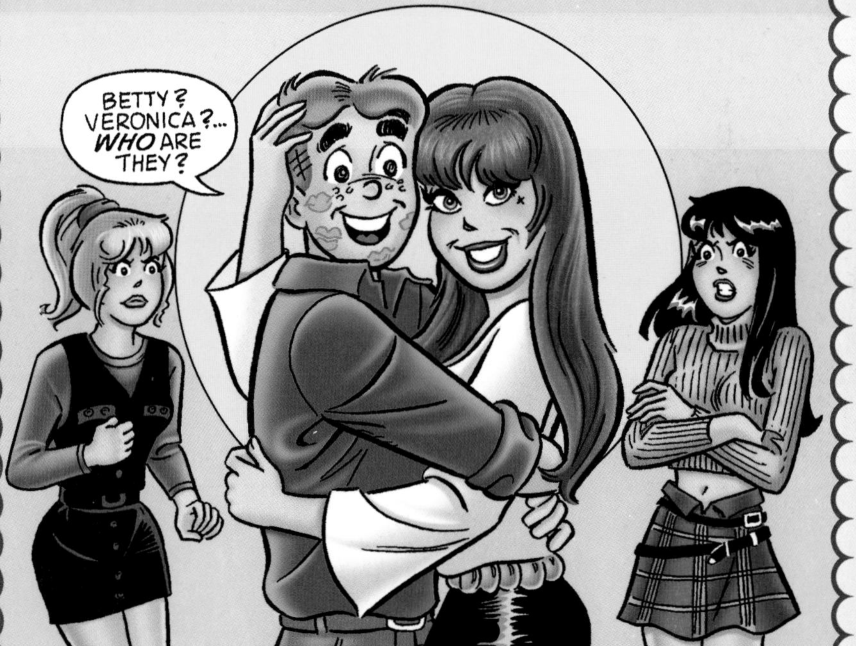
BETTY? VERONICA?... WHO ARE THEY?
Dan Parent & Dan DeCarlo

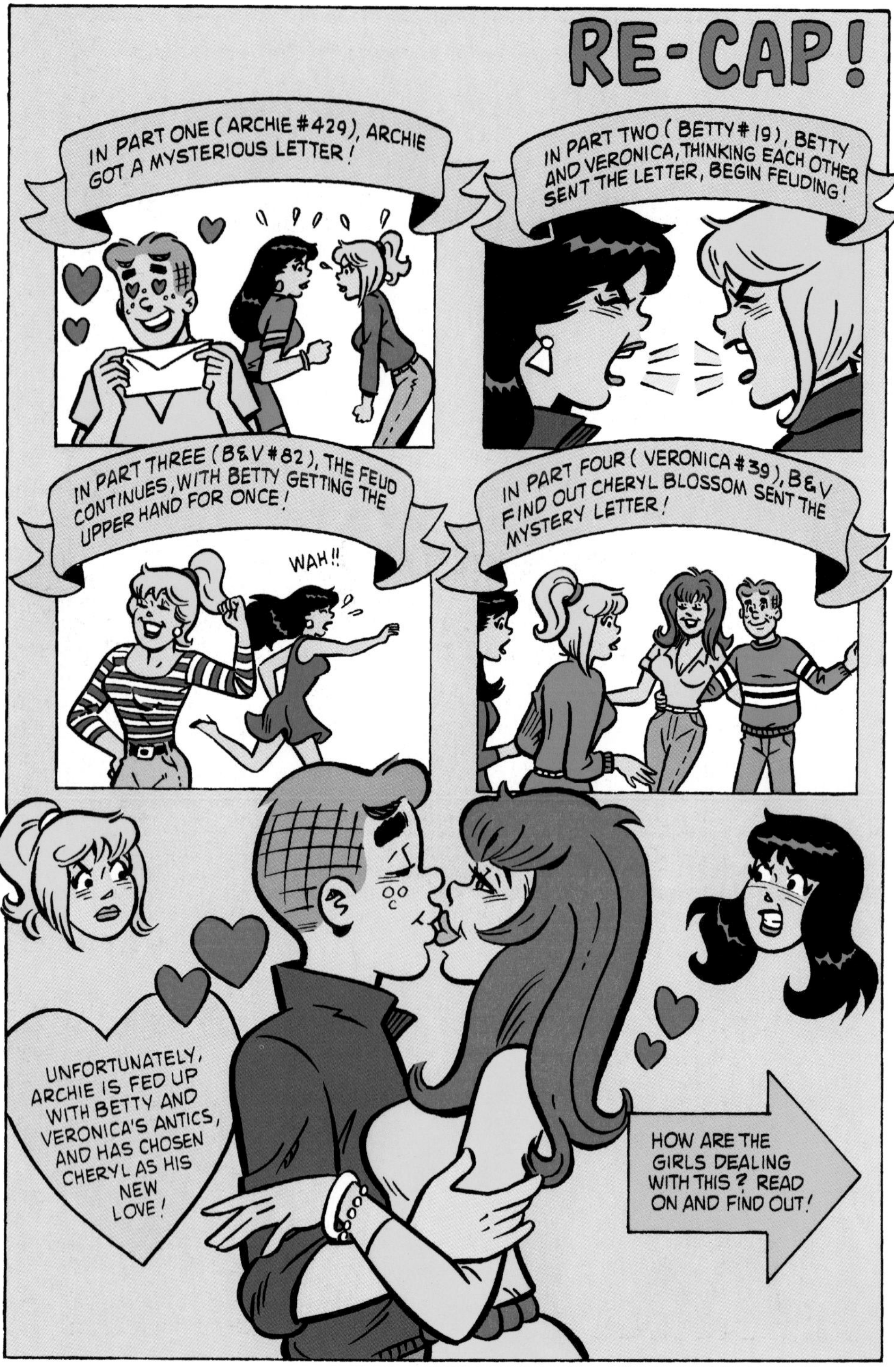
RE-CAP!
IN PART ONE (ARCHIE #429), ARCHIE GOT A MYSTERIOUS LETTER!
IN PART TWO (BETTY #19), BETTY AND VERONICA, THINKING EACH OTHER SENT THE LETTER, BEGIN FEUDING!
IN PART THREE (B&V #82), THE FEUD CONTINUES, WITH BETTY GETTING THE UPPER HAND FOR ONCE!
WAH!!
IN PART FOUR (VERONICA #39), B&V FIND OUT CHERYL BLOSSOM SENT THE MYSTERY LETTER!
UNFORTUNATELY, ARCHIE IS FED UP WITH BETTY AND VERONICA'S ANTICS, AND HAS CHOSEN CHERYL AS HIS NEW LOVE!
HOW ARE THE GIRLS DEALING WITH THIS? READ ON AND FIND OUT!

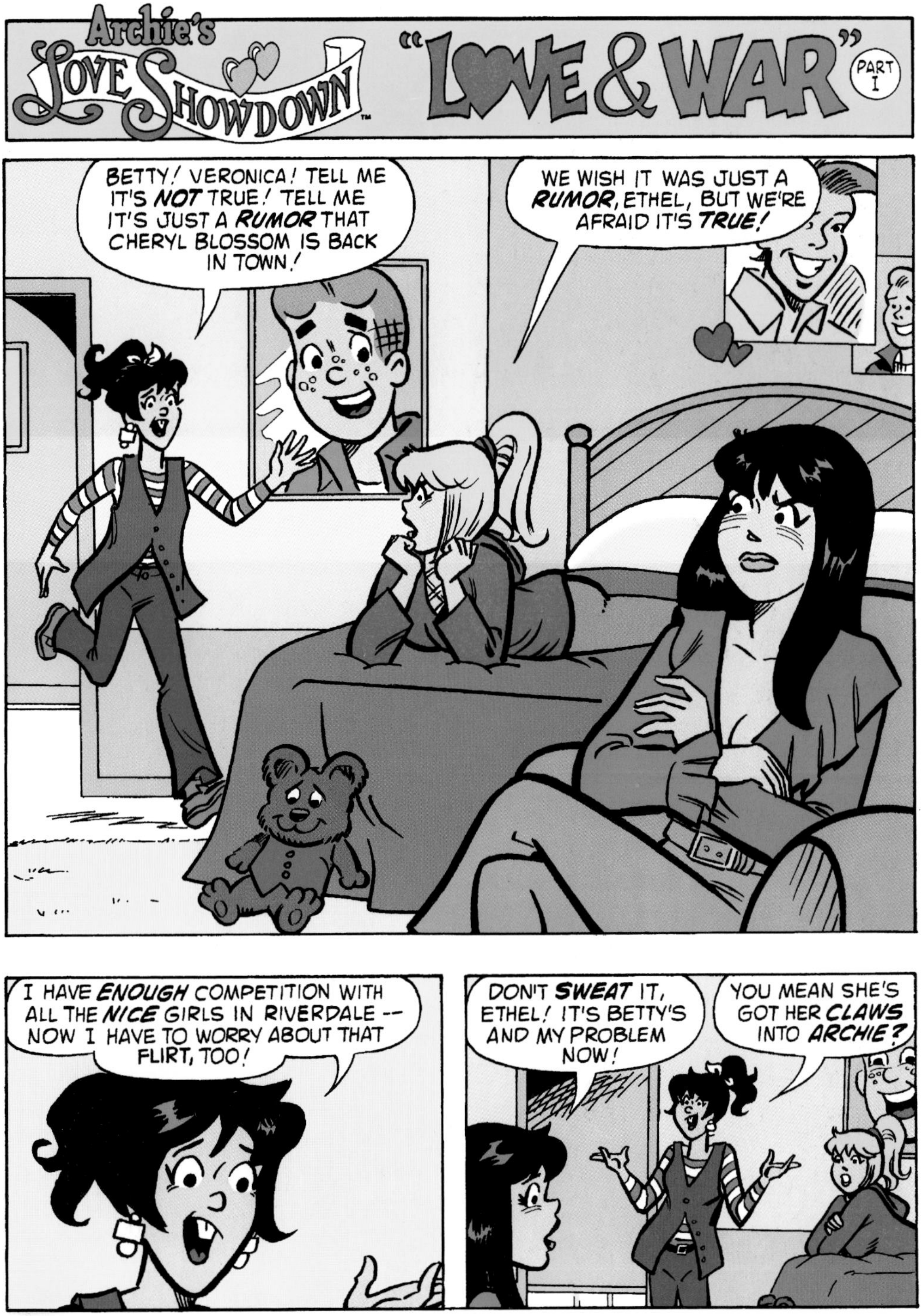

Archie's LOVE SHOWDOWN™
"LOVE & WAR" PART I
BETTY! VERONICA! TELL ME IT'S NOT TRUE! TELL ME IT'S JUST A RUMOR THAT CHERYL BLOSSOM IS BACK IN TOWN!
WE WISH IT WAS JUST A RUMOR, ETHEL, BUT WE'RE AFRAID IT'S TRUE!
I HAVE ENOUGH COMPETITION WITH ALL THE NICE GIRLS IN RIVERDALE -- NOW I HAVE TO WORRY ABOUT THAT FLIRT, TOO!
DON'T SWEAT IT, ETHEL! IT'S BETTY'S AND MY PROBLEM NOW!
YOU MEAN SHE'S GOT HER CLAWS INTO ARCHIE?

ORIGINALLY PRINTED IN LOVE SHOWDOWN SPECIAL, 1994

DAN PARENT • DAN PARENT • MIKE ESPOSITO • BILL YOSHIDA • BARRY GROSSMAN

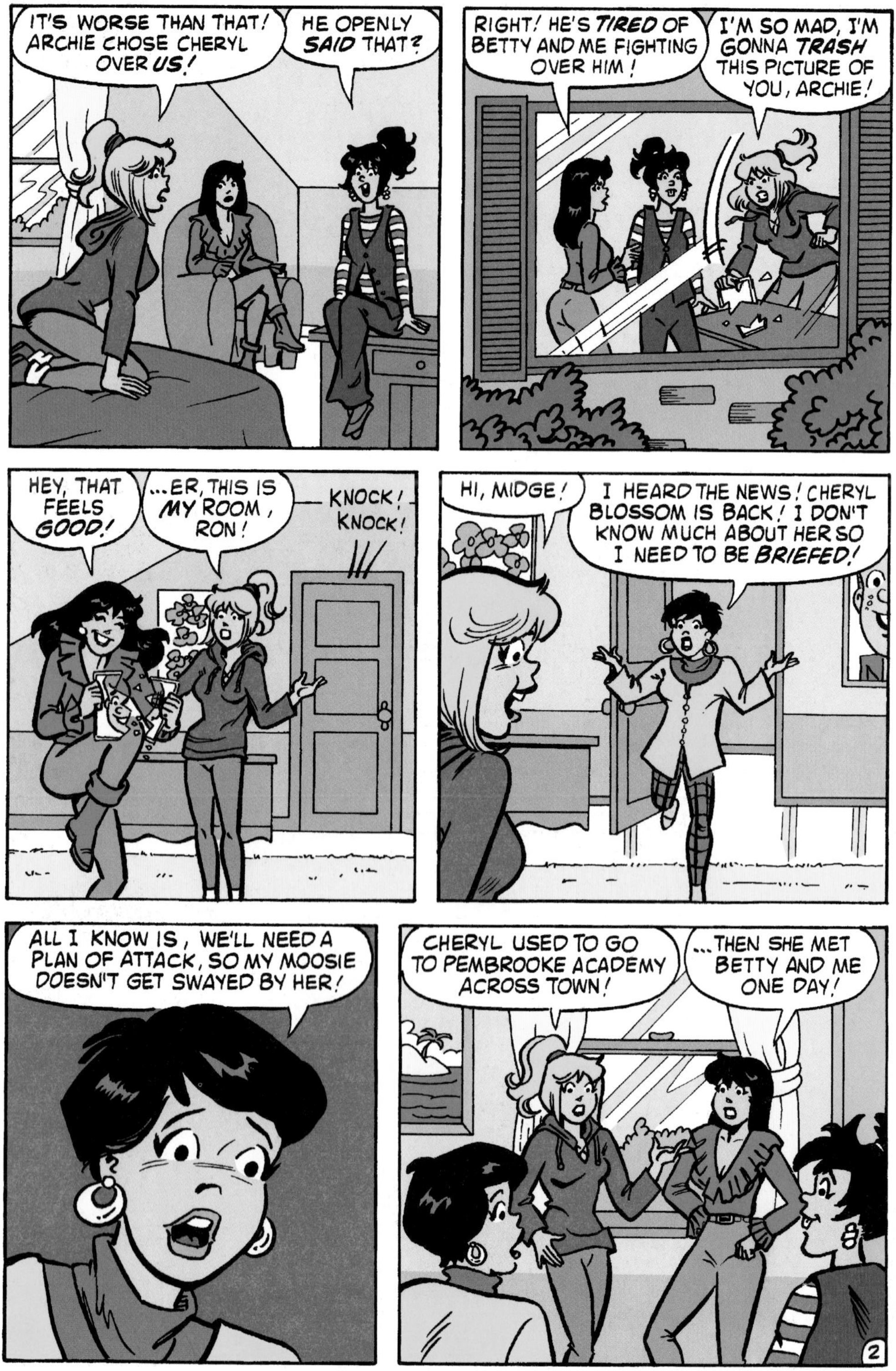
IT'S WORSE THAN THAT! ARCHIE CHOSE CHERYL OVER US!
HE OPENLY SAID THAT?
RIGHT! HE'S TIRED OF BETTY AND ME FIGHTING OVER HIM!
I'M SO MAD, I'M GONNA TRASH THIS PICTURE OF YOU, ARCHIE!
HEY, THAT FEELS GOOD!
...ER, THIS IS MY ROOM, RON!
KNOCK! KNOCK!
HI, MIDGE!
I HEARD THE NEWS! CHERYL BLOSSOM IS BACK! I DON'T KNOW MUCH ABOUT HER SO I NEED TO BE BRIEFED!
ALL I KNOW IS, WE'LL NEED A PLAN OF ATTACK, SO MY MOOSIE DOESN'T GET SWAYED BY HER!
CHERYL USED TO GO TO PEMBROOKE ACADEMY ACROSS TOWN!
...THEN SHE MET BETTY AND ME ONE DAY!
2

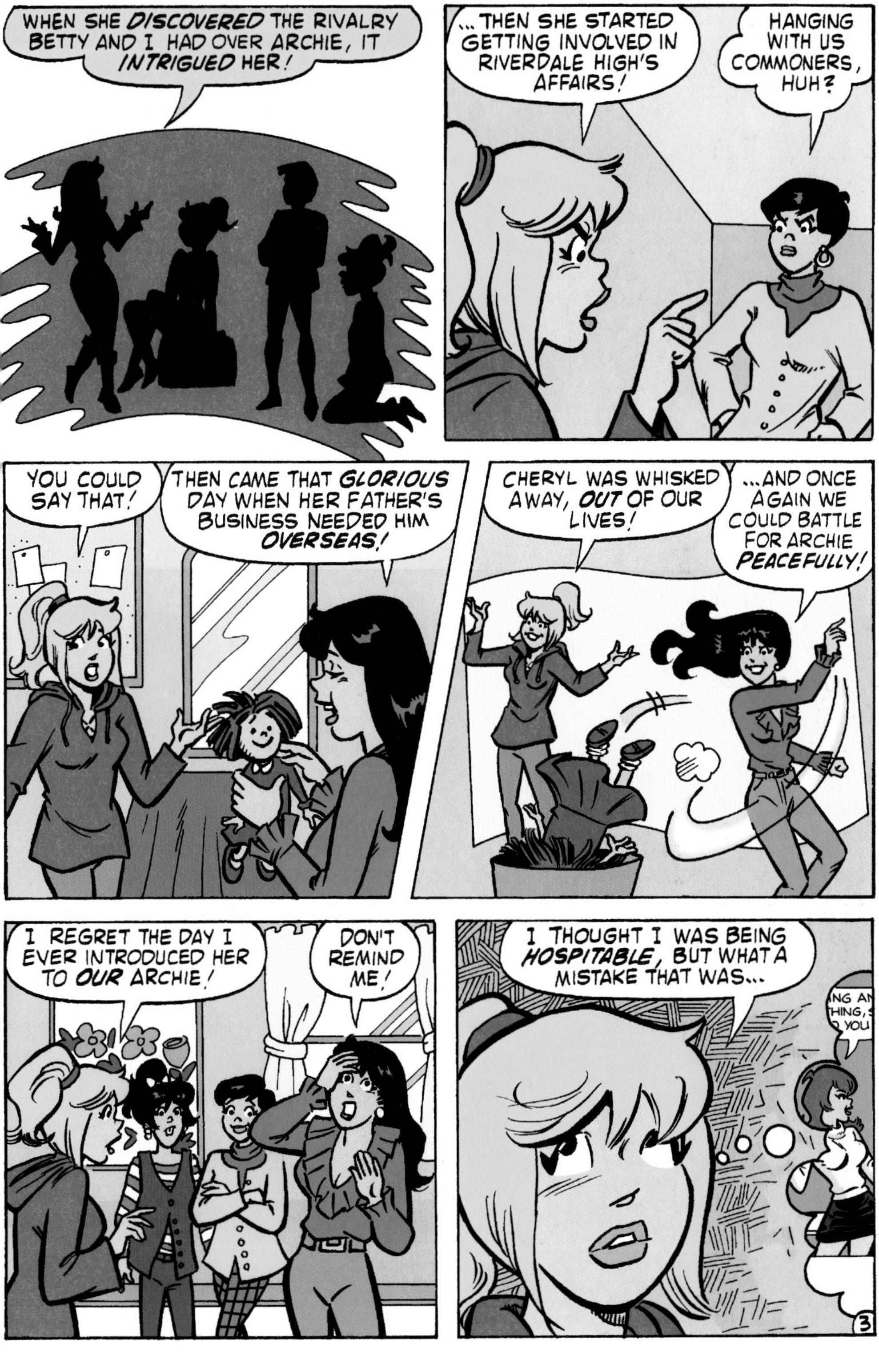
WHEN SHE DISCOVERED THE RIVALRY BETTY AND I HAD OVER ARCHIE, IT INTRIGUED HER!
...THEN SHE STARTED GETTING INVOLVED IN RIVERDALE HIGH'S AFFAIRS!
HANGING WITH US COMMONERS, HUH?
YOU COULD SAY THAT!
THEN CAME THAT GLORIOUS DAY WHEN HER FATHER'S BUSINESS NEEDED HIM OVERSEAS!
CHERYL WAS WHISKED AWAY, OUT OF OUR LIVES!
...AND ONCE AGAIN WE COULD BATTLE FOR ARCHIE PEACEFULLY!
I REGRET THE DAY I EVER INTRODUCED HER TO OUR ARCHIE!
DON'T REMIND ME!
I THOUGHT I WAS BEING HOSPITABLE, BUT WHAT A MISTAKE THAT WAS...
3

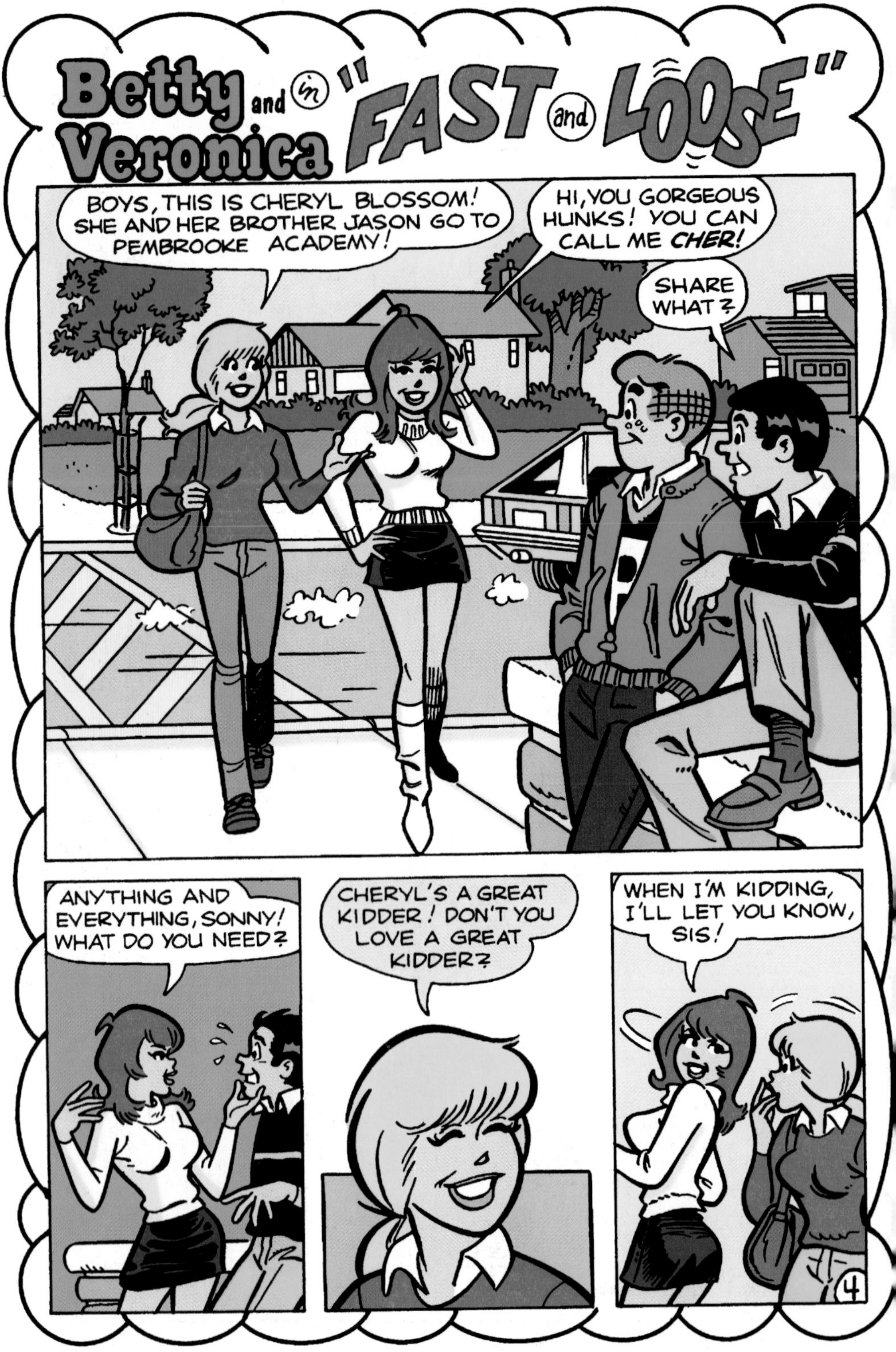
Betty and Veronica in "FAST and LOOSE"
BOYS, THIS IS CHERYL BLOSSOM! SHE AND HER BROTHER JASON GO TO PEMBROOKE ACADEMY!
HI, YOU GORGEOUS HUNKS! YOU CAN CALL ME CHER!
SHARE WHAT?
ANYTHING AND EVERYTHING, SONNY! WHAT DO YOU NEED?
CHERYL'S A GREAT KIDDER! DON'T YOU LOVE A GREAT KIDDER?
WHEN I'M KIDDING, I'LL LET YOU KNOW, SIS!
4

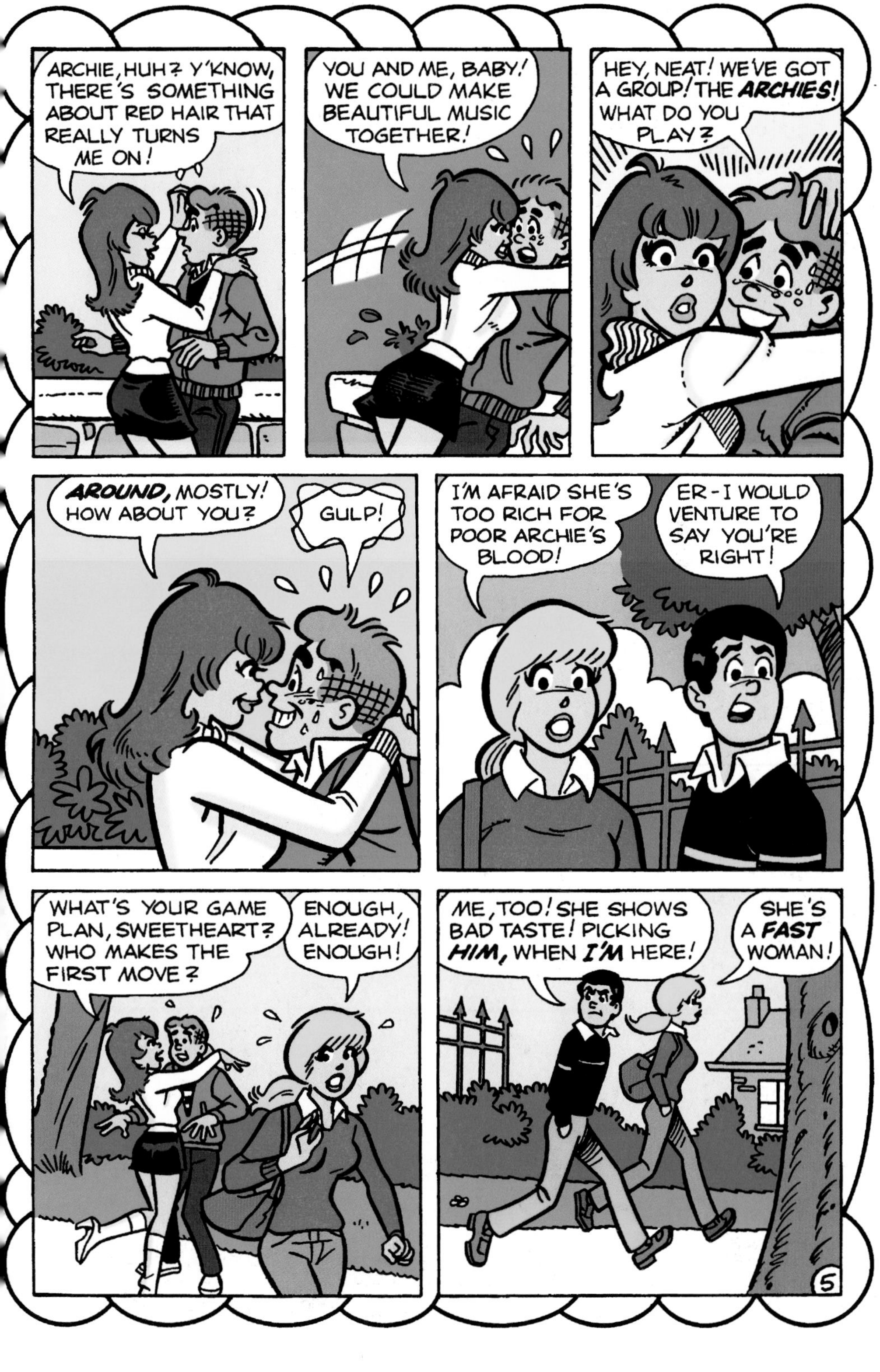
ARCHIE, HUH? Y'KNOW, THERE'S SOMETHING ABOUT RED HAIR THAT REALLY TURNS ME ON!
YOU AND ME, BABY! WE COULD MAKE BEAUTIFUL MUSIC TOGETHER!
HEY, NEAT! WE'VE GOT A GROUP! THE ARCHIES! WHAT DO YOU PLAY?
AROUND, MOSTLY! HOW ABOUT YOU?
GULP!
I'M AFRAID SHE'S TOO RICH FOR POOR ARCHIE'S BLOOD!
ER - I WOULD VENTURE TO SAY YOU'RE RIGHT!
WHAT'S YOUR GAME PLAN, SWEETHEART? WHO MAKES THE FIRST MOVE?
ENOUGH, ALREADY! ENOUGH!
ME, TOO! SHE SHOWS BAD TASTE! PICKING HIM, WHEN I'M HERE!
SHE'S A FAST WOMAN!
5

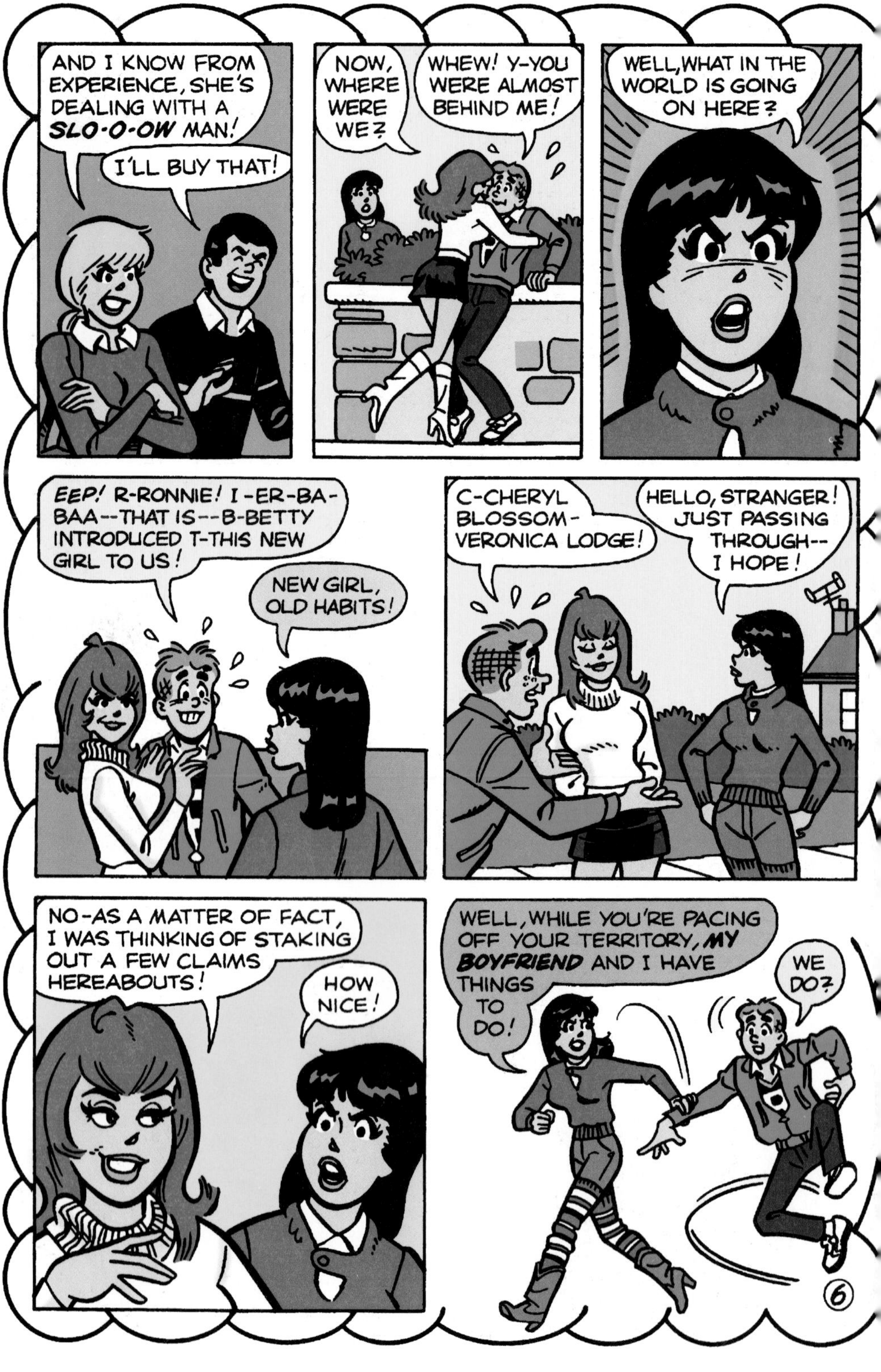
AND I KNOW FROM EXPERIENCE, SHE'S DEALING WITH A SLO-O-OW MAN!
I'LL BUY THAT!
NOW, WHERE WERE WE?
WHEW! Y-YOU WERE ALMOST BEHIND ME!
WELL, WHAT IN THE WORLD IS GOING ON HERE?
EEP! R-RONNIE! I-ER-BA-BAA--THAT IS--B-BETTY INTRODUCED T-THIS NEW GIRL TO US!
NEW GIRL, OLD HABITS!
C-CHERYL BLOSSOM-VERONICA LODGE!
HELLO, STRANGER! JUST PASSING THROUGH--I HOPE!
NO-AS A MATTER OF FACT, I WAS THINKING OF STAKING OUT A FEW CLAIMS HEREABOUTS!
HOW NICE!
WELL, WHILE YOU'RE PACING OFF YOUR TERRITORY, MY BOYFRIEND AND I HAVE THINGS TO DO!
WE DO?
6

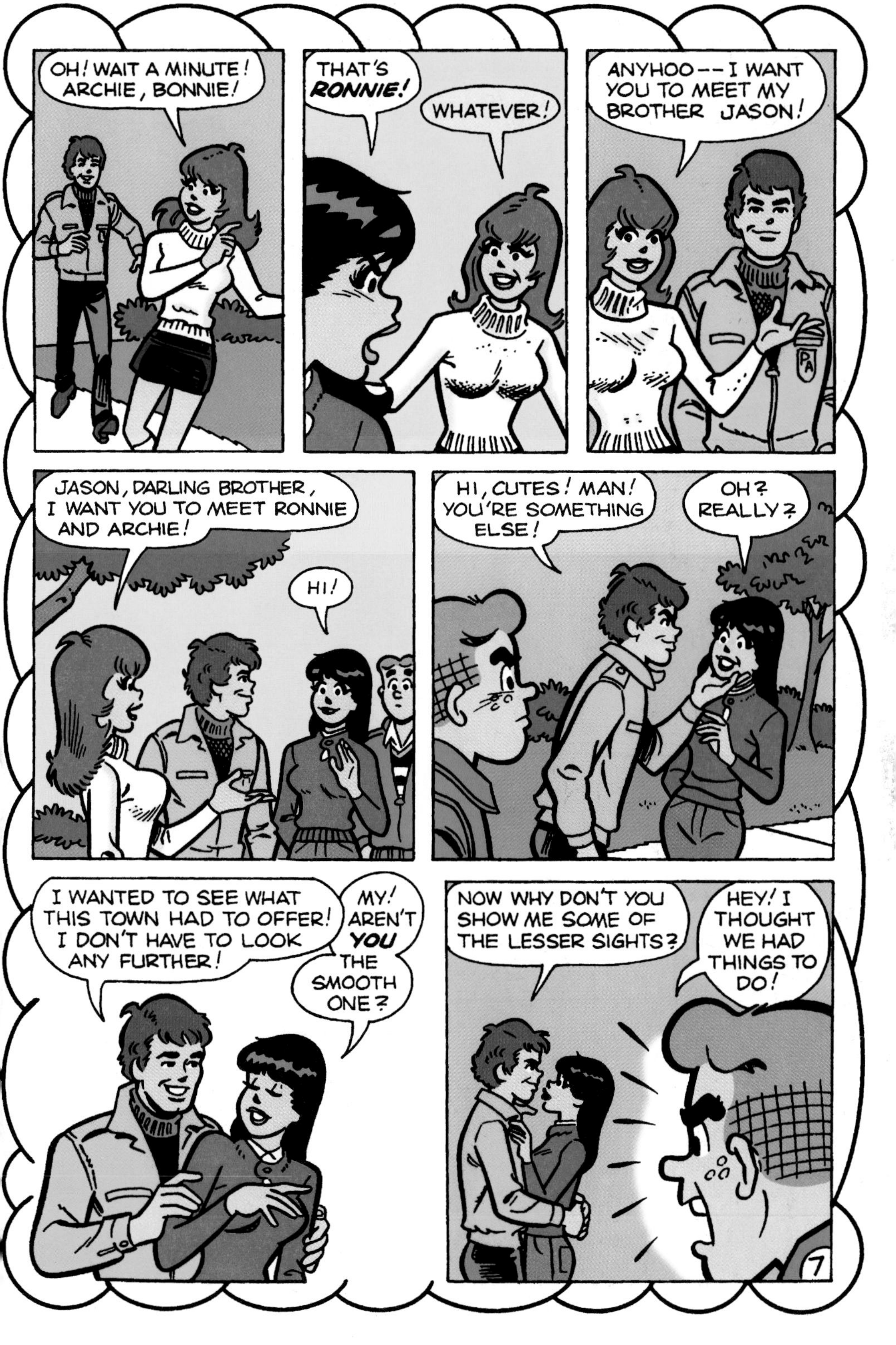
OH! WAIT A MINUTE! ARCHIE, BONNIE!
THAT'S **RONNIE!**
WHATEVER!
ANYHOO -- I WANT YOU TO MEET MY BROTHER JASON!
JASON, DARLING BROTHER, I WANT YOU TO MEET RONNIE AND ARCHIE!
HI!
HI, CUTES! MAN! YOU'RE SOMETHING ELSE!
OH? REALLY?
I WANTED TO SEE WHAT THIS TOWN HAD TO OFFER! I DON'T HAVE TO LOOK ANY FURTHER!
MY! AREN'T **YOU** THE SMOOTH ONE?
NOW WHY DON'T YOU SHOW ME SOME OF THE LESSER SIGHTS?
HEY! I THOUGHT WE HAD THINGS TO DO!
7

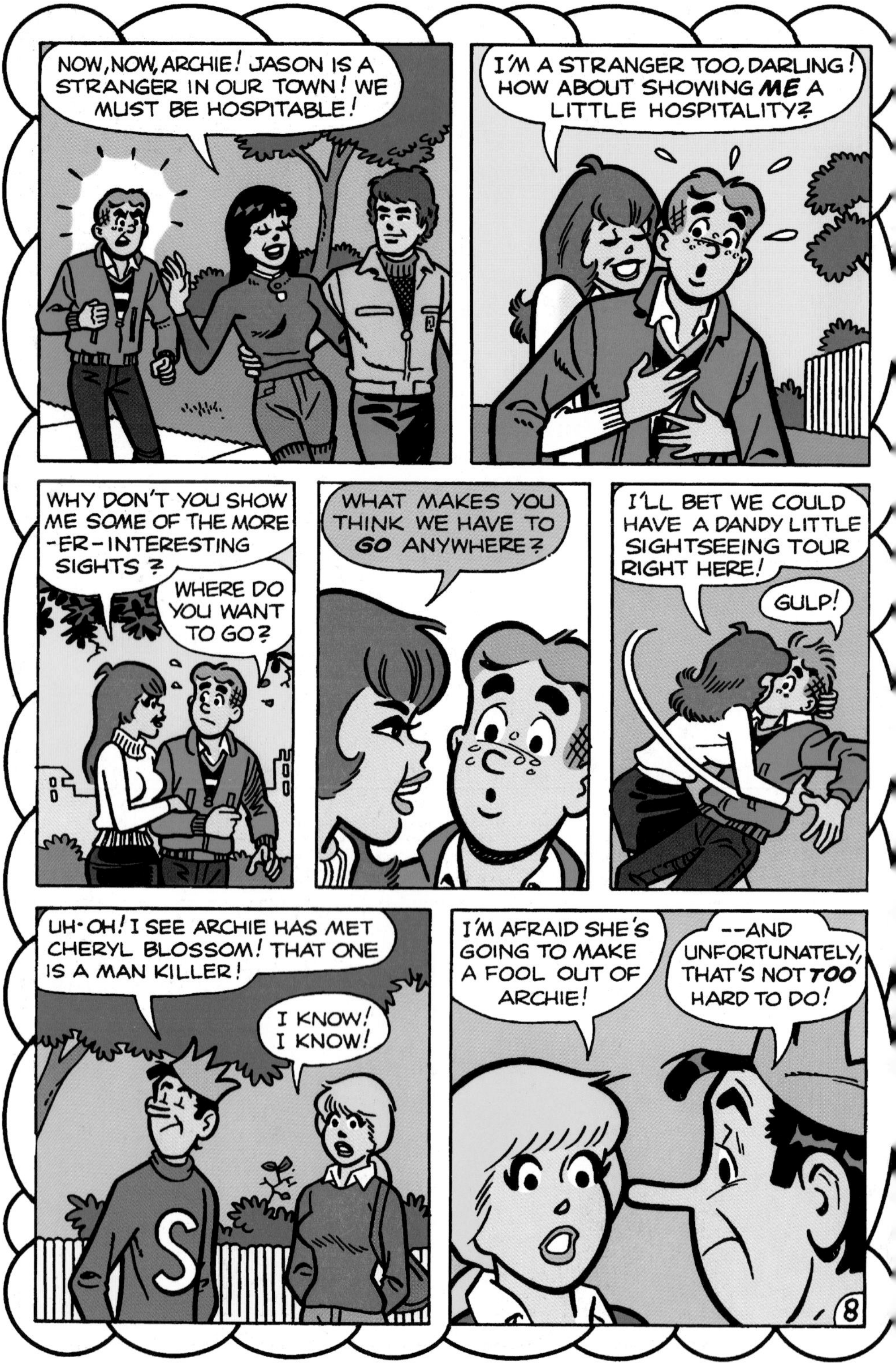
NOW, NOW, ARCHIE! JASON IS A STRANGER IN OUR TOWN! WE MUST BE HOSPITABLE!
I'M A STRANGER TOO, DARLING! HOW ABOUT SHOWING *ME* A LITTLE HOSPITALITY?
WHY DON'T YOU SHOW ME SOME OF THE MORE -ER- INTERESTING SIGHTS?
WHERE DO YOU WANT TO GO?
WHAT MAKES YOU THINK WE HAVE TO *GO* ANYWHERE?
I'LL BET WE COULD HAVE A DANDY LITTLE SIGHTSEEING TOUR RIGHT HERE!
GULP!
UH-OH! I SEE ARCHIE HAS MET CHERYL BLOSSOM! THAT ONE IS A MAN KILLER!
I KNOW! I KNOW!
I'M AFRAID SHE'S GOING TO MAKE A FOOL OUT OF ARCHIE!
--AND UNFORTUNATELY, THAT'S NOT *TOO* HARD TO DO!
8

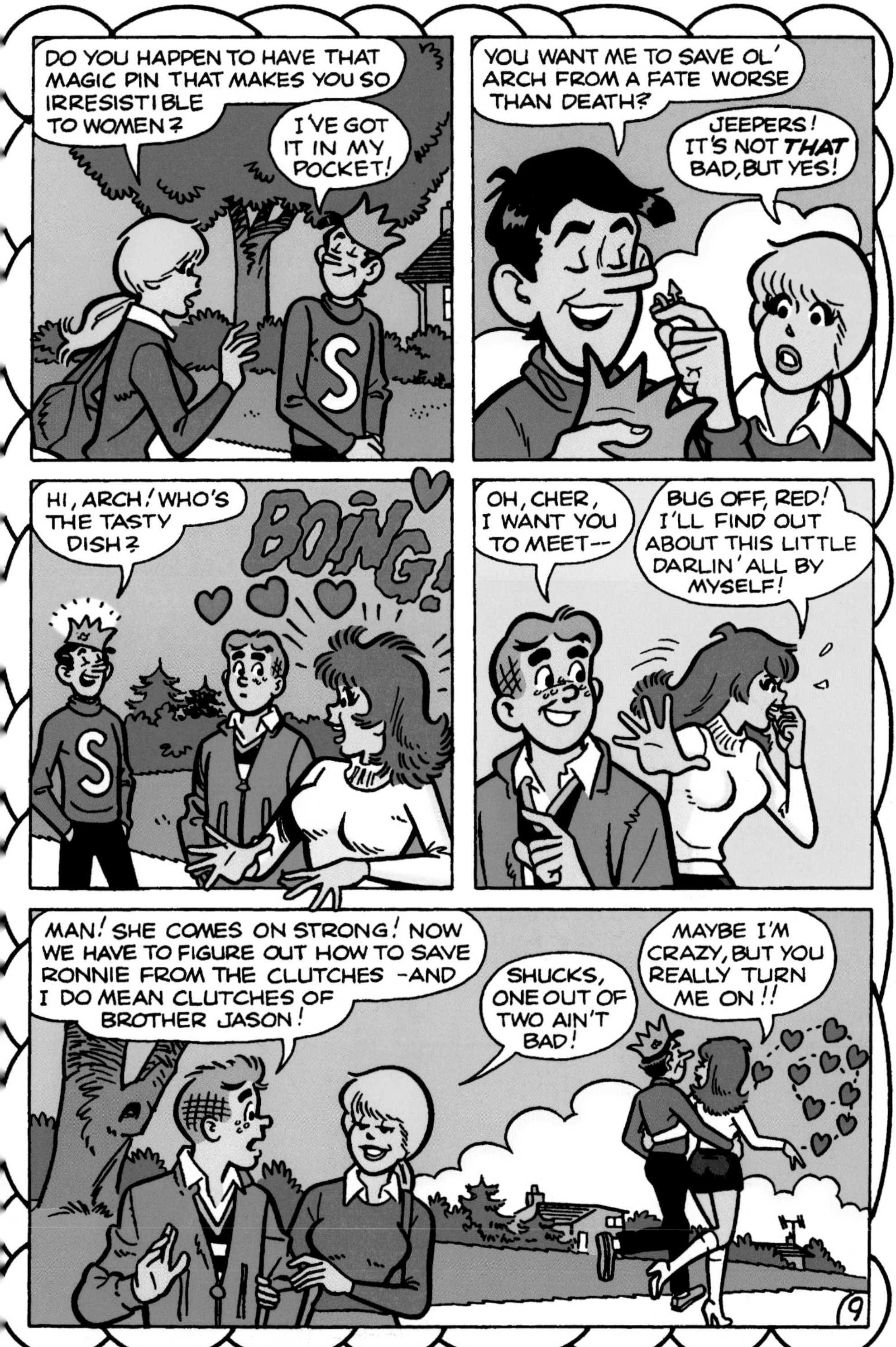
DO YOU HAPPEN TO HAVE THAT MAGIC PIN THAT MAKES YOU SO IRRESISTIBLE TO WOMEN?
I'VE GOT IT IN MY POCKET!
YOU WANT ME TO SAVE OL' ARCH FROM A FATE WORSE THAN DEATH?
JEEPERS! IT'S NOT THAT BAD, BUT YES!
HI, ARCH! WHO'S THE TASTY DISH?
BOING!
OH, CHER, I WANT YOU TO MEET--
BUG OFF, RED! I'LL FIND OUT ABOUT THIS LITTLE DARLIN' ALL BY MYSELF!
MAN! SHE COMES ON STRONG! NOW WE HAVE TO FIGURE OUT HOW TO SAVE RONNIE FROM THE CLUTCHES -AND I DO MEAN CLUTCHES OF BROTHER JASON!
SHUCKS, ONE OUT OF TWO AIN'T BAD!
MAYBE I'M CRAZY, BUT YOU REALLY TURN ME ON!!
9

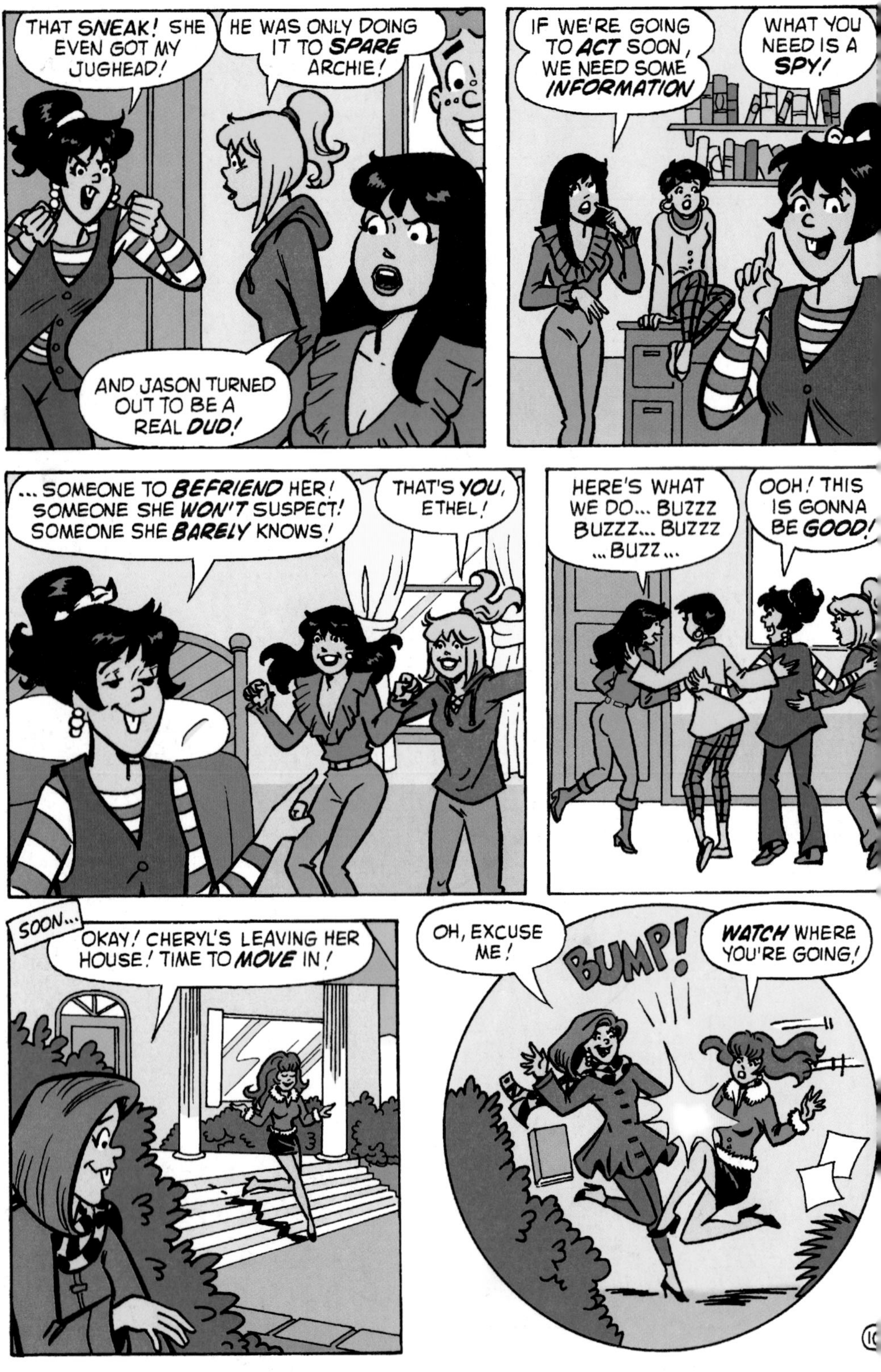

THAT SNEAK! SHE EVEN GOT MY JUGHEAD!
HE WAS ONLY DOING IT TO SPARE ARCHIE!
AND JASON TURNED OUT TO BE A REAL DUD!
IF WE'RE GOING TO ACT SOON, WE NEED SOME INFORMATION
WHAT YOU NEED IS A SPY!
... SOMEONE TO BEFRIEND HER! SOMEONE SHE WON'T SUSPECT! SOMEONE SHE BARELY KNOWS!
THAT'S YOU, ETHEL!
HERE'S WHAT WE DO... BUZZZ BUZZZ... BUZZZ ...BUZZ...
OOH! THIS IS GONNA BE GOOD!
SOON...
OKAY! CHERYL'S LEAVING HER HOUSE! TIME TO MOVE IN!
OH, EXCUSE ME!
BUMP!
WATCH WHERE YOU'RE GOING!

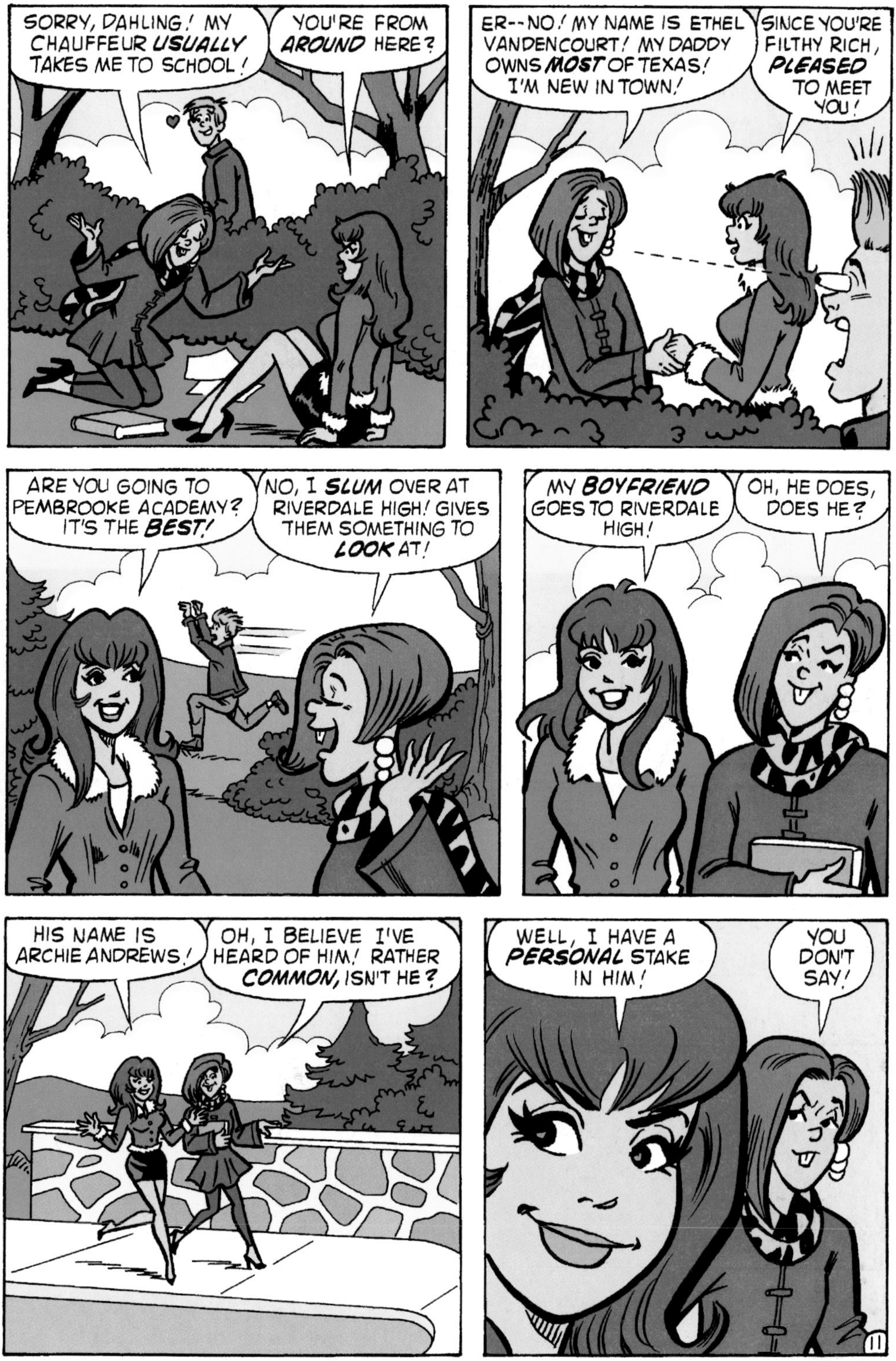
SORRY, DAHLING! MY CHAUFFEUR USUALLY TAKES ME TO SCHOOL!
YOU'RE FROM AROUND HERE?
ER--NO! MY NAME IS ETHEL VANDENCOURT! MY DADDY OWNS MOST OF TEXAS! I'M NEW IN TOWN!
SINCE YOU'RE FILTHY RICH, PLEASED TO MEET YOU!
ARE YOU GOING TO PEMBROOKE ACADEMY? IT'S THE BEST!
NO, I SLUM OVER AT RIVERDALE HIGH! GIVES THEM SOMETHING TO LOOK AT!
MY BOYFRIEND GOES TO RIVERDALE HIGH!
OH, HE DOES, DOES HE?
HIS NAME IS ARCHIE ANDREWS!
OH, I BELIEVE I'VE HEARD OF HIM! RATHER COMMON, ISN'T HE?
WELL, I HAVE A PERSONAL STAKE IN HIM!
YOU DON'T SAY!
11

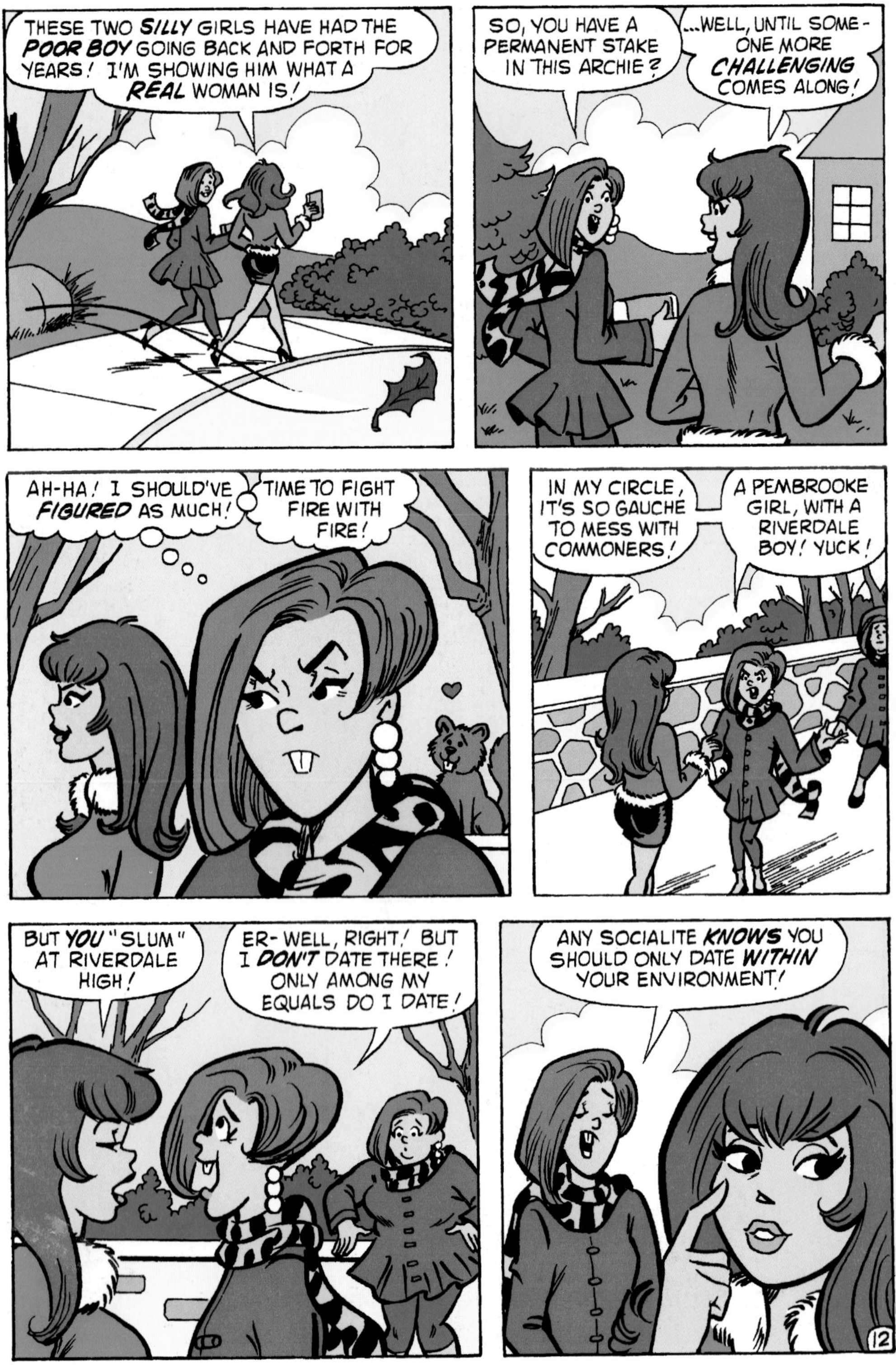
THESE TWO SILLY GIRLS HAVE HAD THE POOR BOY GOING BACK AND FORTH FOR YEARS! I'M SHOWING HIM WHAT A REAL WOMAN IS!
SO, YOU HAVE A PERMANENT STAKE IN THIS ARCHIE?
...WELL, UNTIL SOME-ONE MORE CHALLENGING COMES ALONG!
AH-HA! I SHOULD'VE FIGURED AS MUCH!
TIME TO FIGHT FIRE WITH FIRE!
IN MY CIRCLE, IT'S SO GAUCHE TO MESS WITH COMMONERS!
A PEMBROOKE GIRL, WITH A RIVERDALE BOY! YUCK!
BUT YOU "SLUM" AT RIVERDALE HIGH!
ER-WELL, RIGHT! BUT I DON'T DATE THERE! ONLY AMONG MY EQUALS DO I DATE!
ANY SOCIALITE KNOWS YOU SHOULD ONLY DATE WITHIN YOUR ENVIRONMENT!
12

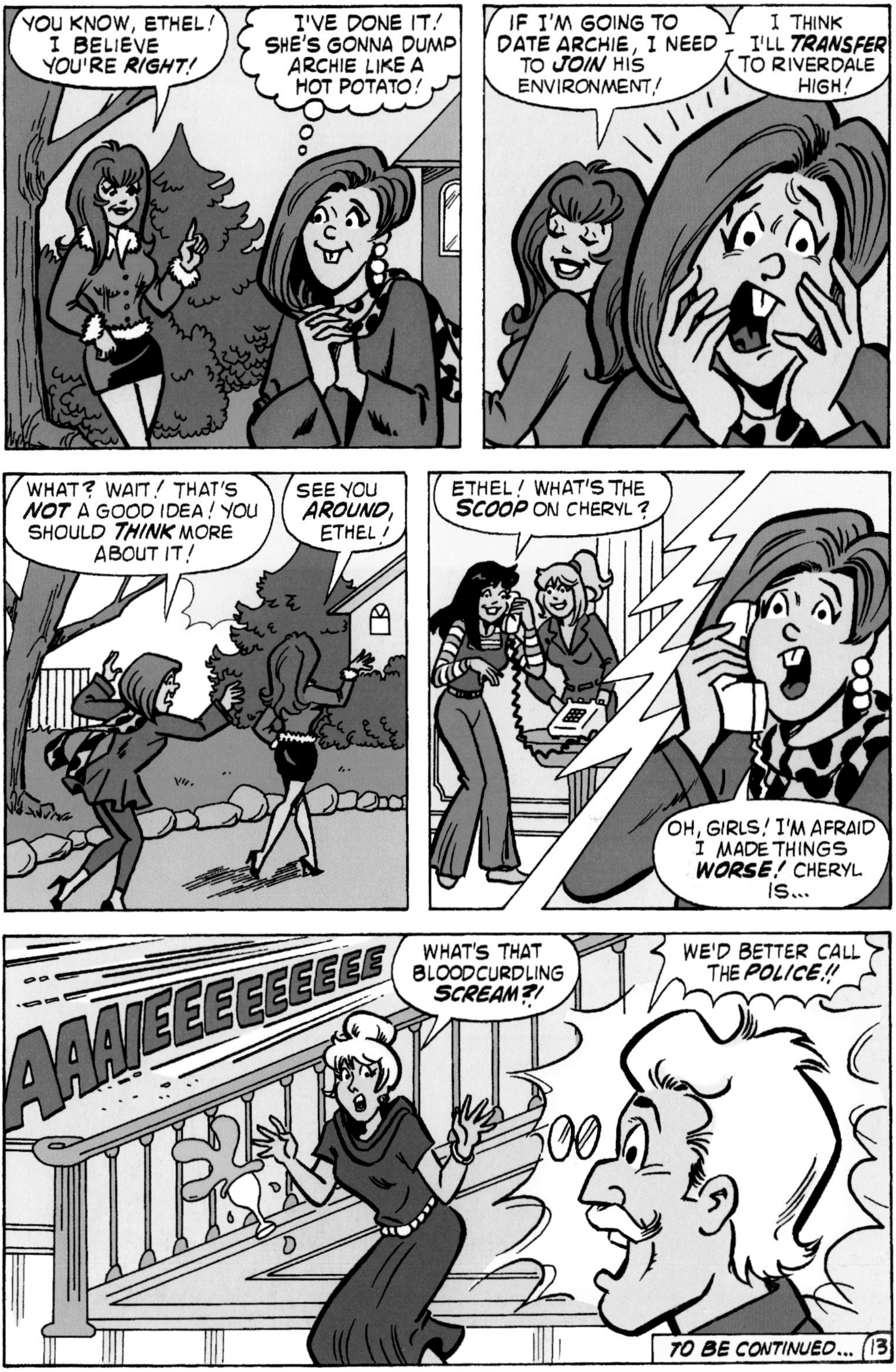
YOU KNOW, ETHEL! I BELIEVE YOU'RE RIGHT!
I'VE DONE IT! SHE'S GONNA DUMP ARCHIE LIKE A HOT POTATO!
IF I'M GOING TO DATE ARCHIE, I NEED TO JOIN HIS ENVIRONMENT!
I THINK I'LL TRANSFER TO RIVERDALE HIGH!
WHAT? WAIT! THAT'S NOT A GOOD IDEA! YOU SHOULD THINK MORE ABOUT IT!
SEE YOU AROUND, ETHEL!
ETHEL! WHAT'S THE SCOOP ON CHERYL?
OH, GIRLS! I'M AFRAID I MADE THINGS WORSE! CHERYL IS...
AAAIEEEEEEEEE
WHAT'S THAT BLOODCURDLING SCREAM?!
WE'D BETTER CALL THE POLICE!!
TO BE CONTINUED...
13

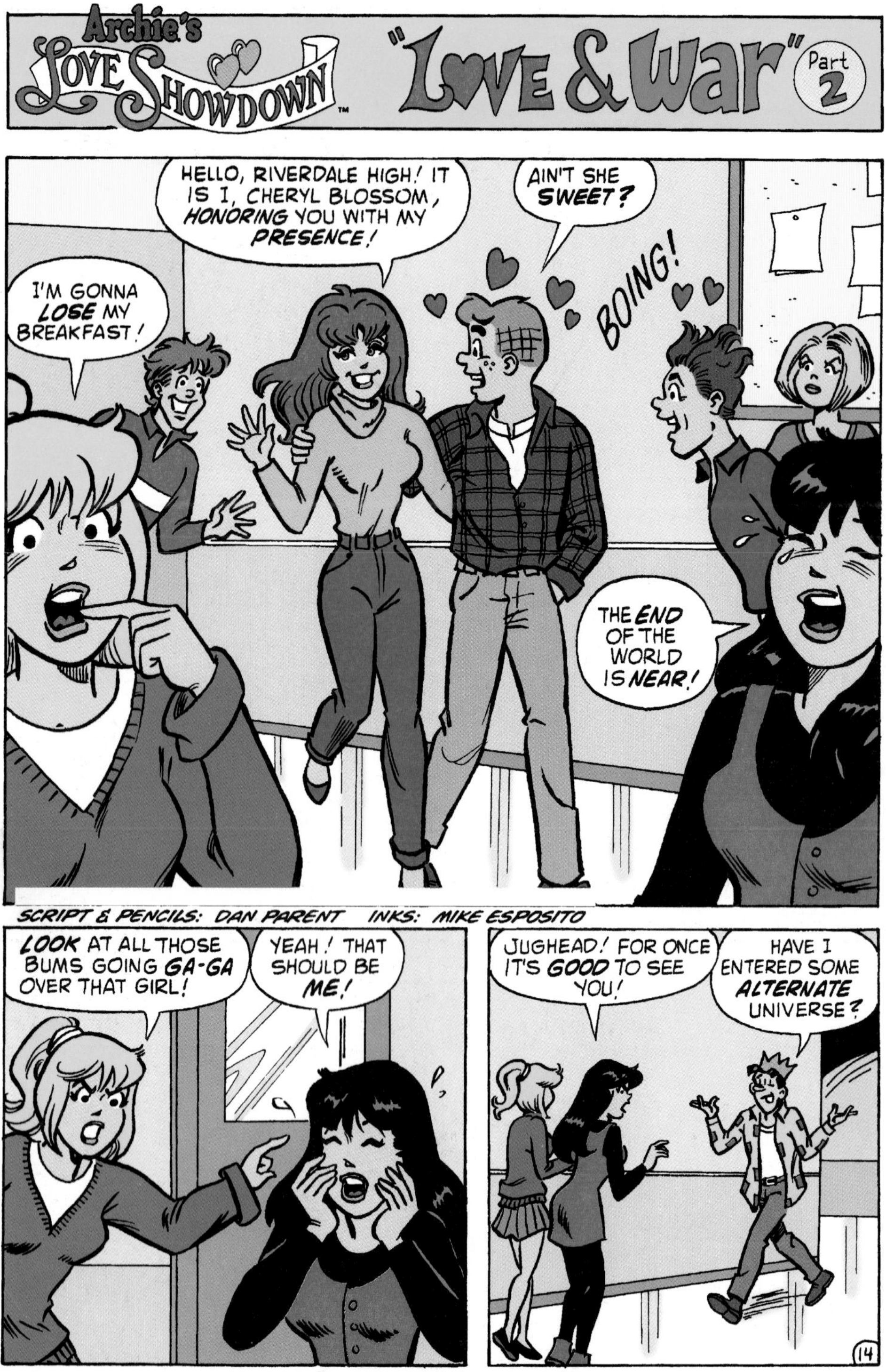
Archie's LOVE SHOWDOWN
"LOVE & WAR" Part 2
HELLO, RIVERDALE HIGH! IT IS I, CHERYL BLOSSOM, HONORING YOU WITH MY PRESENCE!
AIN'T SHE SWEET?
I'M GONNA LOSE MY BREAKFAST!
BOING!
THE END OF THE WORLD IS NEAR!
SCRIPT & PENCILS: DAN PARENT INKS: MIKE ESPOSITO
LOOK AT ALL THOSE BUMS GOING GA-GA OVER THAT GIRL!
YEAH! THAT SHOULD BE ME!
JUGHEAD! FOR ONCE IT'S GOOD TO SEE YOU!
HAVE I ENTERED SOME ALTERNATE UNIVERSE?
14

ORIGINALLY PRINTED IN LOVE SHOWDOWN SPECIAL, 1994

DAN PARENT • DAN PARENT • MIKE ESPOSITO • BILL YOSHIDA • BARRY GROSSMAN

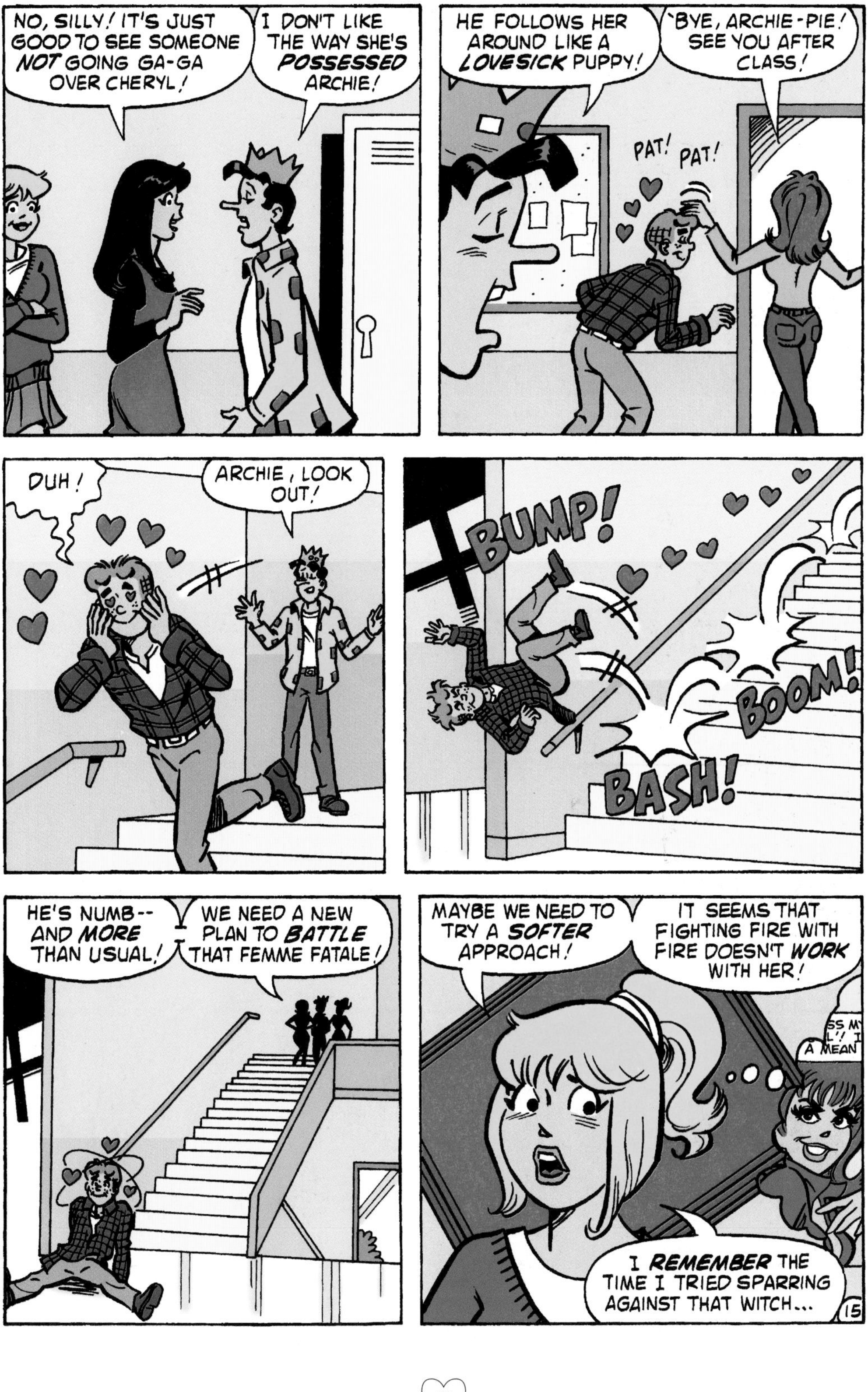
NO, SILLY! IT'S JUST GOOD TO SEE SOMEONE NOT GOING GA-GA OVER CHERYL!
I DON'T LIKE THE WAY SHE'S POSSESSED ARCHIE!
HE FOLLOWS HER AROUND LIKE A LOVESICK PUPPY!
'BYE, ARCHIE-PIE! SEE YOU AFTER CLASS!
PAT! PAT!
DUH!
ARCHIE, LOOK OUT!
BUMP!
BOOM!
BASH!
HE'S NUMB-- AND MORE THAN USUAL!
WE NEED A NEW PLAN TO BATTLE THAT FEMME FATALE!
MAYBE WE NEED TO TRY A SOFTER APPROACH!
IT SEEMS THAT FIGHTING FIRE WITH FIRE DOESN'T WORK WITH HER!
I REMEMBER THE TIME I TRIED SPARRING AGAINST THAT WITCH...
15

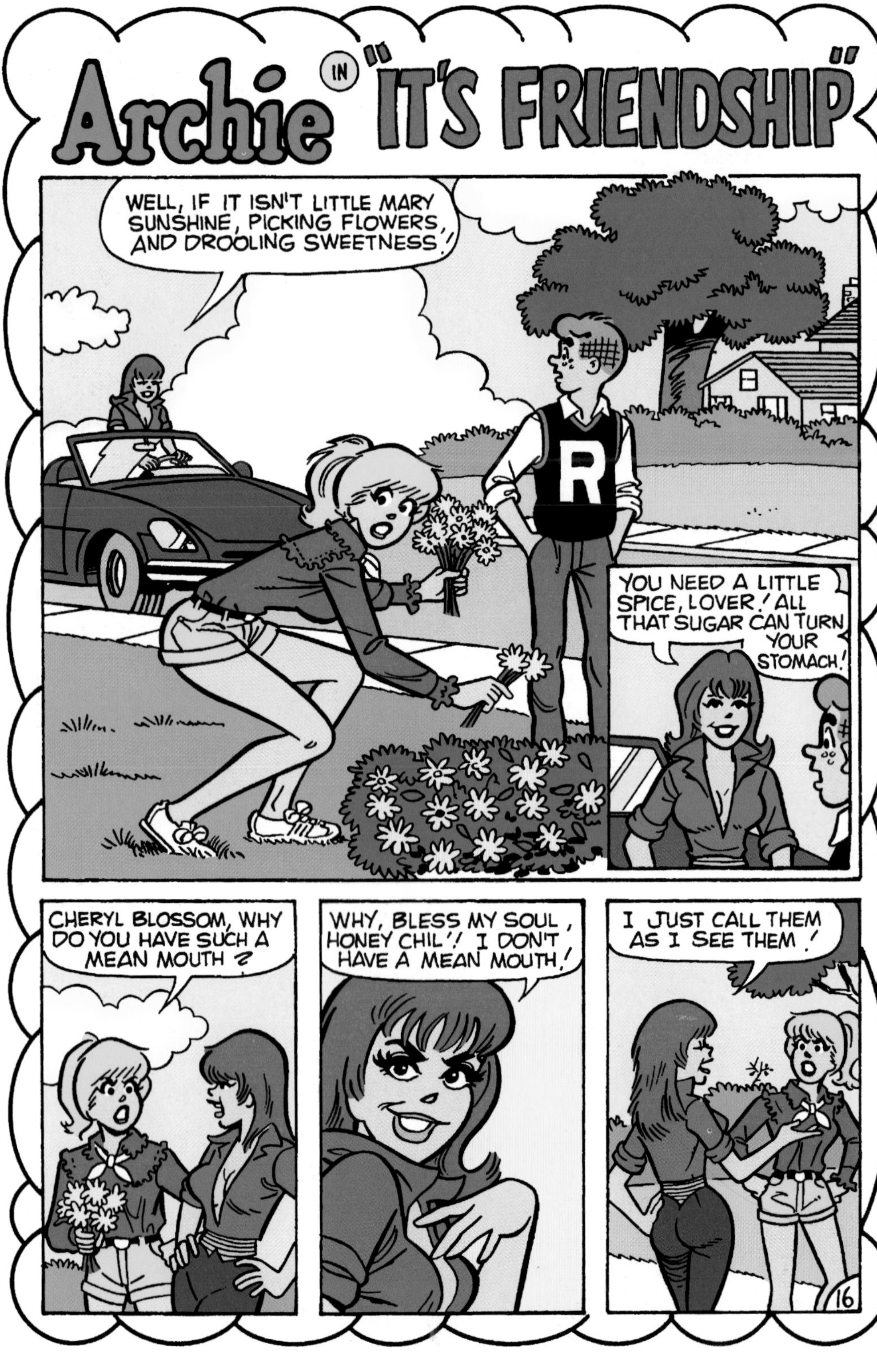
Archie IN "IT'S FRIENDSHIP"
WELL, IF IT ISN'T LITTLE MARY SUNSHINE, PICKING FLOWERS, AND DROOLING SWEETNESS!
R
YOU NEED A LITTLE SPICE, LOVER! ALL THAT SUGAR CAN TURN YOUR STOMACH!
CHERYL BLOSSOM, WHY DO YOU HAVE SUCH A MEAN MOUTH ?
WHY, BLESS MY SOUL, HONEY CHIL'! I DON'T HAVE A MEAN MOUTH!
I JUST CALL THEM AS I SEE THEM!
16

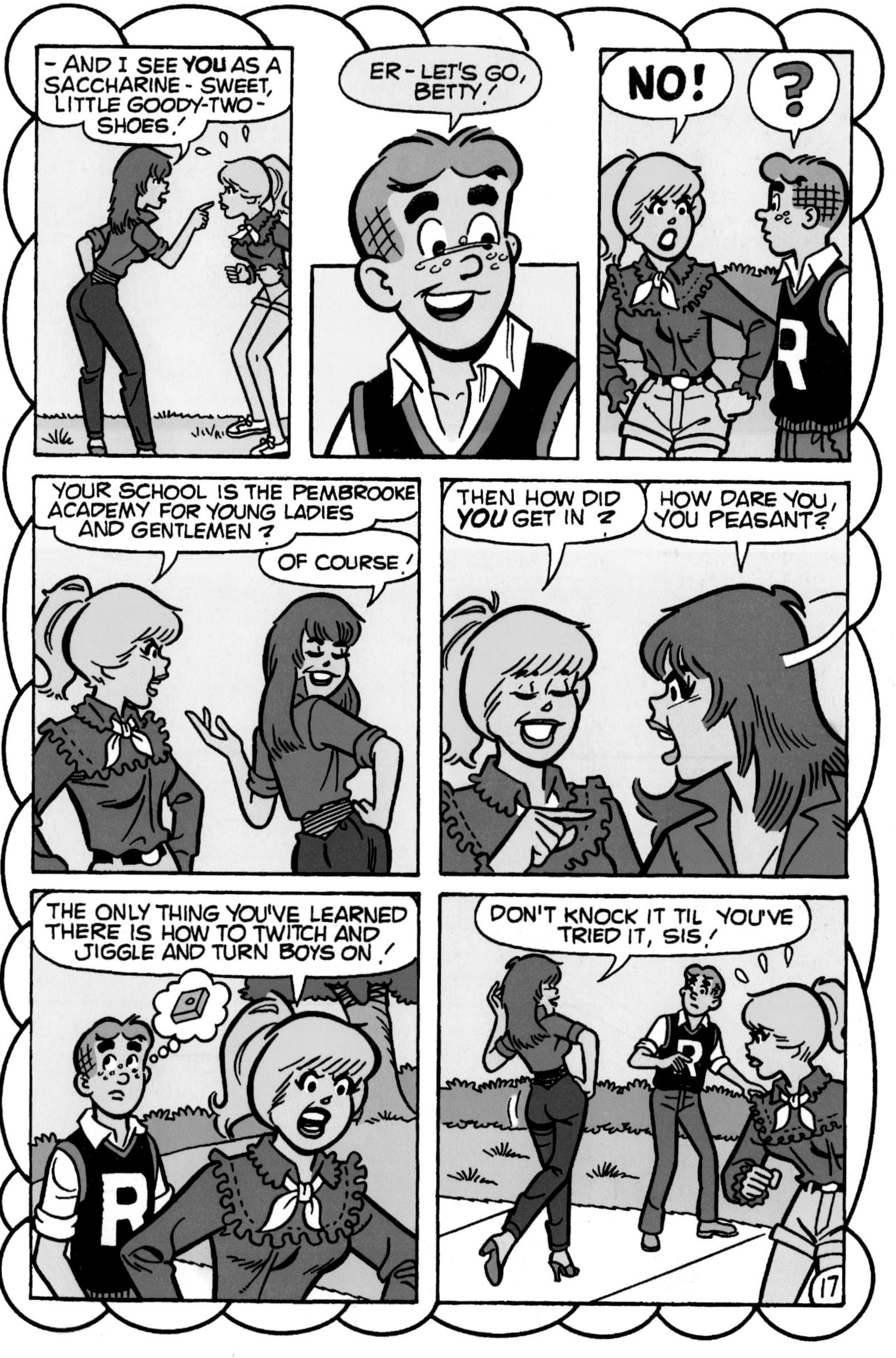
- AND I SEE YOU AS A SACCHARINE - SWEET, LITTLE GOODY-TWO-SHOES!
ER - LET'S GO, BETTY!
NO!
?
YOUR SCHOOL IS THE PEMBROOKE ACADEMY FOR YOUNG LADIES AND GENTLEMEN?
OF COURSE!
THEN HOW DID YOU GET IN?
HOW DARE YOU, YOU PEASANT?
THE ONLY THING YOU'VE LEARNED THERE IS HOW TO TWITCH AND JIGGLE AND TURN BOYS ON!
DON'T KNOCK IT TIL YOU'VE TRIED IT, SIS!
17

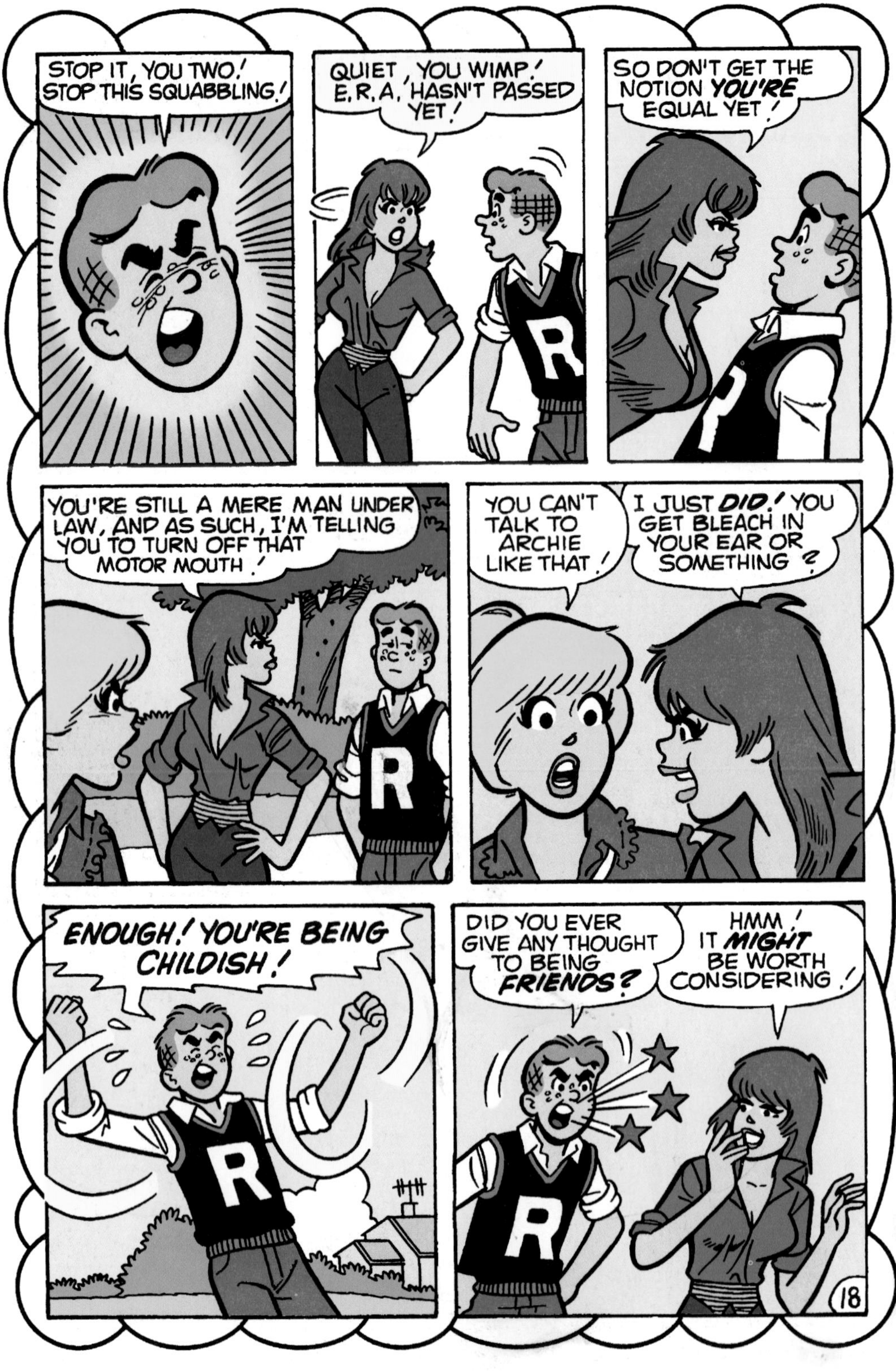
STOP IT, YOU TWO! STOP THIS SQUABBLING!
QUIET, YOU WIMP! E.R.A. HASN'T PASSED YET!
SO DON'T GET THE NOTION YOU'RE EQUAL YET!
YOU'RE STILL A MERE MAN UNDER LAW, AND AS SUCH, I'M TELLING YOU TO TURN OFF THAT MOTOR MOUTH!
YOU CAN'T TALK TO ARCHIE LIKE THAT!
I JUST DID! YOU GET BLEACH IN YOUR EAR OR SOMETHING?
ENOUGH! YOU'RE BEING CHILDISH!
DID YOU EVER GIVE ANY THOUGHT TO BEING FRIENDS?
HMM! IT MIGHT BE WORTH CONSIDERING!
18

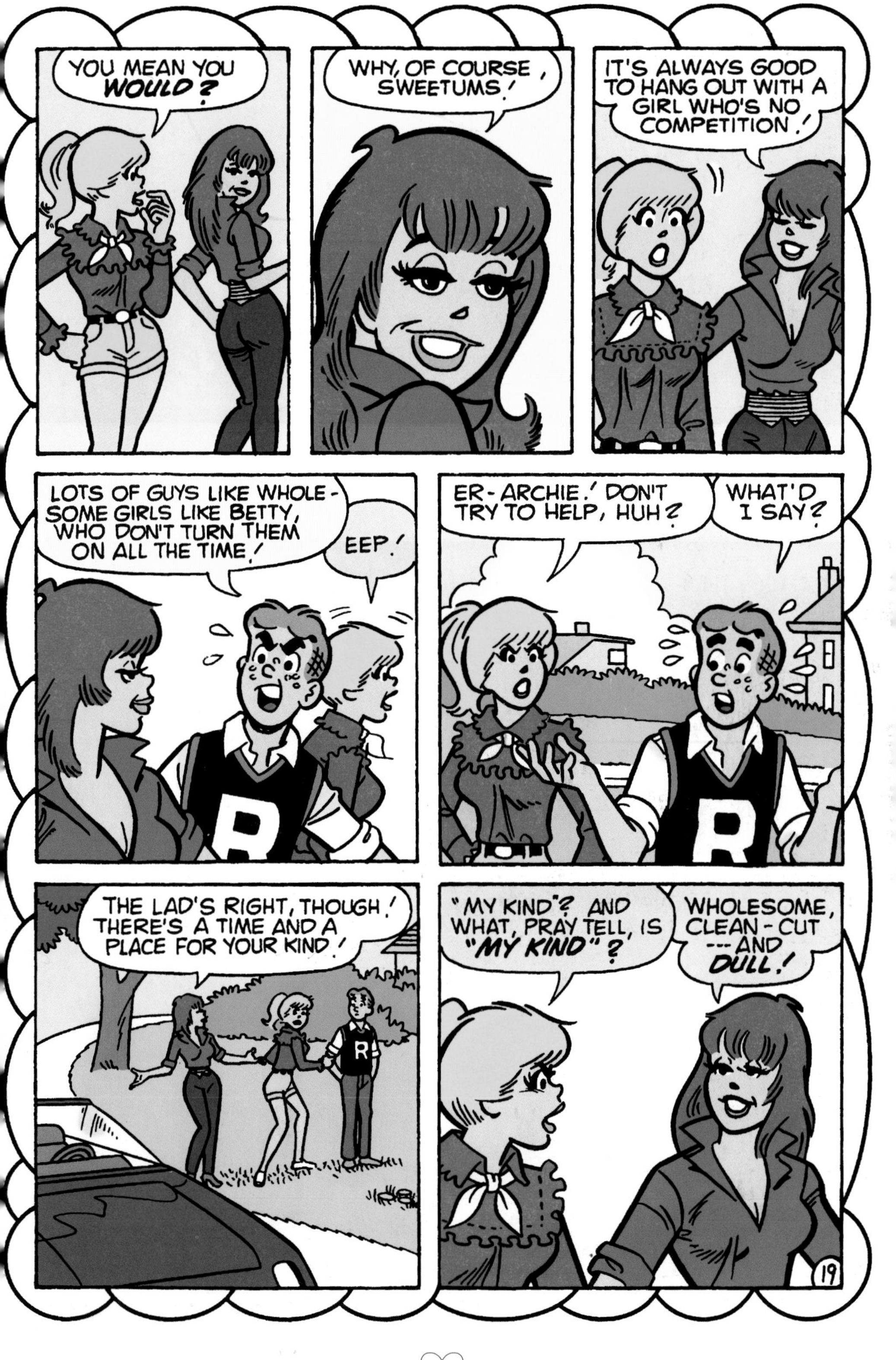
YOU MEAN YOU WOULD?
WHY, OF COURSE, SWEETUMS!
IT'S ALWAYS GOOD TO HANG OUT WITH A GIRL WHO'S NO COMPETITION!
LOTS OF GUYS LIKE WHOLESOME GIRLS LIKE BETTY, WHO DON'T TURN THEM ON ALL THE TIME!
EEP!
ER-ARCHIE! DON'T TRY TO HELP, HUH?
WHAT'D I SAY?
THE LAD'S RIGHT, THOUGH! THERE'S A TIME AND A PLACE FOR YOUR KIND!
"MY KIND"? AND WHAT, PRAY TELL, IS "MY KIND"?
WHOLESOME, CLEAN-CUT --- AND DULL!
19

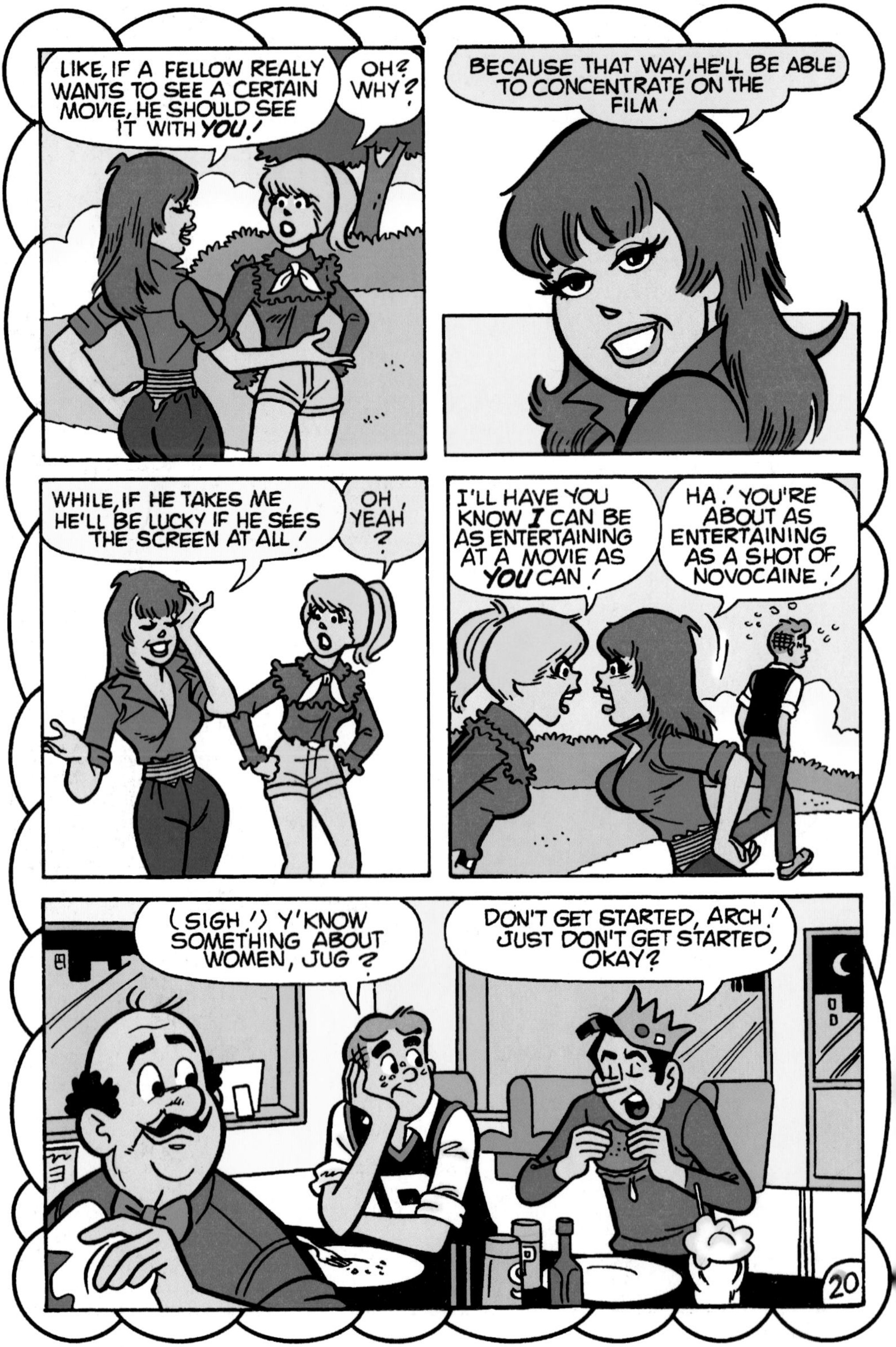
LIKE, IF A FELLOW REALLY WANTS TO SEE A CERTAIN MOVIE, HE SHOULD SEE IT WITH YOU!
OH? WHY?
BECAUSE THAT WAY, HE'LL BE ABLE TO CONCENTRATE ON THE FILM!
WHILE, IF HE TAKES ME, HE'LL BE LUCKY IF HE SEES THE SCREEN AT ALL!
OH, YEAH?
I'LL HAVE YOU KNOW I CAN BE AS ENTERTAINING AT A MOVIE AS YOU CAN!
HA! YOU'RE ABOUT AS ENTERTAINING AS A SHOT OF NOVOCAINE!
(SIGH!) Y'KNOW SOMETHING ABOUT WOMEN, JUG?
DON'T GET STARTED, ARCH! JUST DON'T GET STARTED, OKAY?
20

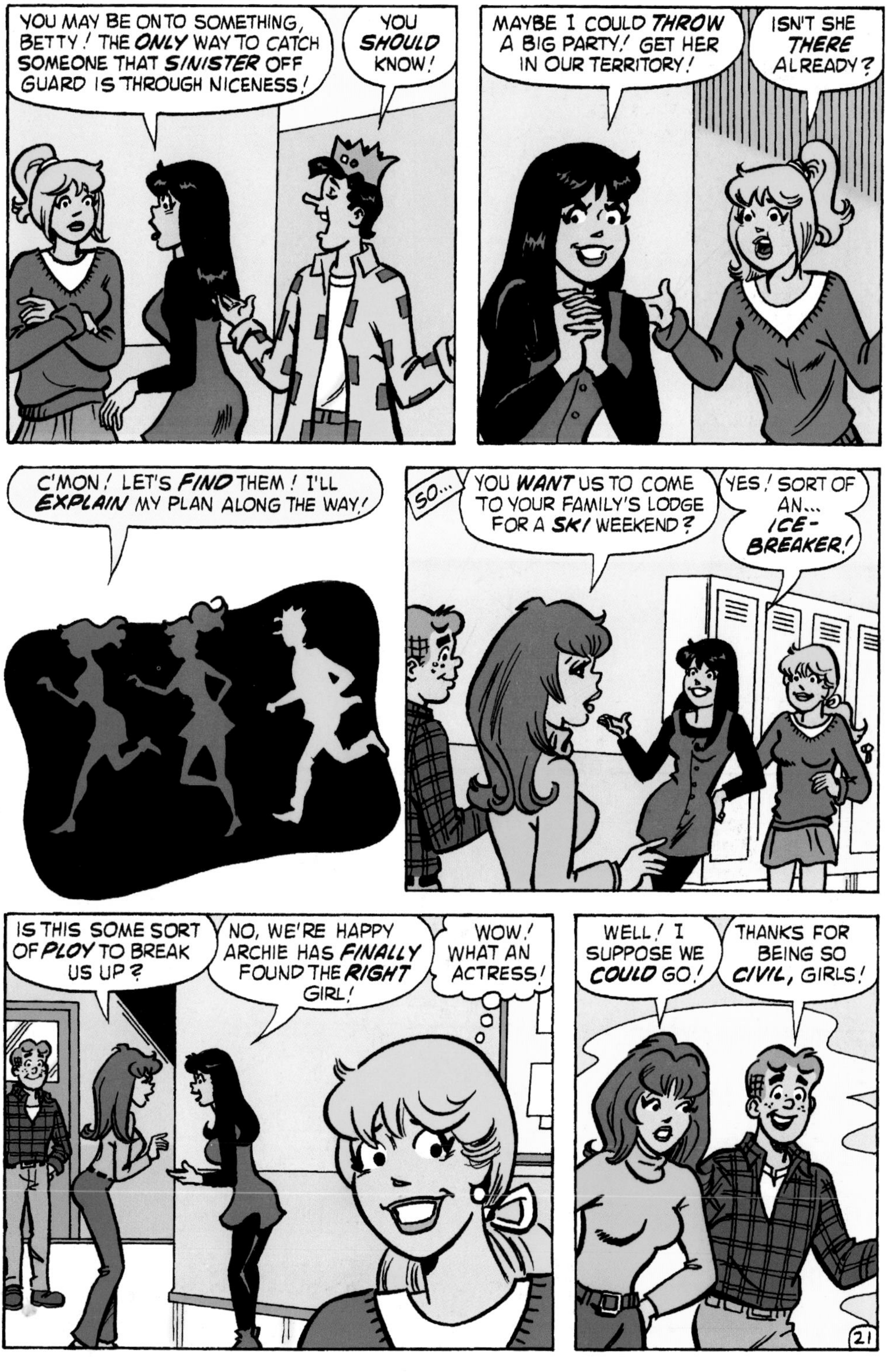

YOU MAY BE ONTO SOMETHING, BETTY! THE ONLY WAY TO CATCH SOMEONE THAT SINISTER OFF GUARD IS THROUGH NICENESS!
YOU SHOULD KNOW!
MAYBE I COULD THROW A BIG PARTY! GET HER IN OUR TERRITORY!
ISN'T SHE THERE ALREADY?
C'MON! LET'S FIND THEM! I'LL EXPLAIN MY PLAN ALONG THE WAY!
SO...
YOU WANT US TO COME TO YOUR FAMILY'S LODGE FOR A SKI WEEKEND?
YES! SORT OF AN... ICE-BREAKER!
IS THIS SOME SORT OF PLOY TO BREAK US UP?
NO, WE'RE HAPPY ARCHIE HAS FINALLY FOUND THE RIGHT GIRL!
WOW! WHAT AN ACTRESS!
WELL! I SUPPOSE WE COULD GO!
THANKS FOR BEING SO CIVIL, GIRLS!
21

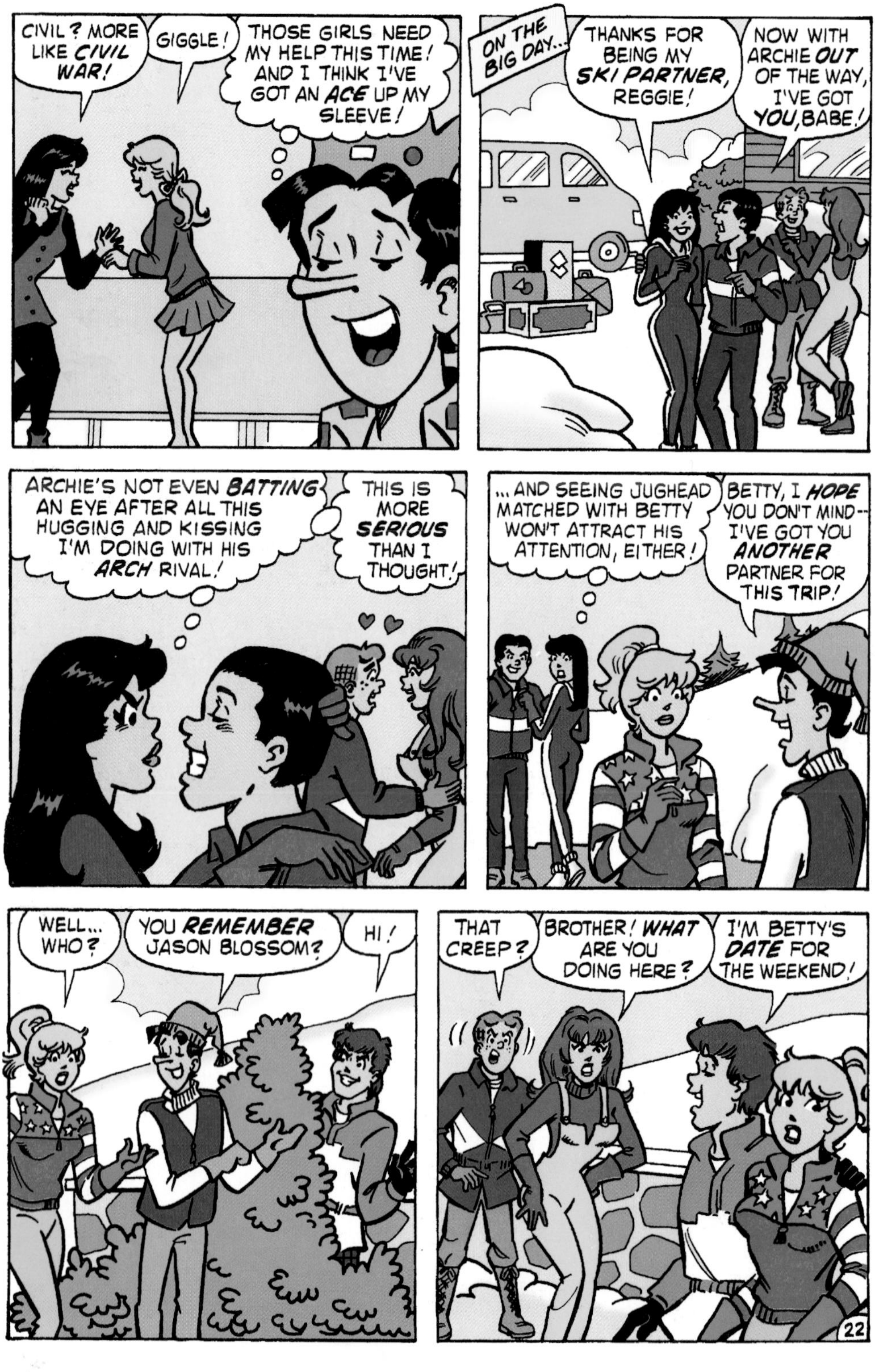
CIVIL? MORE LIKE CIVIL WAR!
GIGGLE!
THOSE GIRLS NEED MY HELP THIS TIME! AND I THINK I'VE GOT AN ACE UP MY SLEEVE!
ON THE BIG DAY...
THANKS FOR BEING MY SKI PARTNER, REGGIE!
NOW WITH ARCHIE OUT OF THE WAY, I'VE GOT YOU, BABE!
ARCHIE'S NOT EVEN BATTING AN EYE AFTER ALL THIS HUGGING AND KISSING I'M DOING WITH HIS ARCH RIVAL!
THIS IS MORE SERIOUS THAN I THOUGHT!
...AND SEEING JUGHEAD MATCHED WITH BETTY WON'T ATTRACT HIS ATTENTION, EITHER!
BETTY, I HOPE YOU DON'T MIND-- I'VE GOT YOU ANOTHER PARTNER FOR THIS TRIP!
WELL... WHO?
YOU REMEMBER JASON BLOSSOM?
HI!
THAT CREEP?
BROTHER! WHAT ARE YOU DOING HERE?
I'M BETTY'S DATE FOR THE WEEKEND!
22

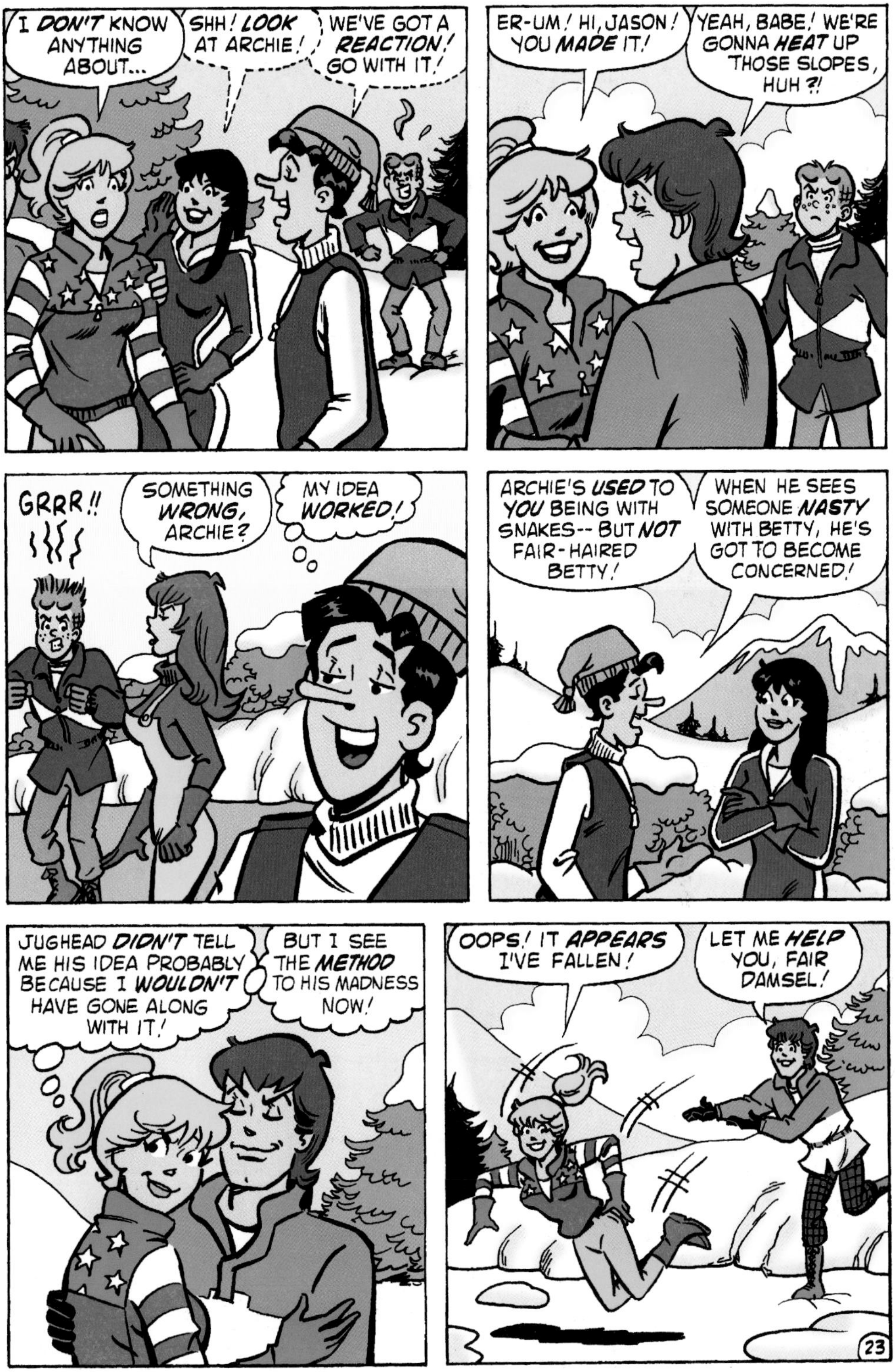
I DON'T KNOW ANYTHING ABOUT...
SHH! LOOK AT ARCHIE!
WE'VE GOT A REACTION! GO WITH IT!
ER-UM! HI, JASON! YOU MADE IT!
YEAH, BABE! WE'RE GONNA HEAT UP THOSE SLOPES, HUH ?!
GRRR!!
SOMETHING WRONG, ARCHIE?
MY IDEA WORKED!
ARCHIE'S USED TO YOU BEING WITH SNAKES-- BUT NOT FAIR-HAIRED BETTY!
WHEN HE SEES SOMEONE NASTY WITH BETTY, HE'S GOT TO BECOME CONCERNED!
JUGHEAD DIDN'T TELL ME HIS IDEA PROBABLY BECAUSE I WOULDN'T HAVE GONE ALONG WITH IT!
BUT I SEE THE METHOD TO HIS MADNESS NOW!
OOPS! IT APPEARS I'VE FALLEN!
LET ME HELP YOU, FAIR DAMSEL!
23

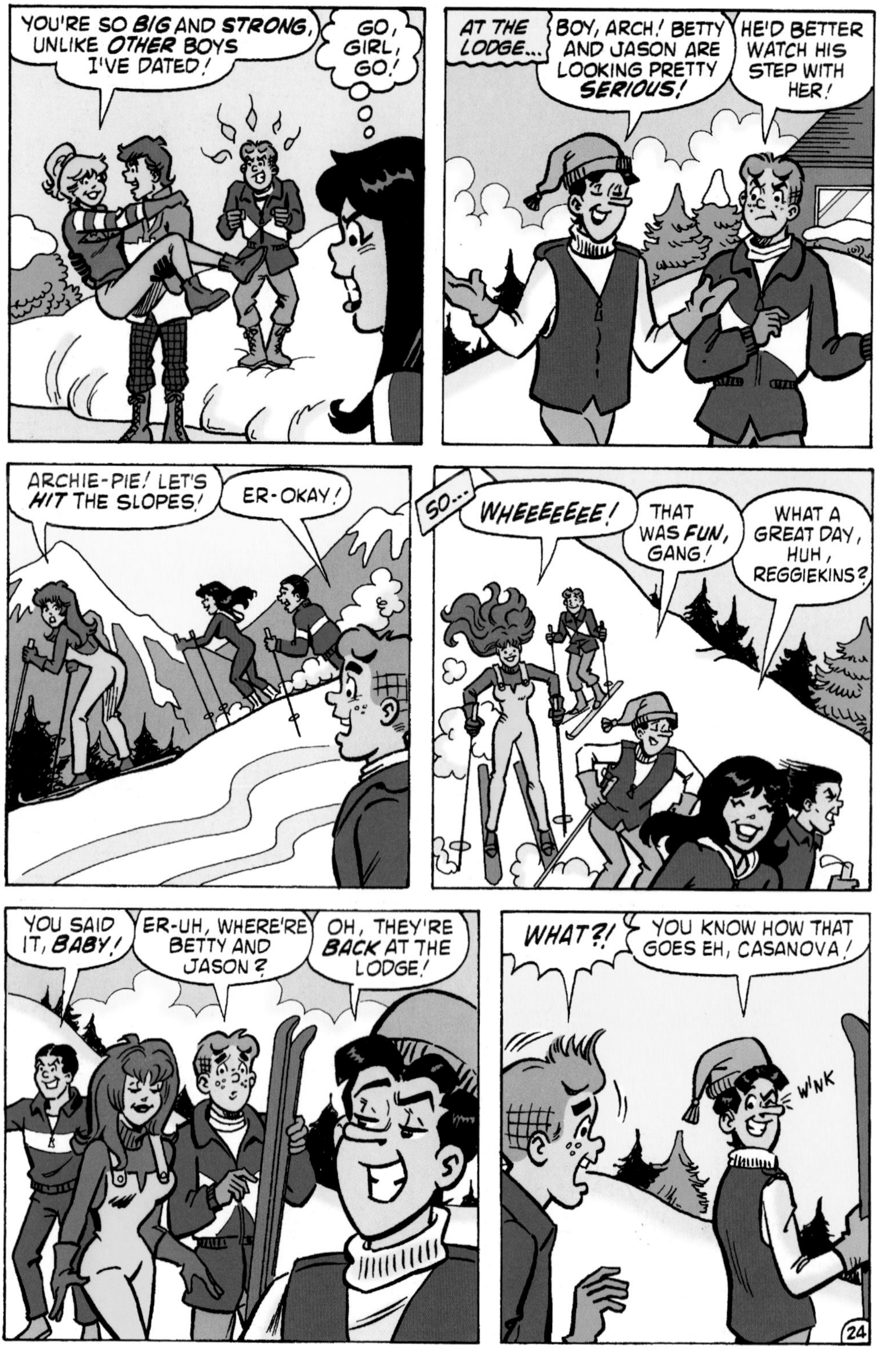
YOU'RE SO BIG AND STRONG, UNLIKE OTHER BOYS I'VE DATED!
GO, GIRL, GO!
AT THE LODGE...
BOY, ARCH! BETTY AND JASON ARE LOOKING PRETTY SERIOUS!
HE'D BETTER WATCH HIS STEP WITH HER!
ARCHIE-PIE! LET'S HIT THE SLOPES!
ER-OKAY!
SO...
WHEEEEEEE!
THAT WAS FUN, GANG!
WHAT A GREAT DAY, HUH, REGGIEKINS?
YOU SAID IT, BABY!
ER-UH, WHERE'RE BETTY AND JASON?
OH, THEY'RE BACK AT THE LODGE!
WHAT?!
YOU KNOW HOW THAT GOES EH, CASANOVA!
WINK
24

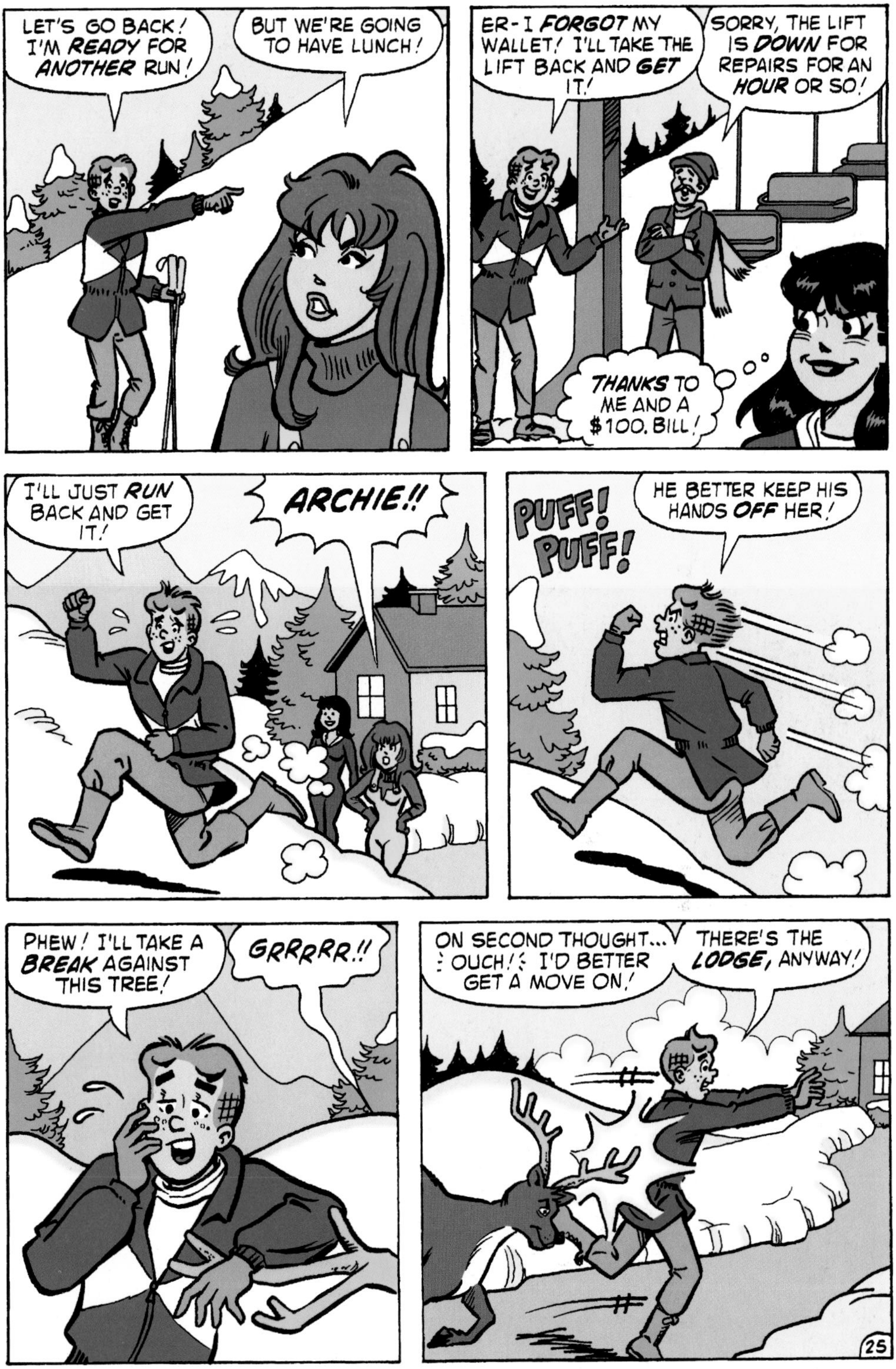
LET'S GO BACK! I'M READY FOR ANOTHER RUN!
BUT WE'RE GOING TO HAVE LUNCH!
ER- I FORGOT MY WALLET! I'LL TAKE THE LIFT BACK AND GET IT!
SORRY, THE LIFT IS DOWN FOR REPAIRS FOR AN HOUR OR SO!
THANKS TO ME AND A $100. BILL!
I'LL JUST RUN BACK AND GET IT!
ARCHIE!!
PUFF! PUFF!
HE BETTER KEEP HIS HANDS OFF HER!
PHEW! I'LL TAKE A BREAK AGAINST THIS TREE!
GRRRRR!!
ON SECOND THOUGHT... OUCH! I'D BETTER GET A MOVE ON!
THERE'S THE LODGE, ANYWAY!
25

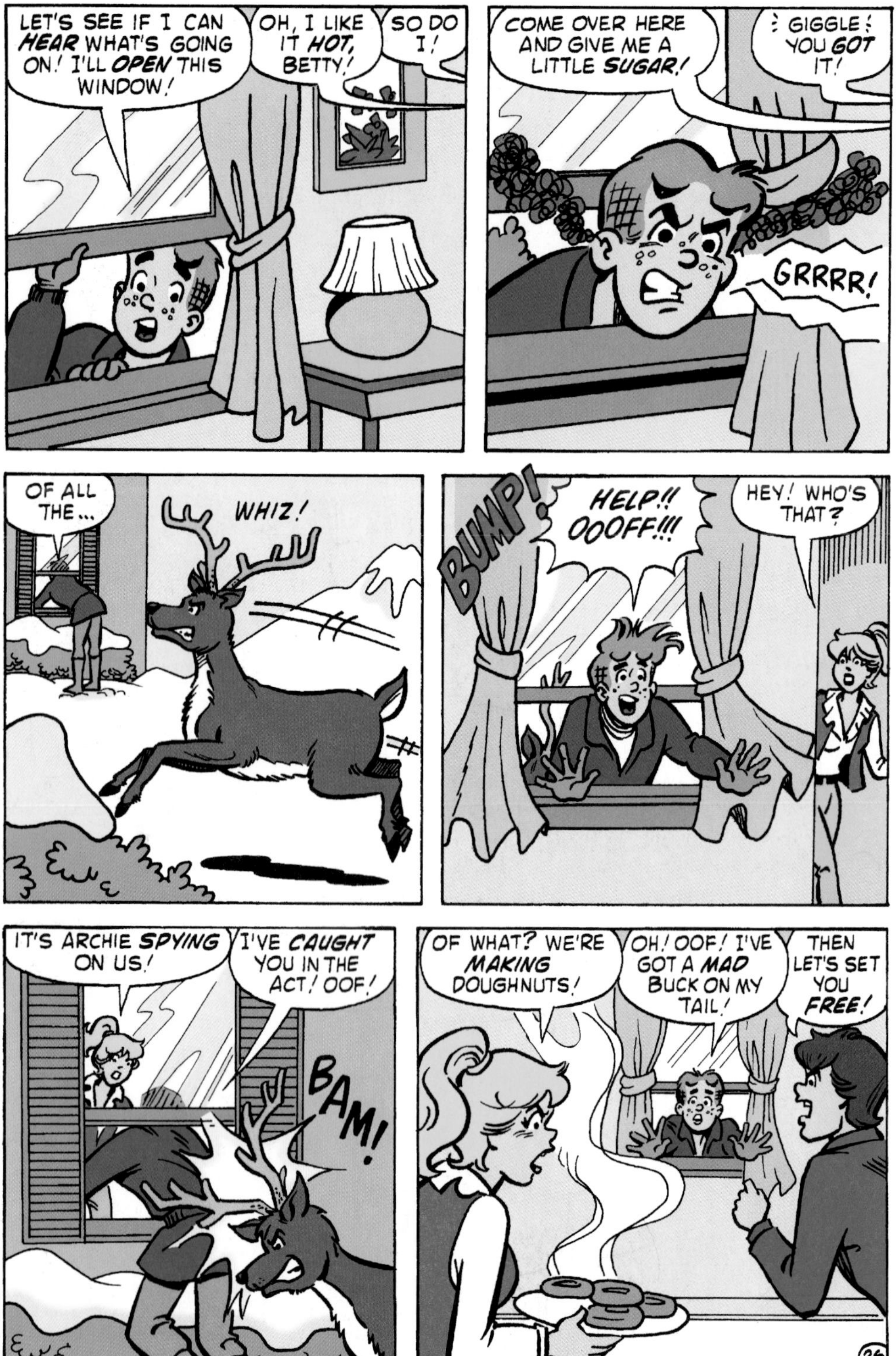
LET'S SEE IF I CAN HEAR WHAT'S GOING ON! I'LL OPEN THIS WINDOW!
OH, I LIKE IT HOT, BETTY!
SO DO I!
COME OVER HERE AND GIVE ME A LITTLE SUGAR!
GIGGLE! YOU GOT IT!
GRRRR!
OF ALL THE...
WHIZ!
BUMP!
HELP!! OOOFF!!!
HEY! WHO'S THAT?
IT'S ARCHIE SPYING ON US!
I'VE CAUGHT YOU IN THE ACT! OOF!
BAM!
OF WHAT? WE'RE MAKING DOUGHNUTS!
OH! OOF! I'VE GOT A MAD BUCK ON MY TAIL!
THEN LET'S SET YOU FREE!
26

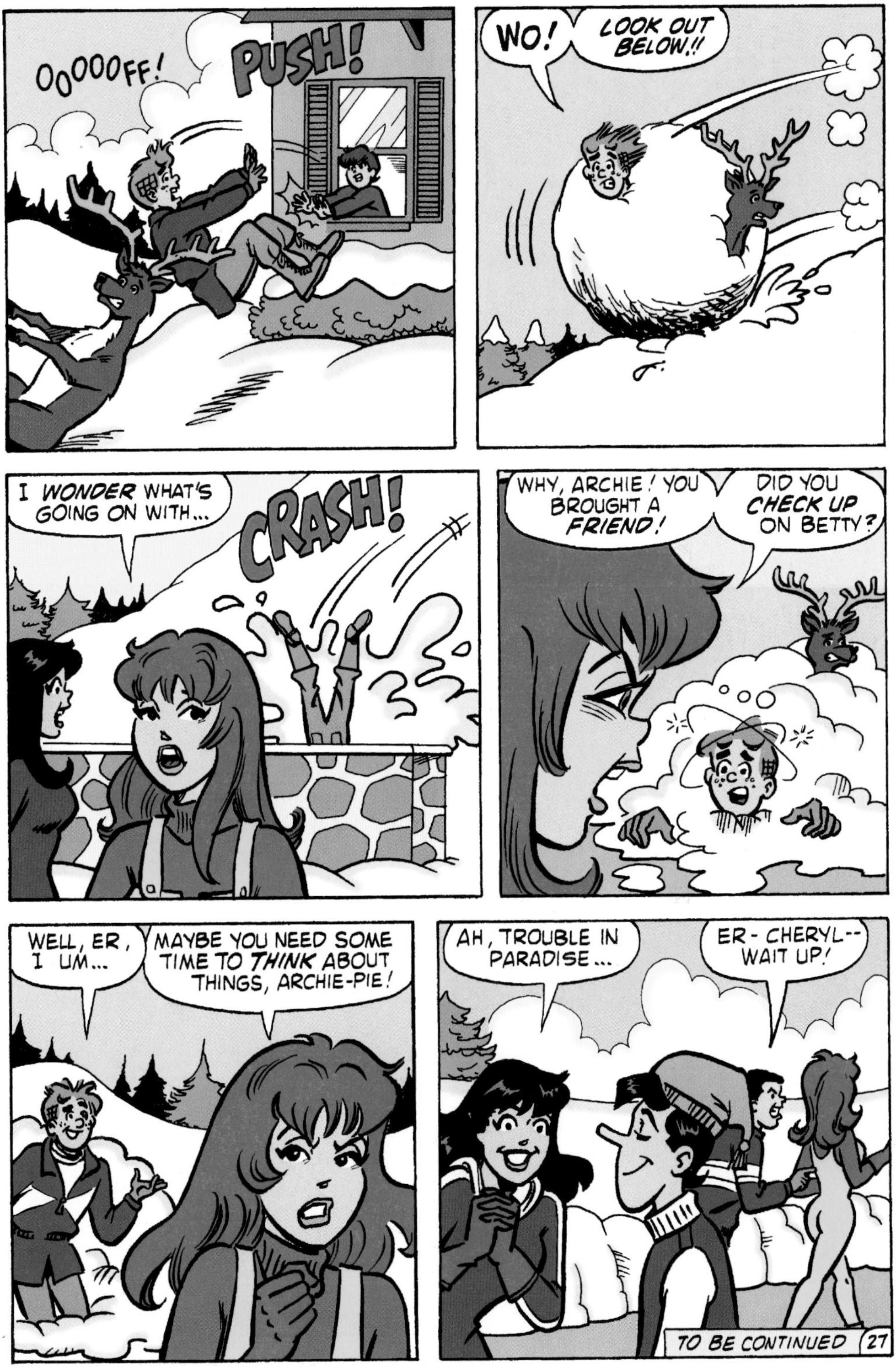
OOOOOFF!
PUSH!
WO!
LOOK OUT BELOW!!
I WONDER WHAT'S GOING ON WITH...
CRASH!
WHY, ARCHIE! YOU BROUGHT A FRIEND!
DID YOU CHECK UP ON BETTY?
WELL, ER, I UM...
MAYBE YOU NEED SOME TIME TO THINK ABOUT THINGS, ARCHIE-PIE!
AH, TROUBLE IN PARADISE...
ER- CHERYL-- WAIT UP!
TO BE CONTINUED
27

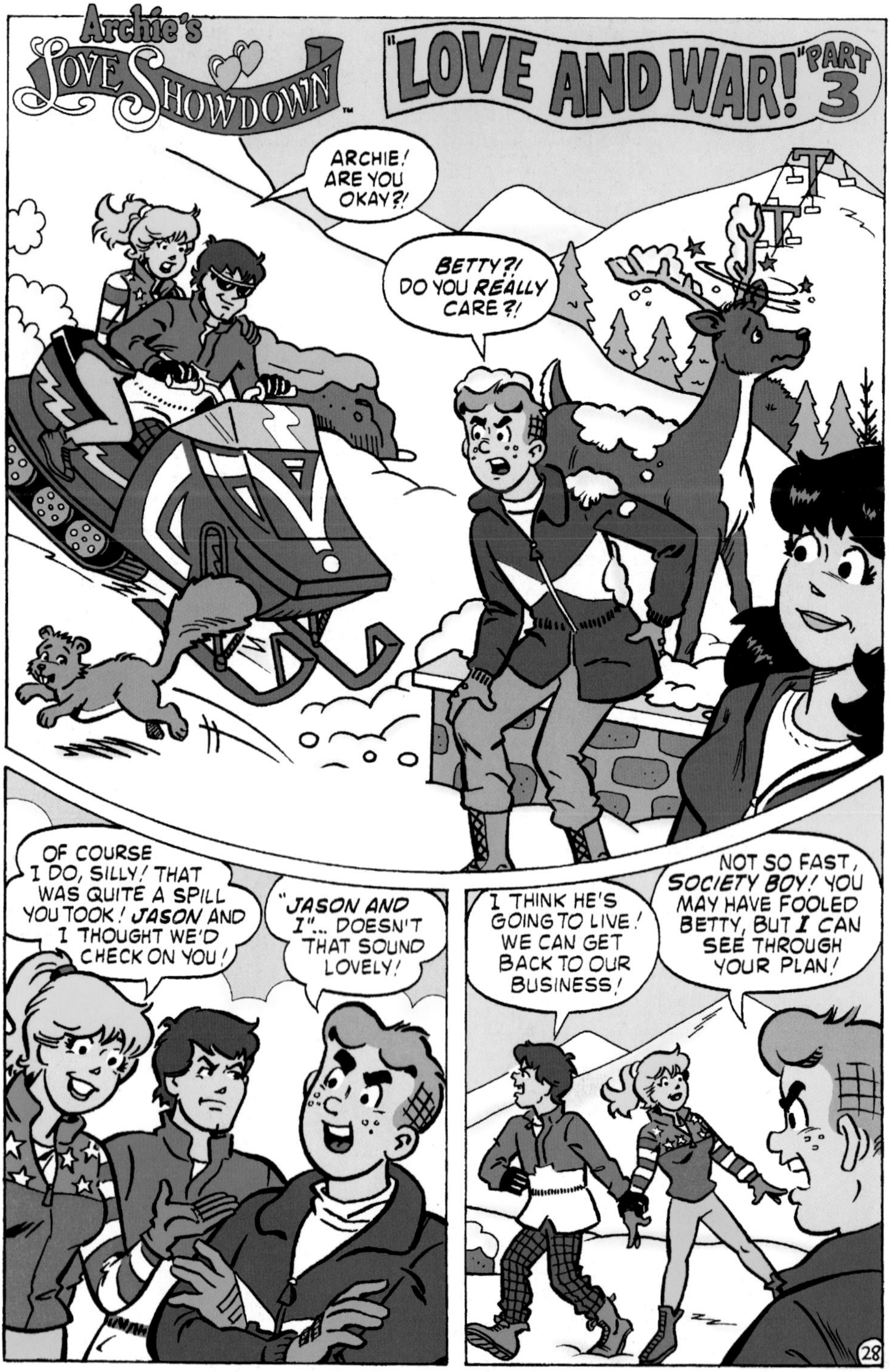
Archie's LOVE SHOWDOWN
"LOVE AND WAR!" PART 3
ARCHIE! ARE YOU OKAY?!
BETTY?! DO YOU REALLY CARE?!
OF COURSE I DO, SILLY! THAT WAS QUITE A SPILL YOU TOOK! JASON AND I THOUGHT WE'D CHECK ON YOU!
"JASON AND I"... DOESN'T THAT SOUND LOVELY!
I THINK HE'S GOING TO LIVE! WE CAN GET BACK TO OUR BUSINESS!
NOT SO FAST, SOCIETY BOY! YOU MAY HAVE FOOLED BETTY, BUT I CAN SEE THROUGH YOUR PLAN!
28

ORIGINALLY PRINTED IN LOVE SHOWDOWN SPECIAL, 1994

BILL GOLLIHER • BILL GOLLIHER • MIKE ESPOSITO • BILL YOSHIDA • BARRY GROSSMAN

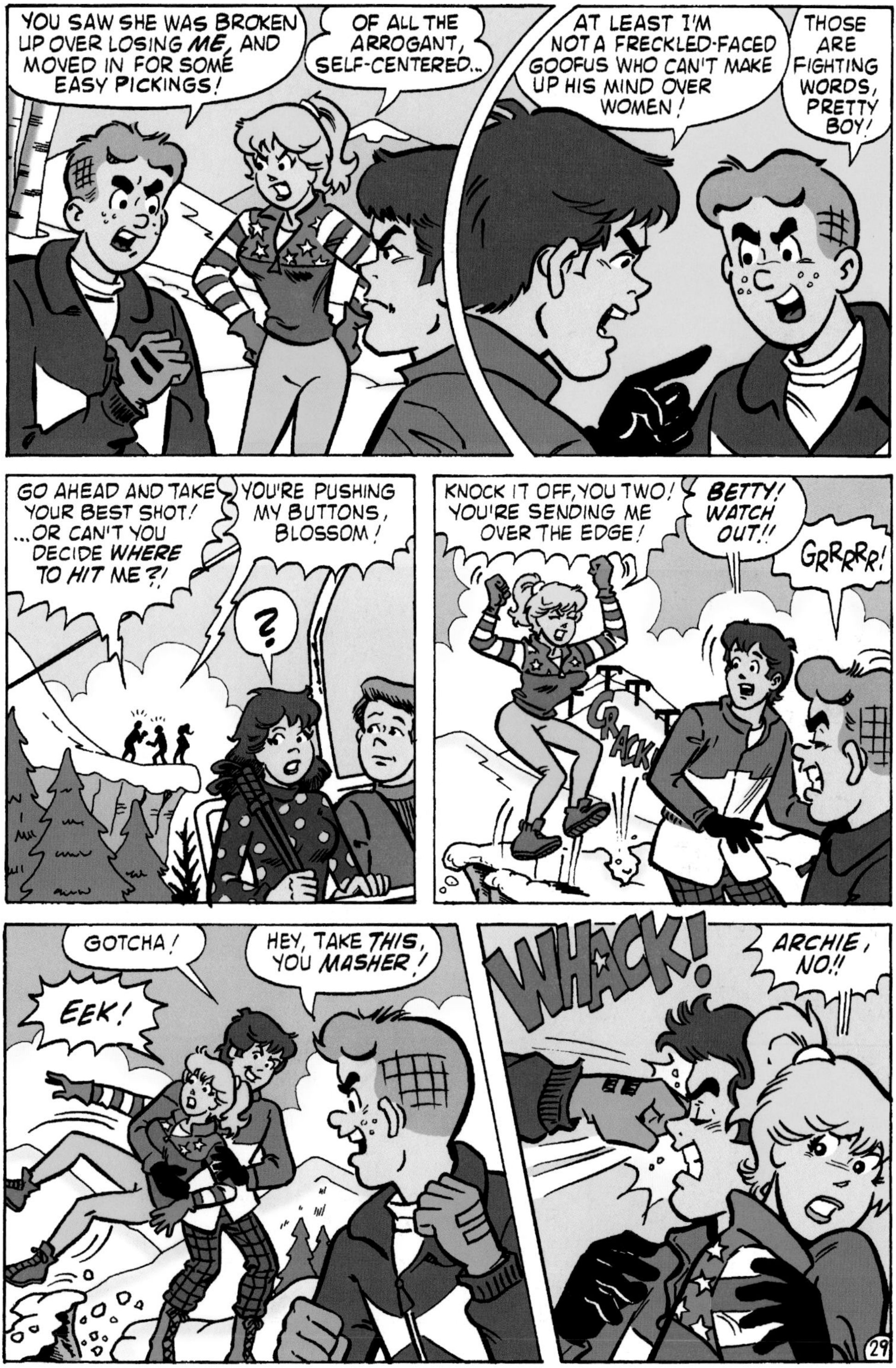
YOU SAW SHE WAS BROKEN UP OVER LOSING ME, AND MOVED IN FOR SOME EASY PICKINGS!
OF ALL THE ARROGANT, SELF-CENTERED...
AT LEAST I'M NOT A FRECKLED-FACED GOOFUS WHO CAN'T MAKE UP HIS MIND OVER WOMEN!
THOSE ARE FIGHTING WORDS, PRETTY BOY!
GO AHEAD AND TAKE YOUR BEST SHOT! ...OR CAN'T YOU DECIDE WHERE TO HIT ME?!
YOU'RE PUSHING MY BUTTONS, BLOSSOM!
?
KNOCK IT OFF, YOU TWO! YOU'RE SENDING ME OVER THE EDGE!
BETTY! WATCH OUT!!
GRRRRR!
CRACK!
GOTCHA!
EEK!
HEY, TAKE THIS, YOU MASHER!
WHACK!
ARCHIE, NO!!
29

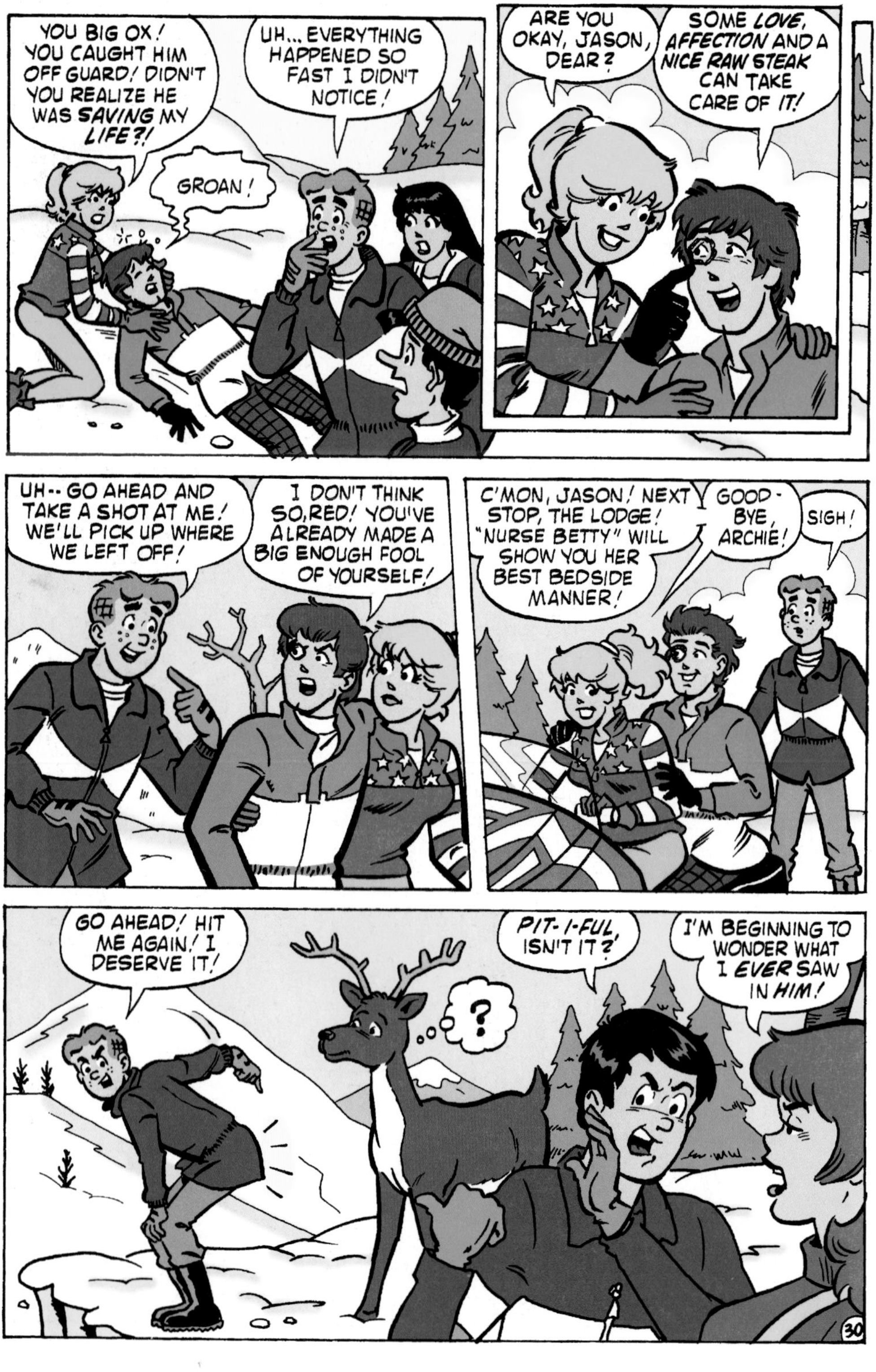

YOU BIG OX! YOU CAUGHT HIM OFF GUARD! DIDN'T YOU REALIZE HE WAS SAVING MY LIFE?!
UH... EVERYTHING HAPPENED SO FAST I DIDN'T NOTICE!
GROAN!
ARE YOU OKAY, JASON, DEAR?
SOME LOVE, AFFECTION AND A NICE RAW STEAK CAN TAKE CARE OF IT!
UH -- GO AHEAD AND TAKE A SHOT AT ME! WE'LL PICK UP WHERE WE LEFT OFF!
I DON'T THINK SO, RED! YOU'VE ALREADY MADE A BIG ENOUGH FOOL OF YOURSELF!
C'MON, JASON! NEXT STOP, THE LODGE! "NURSE BETTY" WILL SHOW YOU HER BEST BEDSIDE MANNER!
GOOD-BYE, ARCHIE!
SIGH!
GO AHEAD! HIT ME AGAIN! I DESERVE IT!
?
PIT-I-FUL, ISN'T IT?
I'M BEGINNING TO WONDER WHAT I EVER SAW IN HIM!
30

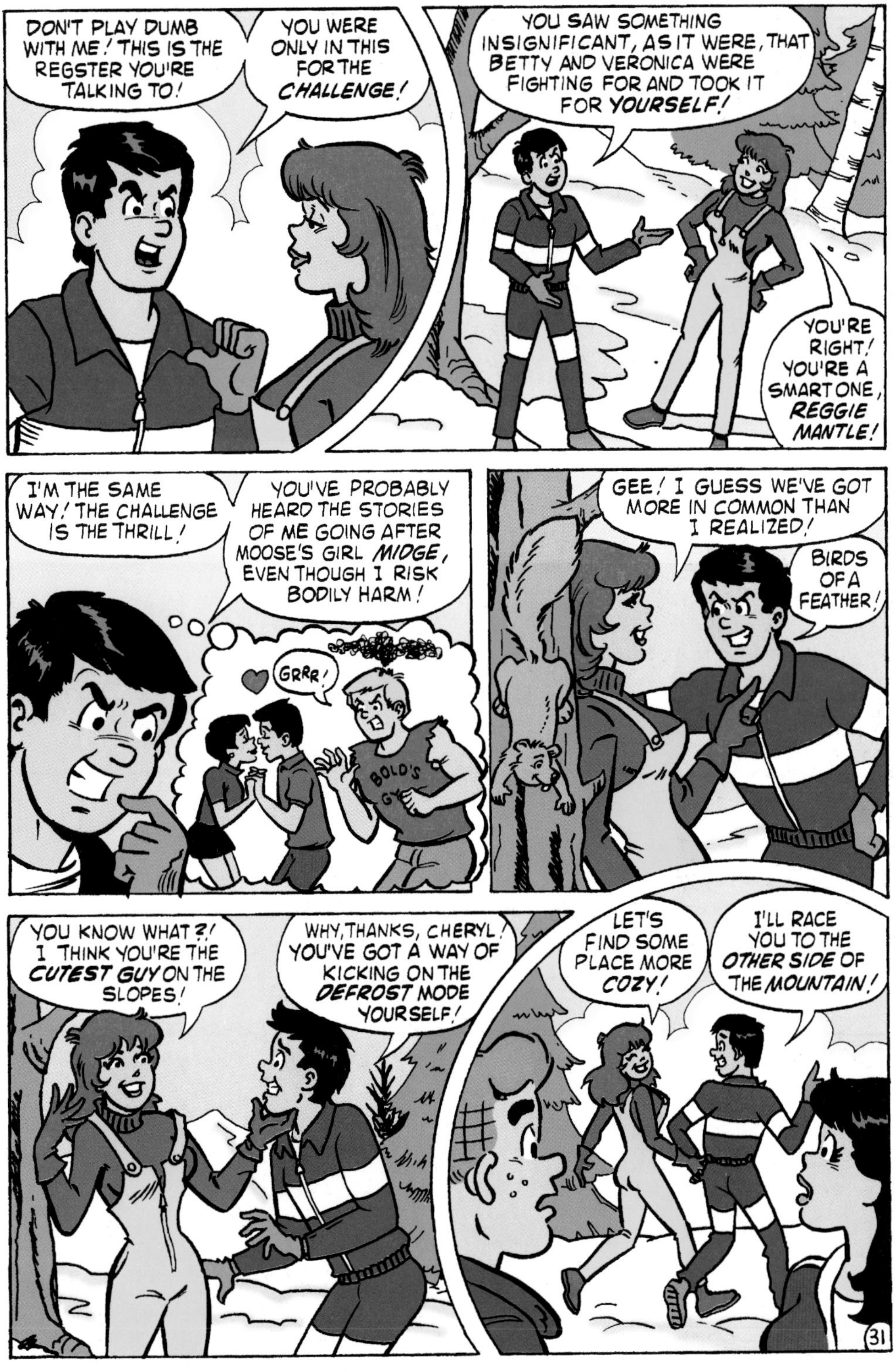

DON'T PLAY DUMB WITH ME! THIS IS THE REGSTER YOU'RE TALKING TO!
YOU WERE ONLY IN THIS FOR THE CHALLENGE!
YOU SAW SOMETHING INSIGNIFICANT, AS IT WERE, THAT BETTY AND VERONICA WERE FIGHTING FOR AND TOOK IT FOR YOURSELF!
YOU'RE RIGHT! YOU'RE A SMART ONE, REGGIE MANTLE!
I'M THE SAME WAY! THE CHALLENGE IS THE THRILL!
YOU'VE PROBABLY HEARD THE STORIES OF ME GOING AFTER MOOSE'S GIRL MIDGE, EVEN THOUGH I RISK BODILY HARM!
GRRR!
BOLD'S GY
GEE! I GUESS WE'VE GOT MORE IN COMMON THAN I REALIZED!
BIRDS OF A FEATHER!
YOU KNOW WHAT?! I THINK YOU'RE THE CUTEST GUY ON THE SLOPES!
WHY, THANKS, CHERYL! YOU'VE GOT A WAY OF KICKING ON THE DEFROST MODE YOURSELF!
LET'S FIND SOME PLACE MORE COZY!
I'LL RACE YOU TO THE OTHER SIDE OF THE MOUNTAIN!
31

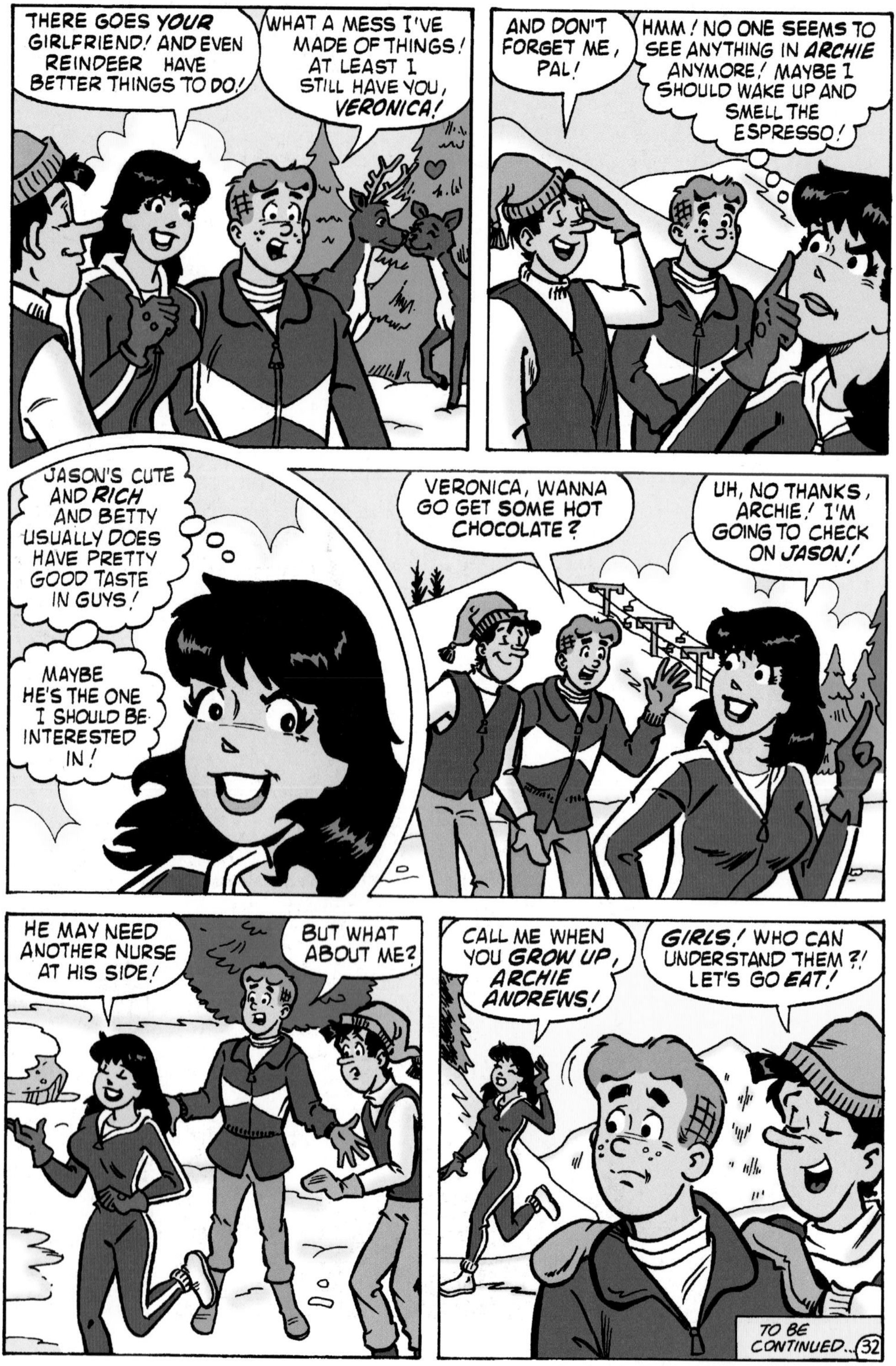
THERE GOES YOUR GIRLFRIEND! AND EVEN REINDEER HAVE BETTER THINGS TO DO!
WHAT A MESS I'VE MADE OF THINGS! AT LEAST I STILL HAVE YOU, VERONICA!
AND DON'T FORGET ME, PAL!
HMM! NO ONE SEEMS TO SEE ANYTHING IN ARCHIE ANYMORE! MAYBE I SHOULD WAKE UP AND SMELL THE ESPRESSO!
JASON'S CUTE AND RICH AND BETTY USUALLY DOES HAVE PRETTY GOOD TASTE IN GUYS!
MAYBE HE'S THE ONE I SHOULD BE INTERESTED IN!
VERONICA, WANNA GO GET SOME HOT CHOCOLATE?
UH, NO THANKS, ARCHIE! I'M GOING TO CHECK ON JASON!
HE MAY NEED ANOTHER NURSE AT HIS SIDE!
BUT WHAT ABOUT ME?
CALL ME WHEN YOU GROW UP, ARCHIE ANDREWS!
GIRLS! WHO CAN UNDERSTAND THEM?! LET'S GO EAT!
TO BE CONTINUED...
32

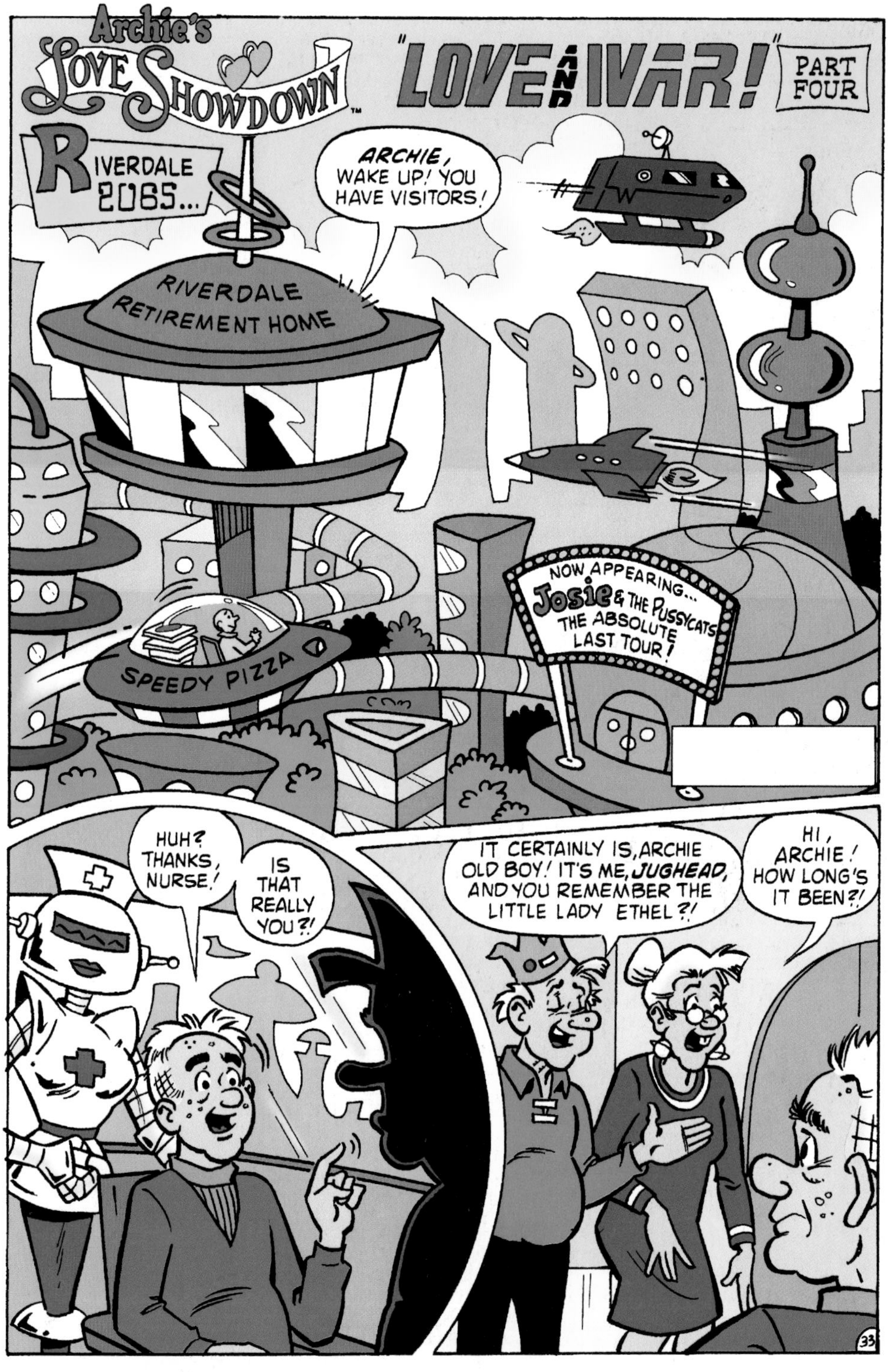
Archie's LOVE SHOWDOWN™
"LOVE AND WAR!"
PART FOUR
RIVERDALE 2065...
ARCHIE, WAKE UP! YOU HAVE VISITORS!
RIVERDALE RETIREMENT HOME
SPEEDY PIZZA
NOW APPEARING... Josie & THE PUSSYCATS THE ABSOLUTE LAST TOUR!
HUH? THANKS, NURSE!
IS THAT REALLY YOU?!
IT CERTAINLY IS, ARCHIE OLD BOY! IT'S ME, JUGHEAD, AND YOU REMEMBER THE LITTLE LADY ETHEL?!
HI, ARCHIE! HOW LONG'S IT BEEN?!
33

ORIGINALLY PRINTED IN LOVE SHOWDOWN SPECIAL, 1994

BILL GOLLIHER • BILL GOLLIHER • MIKE ESPOSITO • BILL YOSHIDA • BARRY GROSSMAN

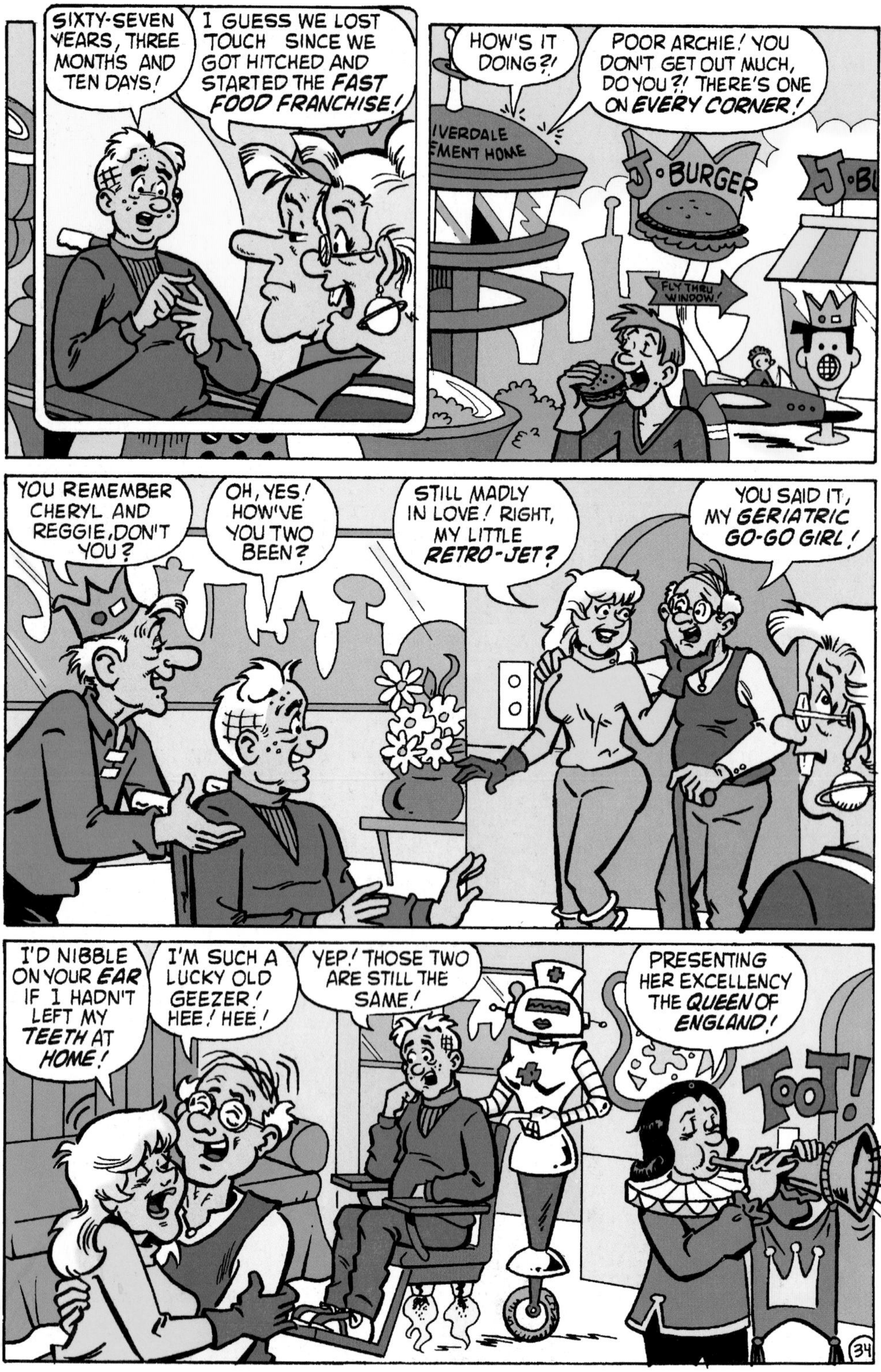
SIXTY-SEVEN YEARS, THREE MONTHS AND TEN DAYS!
I GUESS WE LOST TOUCH SINCE WE GOT HITCHED AND STARTED THE FAST FOOD FRANCHISE!
HOW'S IT DOING?!
POOR ARCHIE! YOU DON'T GET OUT MUCH, DO YOU?! THERE'S ONE ON EVERY CORNER!
J-BURGER
FLY THRU WINDOW!
YOU REMEMBER CHERYL AND REGGIE, DON'T YOU?
OH, YES! HOW'VE YOU TWO BEEN?
STILL MADLY IN LOVE! RIGHT, MY LITTLE RETRO-JET?
YOU SAID IT, MY GERIATRIC GO-GO GIRL!
I'D NIBBLE ON YOUR EAR IF I HADN'T LEFT MY TEETH AT HOME!
I'M SUCH A LUCKY OLD GEEZER! HEE! HEE!
YEP! THOSE TWO ARE STILL THE SAME!
PRESENTING HER EXCELLENCY THE QUEEN OF ENGLAND!
TOOT!
34

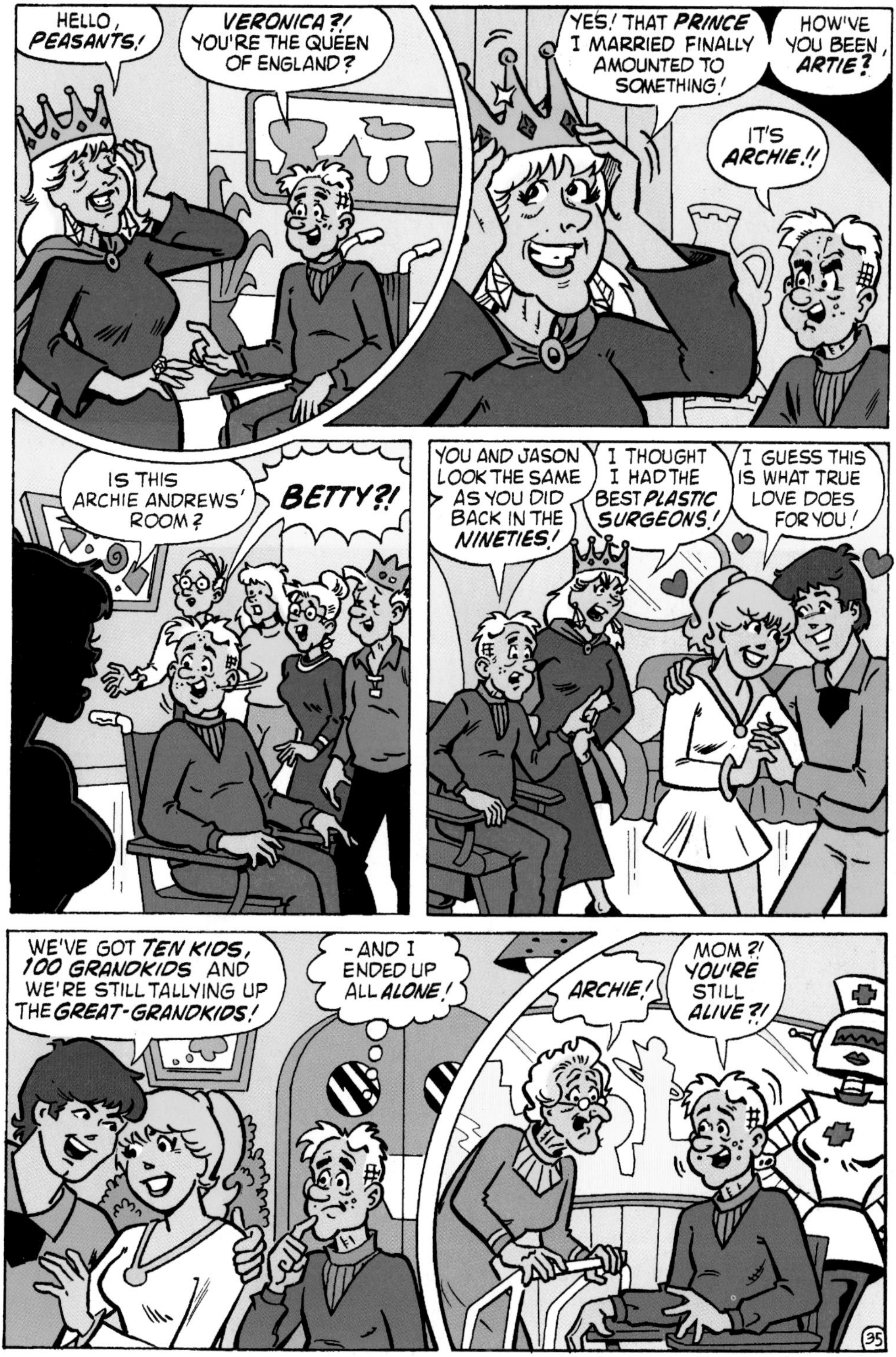

HELLO, PEASANTS!
VERONICA?! YOU'RE THE QUEEN OF ENGLAND?
YES! THAT PRINCE I MARRIED FINALLY AMOUNTED TO SOMETHING!
HOW'VE YOU BEEN, ARTIE?
IT'S ARCHIE!!
IS THIS ARCHIE ANDREWS' ROOM?
BETTY?!
YOU AND JASON LOOK THE SAME AS YOU DID BACK IN THE NINETIES!
I THOUGHT I HAD THE BEST PLASTIC SURGEONS!
I GUESS THIS IS WHAT TRUE LOVE DOES FOR YOU!
WE'VE GOT TEN KIDS, 100 GRANDKIDS AND WE'RE STILL TALLYING UP THE GREAT-GRANDKIDS!
- AND I ENDED UP ALL ALONE!
ARCHIE!
MOM?! YOU'RE STILL ALIVE?!
35

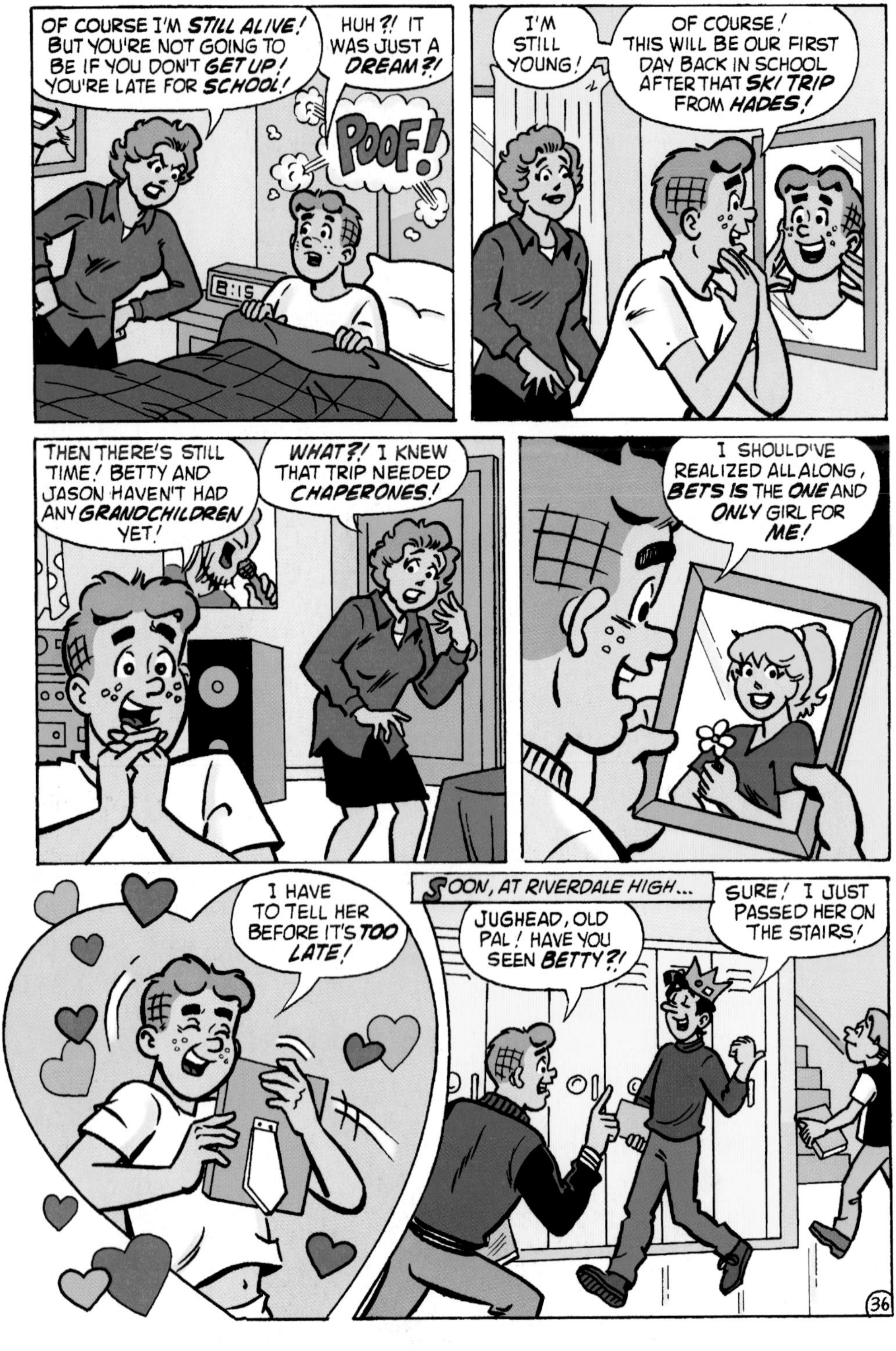
OF COURSE I'M STILL ALIVE! BUT YOU'RE NOT GOING TO BE IF YOU DON'T GET UP! YOU'RE LATE FOR SCHOOL!
HUH?! IT WAS JUST A DREAM?!
POOF!
8:15
I'M STILL YOUNG!
OF COURSE! THIS WILL BE OUR FIRST DAY BACK IN SCHOOL AFTER THAT SKI TRIP FROM HADES!
THEN THERE'S STILL TIME! BETTY AND JASON HAVEN'T HAD ANY GRANDCHILDREN YET!
WHAT?! I KNEW THAT TRIP NEEDED CHAPERONES!
I SHOULD'VE REALIZED ALL ALONG, BETS IS THE ONE AND ONLY GIRL FOR ME!
I HAVE TO TELL HER BEFORE IT'S TOO LATE!
SOON, AT RIVERDALE HIGH...
JUGHEAD, OLD PAL! HAVE YOU SEEN BETTY?!
SURE! I JUST PASSED HER ON THE STAIRS!
36

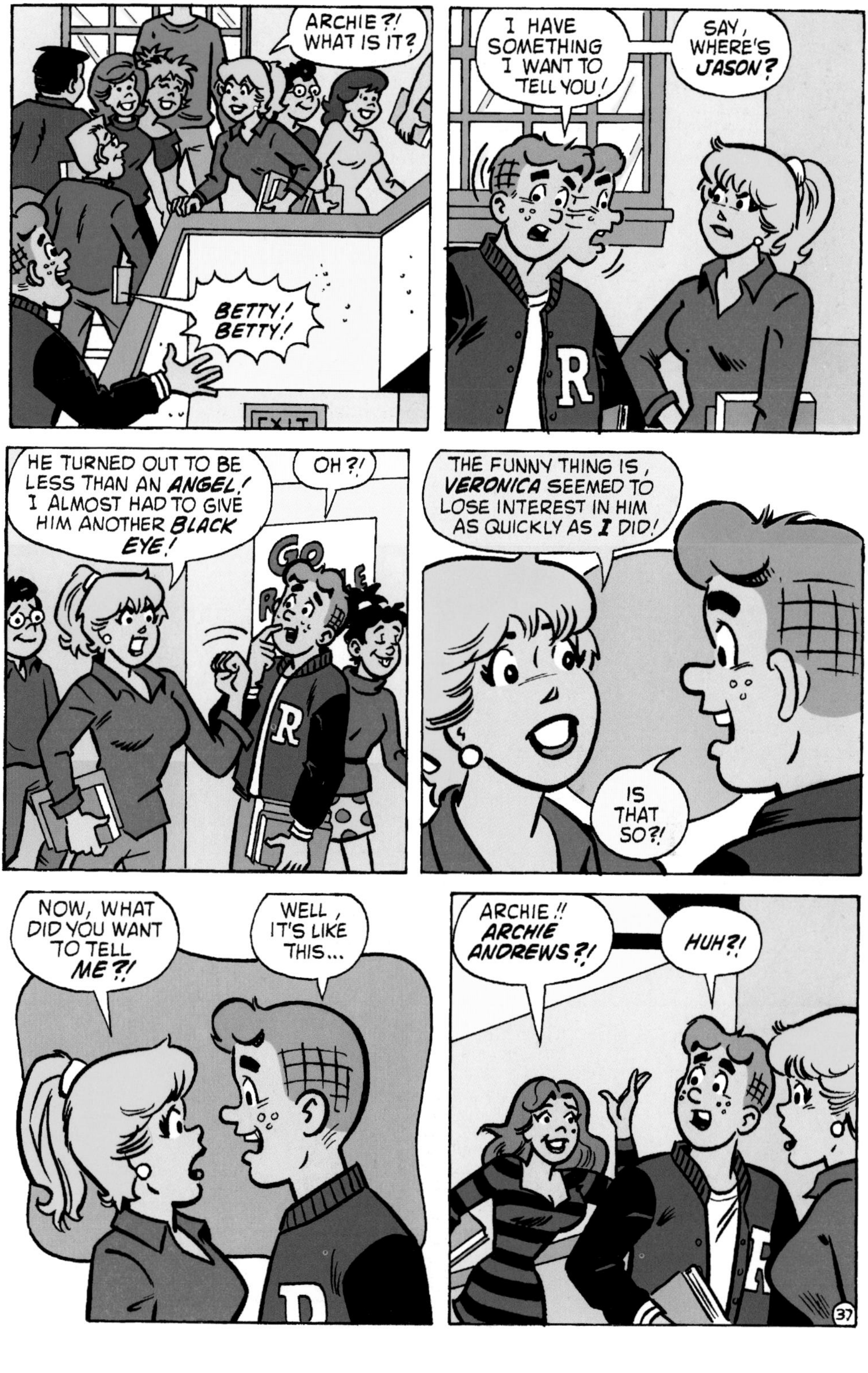
ARCHIE?! WHAT IS IT?
BETTY! BETTY!
EXIT
I HAVE SOMETHING I WANT TO TELL YOU!
SAY, WHERE'S JASON?
HE TURNED OUT TO BE LESS THAN AN ANGEL! I ALMOST HAD TO GIVE HIM ANOTHER BLACK EYE!
OH?!
THE FUNNY THING IS, VERONICA SEEMED TO LOSE INTEREST IN HIM AS QUICKLY AS I DID!
IS THAT SO?!
NOW, WHAT DID YOU WANT TO TELL ME?!
WELL, IT'S LIKE THIS...
ARCHIE!! ARCHIE ANDREWS?!
HUH?!
37

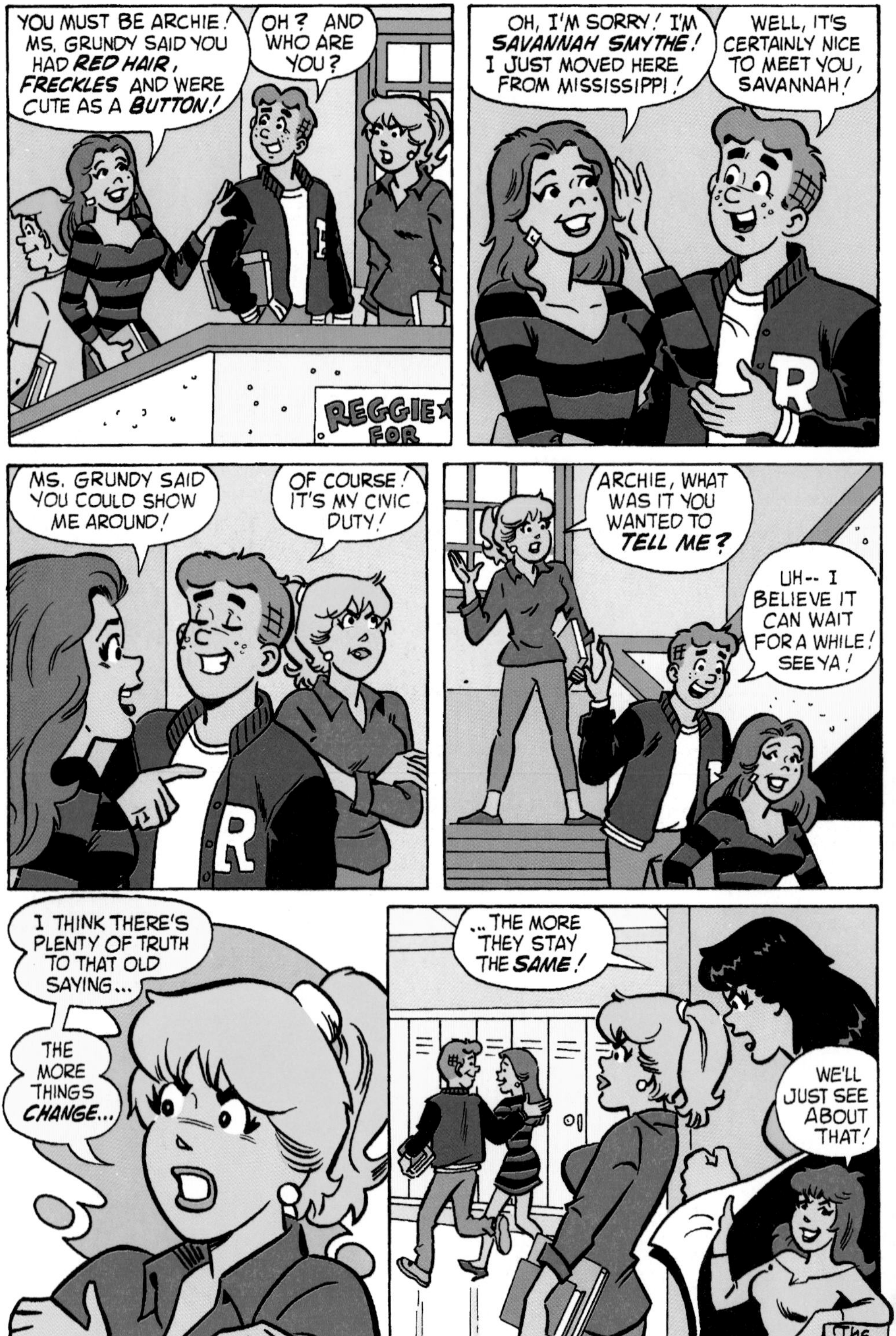

YOU MUST BE ARCHIE! MS. GRUNDY SAID YOU HAD RED HAIR, FRECKLES AND WERE CUTE AS A BUTTON!
OH? AND WHO ARE YOU?
REGGIE FOR
OH, I'M SORRY! I'M SAVANNAH SMYTHE! I JUST MOVED HERE FROM MISSISSIPPI!
WELL, IT'S CERTAINLY NICE TO MEET YOU, SAVANNAH!
MS. GRUNDY SAID YOU COULD SHOW ME AROUND!
OF COURSE! IT'S MY CIVIC DUTY!
ARCHIE, WHAT WAS IT YOU WANTED TO TELL ME?
UH-- I BELIEVE IT CAN WAIT FOR A WHILE! SEE YA!
I THINK THERE'S PLENTY OF TRUTH TO THAT OLD SAYING...
THE MORE THINGS CHANGE...
...THE MORE THEY STAY THE SAME!
WE'LL JUST SEE ABOUT THAT!
THE End

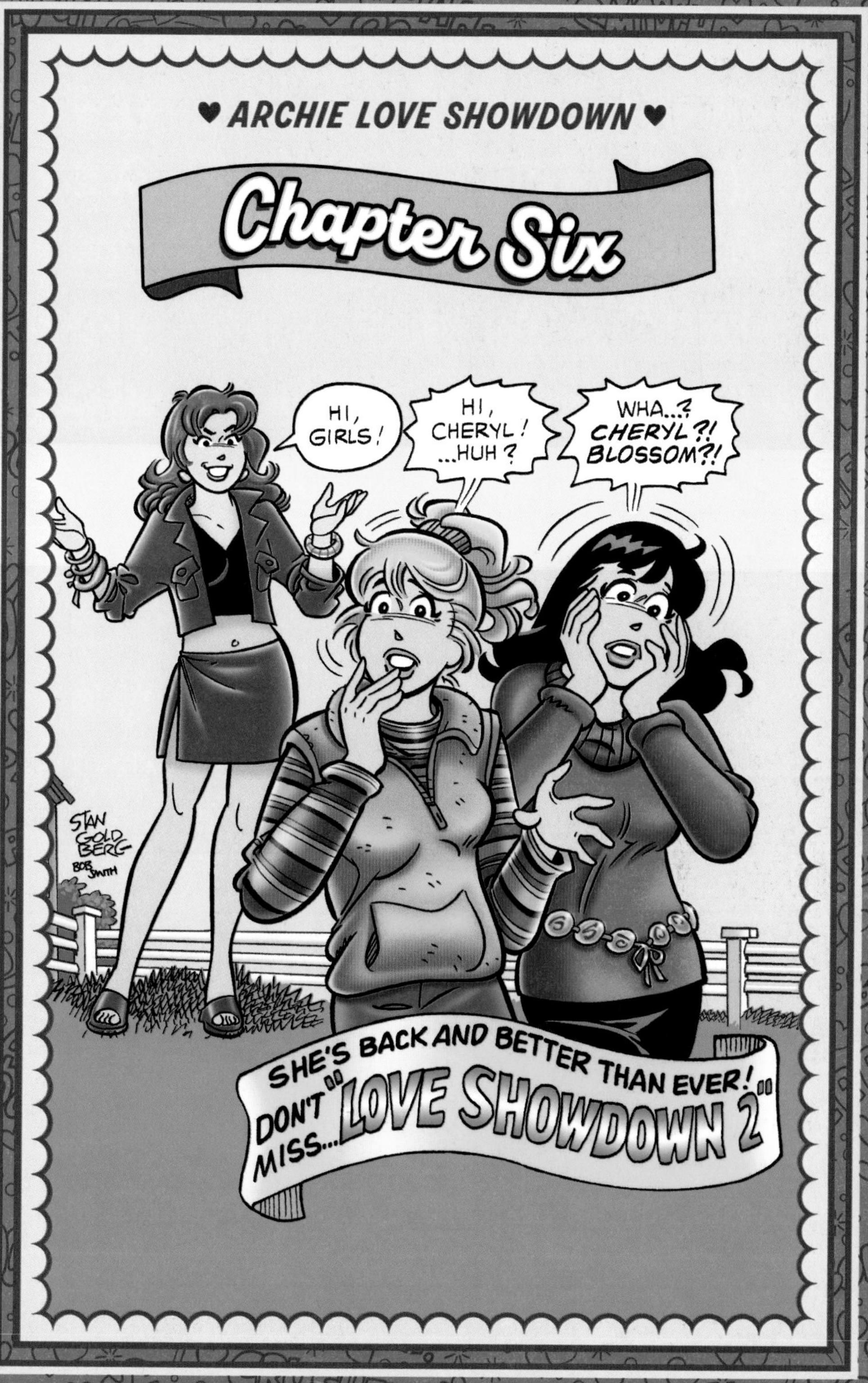
♥ ARCHIE LOVE SHOWDOWN ♥
Chapter Six
HI, GIRLS!
HI, CHERYL! ...HUH?
WHA..? CHERYL?! BLOSSOM?!
STAN GOLDBERG
BOB SMITH
SHE'S BACK AND BETTER THAN EVER!
DON'T MISS..."LOVE SHOWDOWN 2"

Betty and Veronica in "SHE'S BA-A-ACK!"

LOVE SHOWDOWN II

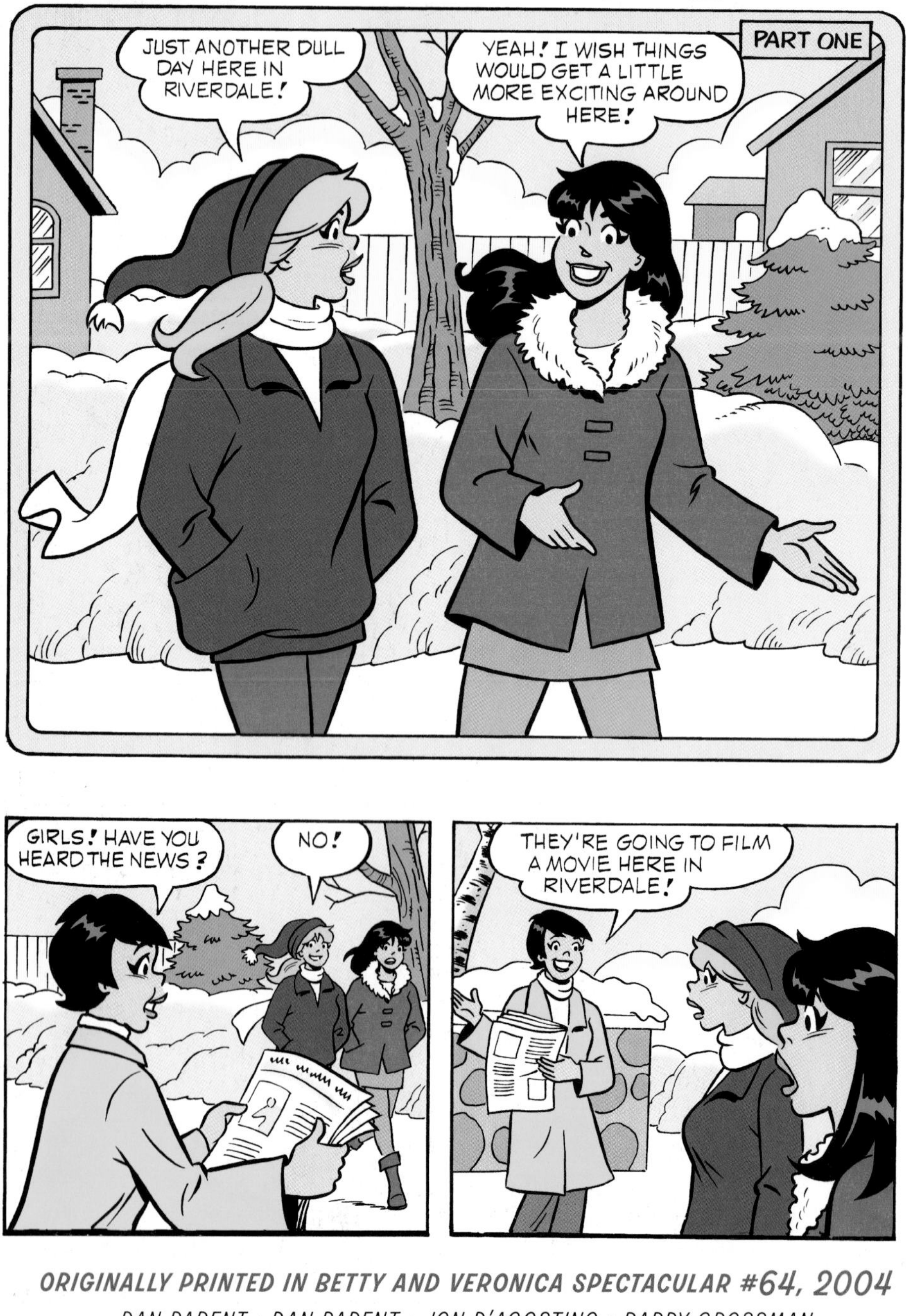

PART ONE
JUST ANOTHER DULL DAY HERE IN RIVERDALE!
YEAH! I WISH THINGS WOULD GET A LITTLE MORE EXCITING AROUND HERE!
GIRLS! HAVE YOU HEARD THE NEWS ?
NO!
THEY'RE GOING TO FILM A MOVIE HERE IN RIVERDALE!

ORIGINALLY PRINTED IN BETTY AND VERONICA SPECTACULAR #64, 2004

DAN PARENT • DAN PARENT • JON D'AGOSTINO • BARRY GROSSMAN

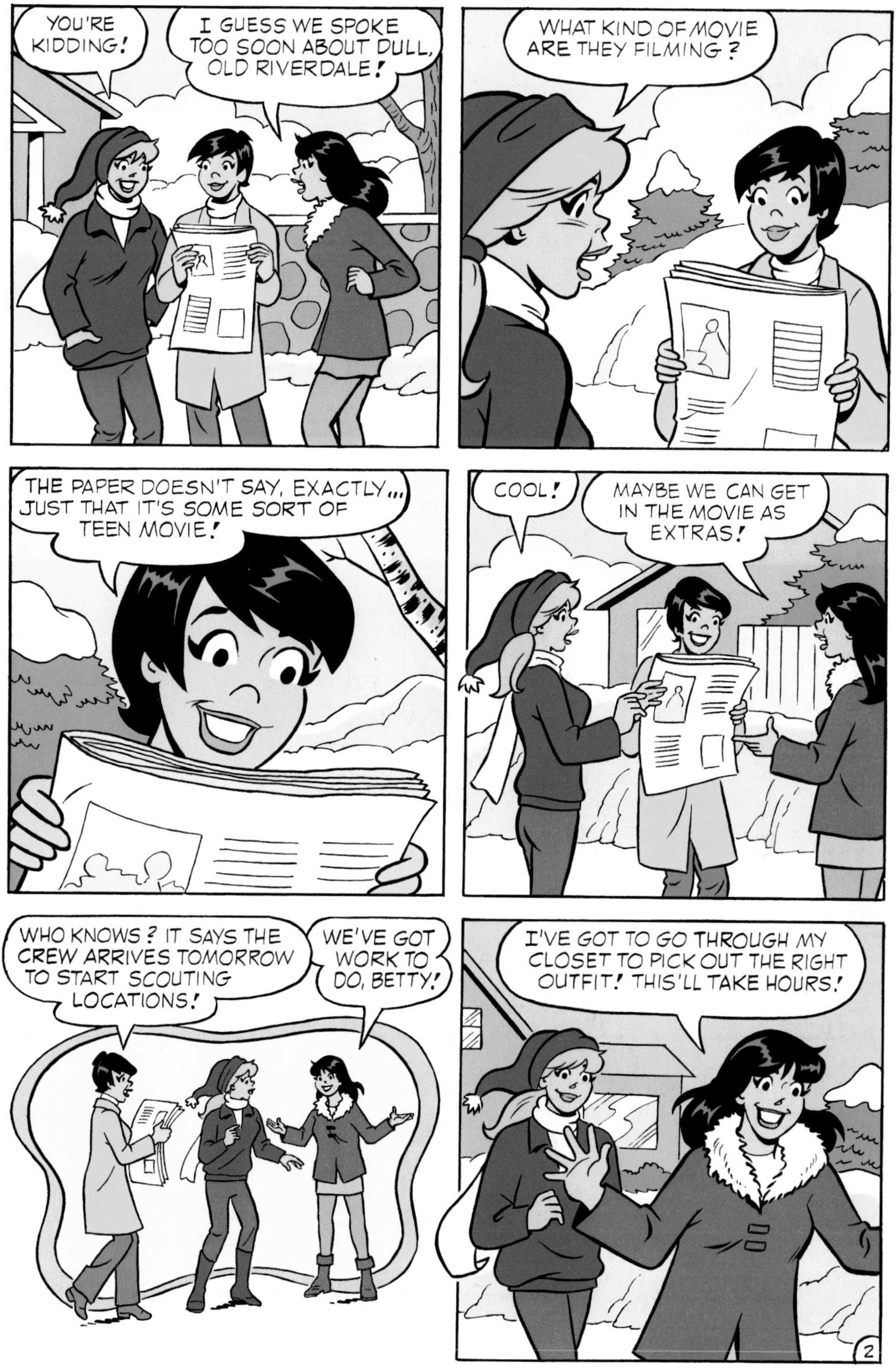

YOU'RE KIDDING!
I GUESS WE SPOKE TOO SOON ABOUT DULL, OLD RIVERDALE!
WHAT KIND OF MOVIE ARE THEY FILMING?
THE PAPER DOESN'T SAY, EXACTLY... JUST THAT IT'S SOME SORT OF TEEN MOVIE!
COOL!
MAYBE WE CAN GET IN THE MOVIE AS EXTRAS!
WHO KNOWS? IT SAYS THE CREW ARRIVES TOMORROW TO START SCOUTING LOCATIONS!
WE'VE GOT WORK TO DO, BETTY!
I'VE GOT TO GO THROUGH MY CLOSET TO PICK OUT THE RIGHT OUTFIT! THIS'LL TAKE HOURS!
2

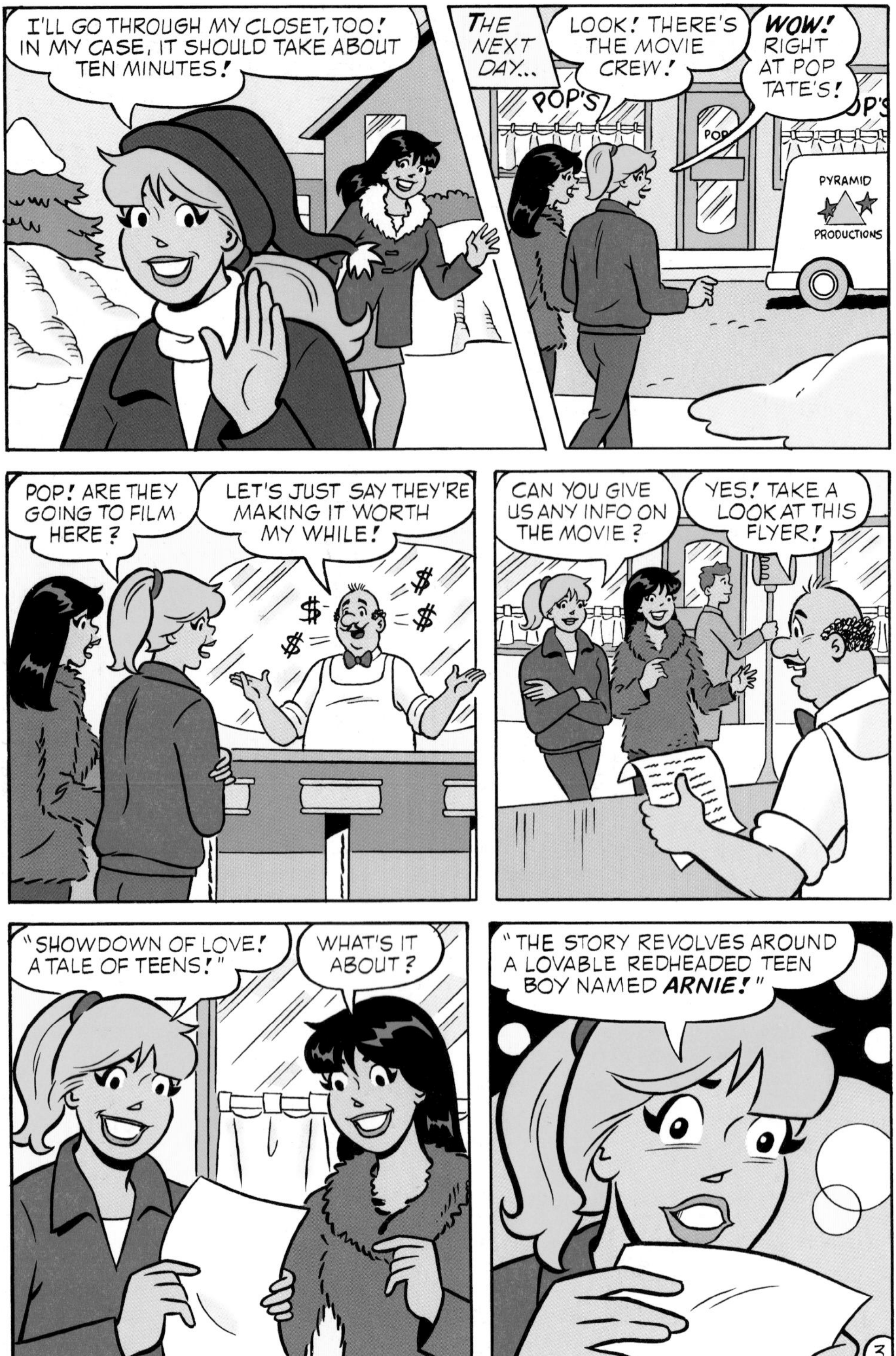
I'LL GO THROUGH MY CLOSET, TOO! IN MY CASE, IT SHOULD TAKE ABOUT TEN MINUTES!
THE NEXT DAY...
LOOK! THERE'S THE MOVIE CREW!
WOW! RIGHT AT POP TATE'S!
POP'S
PYRAMID PRODUCTIONS
POP! ARE THEY GOING TO FILM HERE?
LET'S JUST SAY THEY'RE MAKING IT WORTH MY WHILE!
CAN YOU GIVE US ANY INFO ON THE MOVIE?
YES! TAKE A LOOK AT THIS FLYER!
"SHOWDOWN OF LOVE! A TALE OF TEENS!"
WHAT'S IT ABOUT?
"THE STORY REVOLVES AROUND A LOVABLE REDHEADED TEEN BOY NAMED ARNIE!"
3

THE STORY ALSO INCLUDES HIS TWO GIRLFRIENDS WHO FIGHT OVER HIM, BLONDE-HAIRED *BETSY* AND BRUNETTE *VICTORIA!*

"THE TWO GIRLS SPEND ALL THEIR TIME *FIGHTING* OVER THE RED-HAIRED GOOF BALL!"

HA! WHAT A SILLY IDEA FOR A MOVIE!

WHO'D BUY SUCH A RIDICULOUS PLOT?

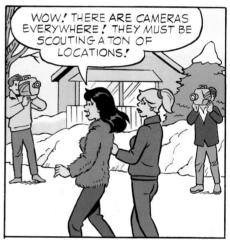

WOW! THERE ARE CAMERAS EVERYWHERE! THEY MUST BE SCOUTING A TON OF LOCATIONS!

ALL RIGHT, GIRLS! WHICH ONE OF YOU DID IT?

HUH? WHAT ARE YOU TALKING ABOUT?

WHO SOLD OUR STORY TO THESE MOVIE PRODUCERS?

4

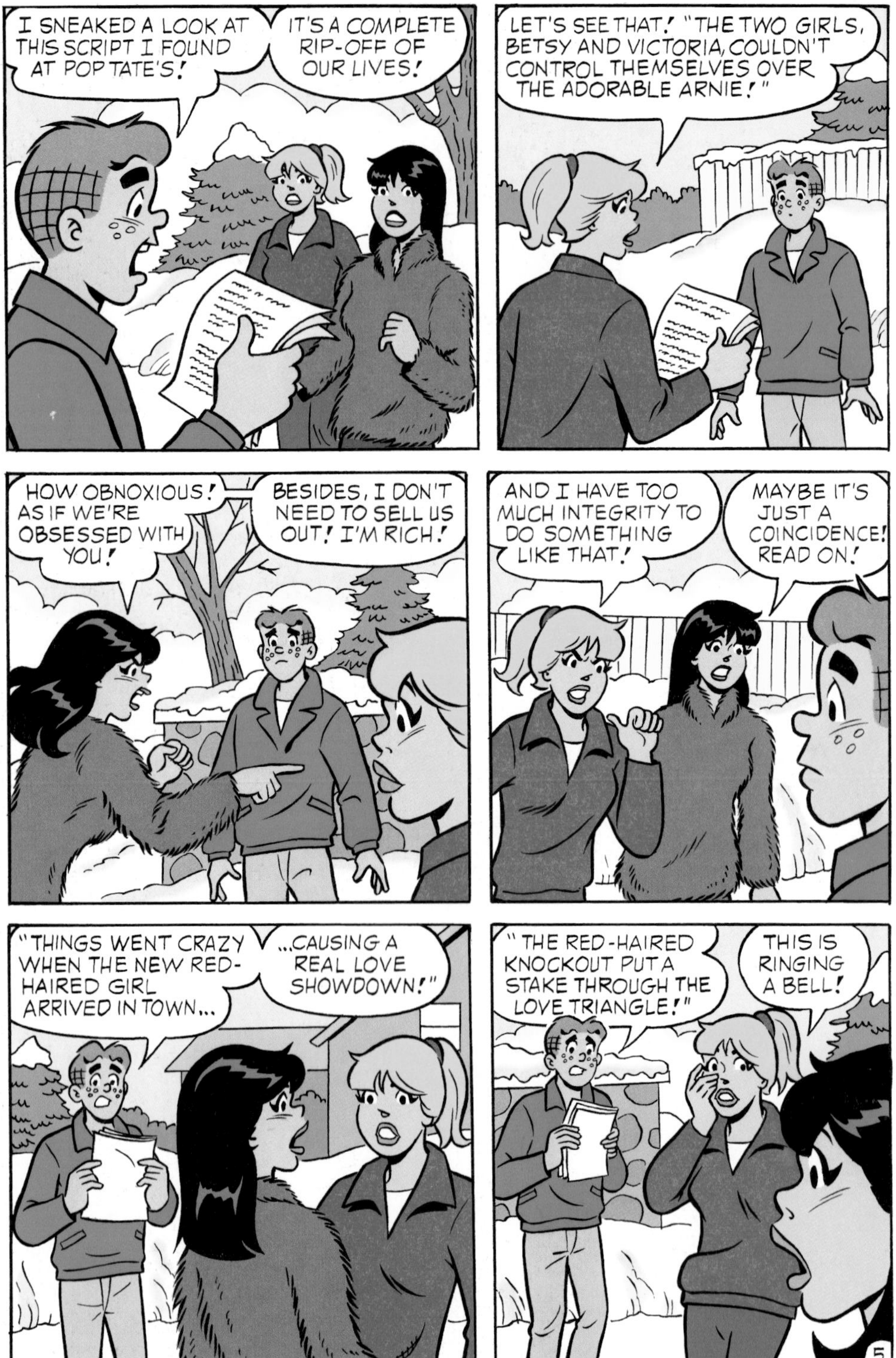

I SNEAKED A LOOK AT THIS SCRIPT I FOUND AT POP TATE'S!
IT'S A COMPLETE RIP-OFF OF OUR LIVES!
LET'S SEE THAT! "THE TWO GIRLS, BETSY AND VICTORIA, COULDN'T CONTROL THEMSELVES OVER THE ADORABLE ARNIE!"
HOW OBNOXIOUS! AS IF WE'RE OBSESSED WITH YOU!
BESIDES, I DON'T NEED TO SELL US OUT! I'M RICH!
AND I HAVE TOO MUCH INTEGRITY TO DO SOMETHING LIKE THAT!
MAYBE IT'S JUST A COINCIDENCE! READ ON!
"THINGS WENT CRAZY WHEN THE NEW RED-HAIRED GIRL ARRIVED IN TOWN...
...CAUSING A REAL LOVE SHOWDOWN!"
"THE RED-HAIRED KNOCKOUT PUT A STAKE THROUGH THE LOVE TRIANGLE!"
THIS IS RINGING A BELL!
5

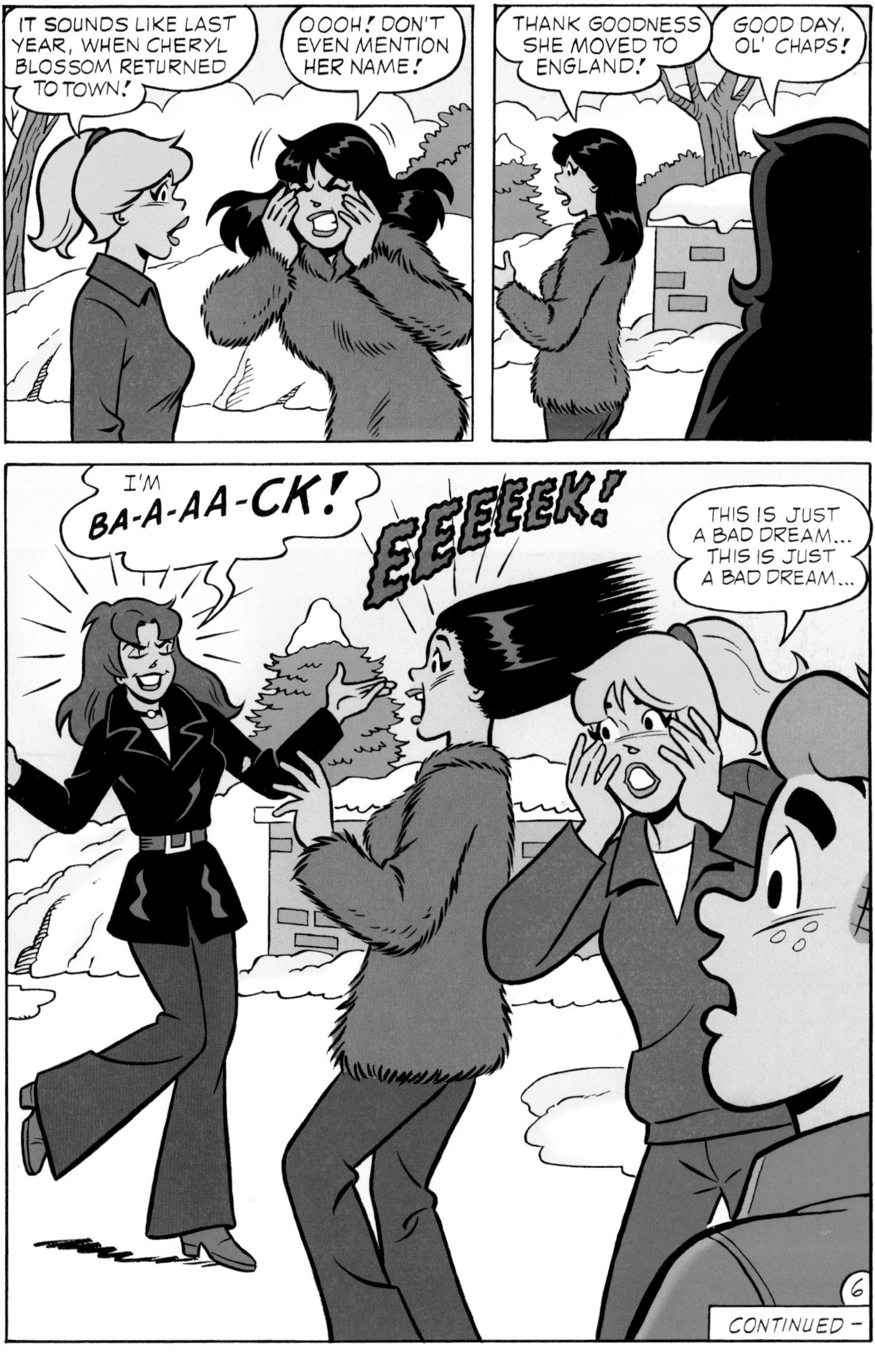

IT SOUNDS LIKE LAST YEAR, WHEN CHERYL BLOSSOM RETURNED TO TOWN!
OOOH! DON'T EVEN MENTION HER NAME!
THANK GOODNESS SHE MOVED TO ENGLAND!
GOOD DAY, OL' CHAPS!
I'M BA-A-AA-CK!
EEEEEK!
THIS IS JUST A BAD DREAM... THIS IS JUST A BAD DREAM...
6
CONTINUED -

Betty and Veronica in "SHE'S BA-A-ACK!"

LOVE SHOWDOWN II

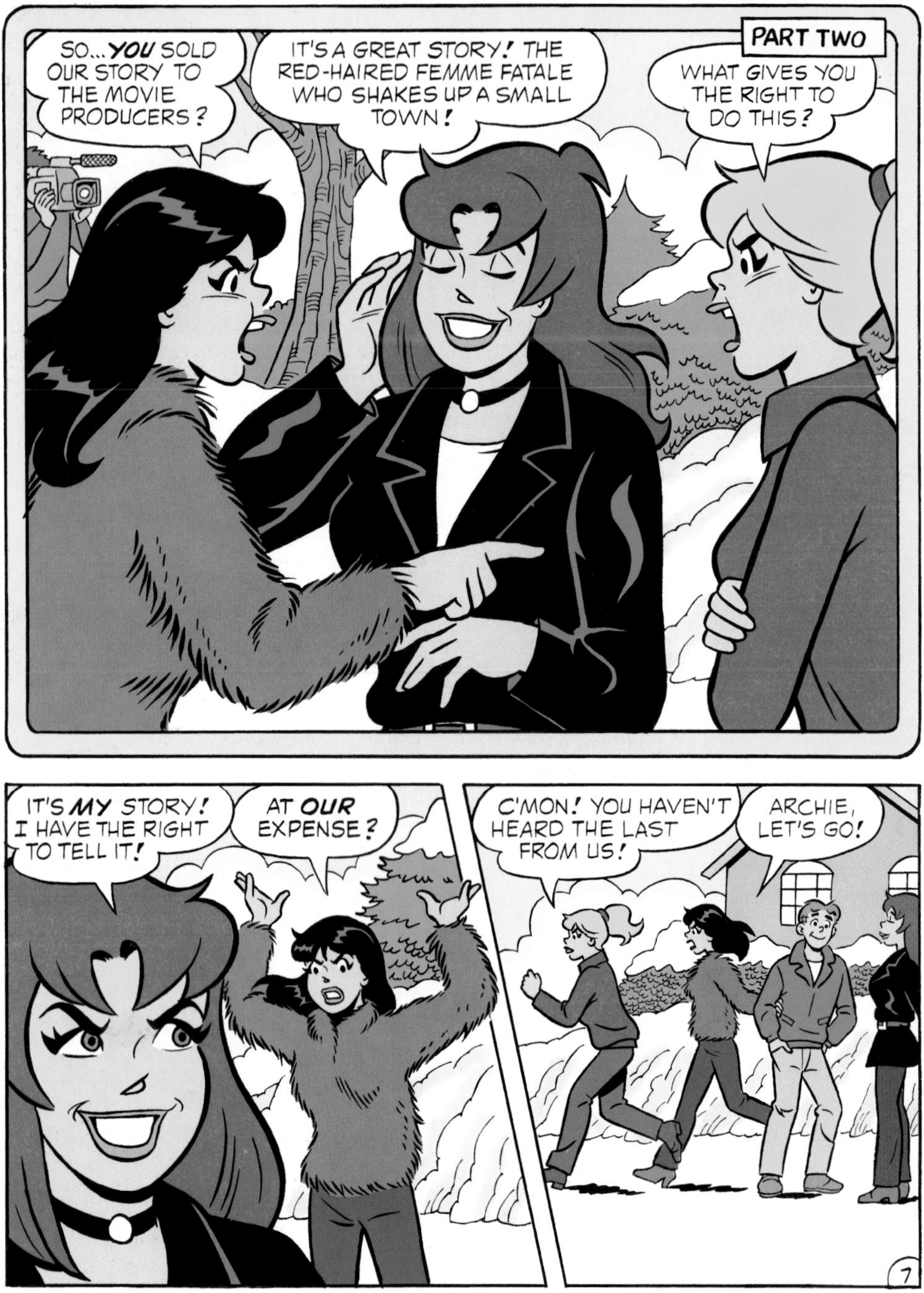
PART TWO
SO... YOU SOLD OUR STORY TO THE MOVIE PRODUCERS?
IT'S A GREAT STORY! THE RED-HAIRED FEMME FATALE WHO SHAKES UP A SMALL TOWN!
WHAT GIVES YOU THE RIGHT TO DO THIS?
IT'S MY STORY! I HAVE THE RIGHT TO TELL IT!
AT OUR EXPENSE?
C'MON! YOU HAVEN'T HEARD THE LAST FROM US!
ARCHIE, LET'S GO!
7

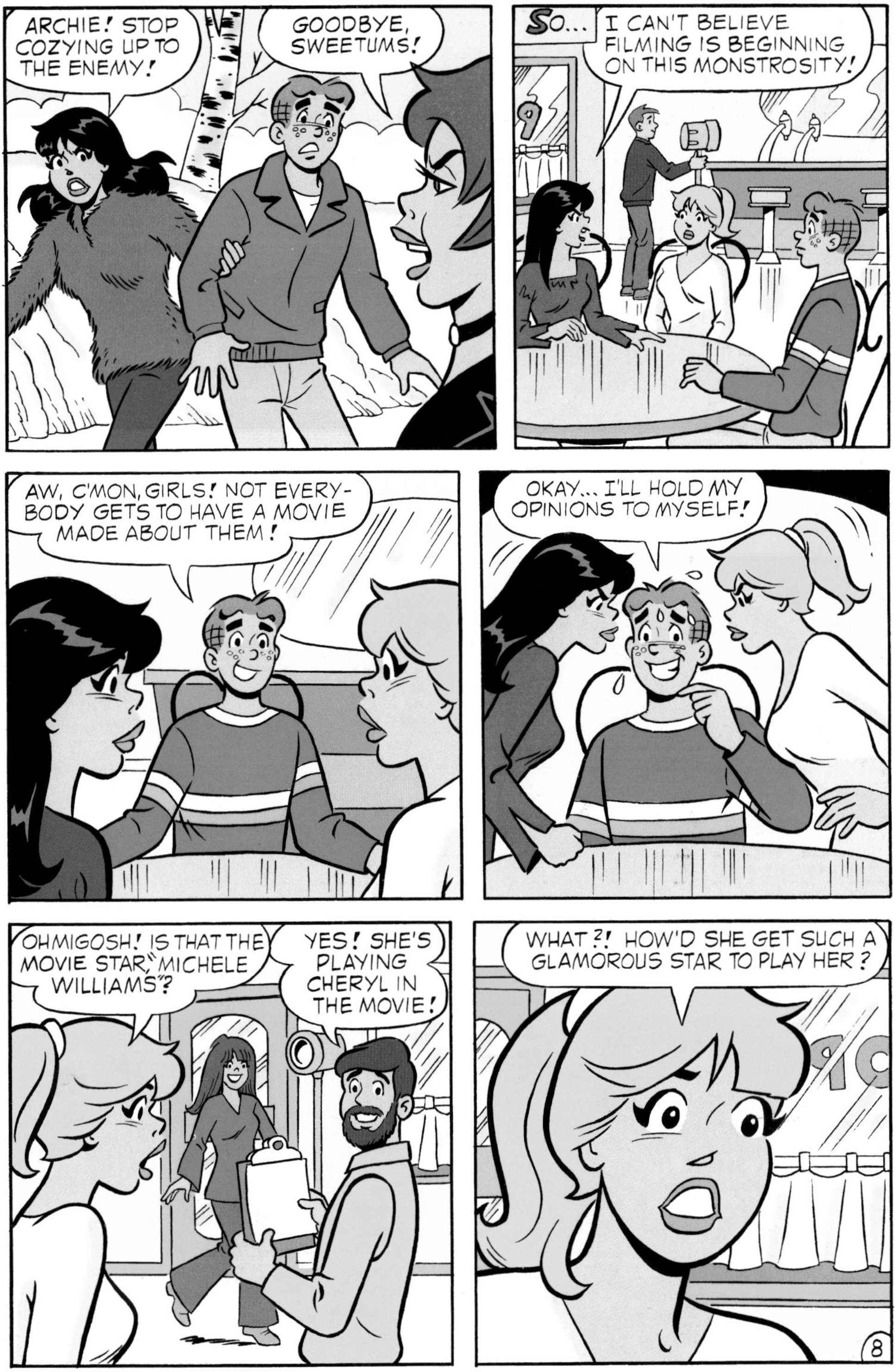
ARCHIE! STOP COZYING UP TO THE ENEMY!
GOODBYE, SWEETUMS!
SO...
I CAN'T BELIEVE FILMING IS BEGINNING ON THIS MONSTROSITY!
AW, C'MON, GIRLS! NOT EVERY-BODY GETS TO HAVE A MOVIE MADE ABOUT THEM!
OKAY... I'LL HOLD MY OPINIONS TO MYSELF!
OHMIGOSH! IS THAT THE MOVIE STAR "MICHELE WILLIAMS"?
YES! SHE'S PLAYING CHERYL IN THE MOVIE!
WHAT?! HOW'D SHE GET SUCH A GLAMOROUS STAR TO PLAY HER?
8

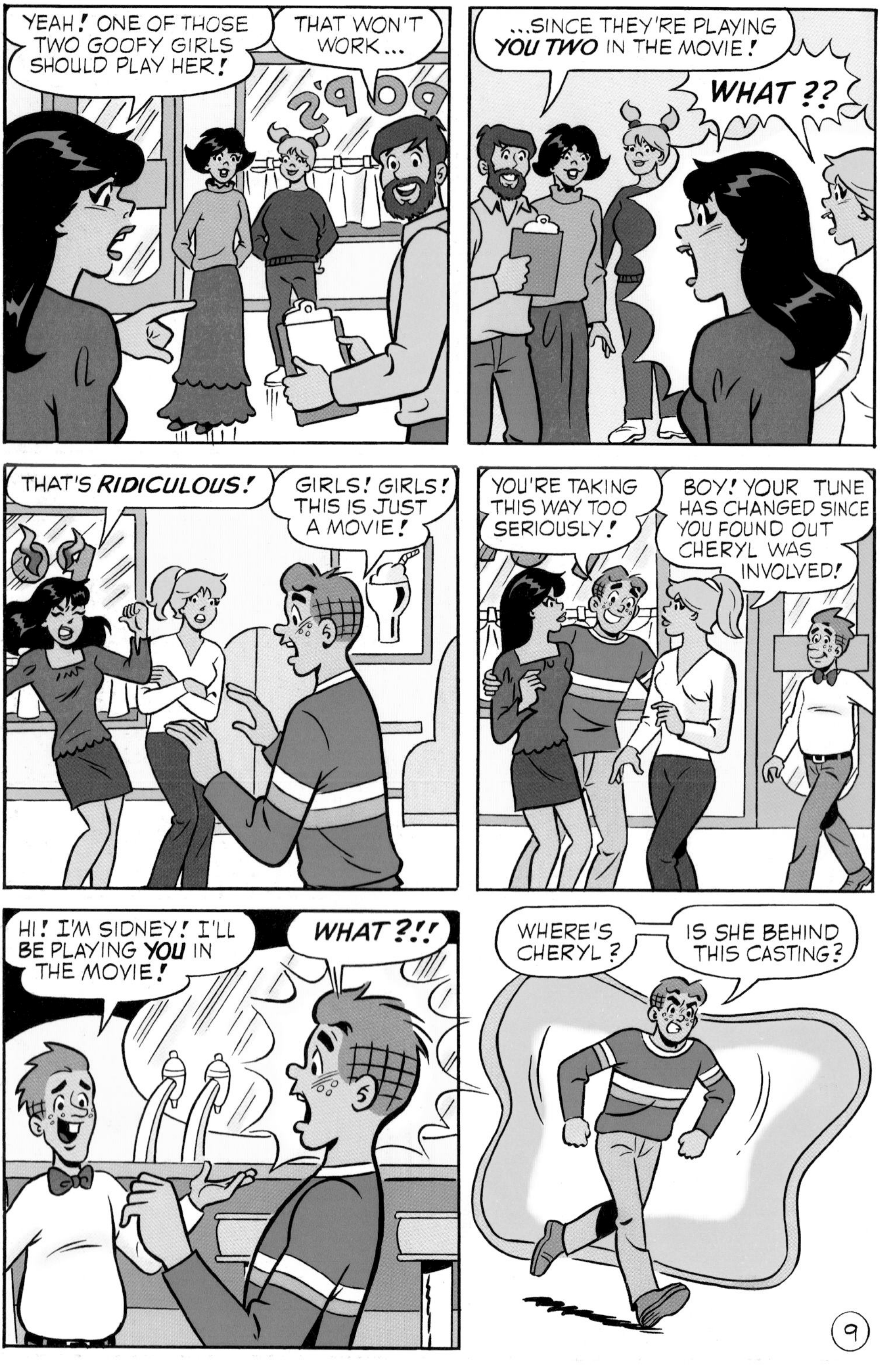
YEAH! ONE OF THOSE TWO GOOFY GIRLS SHOULD PLAY HER!
THAT WON'T WORK...
POP'S
...SINCE THEY'RE PLAYING ***YOU TWO*** IN THE MOVIE!
WHAT??
THAT'S ***RIDICULOUS!***
GIRLS! GIRLS! THIS IS JUST A MOVIE!
YOU'RE TAKING THIS WAY TOO SERIOUSLY!
BOY! YOUR TUNE HAS CHANGED SINCE YOU FOUND OUT CHERYL WAS INVOLVED!
HI! I'M SIDNEY! I'LL BE PLAYING ***YOU*** IN THE MOVIE!
WHAT?!!
WHERE'S CHERYL?
IS SHE BEHIND THIS CASTING?
9

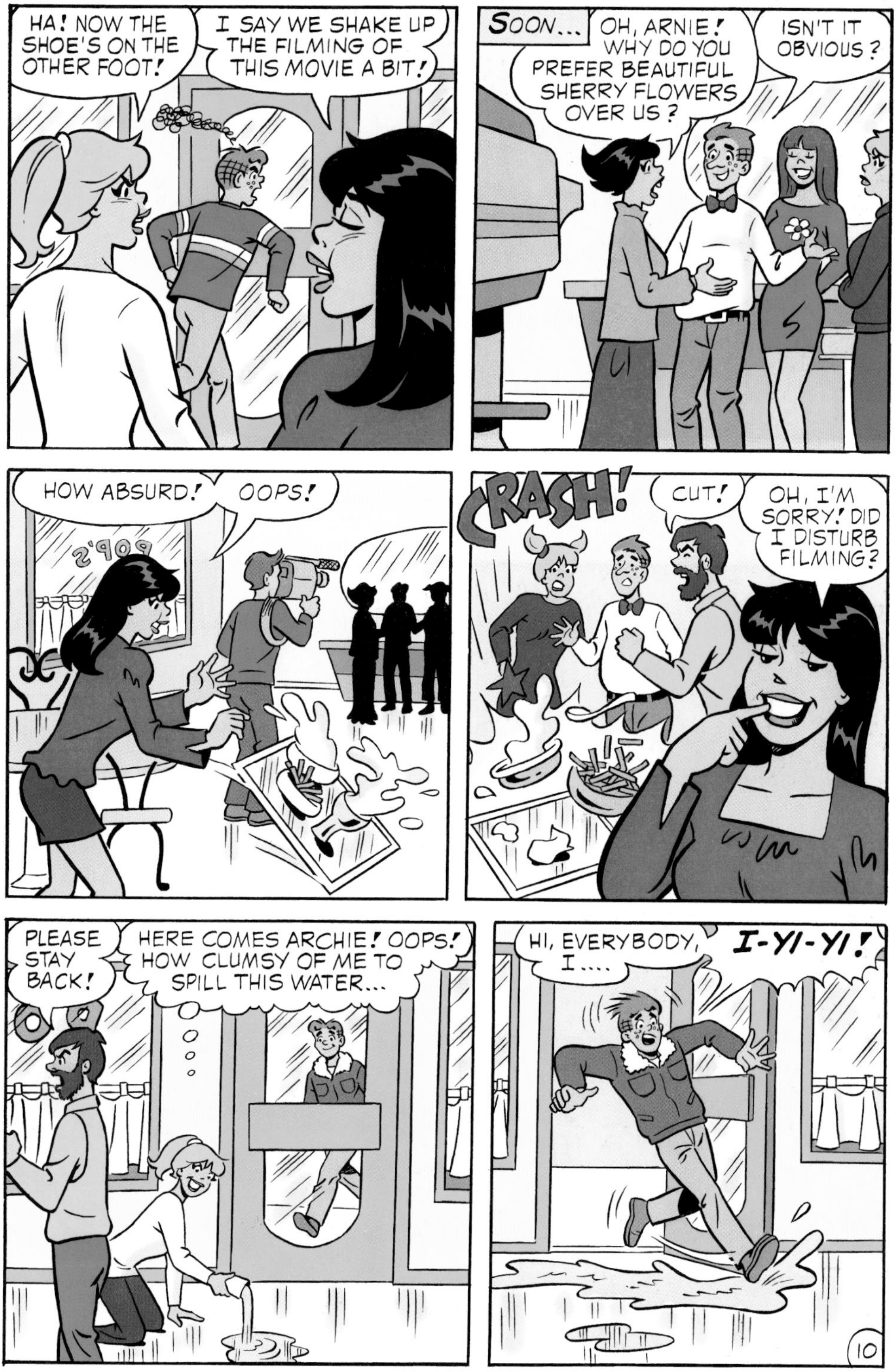

HA! NOW THE SHOE'S ON THE OTHER FOOT!
I SAY WE SHAKE UP THE FILMING OF THIS MOVIE A BIT!
SOON...
OH, ARNIE! WHY DO YOU PREFER BEAUTIFUL SHERRY FLOWERS OVER US?
ISN'T IT OBVIOUS?
HOW ABSURD!
OOPS!
POP'S
CRASH!
CUT!
OH, I'M SORRY! DID I DISTURB FILMING?
PLEASE STAY BACK!
HERE COMES ARCHIE! OOPS! HOW CLUMSY OF ME TO SPILL THIS WATER...
HI, EVERYBODY, I....
I-YI-YI!
10

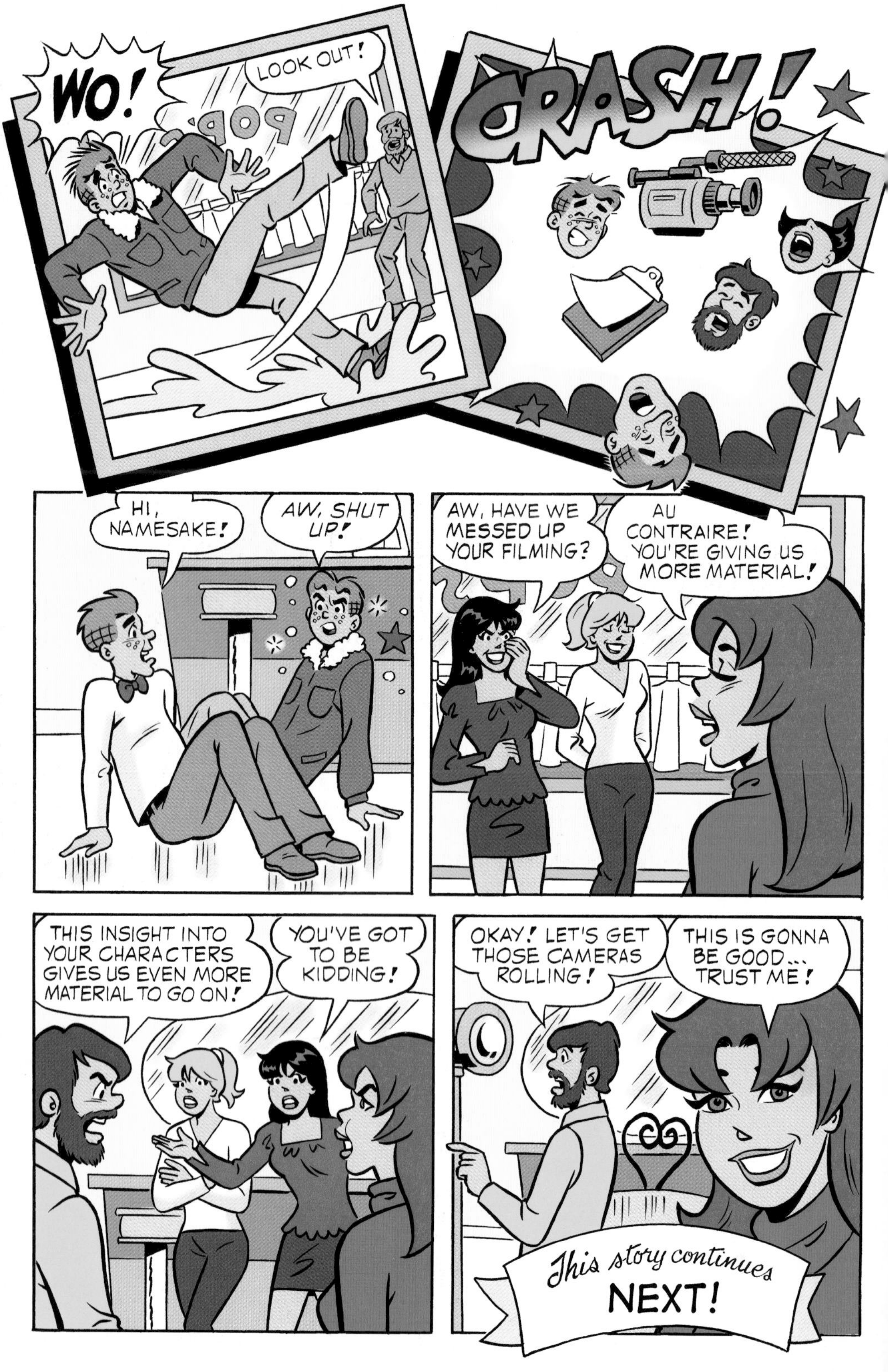
WO!
LOOK OUT!
POP!
CRASH!
HI, NAMESAKE!
AW, SHUT UP!
AW, HAVE WE MESSED UP YOUR FILMING?
AU CONTRAIRE! YOU'RE GIVING US MORE MATERIAL!
THIS INSIGHT INTO YOUR CHARACTERS GIVES US EVEN MORE MATERIAL TO GO ON!
YOU'VE GOT TO BE KIDDING!
OKAY! LET'S GET THOSE CAMERAS ROLLING!
THIS IS GONNA BE GOOD... TRUST ME!
This story continues NEXT!

♥ ARCHIE LOVE SHOWDOWN ♥

Chapter Seven

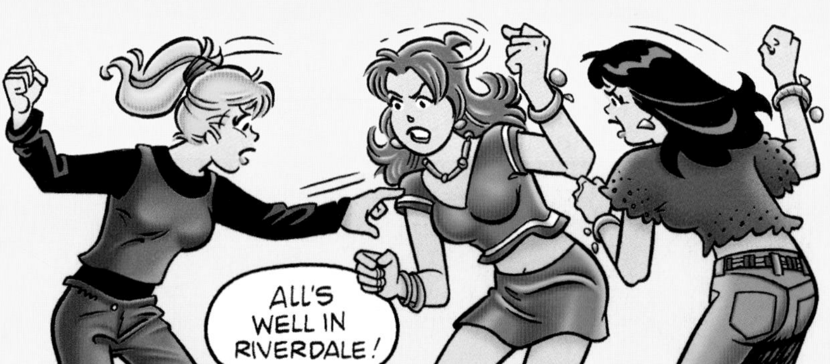
ALL'S WELL IN RIVERDALE!
BETTY, VERONICA AND CHERYL ARE FIGHTING OVER ME AGAIN!
STAN GOLDBERG
BOB SMITH

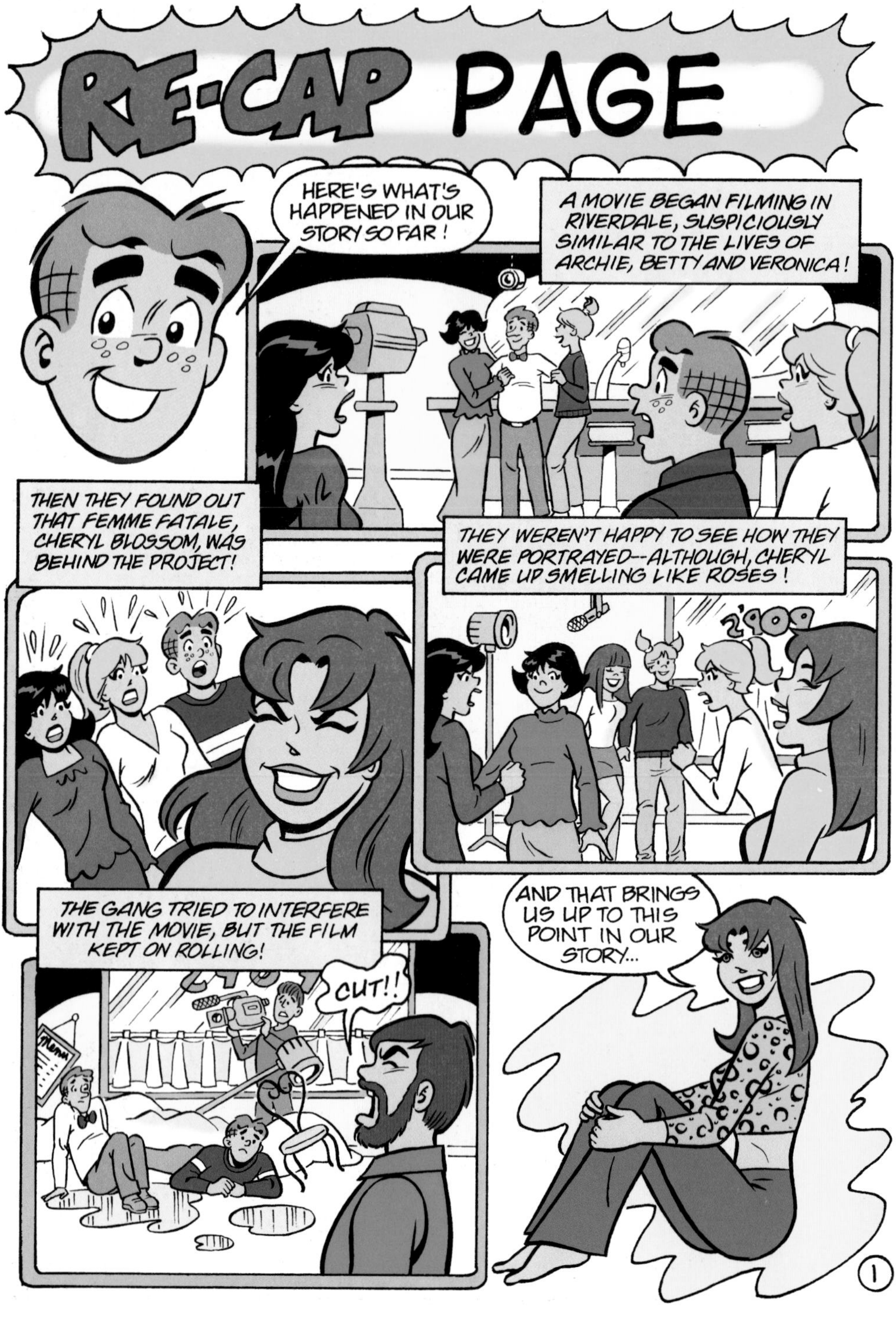
RE-CAP PAGE
HERE'S WHAT'S HAPPENED IN OUR STORY SO FAR!
A MOVIE BEGAN FILMING IN RIVERDALE, SUSPICIOUSLY SIMILAR TO THE LIVES OF ARCHIE, BETTY AND VERONICA!
THEN THEY FOUND OUT THAT FEMME FATALE, CHERYL BLOSSOM, WAS BEHIND THE PROJECT!
THEY WEREN'T HAPPY TO SEE HOW THEY WERE PORTRAYED--ALTHOUGH, CHERYL CAME UP SMELLING LIKE ROSES!
THE GANG TRIED TO INTERFERE WITH THE MOVIE, BUT THE FILM KEPT ON ROLLING!
CUT!!
AND THAT BRINGS US UP TO THIS POINT IN OUR STORY...
1

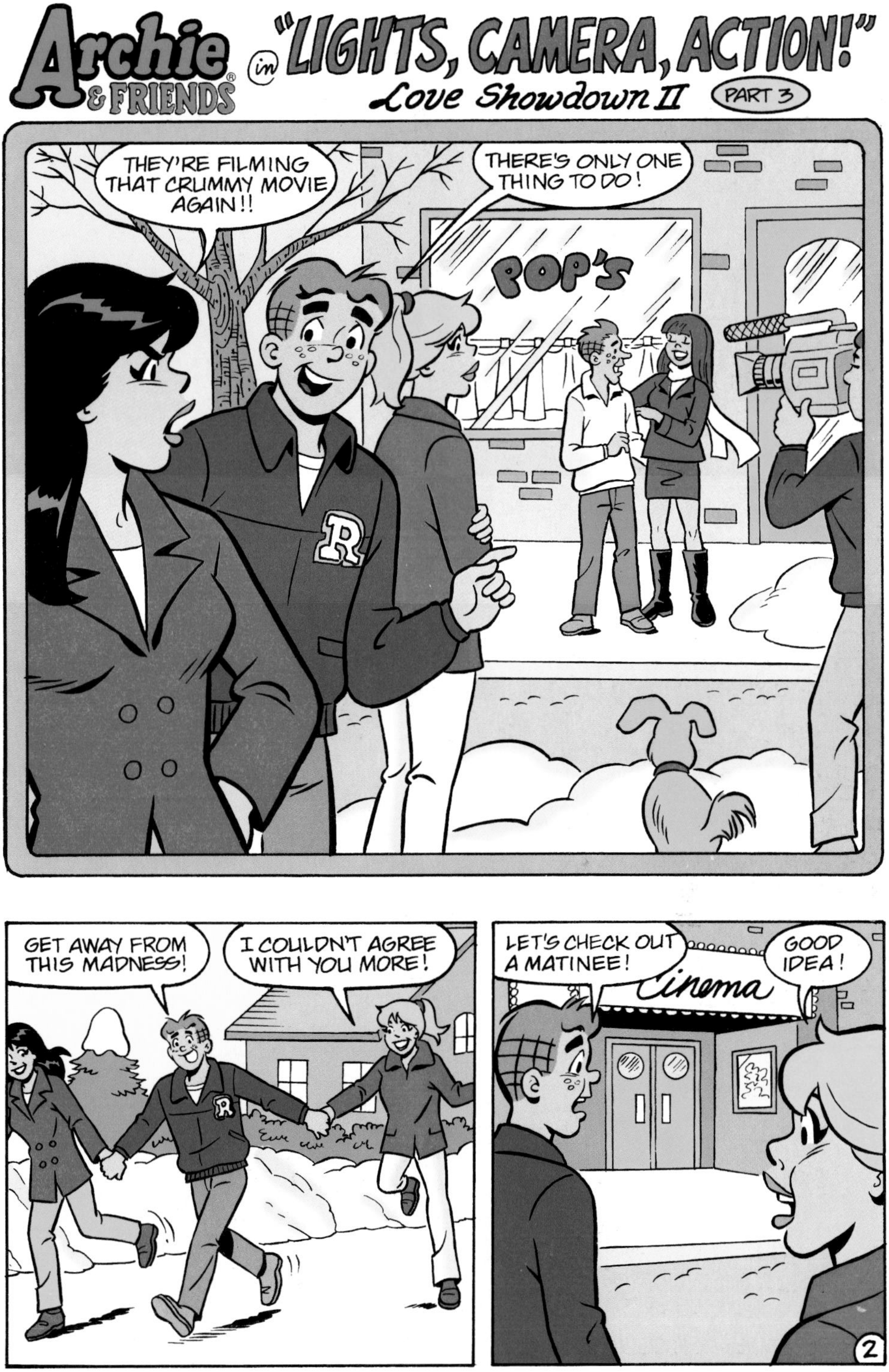

Archie & FRIENDS
in "LIGHTS, CAMERA, ACTION!"
Love Showdown II
PART 3
THEY'RE FILMING THAT CRUMMY MOVIE AGAIN!!
THERE'S ONLY ONE THING TO DO!
POP'S
GET AWAY FROM THIS MADNESS!
I COULDN'T AGREE WITH YOU MORE!
LET'S CHECK OUT A MATINEE!
GOOD IDEA!
Cinema
2

ORIGINALLY PRINTED IN ARCHIE AND FRIENDS #79, MARCH 2004

DAN PARENT • DAN PARENT • JON D'AGOSTINO • VICKIE WILLIAMS • BARRY GROSSMAN

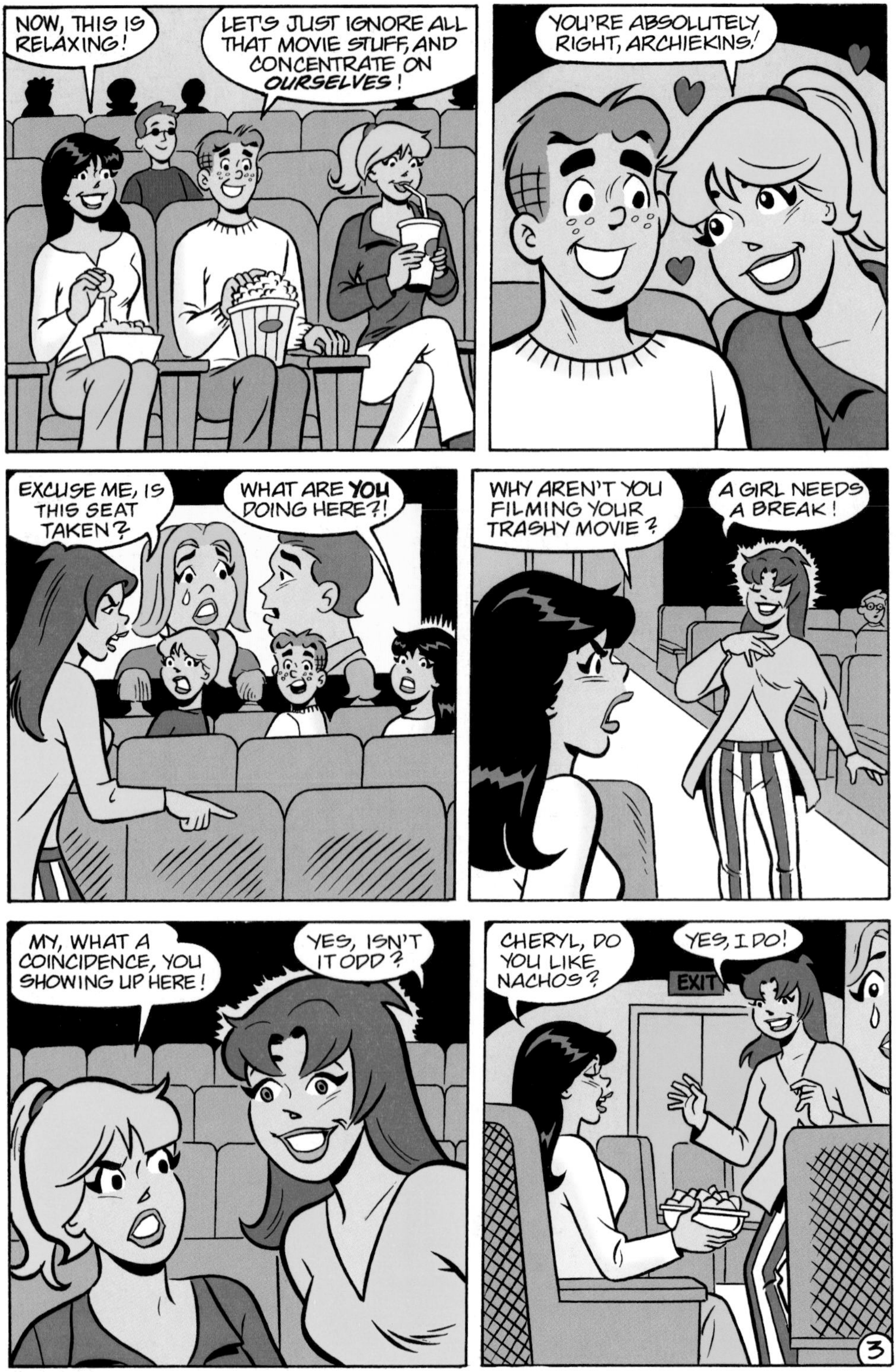
NOW, THIS IS RELAXING!
LET'S JUST IGNORE ALL THAT MOVIE STUFF, AND CONCENTRATE ON OURSELVES!
YOU'RE ABSOLUTELY RIGHT, ARCHIEKINS!
EXCUSE ME, IS THIS SEAT TAKEN?
WHAT ARE YOU DOING HERE?!
WHY AREN'T YOU FILMING YOUR TRASHY MOVIE?
A GIRL NEEDS A BREAK!
MY, WHAT A COINCIDENCE, YOU SHOWING UP HERE!
YES, ISN'T IT ODD?
CHERYL, DO YOU LIKE NACHOS?
YES, I DO!
EXIT
3

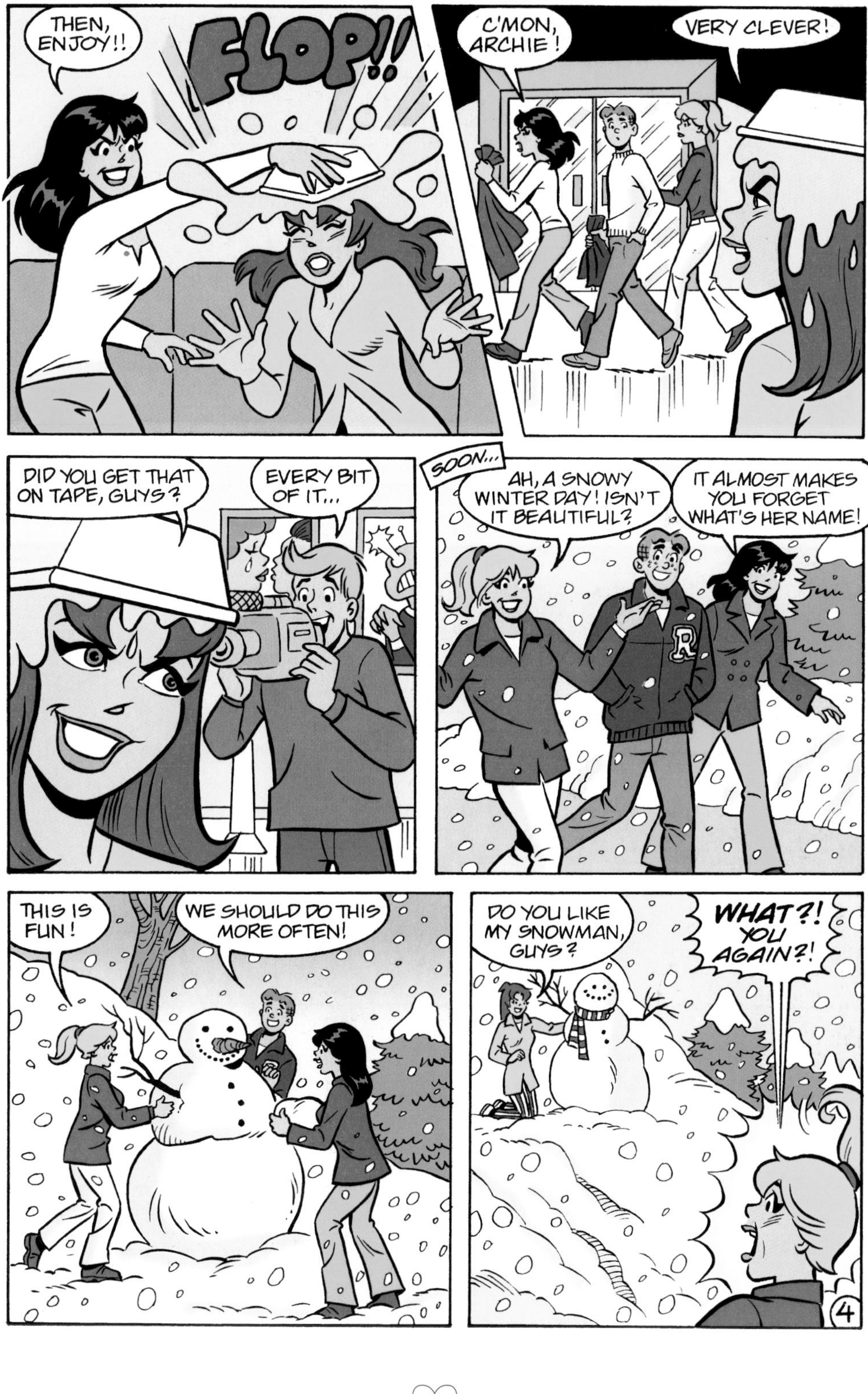
THEN, ENJOY!!
FLOP!!
C'MON, ARCHIE!
VERY CLEVER!
DID YOU GET THAT ON TAPE, GUYS?
EVERY BIT OF IT...
SOON...
AH, A SNOWY WINTER DAY! ISN'T IT BEAUTIFUL?
IT ALMOST MAKES YOU FORGET WHAT'S HER NAME!
THIS IS FUN!
WE SHOULD DO THIS MORE OFTEN!
DO YOU LIKE MY SNOWMAN, GUYS?
WHAT?! YOU AGAIN?!
R
4

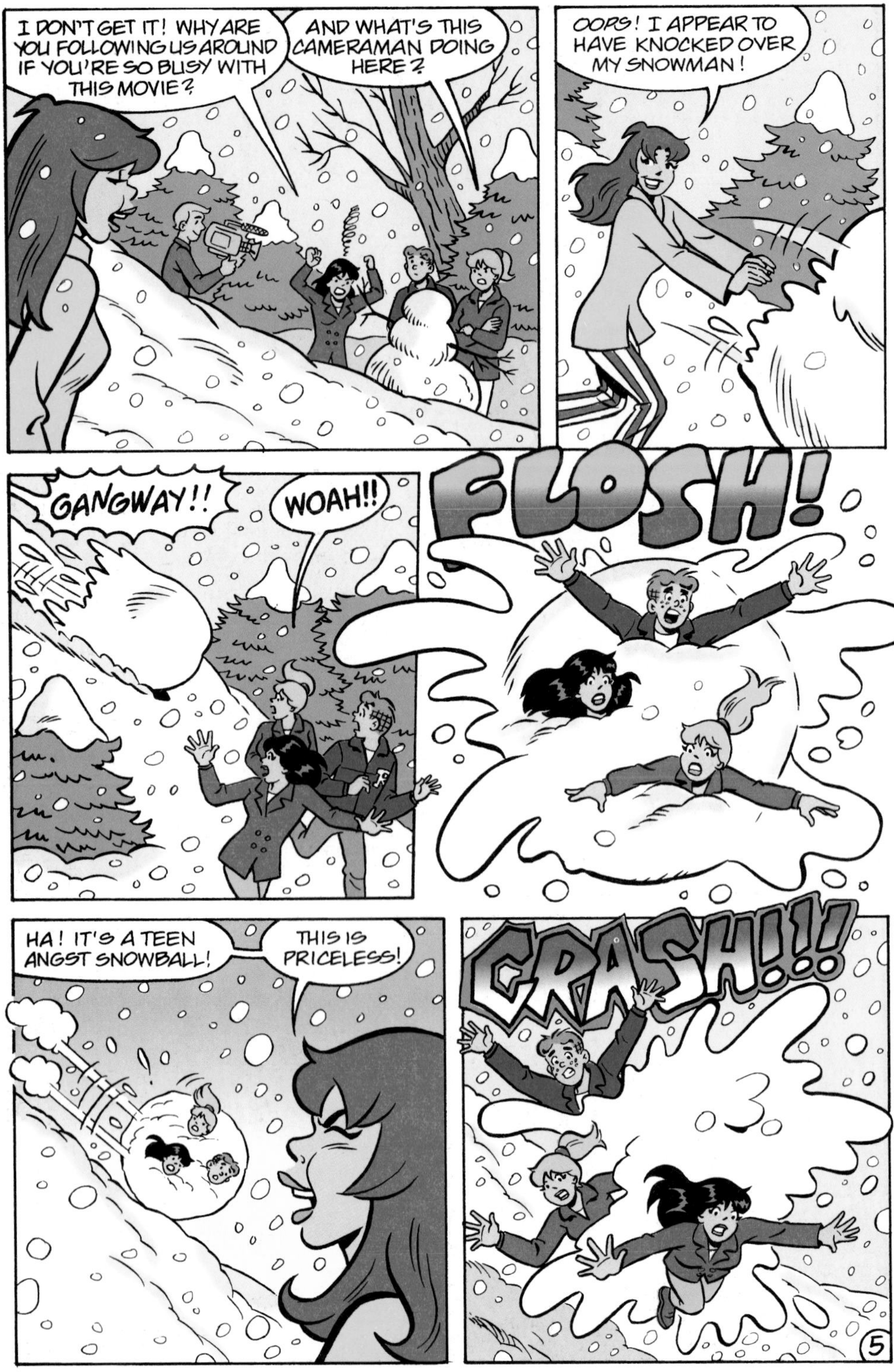

I DON'T GET IT! WHY ARE YOU FOLLOWING US AROUND IF YOU'RE SO BUSY WITH THIS MOVIE?
AND WHAT'S THIS CAMERAMAN DOING HERE?
OOPS! I APPEAR TO HAVE KNOCKED OVER MY SNOWMAN!
GANGWAY!!
WOAH!!
FLOSH!
HA! IT'S A TEEN ANGST SNOWBALL!
THIS IS PRICELESS!
CRASH!!!
5

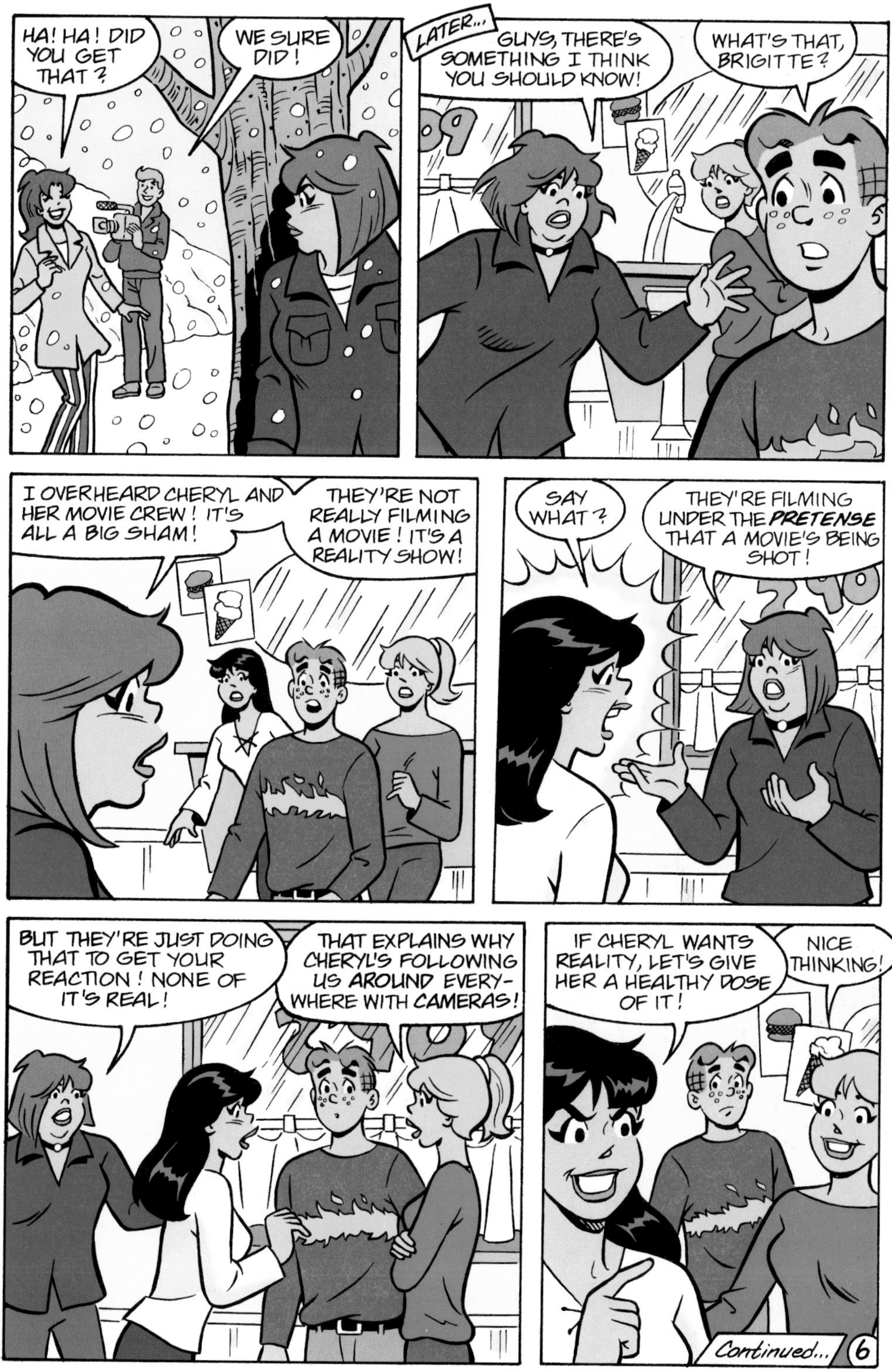
HA! HA! DID YOU GET THAT?
WE SURE DID!
LATER...
GUYS, THERE'S SOMETHING I THINK YOU SHOULD KNOW!
WHAT'S THAT, BRIGITTE?
I OVERHEARD CHERYL AND HER MOVIE CREW! IT'S ALL A BIG SHAM!
THEY'RE NOT REALLY FILMING A MOVIE! IT'S A REALITY SHOW!
SAY WHAT?
THEY'RE FILMING UNDER THE PRETENSE THAT A MOVIE'S BEING SHOT!
BUT THEY'RE JUST DOING THAT TO GET YOUR REACTION! NONE OF IT'S REAL!
THAT EXPLAINS WHY CHERYL'S FOLLOWING US AROUND EVERYWHERE WITH CAMERAS!
IF CHERYL WANTS REALITY, LET'S GIVE HER A HEALTHY DOSE OF IT!
NICE THINKING!
Continued...
6

Archie & Friends in "Lights, Camera, Action!"

Love Showdown II PART 4

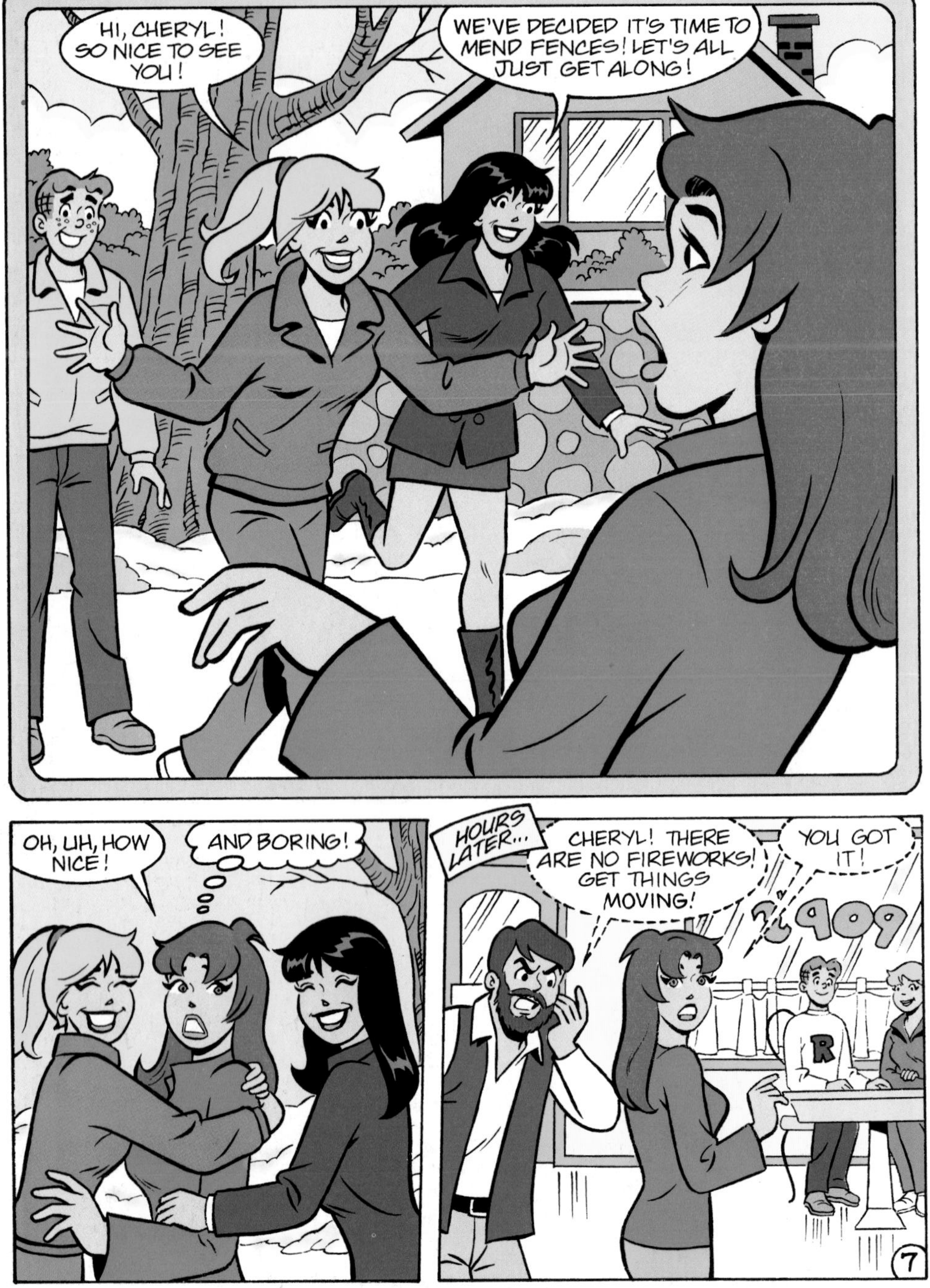
HI, CHERYL! SO NICE TO SEE YOU!
WE'VE DECIDED IT'S TIME TO MEND FENCES! LET'S ALL JUST GET ALONG!
OH, UH, HOW NICE!
AND BORING!
HOURS LATER...
CHERYL! THERE ARE NO FIREWORKS! GET THINGS MOVING!
YOU GOT IT!
R
7

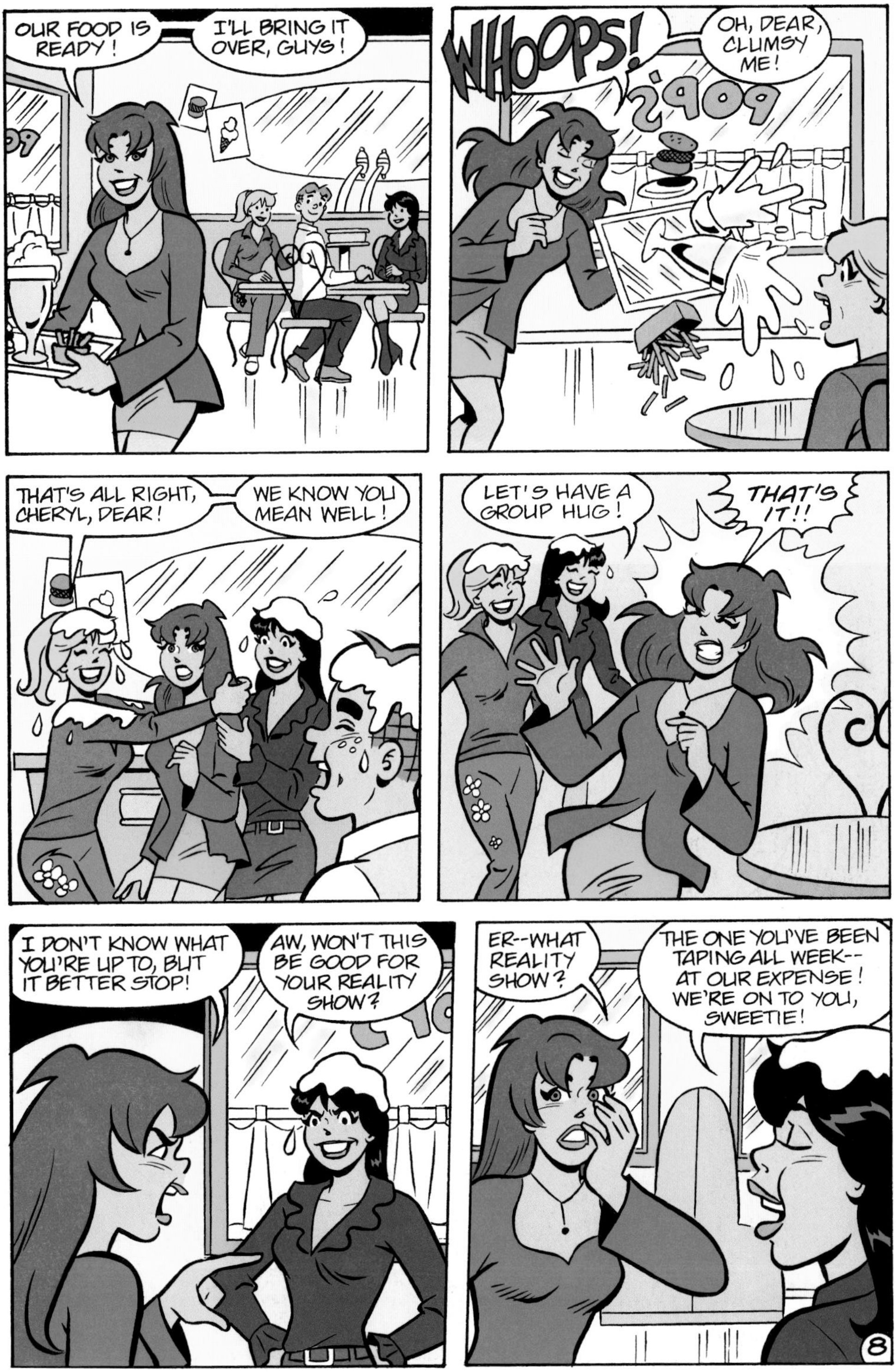

OUR FOOD IS READY!
I'LL BRING IT OVER, GUYS!
WHOOPS!
OH, DEAR, CLUMSY ME!
POP'S
THAT'S ALL RIGHT, CHERYL, DEAR!
WE KNOW YOU MEAN WELL!
LET'S HAVE A GROUP HUG!
THAT'S IT!!
I DON'T KNOW WHAT YOU'RE UP TO, BUT IT BETTER STOP!
AW, WON'T THIS BE GOOD FOR YOUR REALITY SHOW?
ER--WHAT REALITY SHOW?
THE ONE YOU'VE BEEN TAPING ALL WEEK-- AT OUR EXPENSE! WE'RE ON TO YOU, SWEETIE!
8

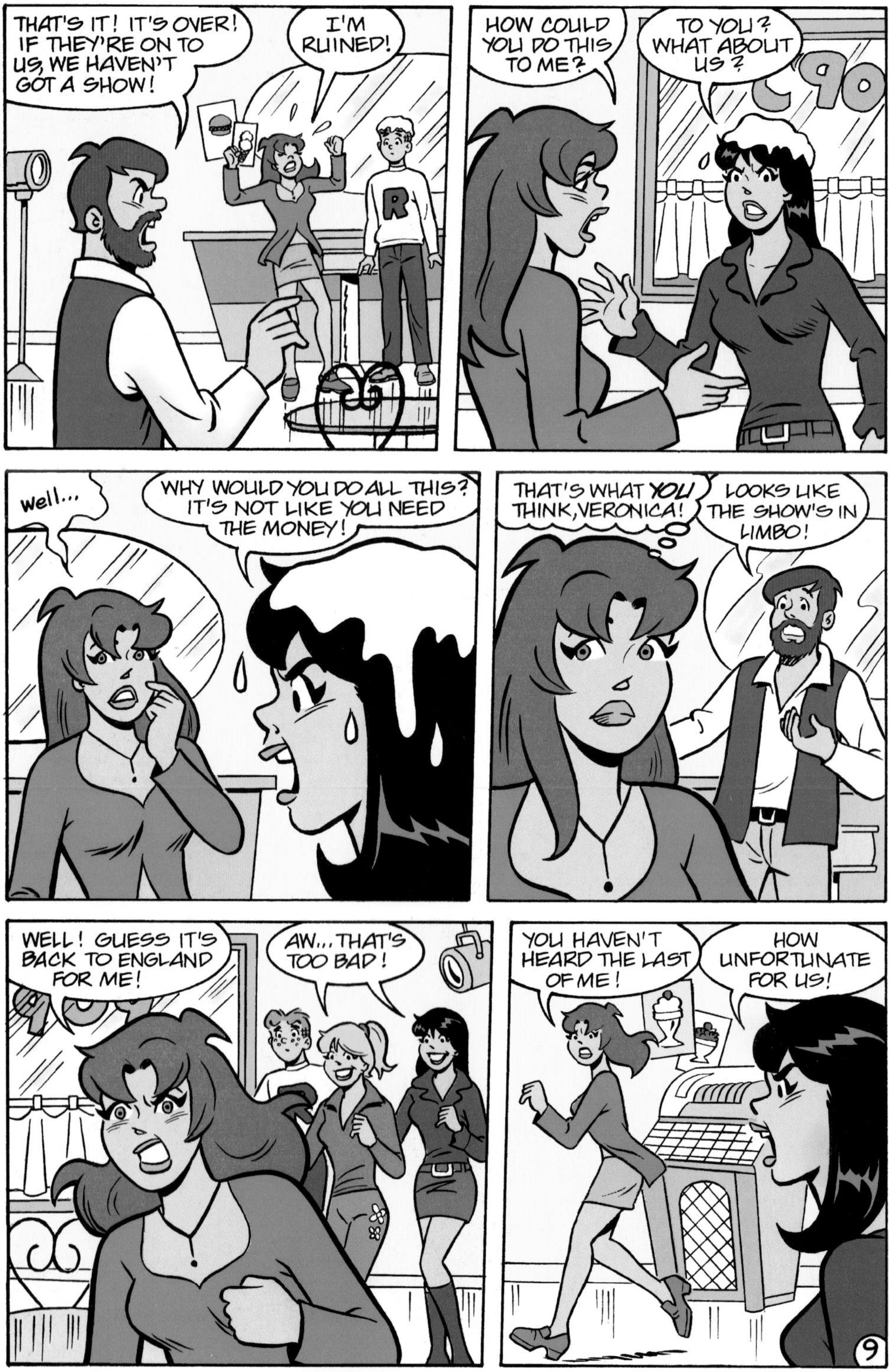
THAT'S IT! IT'S OVER! IF THEY'RE ON TO US, WE HAVEN'T GOT A SHOW!
I'M RUINED!
HOW COULD YOU DO THIS TO ME?
TO YOU? WHAT ABOUT US?
Well...
WHY WOULD YOU DO ALL THIS? IT'S NOT LIKE YOU NEED THE MONEY!
THAT'S WHAT YOU THINK, VERONICA!
LOOKS LIKE THE SHOW'S IN LIMBO!
WELL! GUESS IT'S BACK TO ENGLAND FOR ME!
AW... THAT'S TOO BAD!
YOU HAVEN'T HEARD THE LAST OF ME!
HOW UNFORTUNATE FOR US!
9

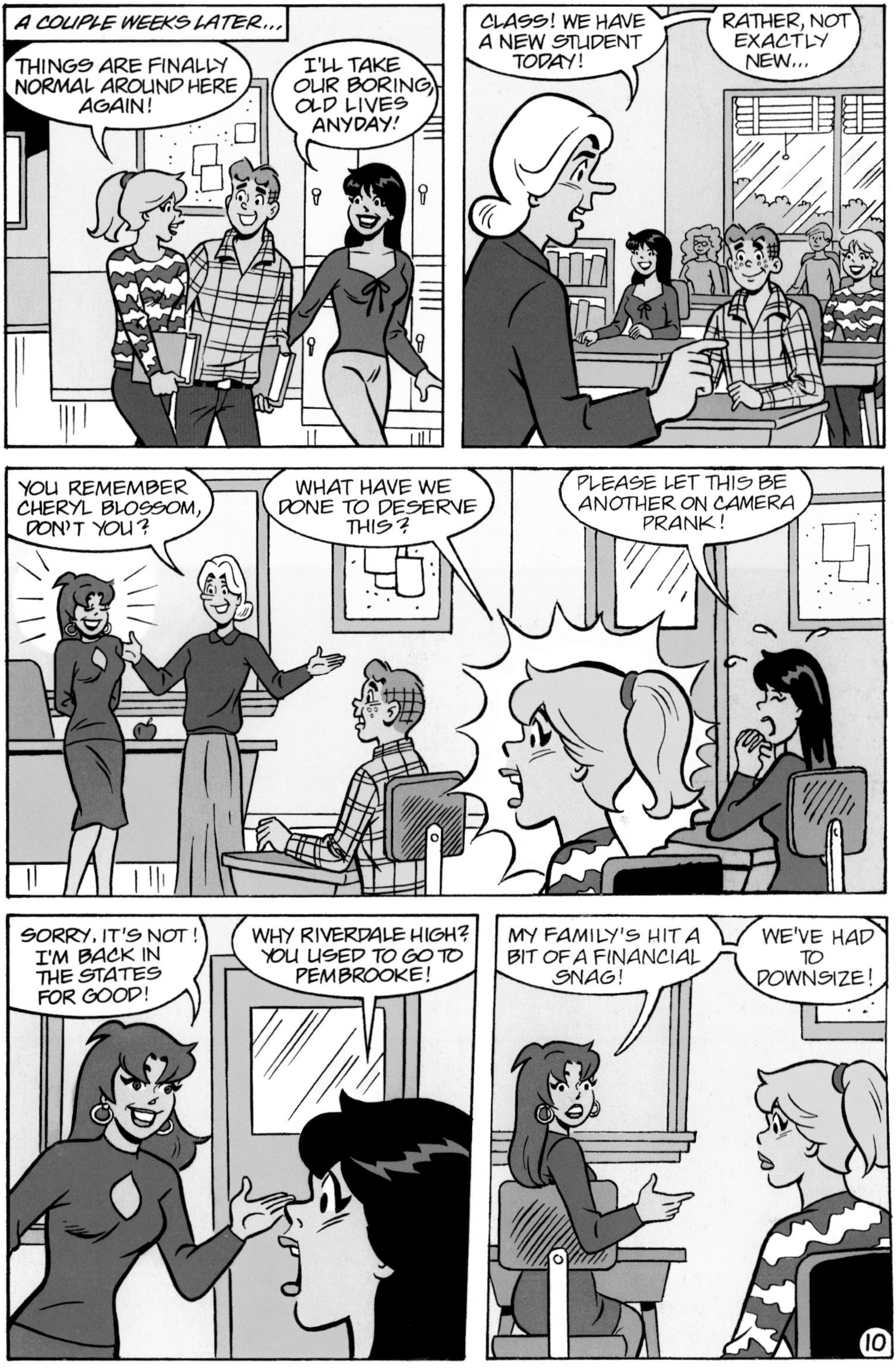
A COUPLE WEEKS LATER...
THINGS ARE FINALLY NORMAL AROUND HERE AGAIN!
I'LL TAKE OUR BORING, OLD LIVES ANYDAY!
CLASS! WE HAVE A NEW STUDENT TODAY!
RATHER, NOT EXACTLY NEW...
YOU REMEMBER CHERYL BLOSSOM, DON'T YOU?
WHAT HAVE WE DONE TO DESERVE THIS?
PLEASE LET THIS BE ANOTHER ON CAMERA PRANK!
SORRY, IT'S NOT! I'M BACK IN THE STATES FOR GOOD!
WHY RIVERDALE HIGH? YOU USED TO GO TO PEMBROOKE!
MY FAMILY'S HIT A BIT OF A FINANCIAL SNAG!
WE'VE HAD TO DOWNSIZE!
10

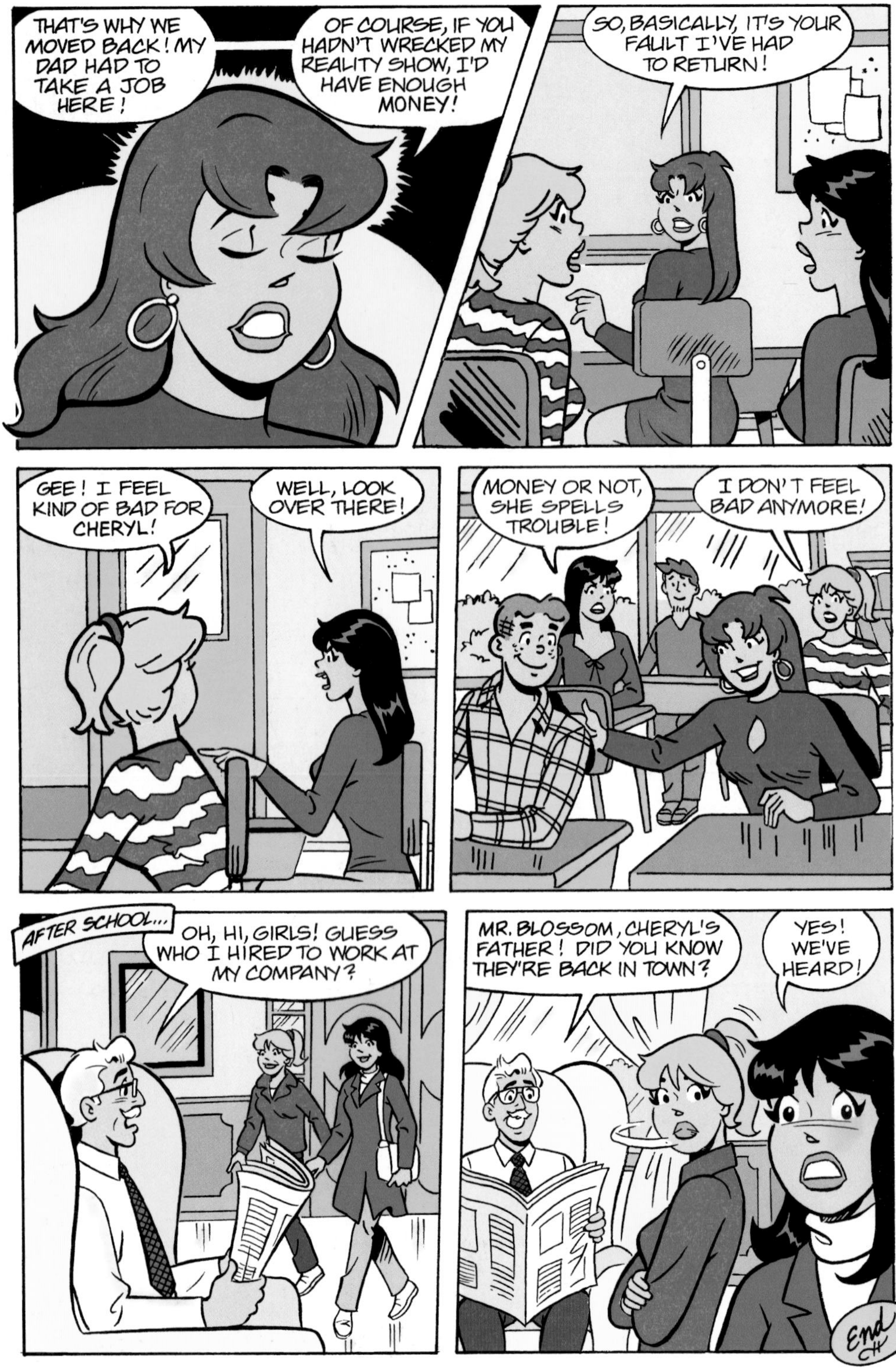
THAT'S WHY WE MOVED BACK! MY DAD HAD TO TAKE A JOB HERE!
OF COURSE, IF YOU HADN'T WRECKED MY REALITY SHOW, I'D HAVE ENOUGH MONEY!
SO, BASICALLY, IT'S YOUR FAULT I'VE HAD TO RETURN!
GEE! I FEEL KIND OF BAD FOR CHERYL!
WELL, LOOK OVER THERE!
MONEY OR NOT, SHE SPELLS TROUBLE!
I DON'T FEEL BAD ANYMORE!
AFTER SCHOOL...
OH, HI, GIRLS! GUESS WHO I HIRED TO WORK AT MY COMPANY?
MR. BLOSSOM, CHERYL'S FATHER! DID YOU KNOW THEY'RE BACK IN TOWN?
YES! WE'VE HEARD!
End

♥ BONUS CONTENT ♥

Archie®
Love Showdown

The 1990s were a time of rapid change in the comics industry. As the decade progressed, publishers attempted to keep up with their competitors as gimmicks ranging from holographic covers to major events designed to shake up the status quo were carefully planned and executed. All this was occurring while the Internet began to become a part of everyday life, forever changing the way we buy and read comics.

Having just come out of a period of creative experimentation that resulted in fan-favorite titles like *Jughead's Time Police* and *Dilton's Strange Science*, Archie Comics entered the event comic fray with 1994's *Love Showdown*. Published across the titles *Archie* #429, *Betty* #19, *Betty and Veronica* #82, and *Veronica* #39, this storyline attempted to do the impossible: Make Archie choose between Betty and Veronica once and for all.

The primary writers and artists for this landmark miniseries were Archie legends Dan Parent and Bill Golliher. For the saga's 30th anniversary, they shared their thoughts on this iconic comic, its sequels, and the Love Showdown's enduring legacy.

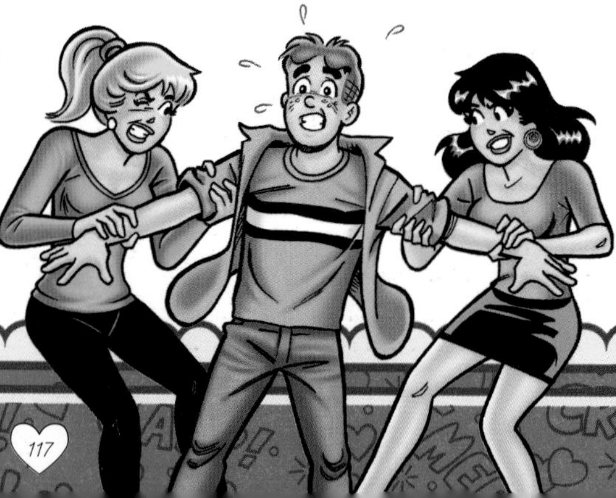

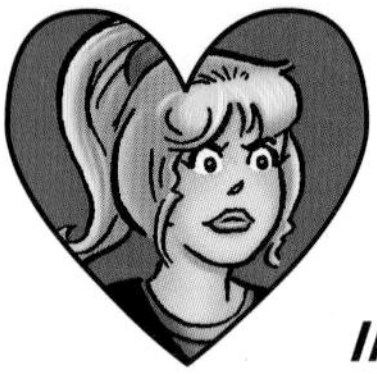

THE LOVE SHOWDOWN REVEALED

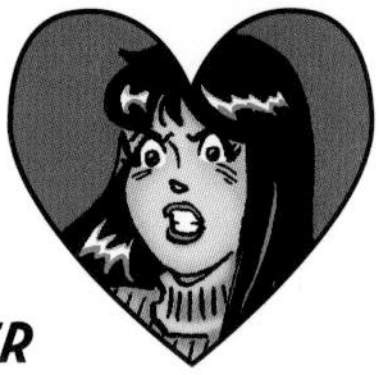

INTERVIEW WITH DAN PARENT AND BILL GOLLIHER

How did you first get involved with working on *Love Showdown*?

Dan Parent: The editors told us to come up with a multi-arc story that would cross over into different titles. Archie hadn't really done that before, but a few other companies had started doing the crossover events and things like that. We just wanted to do something that would cross over into like four or five Archie titles.

Bill Golliher: It was not long after the death of Superman, and the owners and the editor were trying to come up with something to get some headlines for Archie. They asked Dan and I to come up with some ideas. We were both Cheryl fans from back in the day, she was introduced in the early '80s and then disappeared after a few years and faded into the background. We thought it might be a good time to bring her back. Then the kicker was that Archie was finally going to decide on one of the girls. Everybody would assume it would be Betty or Veronica, and then it was Cheryl.

DP: And that was the basic premise we came up with, that Archie was going to choose somebody other than Betty and Veronica.

With this being such a big event for the company and the storyline spanning the multiple titles, did the ambitiousness of the project impact your creative approach to it at all?

DP: We thought it would be an interesting project from a creative standpoint, but we didn't really think it would become a big event. If there had been pressure to make it a big event, then it might've stifled the creativity, but there wasn't any of that.

BG: It was fun working with the Cheryl character and her interactions with Betty and Veronica, or especially Veronica, because they had a conflict going on.

How did the creative process work in terms of who was telling what story and dividing up the writing tasks?

DP: We just mapped out the storyline. We had it tightly plotted so that I could write one issue and Bill could write the other issue to where it would flow pretty seamlessly.

BG: We've always been good friends since our Kubert school days, and we wound up both working at Archie. So we were spending a lot of time together, and we had a lot of time to talk about it and develop it so that worked out well.

Let's talk about Cheryl Blossom. She isn't so much a character as she is a force of nature. Was it challenging to write for her?

DP: Writing her character just is very easy. She's a pretty blunt character. What you see is what you get kind of thing. It was very easy to write her. The main issue was just allowing the powers that be to let us bring her back. She had been cast away for a reason, because she was considered to be too risque of a character.

BG: No, I don't think so. I went back before we actually wrote it and read more of her (previous) dialogue and kind of got an idea of where she was coming from. It's almost like Veronica squared.

Looking back 30 years on, how do you feel about this project and its enduring legacy?

DP: It's great that it's endured this long and that it got the coverage it did. As regular comic book artists and writers, we weren't used to any sort of attention. This was all over mainstream news. We were on *Good Morning America*, *Extra*, and *Entertainment Tonight* being interviewed. It just was out of the norm.

But another thing I appreciate more about Love Showdown is that a lot of people started reading Archie at that point. I see a lot of people at shows who will say, "Oh yeah, Love Showdown. That's what got me reading Archie Comics." So, that was a great benefit from it.

BG: I think it surprised us that it did get the attention that it did. And I don't know if it was the times, because of the death of Superman that people were paying more attention to comics, but it was just wild that it got that much attention. It was a lot of fun.

Interview by CHRIS CUMMINS

Betty vs Veronica

Through the ages

SMACK!

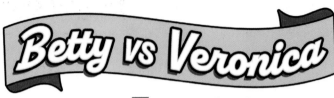

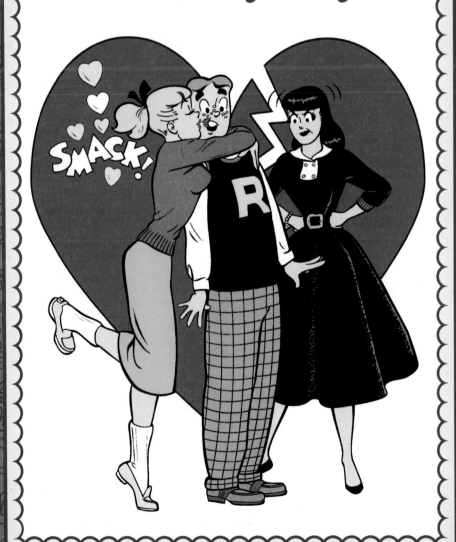

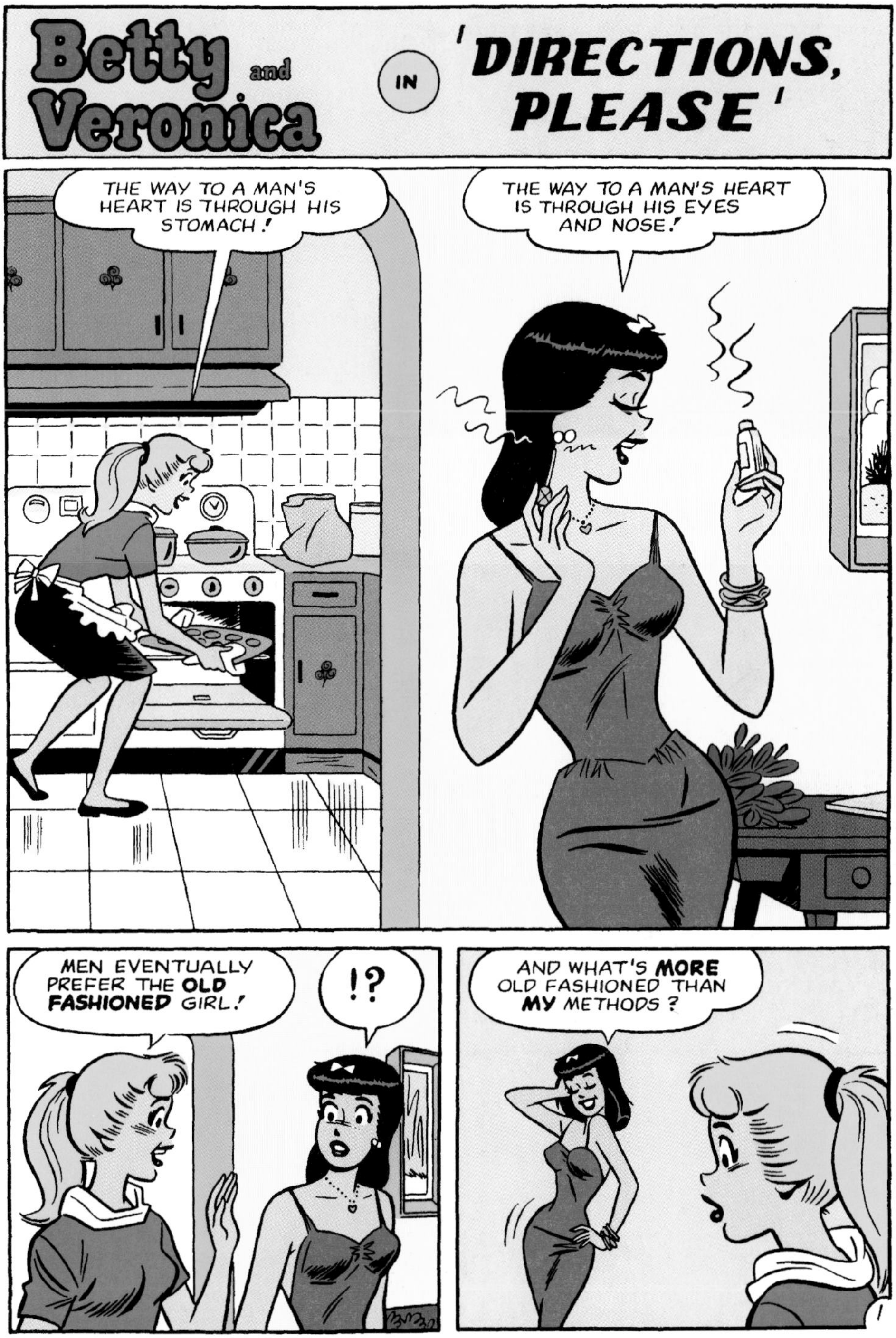
Betty and Veronica
IN
'DIRECTIONS, PLEASE'
THE WAY TO A MAN'S HEART IS THROUGH HIS STOMACH!
THE WAY TO A MAN'S HEART IS THROUGH HIS EYES AND NOSE!
MEN EVENTUALLY PREFER THE **OLD FASHIONED** GIRL!
!?
AND WHAT'S **MORE** OLD FASHIONED THAN **MY** METHODS?
1

ORIGINALLY PRINTED IN ARCHIE'S GIRLS BETTY & VERONICA #91, JULY 1963

FRANK DOYLE • DAN DECARLO • RUDY LAPICK • VINCENT DECARLO

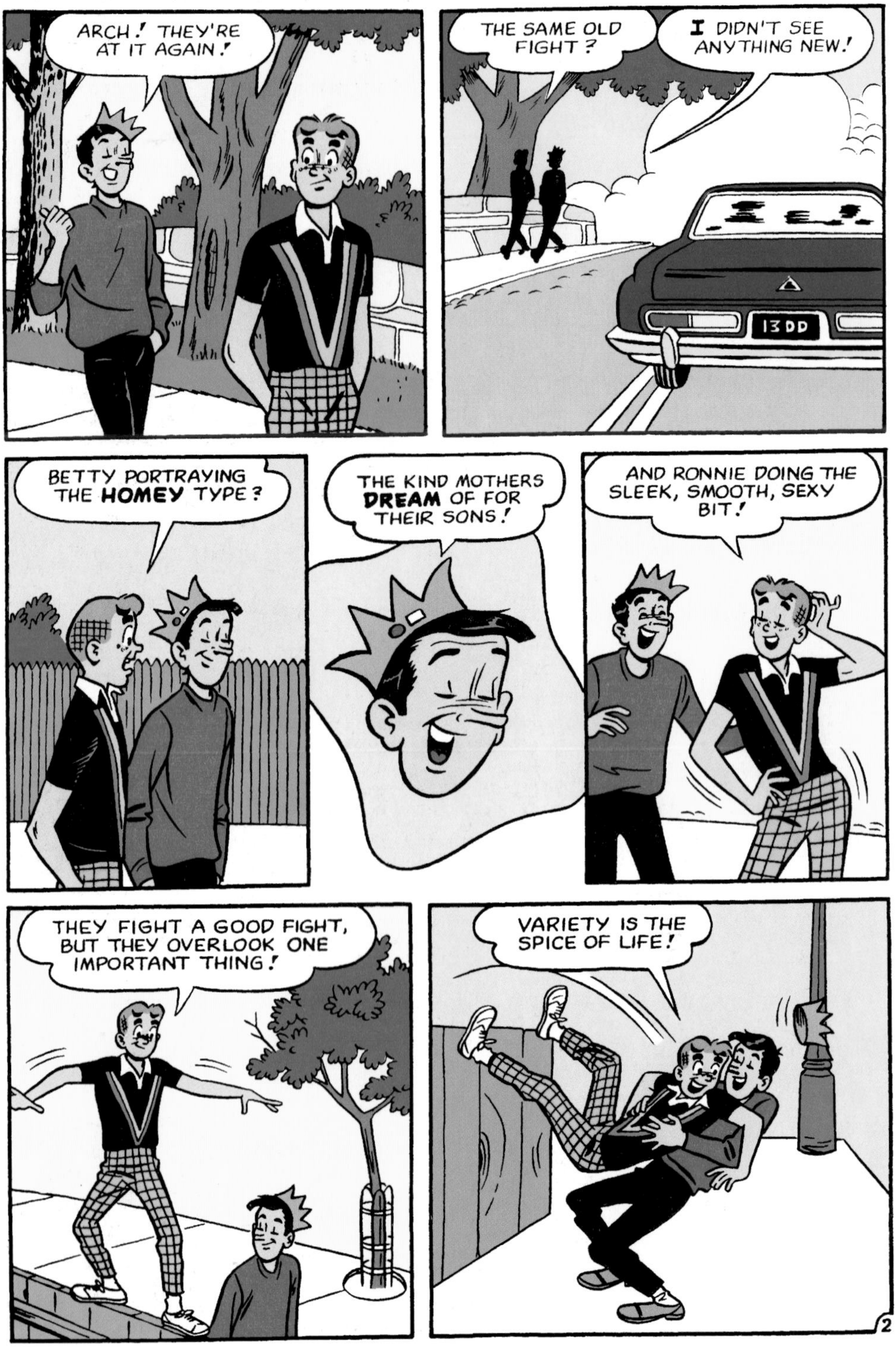

ARCH! THEY'RE AT IT AGAIN!
THE SAME OLD FIGHT?
I DIDN'T SEE ANYTHING NEW!
13 DD
BETTY PORTRAYING THE HOMEY TYPE?
THE KIND MOTHERS DREAM OF FOR THEIR SONS!
AND RONNIE DOING THE SLEEK, SMOOTH, SEXY BIT!
THEY FIGHT A GOOD FIGHT, BUT THEY OVERLOOK ONE IMPORTANT THING!
VARIETY IS THE SPICE OF LIFE!
2

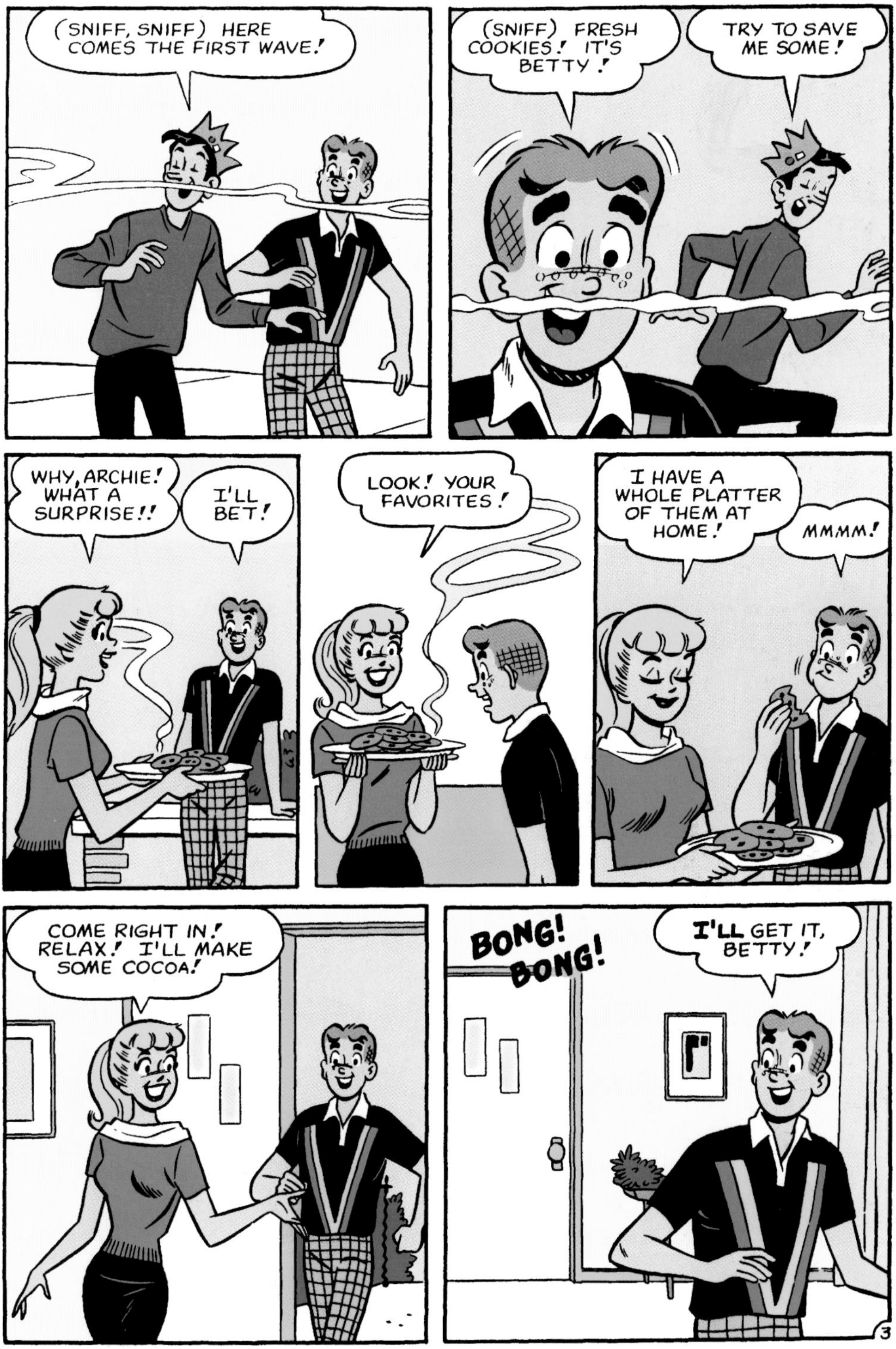
(SNIFF, SNIFF) HERE COMES THE FIRST WAVE!
(SNIFF) FRESH COOKIES! IT'S BETTY!
TRY TO SAVE ME SOME!
WHY, ARCHIE! WHAT A SURPRISE!!
I'LL BET!
LOOK! YOUR FAVORITES!
I HAVE A WHOLE PLATTER OF THEM AT HOME!
MMMM!
COME RIGHT IN! RELAX! I'LL MAKE SOME COCOA!
BONG! BONG!
I'LL GET IT, BETTY!
3

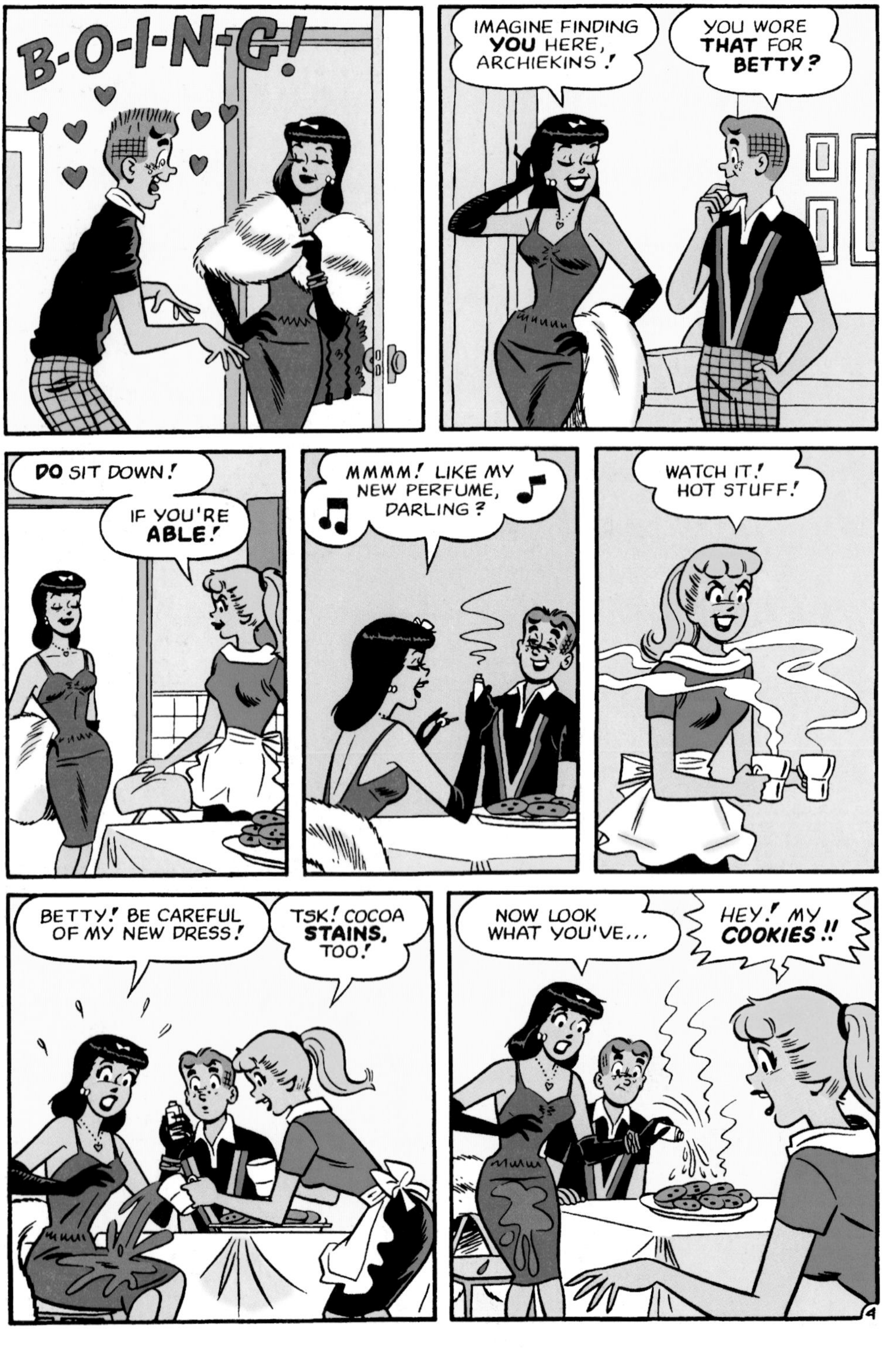
B-O-I-N-G!
IMAGINE FINDING YOU HERE, ARCHIEKINS!
YOU WORE THAT FOR BETTY?
DO SIT DOWN!
IF YOU'RE ABLE!
MMMM! LIKE MY NEW PERFUME, DARLING?
WATCH IT! HOT STUFF!
BETTY! BE CAREFUL OF MY NEW DRESS!
TSK! COCOA STAINS, TOO!
NOW LOOK WHAT YOU'VE...
HEY! MY COOKIES!!
4

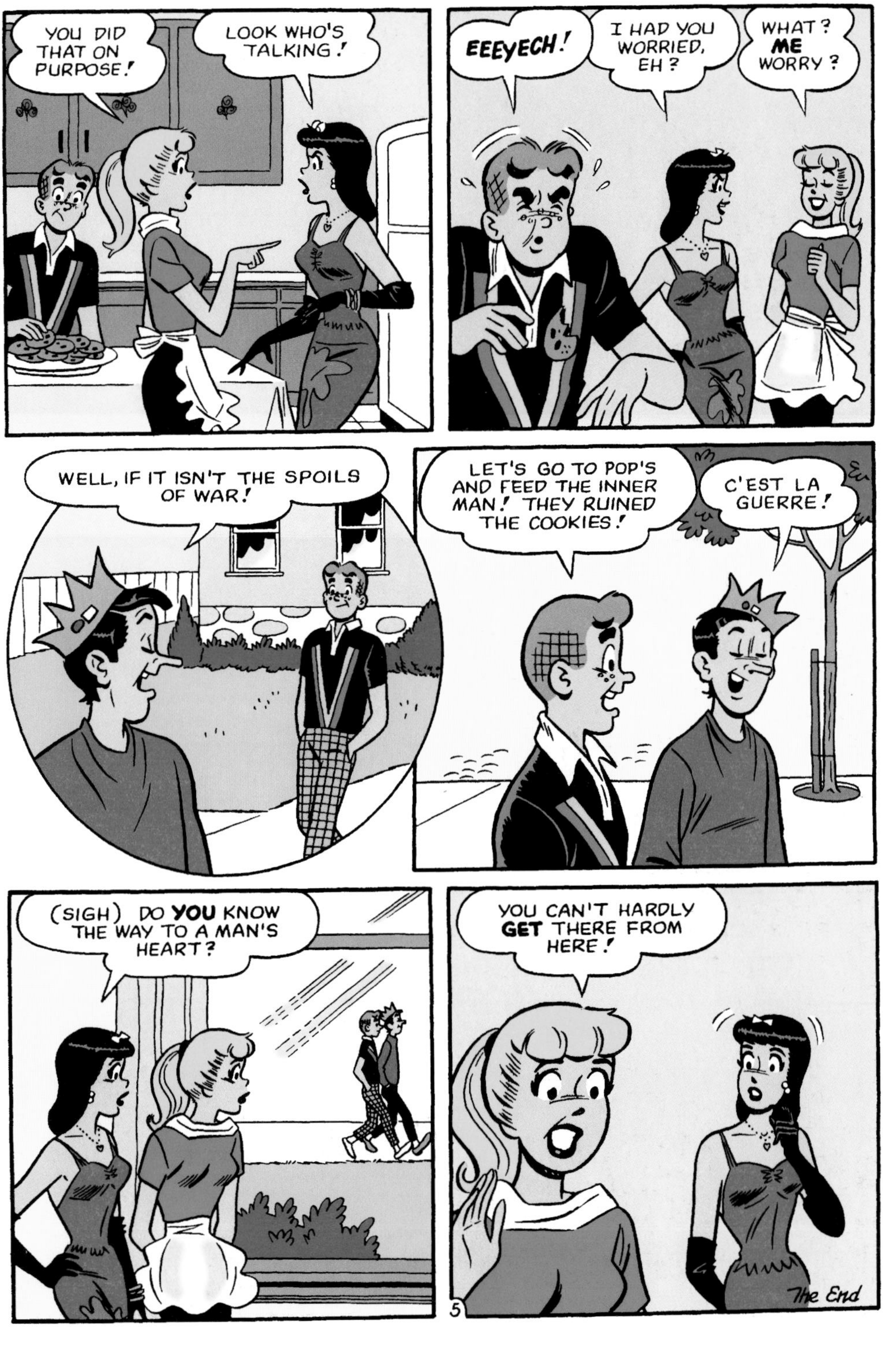
YOU DID THAT ON PURPOSE!
LOOK WHO'S TALKING!
EEEYECH!
I HAD YOU WORRIED, EH?
WHAT? **ME** WORRY?
WELL, IF IT ISN'T THE SPOILS OF WAR!
LET'S GO TO POP'S AND FEED THE INNER MAN! THEY RUINED THE COOKIES!
C'EST LA GUERRE!
(SIGH) DO **YOU** KNOW THE WAY TO A MAN'S HEART?
YOU CAN'T HARDLY **GET** THERE FROM HERE!
5
The End

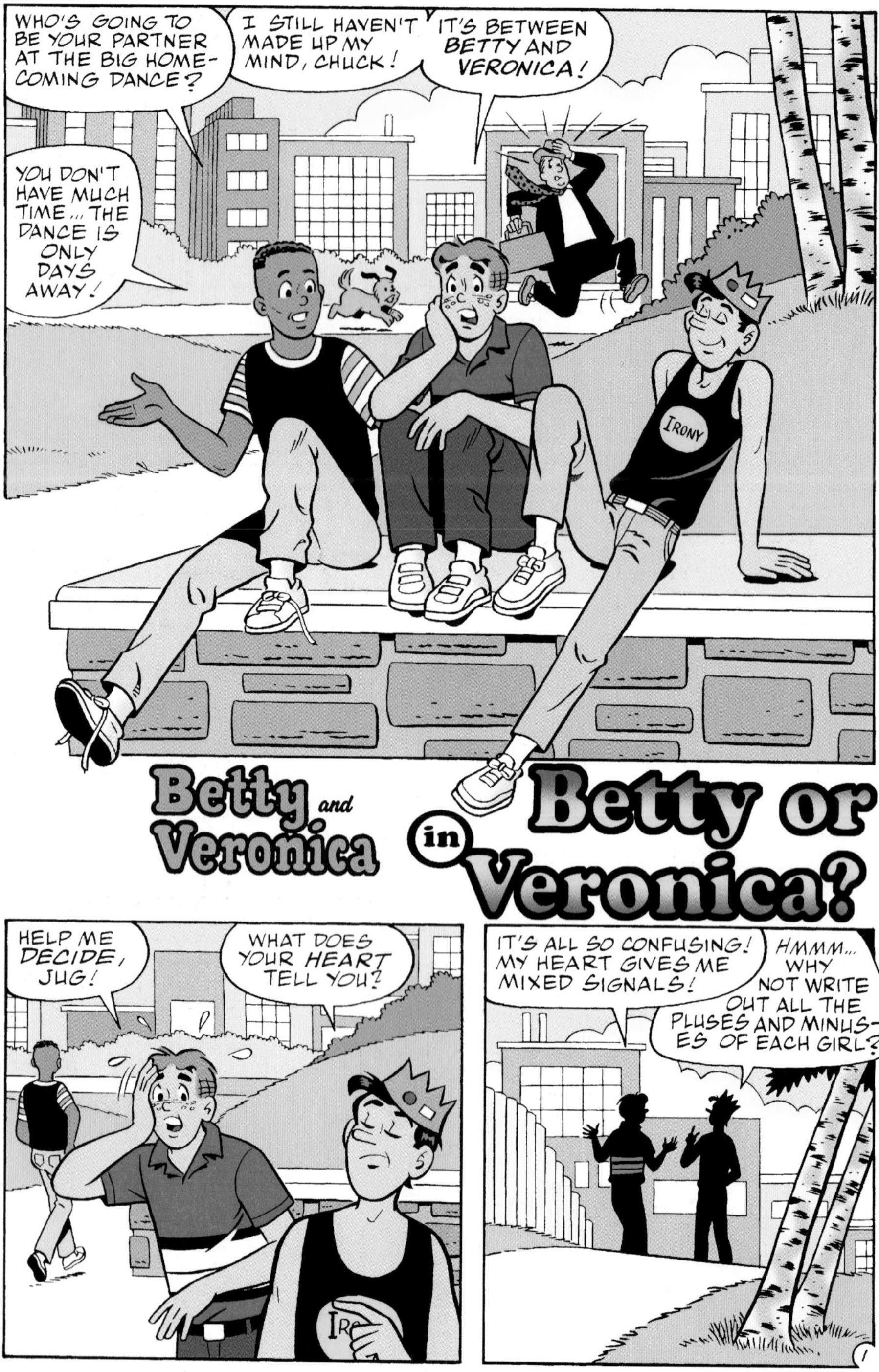

WHO'S GOING TO BE YOUR PARTNER AT THE BIG HOME-COMING DANCE?
I STILL HAVEN'T MADE UP MY MIND, CHUCK!
IT'S BETWEEN BETTY AND VERONICA!
YOU DON'T HAVE MUCH TIME... THE DANCE IS ONLY DAYS AWAY!
IRONY
Betty and Veronica in Betty or Veronica?
HELP ME DECIDE, JUG!
WHAT DOES YOUR HEART TELL YOU?
IT'S ALL SO CONFUSING! MY HEART GIVES ME MIXED SIGNALS!
HMMM... WHY NOT WRITE OUT ALL THE PLUSES AND MINUSES OF EACH GIRL?
1

ORIGINALLY PRINTED IN BETTY & VERONICA DOUBLE DIGEST #136, OCTOBER 2005

GEORGE GLADIR • PAT KENNEDY • JON D'AGOSTINO • JACK MORELLI • BARRY GROSSMAN

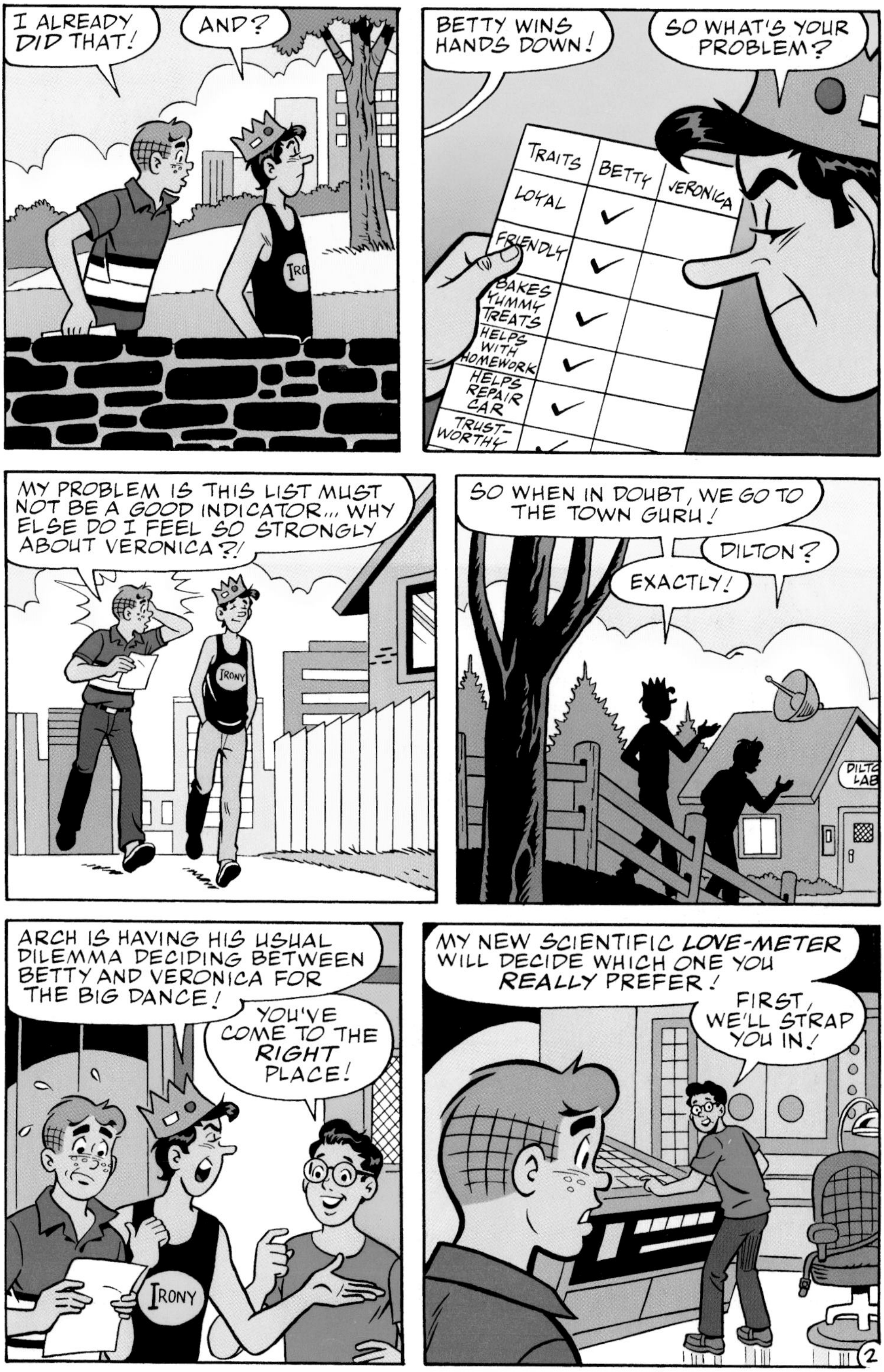
I ALREADY DID THAT!
AND?
BETTY WINS HANDS DOWN!
SO WHAT'S YOUR PROBLEM?
TRAITS
BETTY
VERONICA
LOYAL
FRIENDLY
BAKES YUMMY TREATS
HELPS WITH HOMEWORK
HELPS REPAIR CAR
TRUST-WORTHY
MY PROBLEM IS THIS LIST MUST NOT BE A GOOD INDICATOR... WHY ELSE DO I FEEL SO STRONGLY ABOUT VERONICA?!
IRONY
SO WHEN IN DOUBT, WE GO TO THE TOWN GURU!
DILTON?
EXACTLY!
ARCH IS HAVING HIS USUAL DILEMMA DECIDING BETWEEN BETTY AND VERONICA FOR THE BIG DANCE!
YOU'VE COME TO THE RIGHT PLACE!
IRONY
MY NEW SCIENTIFIC LOVE-METER WILL DECIDE WHICH ONE YOU REALLY PREFER!
FIRST, WE'LL STRAP YOU IN!
2

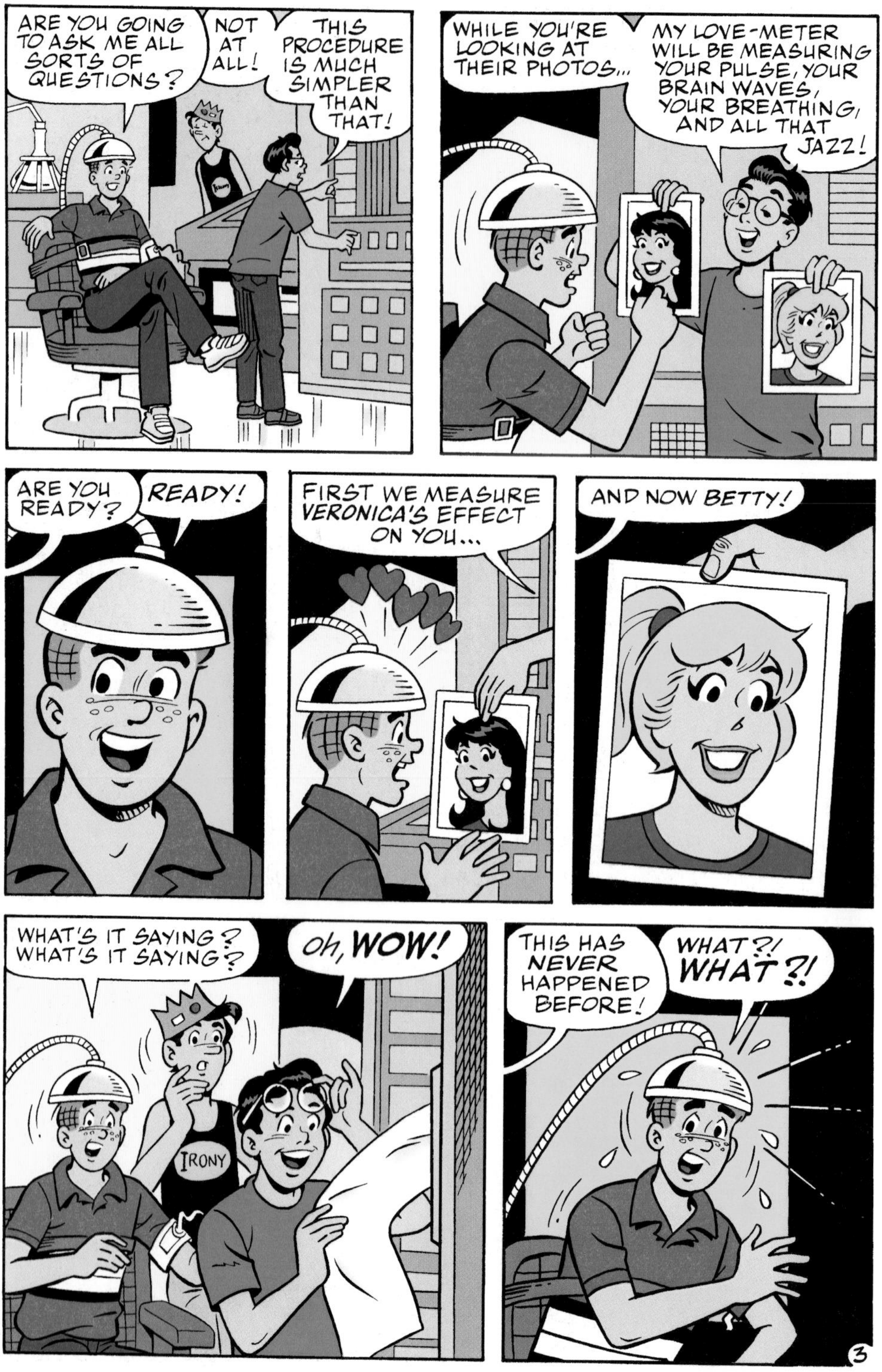

ARE YOU GOING TO ASK ME ALL SORTS OF QUESTIONS?
NOT AT ALL!
THIS PROCEDURE IS MUCH SIMPLER THAN THAT!
WHILE YOU'RE LOOKING AT THEIR PHOTOS...
MY LOVE-METER WILL BE MEASURING YOUR PULSE, YOUR BRAIN WAVES, YOUR BREATHING, AND ALL THAT JAZZ!
ARE YOU READY?
READY!
FIRST WE MEASURE VERONICA'S EFFECT ON YOU...
AND NOW BETTY!
WHAT'S IT SAYING? WHAT'S IT SAYING?
oh, WOW!
IRONY
THIS HAS NEVER HAPPENED BEFORE!
WHAT?! WHAT?!
3

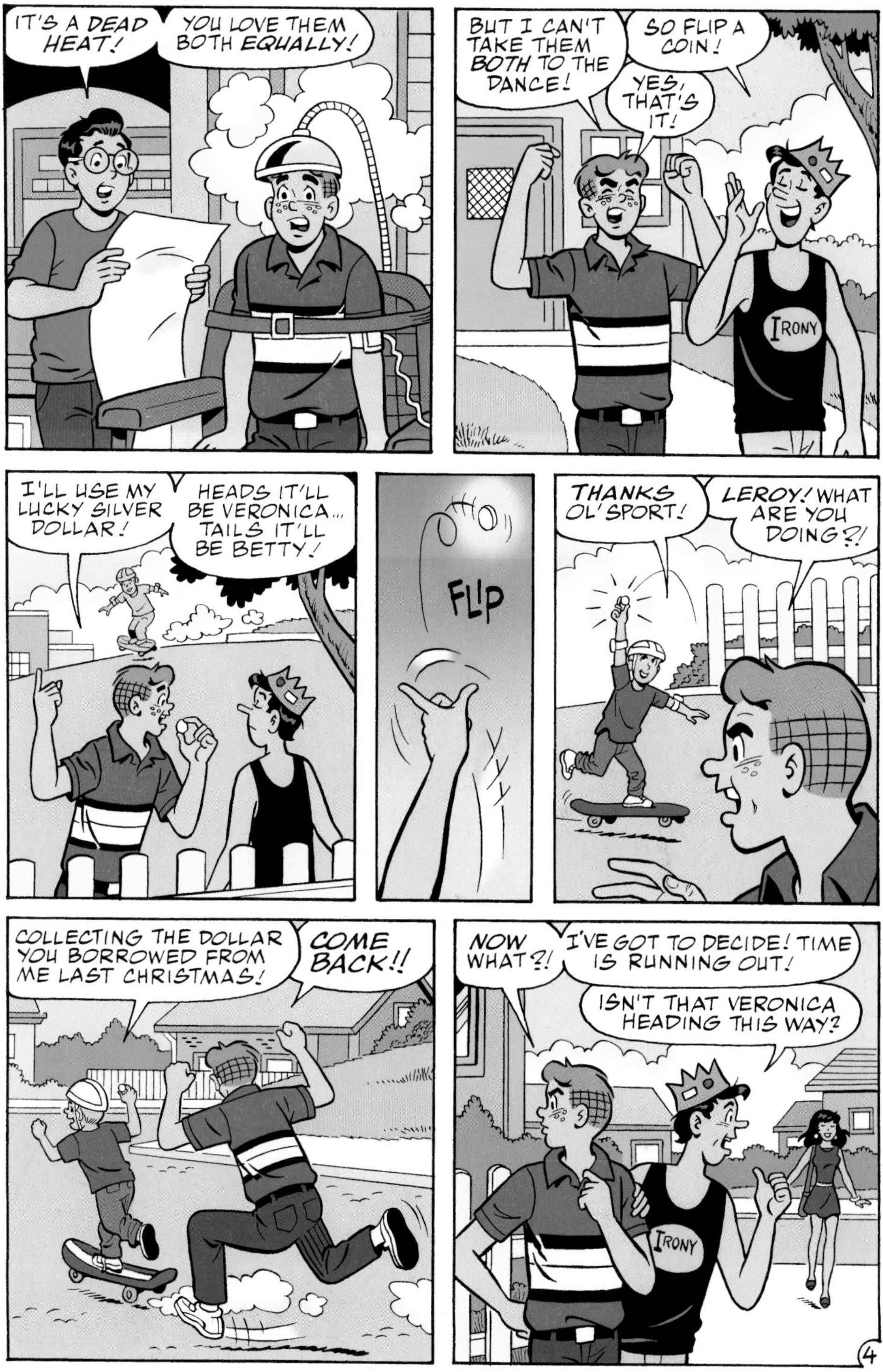
IT'S A DEAD HEAT!
YOU LOVE THEM BOTH EQUALLY!
BUT I CAN'T TAKE THEM BOTH TO THE DANCE!
SO FLIP A COIN!
YES, THAT'S IT!
IRONY
I'LL USE MY LUCKY SILVER DOLLAR!
HEADS IT'LL BE VERONICA... TAILS IT'LL BE BETTY!
FLIP
THANKS OL' SPORT!
LEROY! WHAT ARE YOU DOING?!
COLLECTING THE DOLLAR YOU BORROWED FROM ME LAST CHRISTMAS!
COME BACK!!
NOW WHAT?!
I'VE GOT TO DECIDE! TIME IS RUNNING OUT!
ISN'T THAT VERONICA HEADING THIS WAY?
IRONY
4

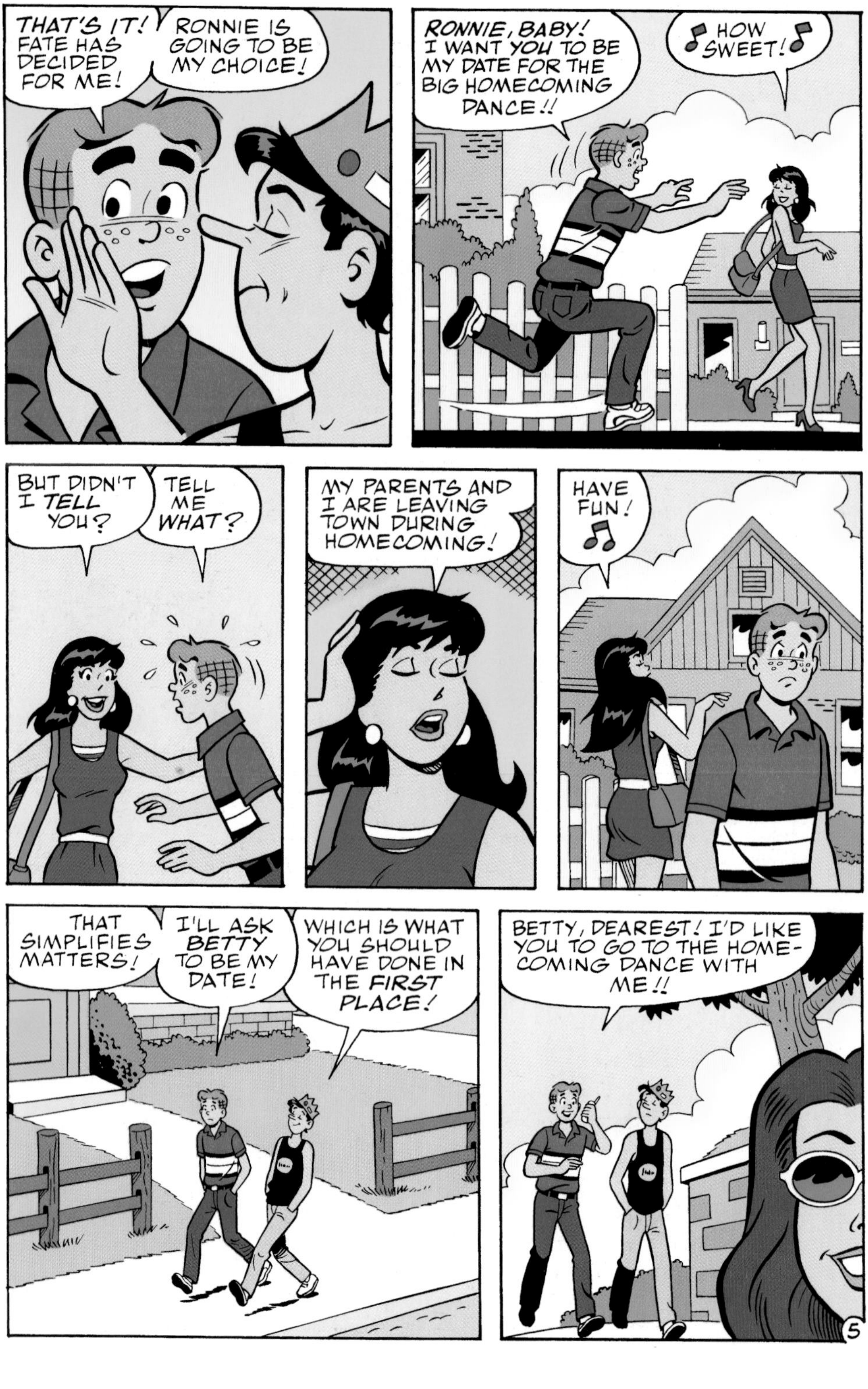
THAT'S IT! FATE HAS DECIDED FOR ME!
RONNIE IS GOING TO BE MY CHOICE!
RONNIE, BABY! I WANT YOU TO BE MY DATE FOR THE BIG HOMECOMING DANCE!!
HOW SWEET!
BUT DIDN'T I TELL YOU?
TELL ME WHAT?
MY PARENTS AND I ARE LEAVING TOWN DURING HOMECOMING!
HAVE FUN!
THAT SIMPLIFIES MATTERS!
I'LL ASK BETTY TO BE MY DATE!
WHICH IS WHAT YOU SHOULD HAVE DONE IN THE FIRST PLACE!
BETTY, DEAREST! I'D LIKE YOU TO GO TO THE HOME-COMING DANCE WITH ME!!
5

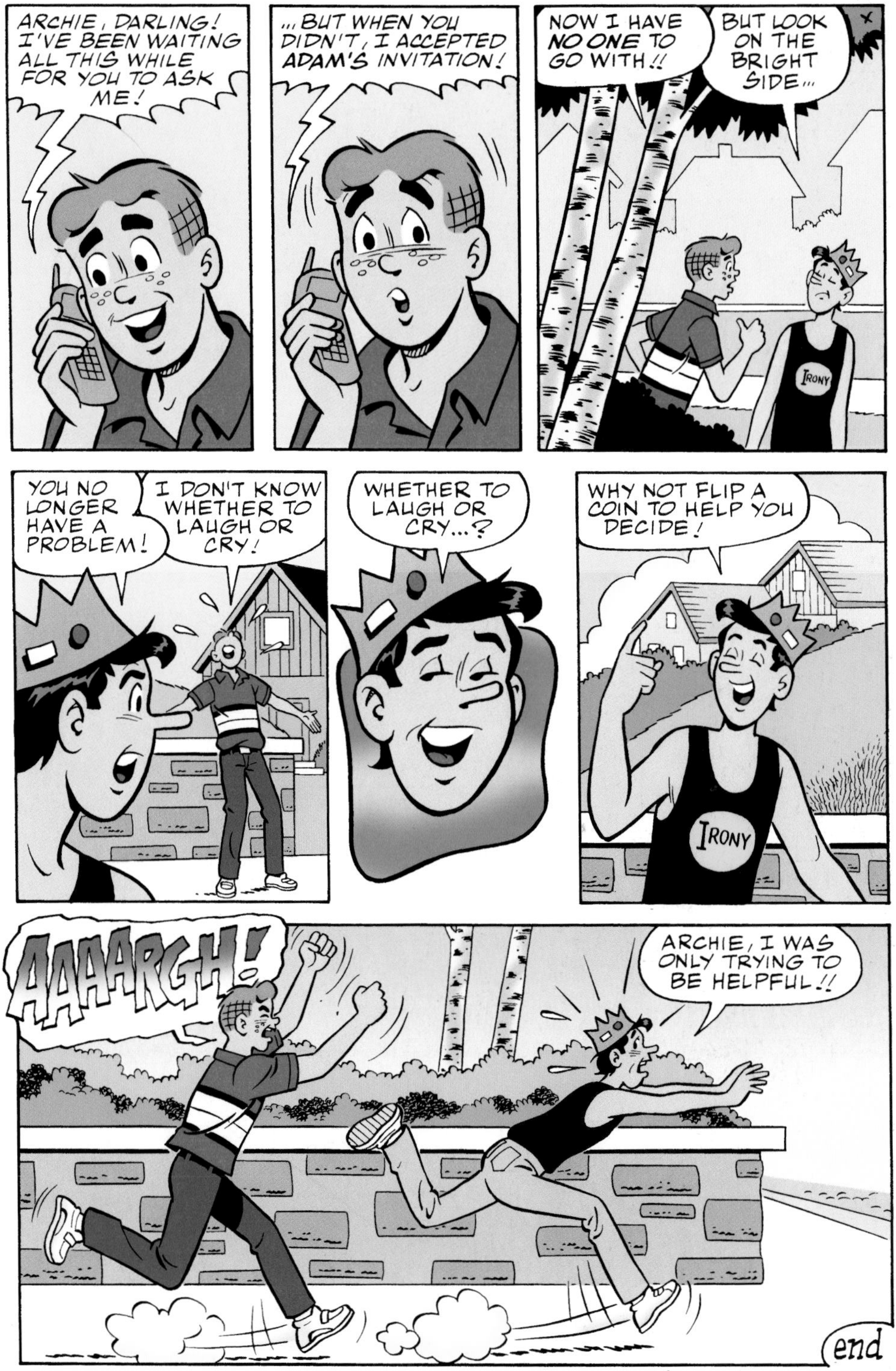
ARCHIE, DARLING! I'VE BEEN WAITING ALL THIS WHILE FOR YOU TO ASK ME!
...BUT WHEN YOU DIDN'T, I ACCEPTED ADAM'S INVITATION!
NOW I HAVE NO ONE TO GO WITH!!
BUT LOOK ON THE BRIGHT SIDE...
IRONY
YOU NO LONGER HAVE A PROBLEM!
I DON'T KNOW WHETHER TO LAUGH OR CRY!
WHETHER TO LAUGH OR CRY...?
WHY NOT FLIP A COIN TO HELP YOU DECIDE!
IRONY
AAAARGH!
ARCHIE, I WAS ONLY TRYING TO BE HELPFUL!!
end

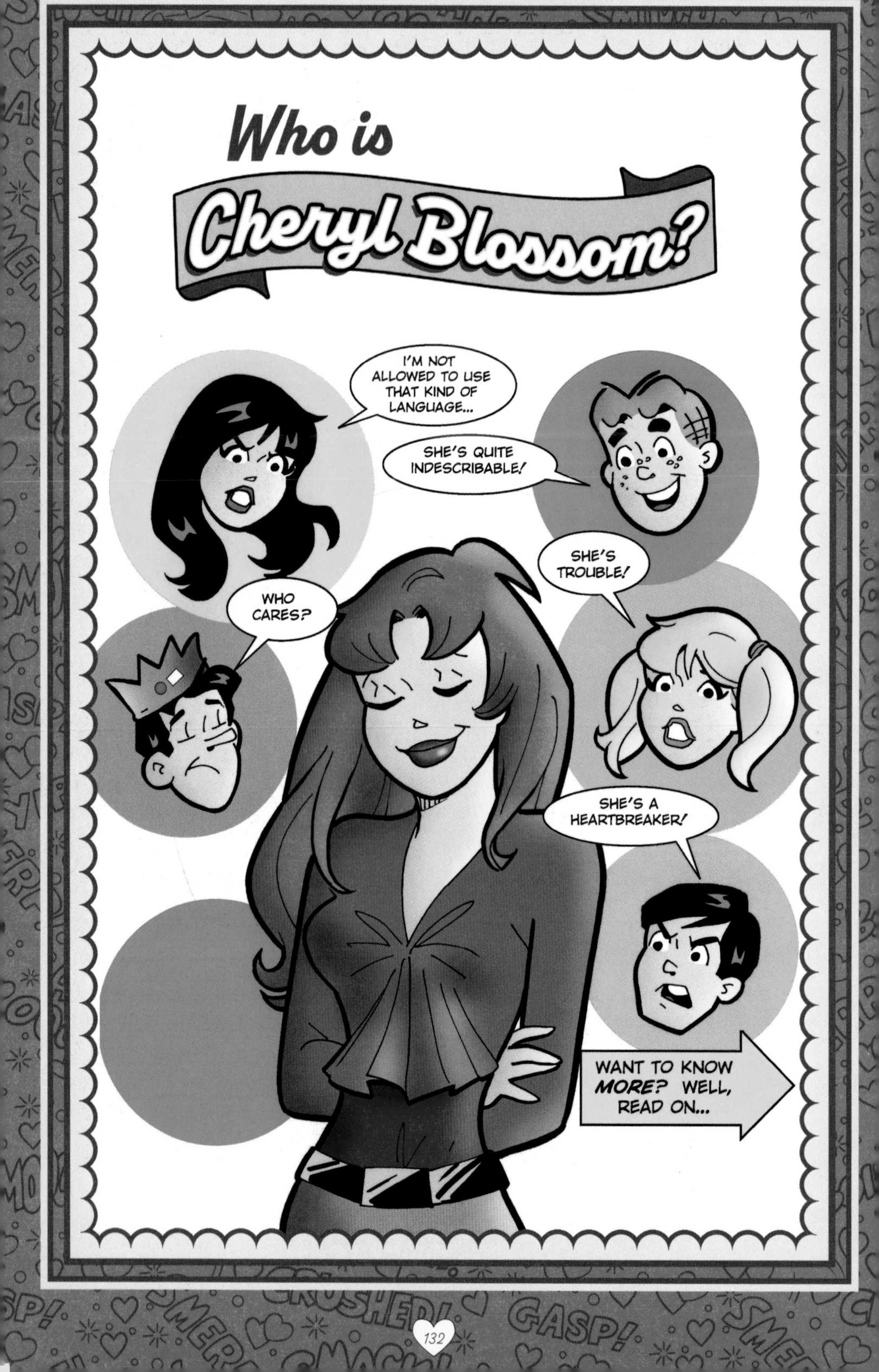
Who is
Cheryl Blossom?
I'M NOT ALLOWED TO USE THAT KIND OF LANGUAGE...
SHE'S QUITE INDESCRIBABLE!
SHE'S TROUBLE!
WHO CARES?
SHE'S A HEARTBREAKER!
WANT TO KNOW MORE? WELL, READ ON...

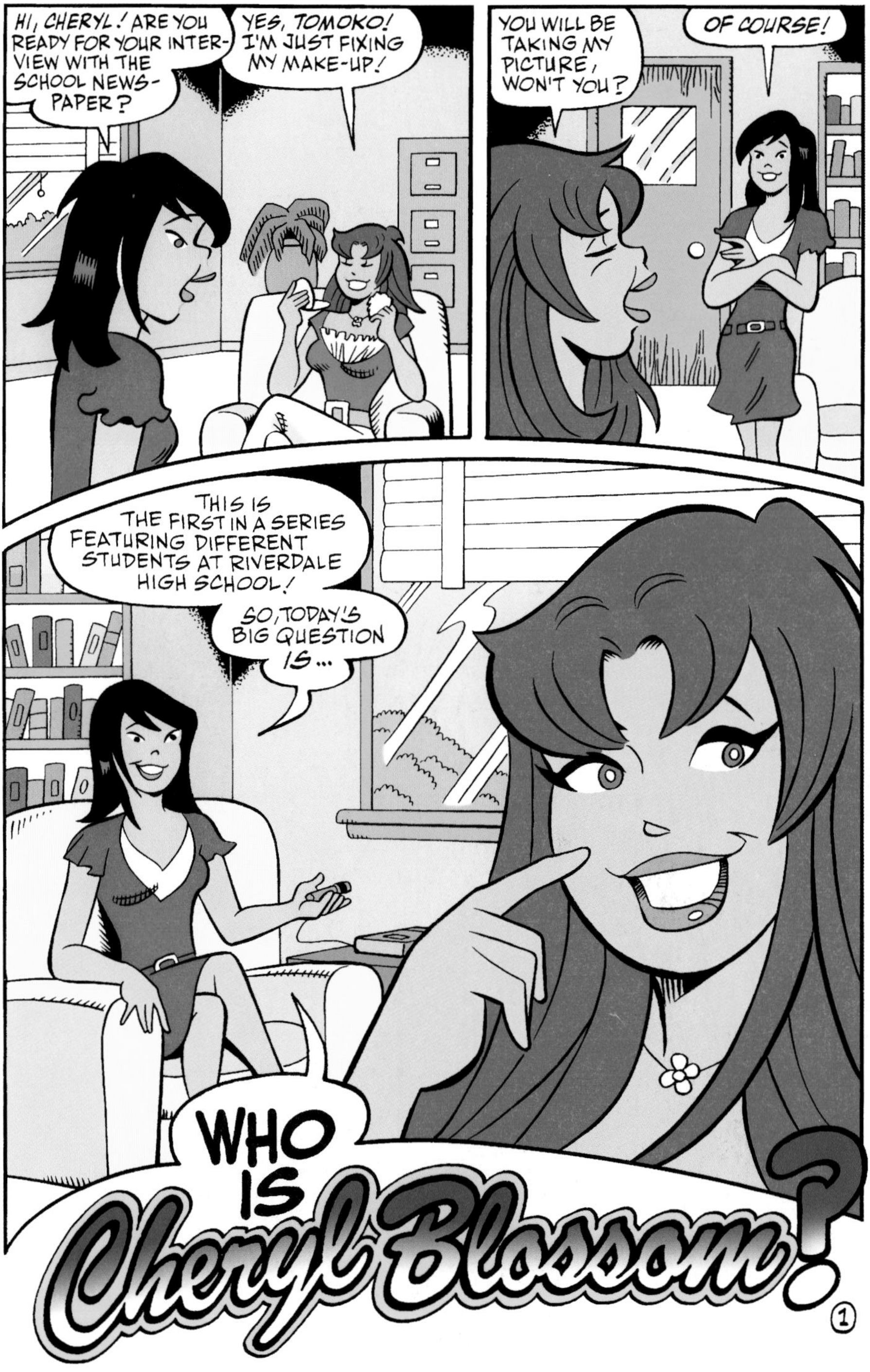
HI, CHERYL! ARE YOU READY FOR YOUR INTER-VIEW WITH THE SCHOOL NEWS-PAPER?
YES, TOMOKO! I'M JUST FIXING MY MAKE-UP!
YOU WILL BE TAKING MY PICTURE, WON'T YOU?
OF COURSE!
THIS IS THE FIRST IN A SERIES FEATURING DIFFERENT STUDENTS AT RIVERDALE HIGH SCHOOL!
SO, TODAY'S BIG QUESTION IS...
WHO IS Cheryl Blossom?!
1

ORIGINALLY PRINTED IN BETTY & VERONICA DOUBLE DIGEST #160, 2008

DAN PARENT • DAN PARENT • JIM AMASH • JACK MORELLI • BARRY GROSSMAN

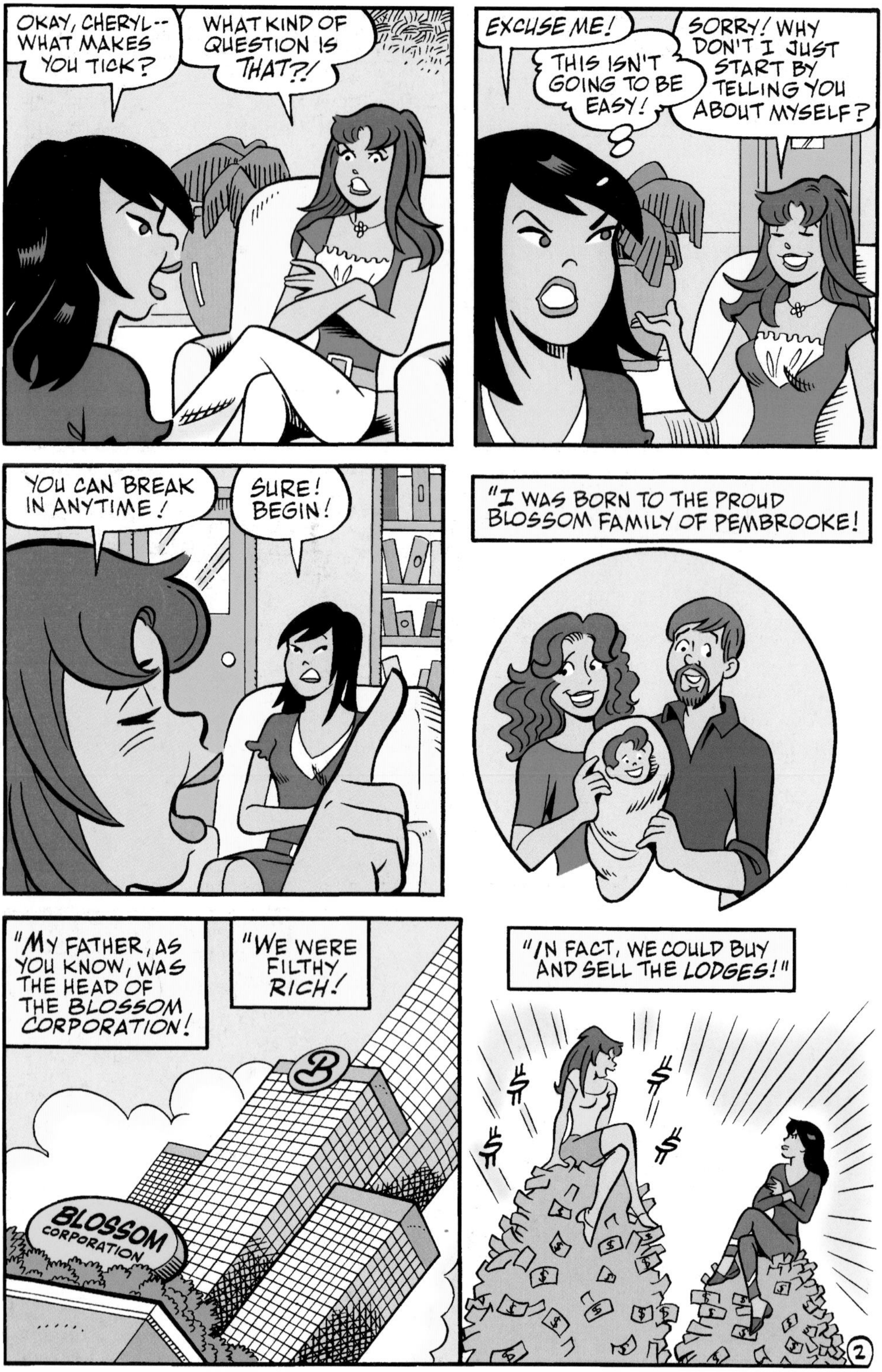
OKAY, CHERYL-- WHAT MAKES YOU TICK?
WHAT KIND OF QUESTION IS THAT?!
EXCUSE ME!
THIS ISN'T GOING TO BE EASY!
SORRY! WHY DON'T I JUST START BY TELLING YOU ABOUT MYSELF?
YOU CAN BREAK IN ANYTIME!
SURE! BEGIN!
"I WAS BORN TO THE PROUD BLOSSOM FAMILY OF PEMBROOKE!
"MY FATHER, AS YOU KNOW, WAS THE HEAD OF THE BLOSSOM CORPORATION!
"WE WERE FILTHY RICH!
BLOSSOM CORPORATION
"IN FACT, WE COULD BUY AND SELL THE LODGES!"
2

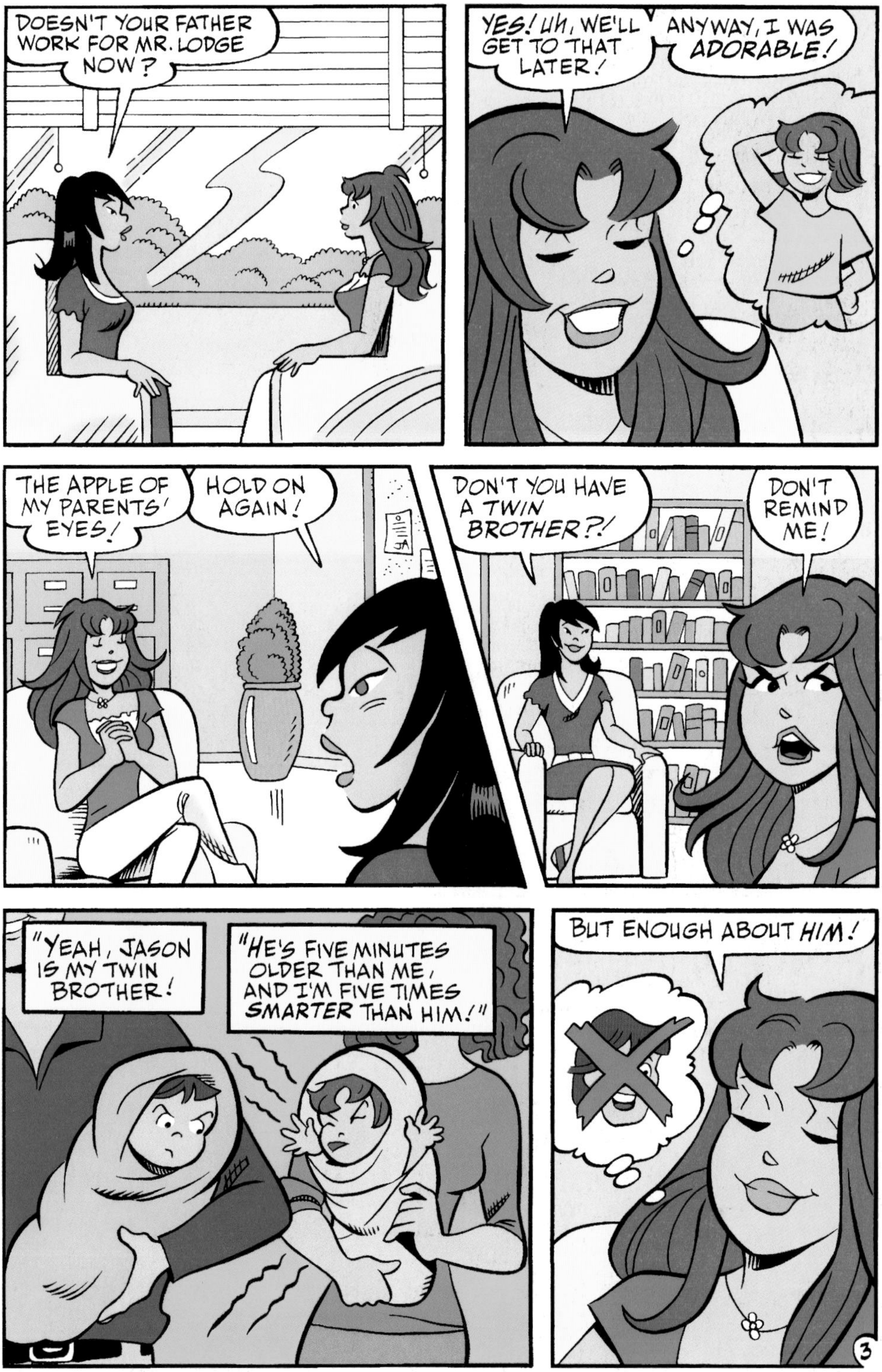
DOESN'T YOUR FATHER WORK FOR MR. LODGE NOW?
YES! UH, WE'LL GET TO THAT LATER!
ANYWAY, I WAS ADORABLE!
THE APPLE OF MY PARENTS' EYES!
HOLD ON AGAIN!
DON'T YOU HAVE A TWIN BROTHER?!
DON'T REMIND ME!
"YEAH, JASON IS MY TWIN BROTHER!
"HE'S FIVE MINUTES OLDER THAN ME, AND I'M FIVE TIMES SMARTER THAN HIM!"
BUT ENOUGH ABOUT HIM!
3

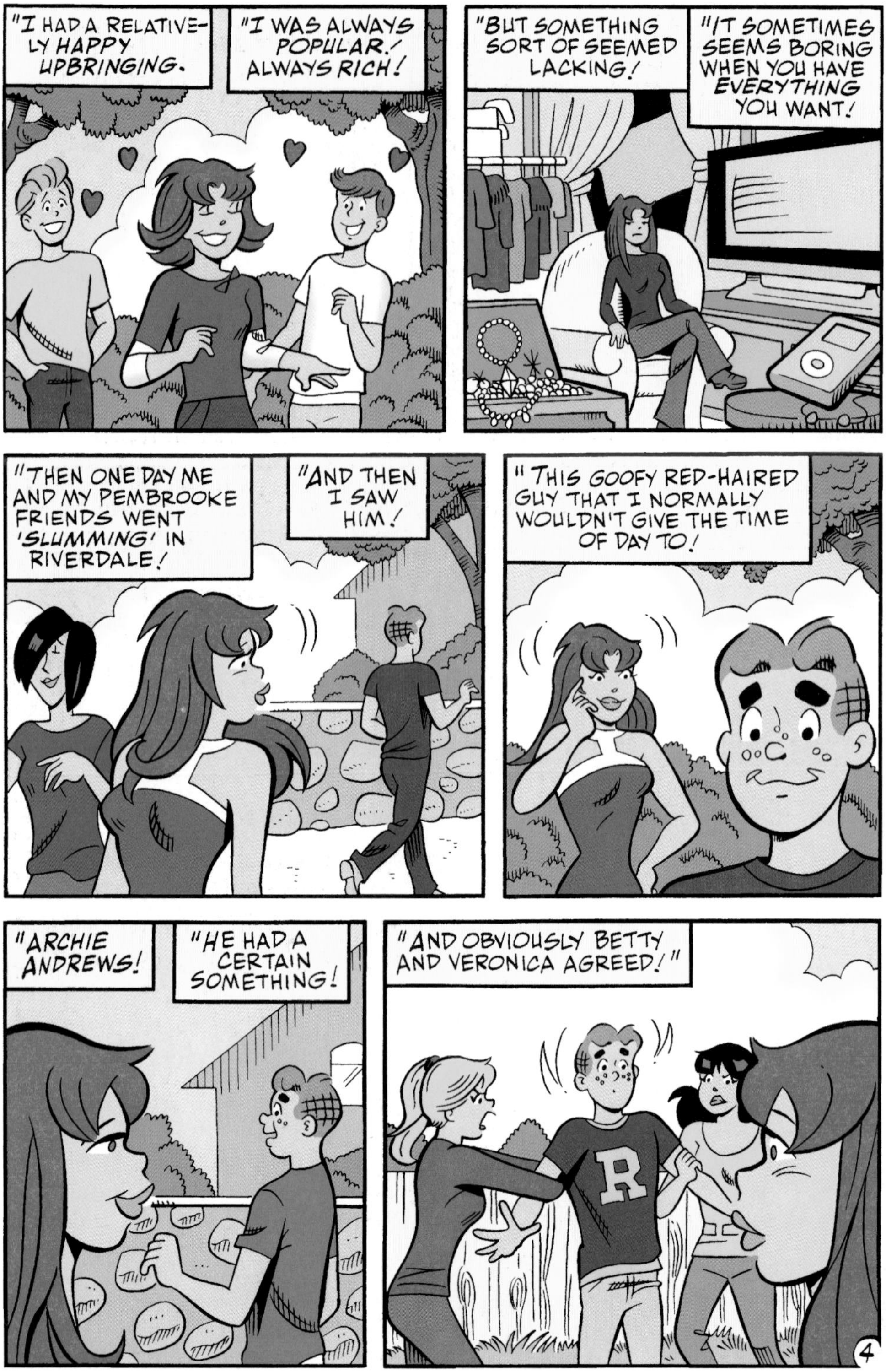
"I HAD A RELATIVE-LY HAPPY UPBRINGING.
"I WAS ALWAYS POPULAR! ALWAYS RICH!
"BUT SOMETHING SORT OF SEEMED LACKING!
"IT SOMETIMES SEEMS BORING WHEN YOU HAVE EVERYTHING YOU WANT!
"THEN ONE DAY ME AND MY PEMBROOKE FRIENDS WENT 'SLUMMING' IN RIVERDALE!
"AND THEN I SAW HIM!
"THIS GOOFY RED-HAIRED GUY THAT I NORMALLY WOULDN'T GIVE THE TIME OF DAY TO!
"ARCHIE ANDREWS!
"HE HAD A CERTAIN SOMETHING!
"AND OBVIOUSLY BETTY AND VERONICA AGREED!"
R
4

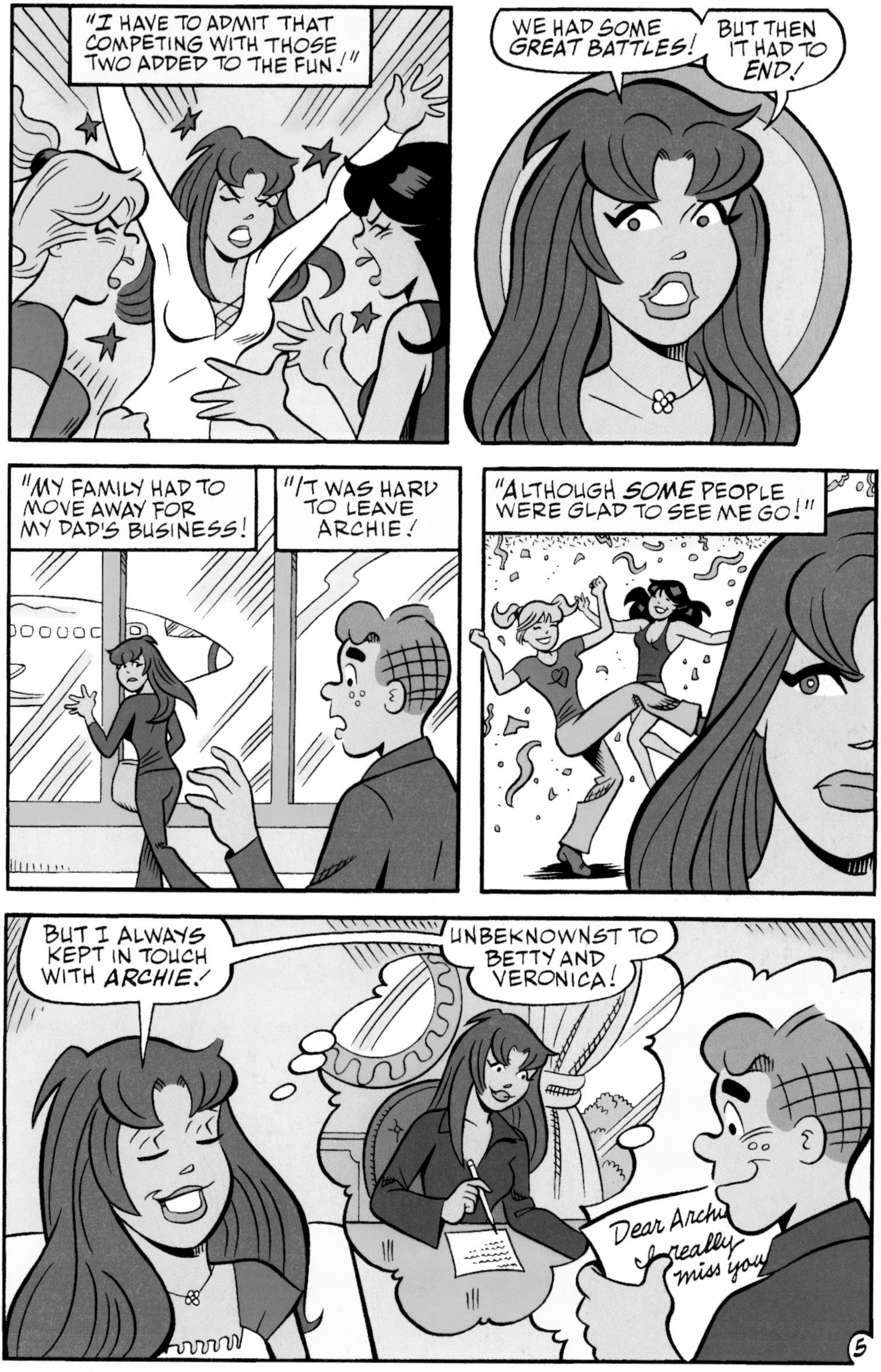
"I HAVE TO ADMIT THAT COMPETING WITH THOSE TWO ADDED TO THE FUN!"
WE HAD SOME GREAT BATTLES!
BUT THEN IT HAD TO END!
"MY FAMILY HAD TO MOVE AWAY FOR MY DAD'S BUSINESS!
"IT WAS HARD TO LEAVE ARCHIE!
"ALTHOUGH SOME PEOPLE WERE GLAD TO SEE ME GO!"
BUT I ALWAYS KEPT IN TOUCH WITH ARCHIE!
UNBEKNOWNST TO BETTY AND VERONICA!
Dear Archi
I really miss you
5

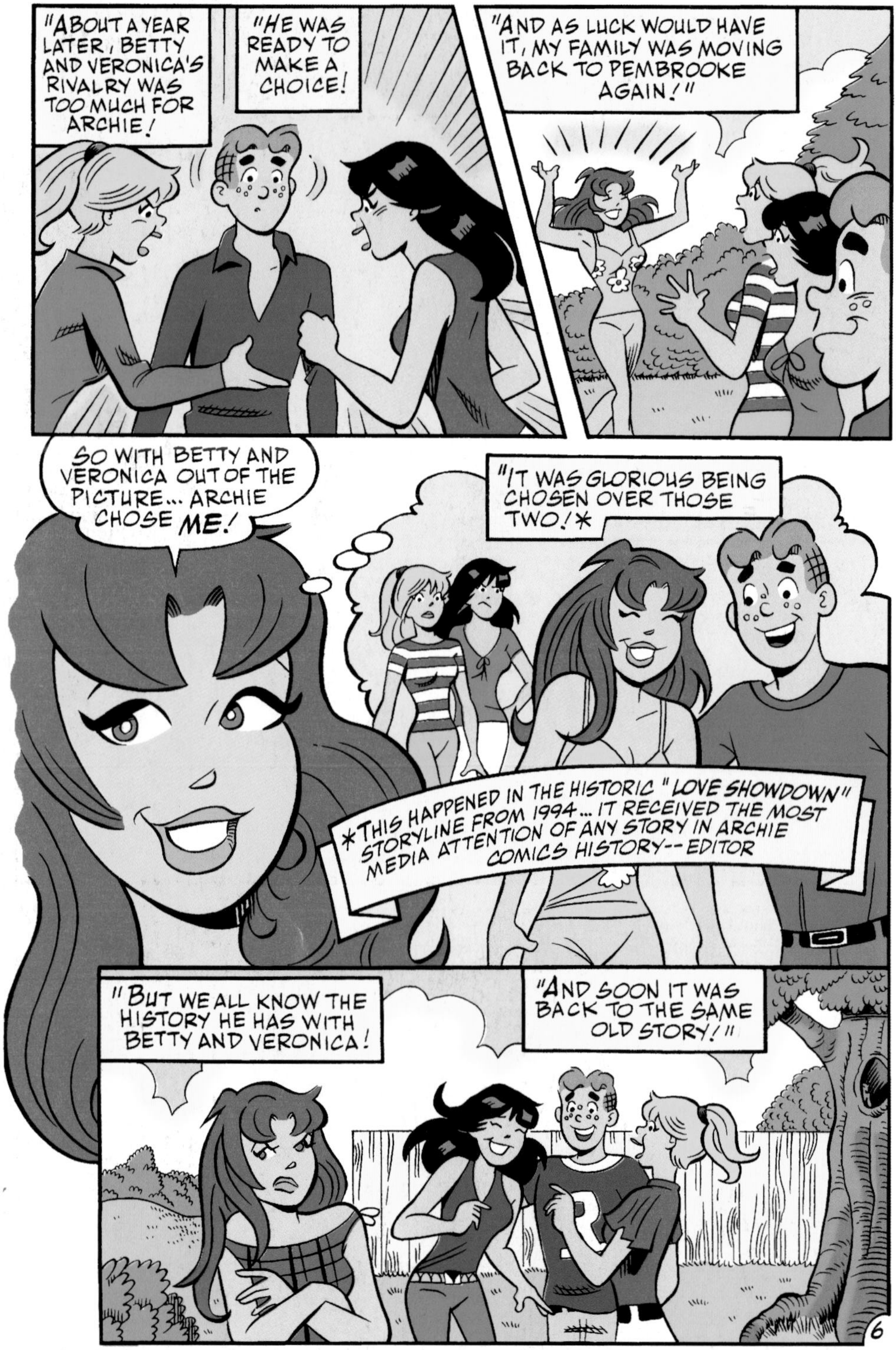
"ABOUT A YEAR LATER, BETTY AND VERONICA'S RIVALRY WAS TOO MUCH FOR ARCHIE!
"HE WAS READY TO MAKE A CHOICE!
"AND AS LUCK WOULD HAVE IT, MY FAMILY WAS MOVING BACK TO PEMBROOKE AGAIN!"
SO WITH BETTY AND VERONICA OUT OF THE PICTURE... ARCHIE CHOSE ME!
"IT WAS GLORIOUS BEING CHOSEN OVER THOSE TWO!*
*THIS HAPPENED IN THE HISTORIC "LOVE SHOWDOWN" STORYLINE FROM 1994... IT RECEIVED THE MOST MEDIA ATTENTION OF ANY STORY IN ARCHIE COMICS HISTORY-- EDITOR
"BUT WE ALL KNOW THE HISTORY HE HAS WITH BETTY AND VERONICA!
"AND SOON IT WAS BACK TO THE SAME OLD STORY!"
6

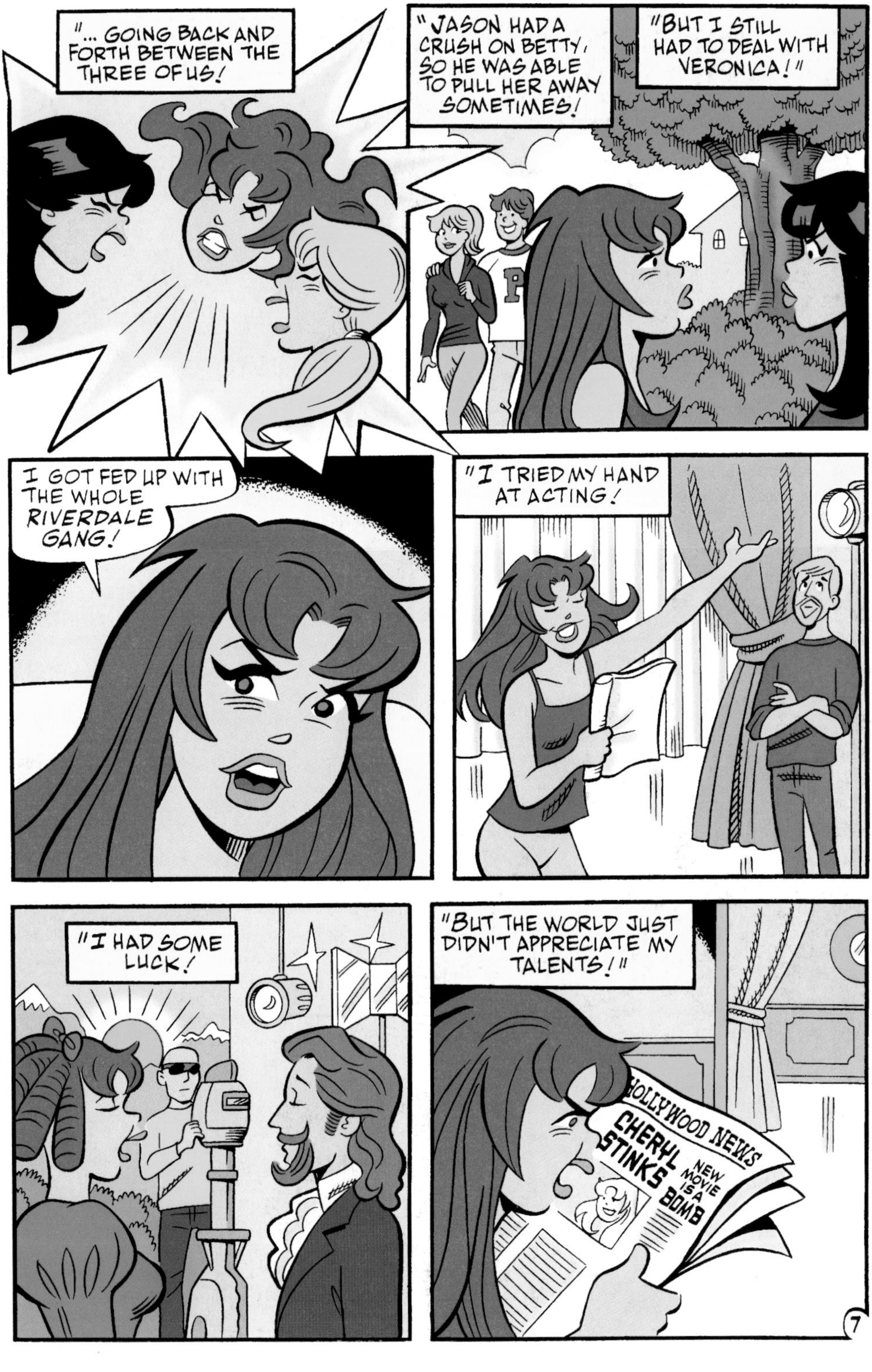
"... GOING BACK AND FORTH BETWEEN THE THREE OF US!
"JASON HAD A CRUSH ON BETTY, SO HE WAS ABLE TO PULL HER AWAY SOMETIMES!
"BUT I STILL HAD TO DEAL WITH VERONICA!"
I GOT FED UP WITH THE WHOLE RIVERDALE GANG!
"I TRIED MY HAND AT ACTING!
"I HAD SOME LUCK!
"BUT THE WORLD JUST DIDN'T APPRECIATE MY TALENTS!"
HOLLYWOOD NEWS
CHERYL STINKS
NEW MOVIE IS A BOMB
7

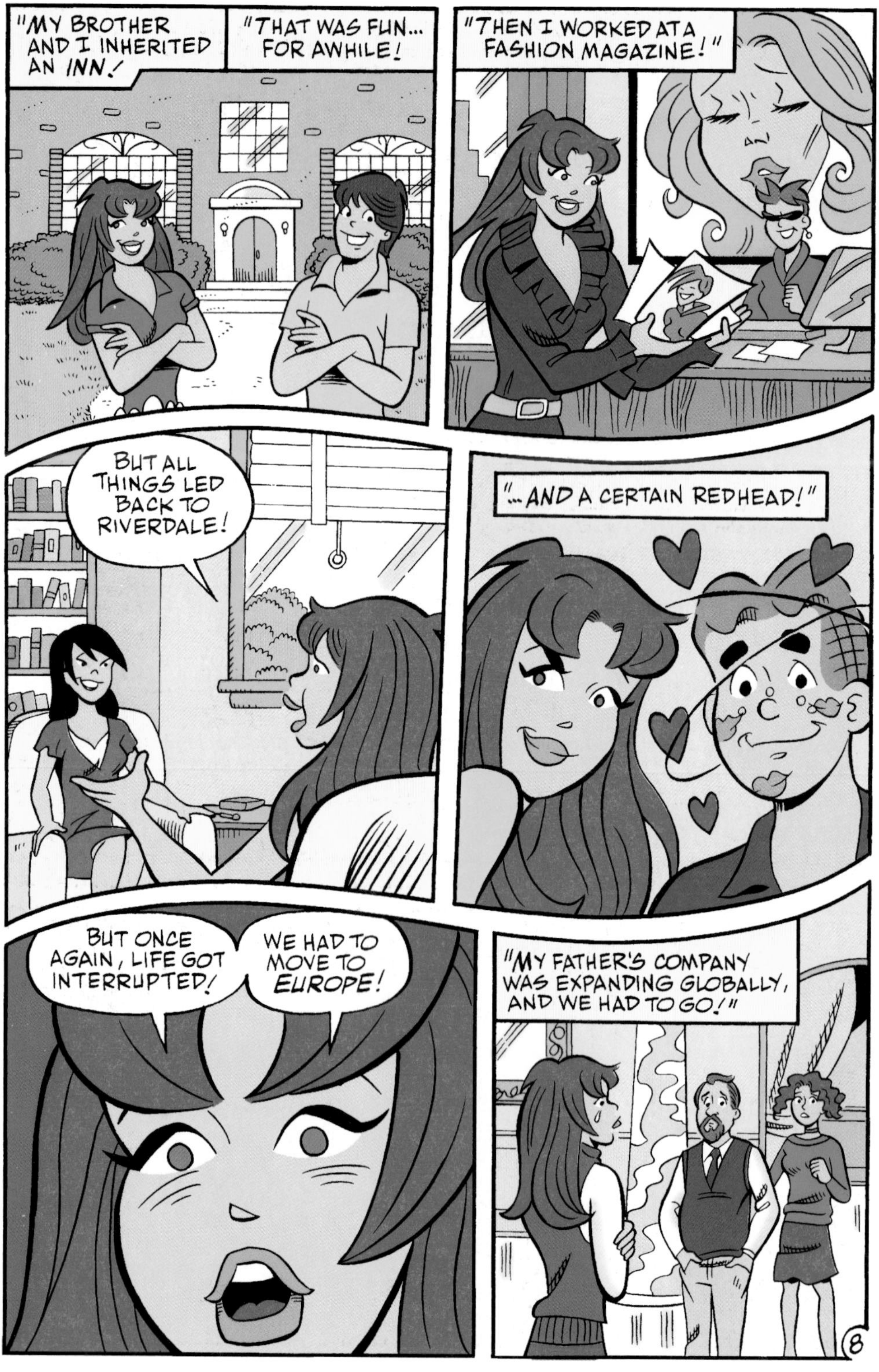
"MY BROTHER AND I INHERITED AN INN!
"THAT WAS FUN... FOR AWHILE!
"THEN I WORKED AT A FASHION MAGAZINE!"
BUT ALL THINGS LED BACK TO RIVERDALE!
"...AND A CERTAIN REDHEAD!"
BUT ONCE AGAIN, LIFE GOT INTERRUPTED!
WE HAD TO MOVE TO EUROPE!
"MY FATHER'S COMPANY WAS EXPANDING GLOBALLY, AND WE HAD TO GO!"
8

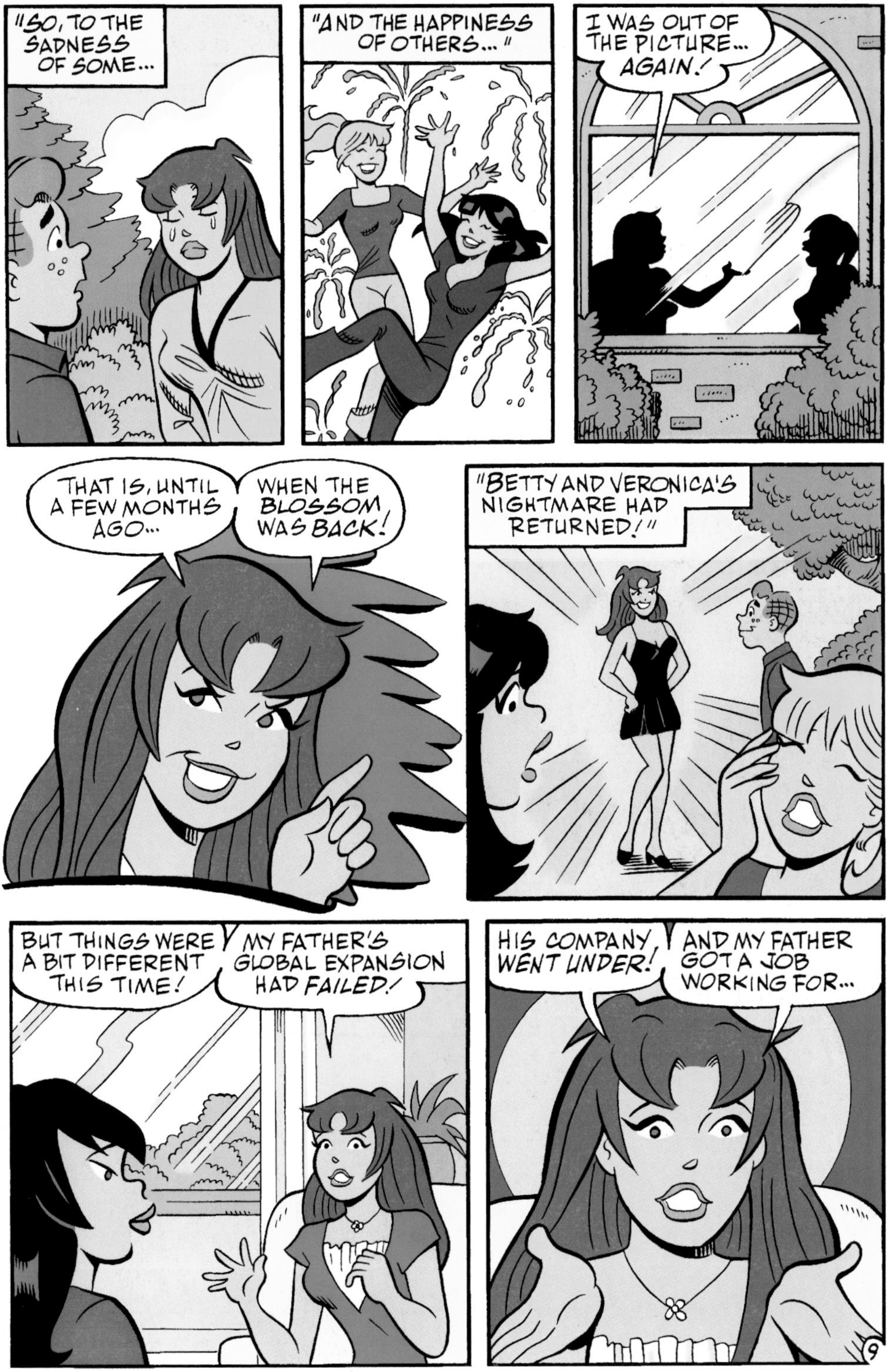
"SO, TO THE SADNESS OF SOME...
"AND THE HAPPINESS OF OTHERS..."
I WAS OUT OF THE PICTURE... AGAIN!
THAT IS, UNTIL A FEW MONTHS AGO...
WHEN THE BLOSSOM WAS BACK!
"BETTY AND VERONICA'S NIGHTMARE HAD RETURNED!"
BUT THINGS WERE A BIT DIFFERENT THIS TIME!
MY FATHER'S GLOBAL EXPANSION HAD FAILED!
HIS COMPANY WENT UNDER!
AND MY FATHER GOT A JOB WORKING FOR...
9

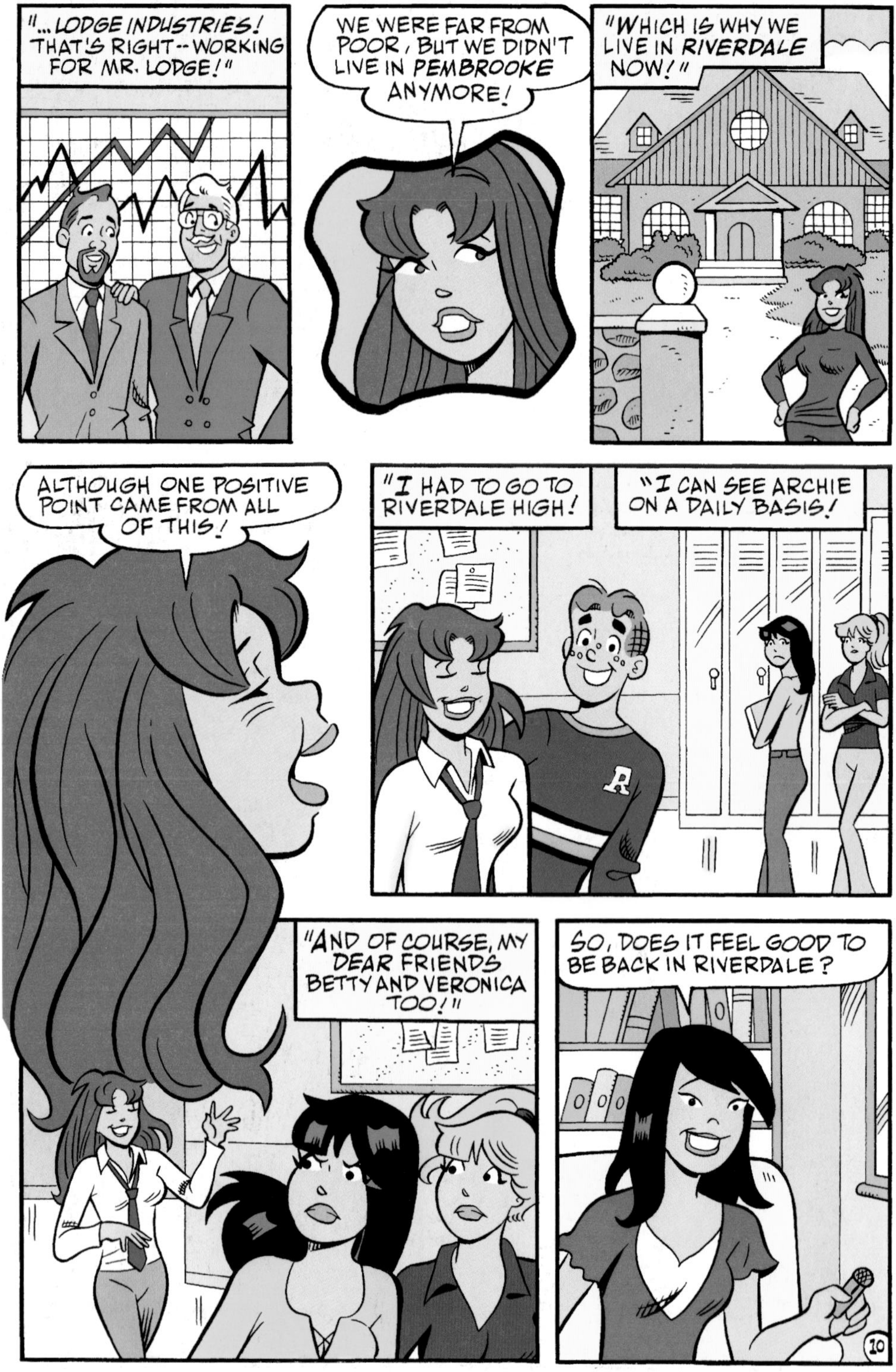
"...LODGE INDUSTRIES! THAT'S RIGHT--WORKING FOR MR. LODGE!"
WE WERE FAR FROM POOR, BUT WE DIDN'T LIVE IN PEMBROOKE ANYMORE!
"WHICH IS WHY WE LIVE IN RIVERDALE NOW!"
ALTHOUGH ONE POSITIVE POINT CAME FROM ALL OF THIS!
"I HAD TO GO TO RIVERDALE HIGH!
"I CAN SEE ARCHIE ON A DAILY BASIS!
"AND OF COURSE, MY DEAR FRIENDS BETTY AND VERONICA TOO!"
SO, DOES IT FEEL GOOD TO BE BACK IN RIVERDALE?
10

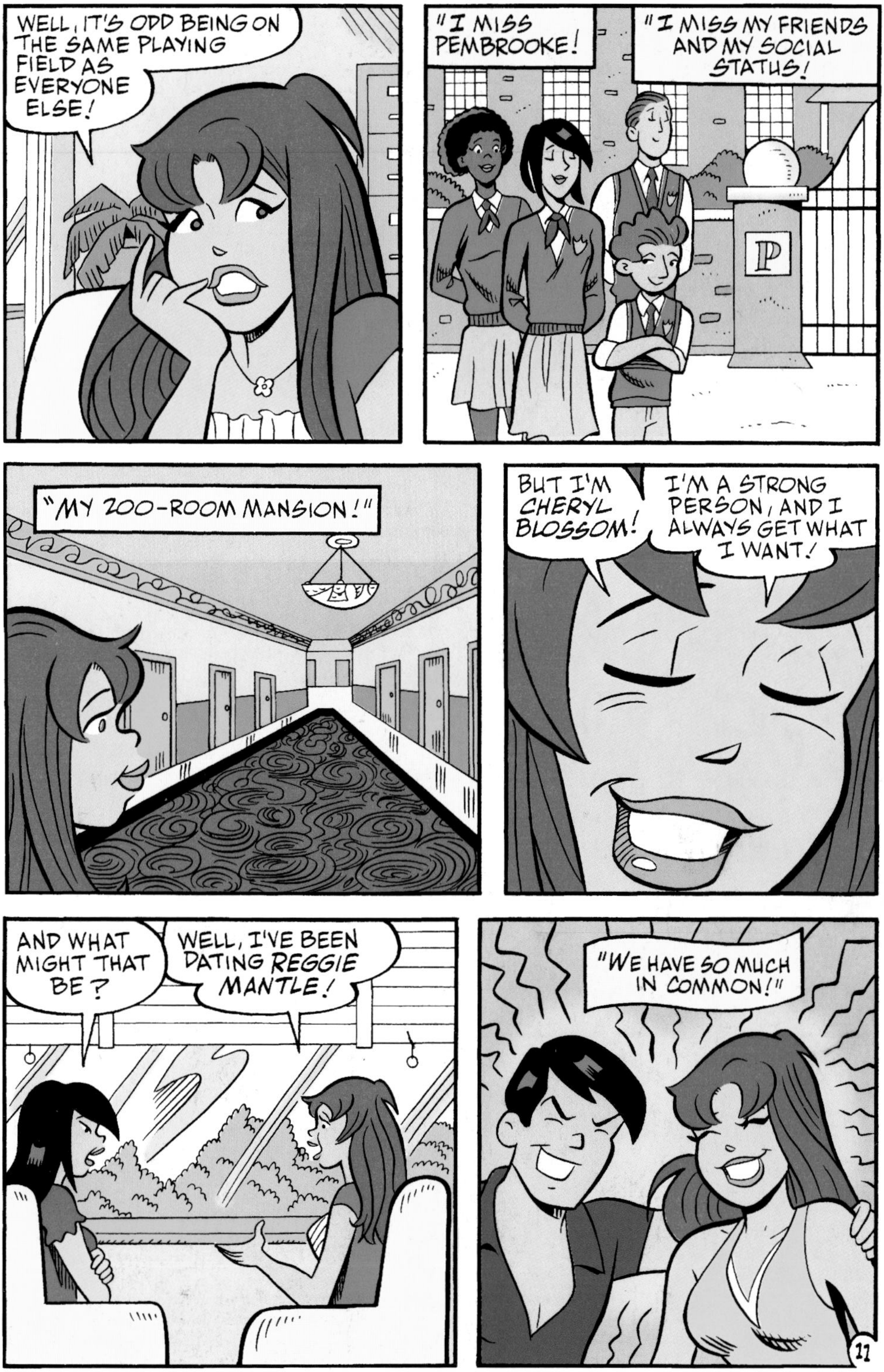
WELL, IT'S ODD BEING ON THE SAME PLAYING FIELD AS EVERYONE ELSE!
"I MISS PEMBROOKE!
"I MISS MY FRIENDS AND MY SOCIAL STATUS!
P
"MY 200-ROOM MANSION!"
BUT I'M CHERYL BLOSSOM!
I'M A STRONG PERSON, AND I ALWAYS GET WHAT I WANT!
AND WHAT MIGHT THAT BE?
WELL, I'VE BEEN DATING REGGIE MANTLE!
"WE HAVE SO MUCH IN COMMON!"
11

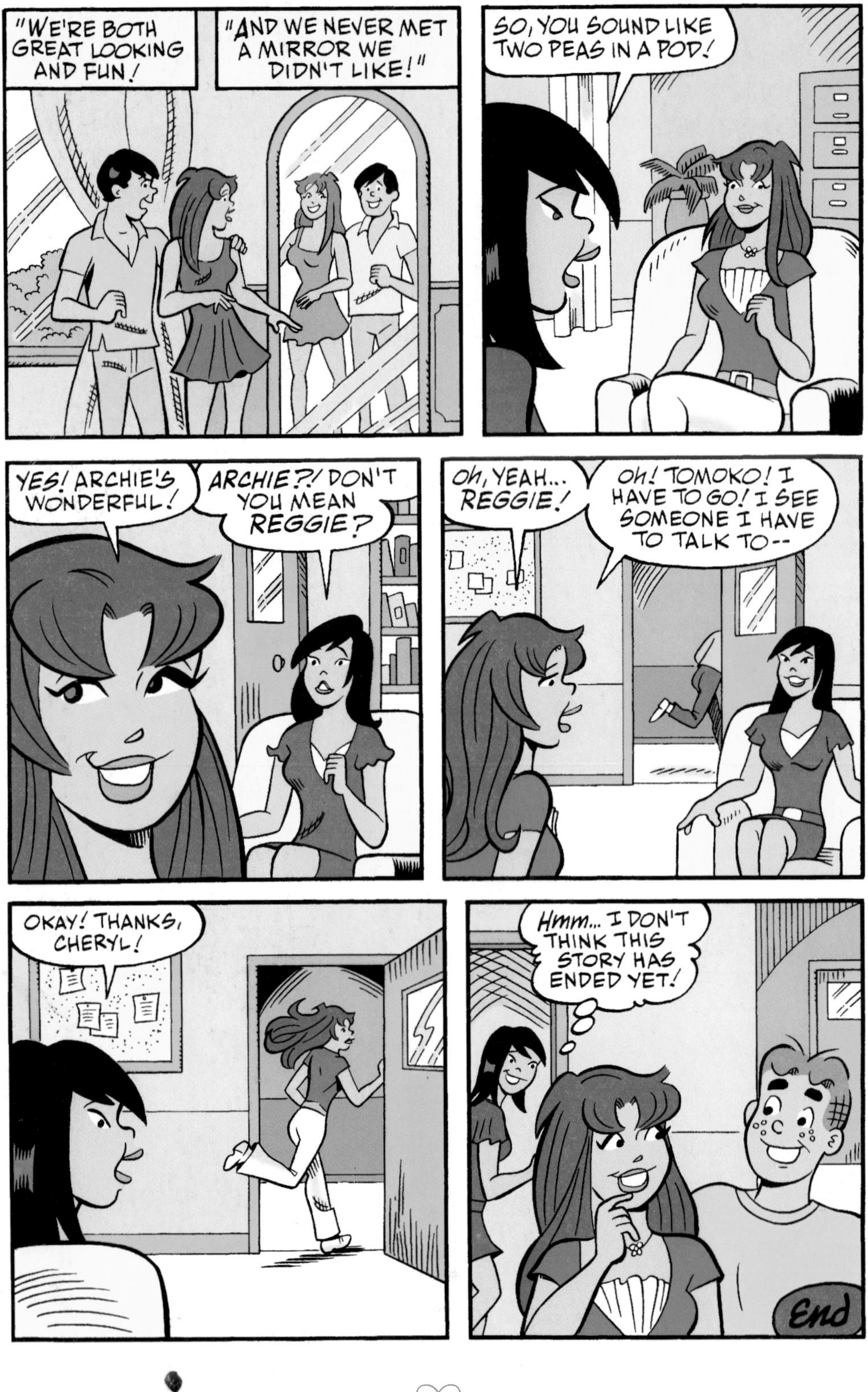

"WE'RE BOTH GREAT LOOKING AND FUN!
"AND WE NEVER MET A MIRROR WE DIDN'T LIKE!"
SO, YOU SOUND LIKE TWO PEAS IN A POD!
YES! ARCHIE'S WONDERFUL!
ARCHIE?! DON'T YOU MEAN REGGIE?
Oh, YEAH... REGGIE!
Oh! TOMOKO! I HAVE TO GO! I SEE SOMEONE I HAVE TO TALK TO--
OKAY! THANKS, CHERYL!
Hmm... I DON'T THINK THIS STORY HAS ENDED YET!
End